PRAISE FOR RADIANT

Township Public Library
D0612384

Sumner-Smith's excellent, subtle, wringing world-building abilities are supported by her clean, clear, precise wordcrafting. *Radiant* is a book that is both a joy and a pleasure to read, with a breathtaking climax that rivals the greatest scenery pieces of the blockbuster films, and an ending that is both satisfying and intriguing, which promises a greater world filled with bigger and brighter mysteries for Xhea, Shai, and all those who dwell in the Lower City, a place—now that Xhea and Shai are in it—is no longer without hope." —J. M. Frey, award-winning author of *Triptych*

"If C. J. Cherryh wrote fantasy with a futuristic feel, it would have a lot in common with this book, especially the protagonist. Excellent work, and recommended." —Michelle Sagara, *New York Times* bestselling author of The Chronicles of Elantra series

"Finally! A *Blade Runner* for the fantasy crowd. Magic as you've never seen it before." —Violette Malan, author of the Dhulyn and Parno series and the Mirror Lands series

"This beautifully written page turner is topnotch. A world that comes alive, rich and magical; characters you want to spend time with; a heroine to root for; trust, friendship, and belonging—*Radiant* has it all! Fantasy not your cup of tea? You should read this one anyway; it deserves space on every bookshelf. Where's the next one?" —Ed Greenwood, creator of The Forgotten Realms® and *New York Times* bestselling author of *Spellfire*, *The Herald*, and many others

"A first novel *Radiant* may be, but by a writer at the top of her craft. Be taken to breathless heights of imagination. Feel your heart pound until it almost breaks, then sigh for joy. This, dear readers, is the story you mustn't miss and will never forget. Recommended? No. I insist. Read *Radiant*." —Julie E. Czerneda, author of *A Turn of Light*

oln Township Public Library
2099 W. John Beers Rd
Stevensville, MI 49127
(269) 429-9575

"An imaginative and original tale of struggle, sacrifice, and friendship within a harsh cultural landscape. *Radiant* is a vibrant debut, infused with pure magic and strong characters." —Amanda Sun, author of *Rain*

"With a clean, evocative style . . . a clever transposition of corporate warfare into a feudal future, and a strong, complementary pair of protagonists, Sumner-Smith's Tower Trilogy is off to a captivating start." —*Publisher's Weekly*, starred review

"Thank goodness this is the first book in a trilogy, because you'll definitely be wanting more when you're done." —*Girls in Capes*

RADIANT

KARINA SUMNER-SMITH

RADIANT

TOWERS TRILOGY BOOK ONE

Lincoln Township Public Library
2099 W. John Beers Rd.
Stevensville, MI 49127
(269) 429-9575

Talos Press

Copyright © 2014 by Karina Sumner-Smith

All rights reserved. No part of this book may be reproduced in any manner without the express written consent of the publisher, except in the case of brief excerpts in critical reviews or articles. All inquiries should be addressed to Skyhorse Publishing, 307 West 36th Street, 11th Floor, New York, NY 10018.

Talos Press books may be purchased in bulk at special discounts for sales promotion, corporate gifts, fund-raising, or educational purposes. Special editions can also be created to specifications. For details, contact the Special Sales Department, Skyhorse Publishing, 307 West 36th Street, 11th Floor, New York, NY 10018 or info@skyhorsepublishing.com.

Talos Press® is a registered trademark of Skyhorse Publishing, Inc.®, a Delaware corporation.

Visit our website at www.skyhorsepublishing.com.

10 9 8 7 6 5 4 3 2

Library of Congress Cataloging-in-Publication Data is available on file.

Cover design by Rain Saukas
Cover illustration credit Rain Saukas

Print ISBN: 978-1-940456-10-2
Ebook ISBN: 978-1-940456-19-5

Printed in the United States of America

Dedicated with love to my parents,
Lindy and Martin,
for always believing.

Part One

Chapter One

Curled in a concrete alcove that had once been a doorway, Xhea watched the City man make his awkward way through the market tents, dragging a ghost behind him. Magic sparkled above his head like an upturned tulip, deflecting the heavy rain and letting it pour to the ground to trace a circle in the puddles at his feet. He was, of course, watching her.

It was not his attention that had caught Xhea's notice, nor his poor attempt to blend into the crowd, but the ghost tethered to him with a line of energy more felt than seen. The dead girl couldn't have been much older than Xhea herself—sixteen, Xhea supposed, perhaps seventeen—and she floated an arm's span above the man's head like a girl-shaped helium balloon.

For fifteen minutes the man had circled, pretending to shop. As if a City man had any use for reclaimed nails, half rusted and pounded straight; for prayer flags, or charms of electrical wire and bone. What was it, Xhea wondered, that made the ghost-afflicted wait for the darkest, rainiest days to seek her out? She snorted softly, a sound without care or pity. They didn't want to be seen with her, that was the truth of it, as if her very presence left a shadow that wouldn't burn away.

As she waited, Xhea tied a coin to the end of a braid of her hair with a bit of tattered ribbon. The coin was an old and dirty thing she'd found in the abandoned shopping corridors that wound beneath the Lower City. Once it would have bought her bread, cigarettes, a warm place to sleep. Now it was nothing but a bit of shiny metal that watched with the pressed eyes of a dead Queen, its only magic a sense of the past that hung about it like the faint scent of something sweet.

She had started braiding another length of dark hair before the man made the decision to approach. He walked toward her with his head down, as if a slumped posture might make him any less conspicuous, as if half the market didn't watch him go. He came to stand before her narrow shelter and stared without speaking, the heavy rain falling between them like a beaded curtain.

Xhea eyed him in silence: his polished shoes, dotted with water; the neat line of his jacket; the monogrammed cuffs that peeked from his jacket sleeves. Only the clean cut of his tailored pants was marred, and that by the slow curl of his fists within the pockets. He straightened, pulling himself upright as if to get every intimidating inch from his average-sized frame.

She held his gaze as she pulled a cigarette from one of her oversized jacket's many pockets and placed it against her lips. From another pocket she drew forth a single match, thankfully dry, which she struck with a practiced flick. Cigarette lit, Xhea leaned back against the concrete.

"Well?" the City man said.

She exhaled. "Well what?"

"Aren't you going to help me? I have a ghost."

"I can see that," Xhea said, and returned the cigarette to her lips. She smoked in contented silence.

"Hey," he said at last, shifting his weight. "I'm talking to you."

"I can see that too."

"I was told," he said, as if she were far younger than her apparent years and dreadfully slow, "that you can help people with ghosts."

Xhea snorted and flicked away a bit of ash. "Try asking nicely. Try saying 'please.' You're the one who needs help here, not me."

The man looked from her braid-tangled hair to her dirt-crusted nails and all the mismatched layers of clothing in between, disbelief plain. "Look, I came here—" he started, then shook himself. "What am I doing?" he muttered. He turned away, running his hand through his thinning hair as he walked. Yet his ghost remained, her tether stretching: a clear indication that the man would return.

Xhea smoked slowly, watching the ghost. She floated, serene, eyes closed and legs folded beneath her, lost in dreams. The ghost's hair was pale, her skin paler still, each appearing in Xhea's black-and-white vision as a faintly luminescent gray. The ghost girl's dress was more vivid, hanging in loose folds that appeared almost to shimmer, the fabric untouched by rain.

Red, Xhea guessed, from the energy it exuded. She rather appreciated the contrast.

What was their story, she wondered. Too young to be his wife, unless his tastes ran to the illegal; too calm to be the victim of a hit and run or the unlucky bystander in a spell gone awry. His daughter, maybe. How touching.

Had illness taken her? But no, these were City folk, through and through. Illness was rare in the City, true disease rarer still, health and long life all but guaranteed by their magic. Suicide, then? Perhaps her father had killed her.

Xhea exhaled a long breath of smoke as the man again approached. *Come to my temple*, she thought to him mockingly. Three walls of concrete and one of rain; a cloud of tobacco for incense. *Come pray for your ghost.*

He stood before her for a long moment, staring. "You're too young to be smoking," he said. The words were slow, tired: an admission of defeat.

"And she's too young to be dead." Xhea nodded toward the ghost that once more hovered above his left shoulder. The coins in her hair clinked with the movement. She had to give him this: he didn't flinch as she gestured toward his ghost; didn't look above his head as if her attention might have brought the invisible to light.

"So tell me," Xhea said. "Why do you want my help? Do you want her gone, your pale ghost? Exorcised? Maybe there's something you need to say to her—or something you think she has to say to you?"

The man watched her in an angry, uncomfortable silence.

"Ah." Xhea sighed. "Don't know, do you? Just came to see what the freak girl had to offer."

It was only then that she realized how thin his umbrella of magic had become, fading in his exhaustion, or that the circles beneath his eyes were dark as bruises. She squelched what little sympathy she felt. Even if he had lost everything, if everyone he loved had died, he still had magic, a gift of nature and blood. With that power, doors opened to his touch; vendors could sell him food; the City acknowledged he existed. He was, in a word, normal.

Unlike Xhea. There was no brightness in her, no magic, only a dark stillness in the depths of her stomach; an ache, like hunger, that she could only think of as absence.

"I'll tell you what," she said. "I'll take your ghost for a day, maybe two, give you a little break." No more flickers at the edges of his vision, or the feeling he was being watched; no more whispers half-heard—or whatever it was he could sense. Each felt their haunting a little differently. "If that turns out okay, we can discuss something more permanent." Or she could offer him more temporary arrangements, and more, turning his indecision into months of steady business. She suppressed a grin.

"How much," he said brusquely.

"A week's worth of food chits, and five hundred unshaped renai."

"Five hundred!"

"You'd use less to get a taxi across the City."

"But unshaped?" he asked, confused that she didn't want the renai—the magical currency—to be spelled to her own power signature, but raw. "Why?"

"I didn't ask how you got a ghost," Xhea said. "Don't ask what I'll do with the payment."

His umbrella flickered and failed, and the rain poured down on his unprotected head. Xhea watched as, to her eyes, his hair and clothing changed from mottled grays to tones of charcoal and black, the fabric slicking to his shoulders and arms and the slight paunch at his waistband. Water dribbled in his eyes and trickled from his nose as he stared.

"What they say about you is true, then," he said, his voice low. "You *are* a freak. No magic in you at all."

Xhea ground her cigarette against the wet concrete, watching the ember sizzle and dull to black. A line of smoke rose upward, vanishing.

"You're the one standing in the rain."

A deal was struck. The rest was only negotiation.

Changing the anchor of a ghost's tether wasn't easy, but it was one thing Xhea could do well, a knack honed by years of practice. Ghosts remained in the living world because of unfinished business, something they couldn't leave behind. What few knew was that they were literally bound to that unfinished business.

Unless, of course, you had a really sharp knife. Xhea's knife was silver, with a narrow blade that folded into a handle inlaid with mother of pearl. The handle's sheen had been dulled by the touch of countless hands, but the blade was polished mirror-bright, its maker's mark worn to a mere squiggle in the metal.

The man, soaked to the bone, stood rigidly as Xhea climbed onto an overturned fruit crate, knife extended, and examined the tether above his head.

"Don't cut me," he said.

"Don't complain," she replied.

Carefully, Xhea closed her hand around the near-invisible tether. It felt like little more than a length of slippery air and vibrated at her touch like a plucked guitar string. Holding it steady, she probed with the tip of her knife for weakness. As she shifted, her jacket rattled: the pockets were full to overflowing with a week's worth of chits, small plastic discs imbued with just enough magic to buy a single meal. They were designed for children too young to understand the value of their own magic, more likely to weaken themselves buying candy or be drained by a predator than to buy a balanced meal. Though she appeared younger than her age, Xhea knew she still looked too old to be using chits. She couldn't bring herself to care. With no magic of her own, she had no other way to buy food; it was that, steal, or starve.

The rest of the payment had been spelled to transfer to her upon completion of their transaction. A small sphere of magic— nearly five hundred renai, the man's inclination to bargain being weak at best—now floated above Xhea's head like her own shining ghost, awaiting its time to leap into her body.

There. Her silver knife slid into a weak section of the tether a few hands' length from its anchor in the man's chest, and the line's vibration quickened at the blade's intrusion. She slid her hand down the length until she could touch that weakness with both fingers and knife, feeling for details that even her eyes could not see.

The City man looked from the knife to Xhea's face, then closed his eyes. "Hurry," he said. "Please just . . . hurry."

The blade flashed down. The ghost's eyes flew open and she recoiled, springing back to the end of the tether that Xhea refused to release. The ghost opened her mouth as if to scream, her once-perfect calm gone, but no sound emerged. Their eyes met. Locked. The ghost's eyes were pale too, Xhea saw; bright silver to her vision, reduced to but a thin ring by fear-widened pupils. Yet she only watched in silence as Xhea fought the tether, drawing it down and pressing the severed end to her own chest. It sank into her like rain into a storm sewer, vanishing completely.

The City man turned to her, Xhea's position on the crate bringing their eyes to a level. He reached out to grasp the wrist of Xhea's knife hand—and jerked back as if shocked. She acknowledged neither touch nor recoil.

"That's it?"

"You want to pay more?"

"I—"

"Then that's it."

He stared at her, and took a long, shuddering breath. The rain had slowed to little more than a drizzle. He stepped back from her concrete shelter and into the middle of the street. For a moment he stood, watching with an expression that she could not name, then walked away without another word.

"Two days," Xhea called after him. "She'll return to you in two days, unless you come back."

There was no reply, only the sight of his hunched back vanishing into the market crowd.

His absence was a signal. Xhea's payment brightened, then sped forward and slammed into the center of her forehead. She gasped as the magic washed over her, through her; she stumbled back, lost her footing on the crate, and fell. There was a roaring in her ears like floodwaters' rush, and she tasted bile as her stomach attempted to return what little she'd eaten that day.

"Breathe," Xhea whispered. Her head spun. She reached out to grab at the concrete wall as a sudden rush of vertigo seemed to flip the world on its side and tilt it back again. She gagged and clutched at her stomach. "Breathe . . . breathe . . ."

It was in these moments with raw magic coursing through her body that she always swore she would never ask for renai in payment again—never demand it, never crave it. With no magic of her own, it was a waste, a rush, a surge of power without purpose or end. Helpless to process the renai or make it her own, her body fought the onslaught. Next time, she thought, gagging and shuddering—next time she'd stick to food chits and pity, everything else be blighted.

Then the vertigo began to subside, and the nausea eased; Xhea took one long, slow breath, and another. In the sudden quiet, she heard the rain begin again, a faint patter against the concrete, and the wind as it sighed through the Lower City's corridors of broken glass and twisted steel.

She felt . . . she almost had to struggle for the word . . . alive. With the bright magic burning within her, she felt no darkness in her center, no stillness. She was light, empty, on fire. *This*, she thought, *is what it must feel like to be normal.*

Xhea opened her eyes. Instead of a world of unending grays, she saw color. The brilliance made her breath catch—even now, after so many times. She stared upward, unsure if she wanted to shield her eyes or never close them again.

She saw only glimpses of the floating Towers of the City above—the shadows of the lowest few, the downward points of defensive spires—but even those were jewel bright, gold and green and blue. Closer, the ghost had resumed her meditative pose, legs curled beneath her as she looked down at Xhea's fallen form in no little confusion. The ghost's pale hair was blond, her silver eyes a light and luminous blue, but it was her dress that made Xhea stare. It was not the gray she'd seen, nor the red she'd imagined, but a rich plum like new blossoms.

"That looked like it hurt," the ghost said, her voice tentative.

"A good observation."

Xhea felt that she had but to lift her arms to float beside the ghost, untethered by weight or the world. Reality had other ideas. It took her three tries and the assistance of the wall to gain her feet, and even then she stood swaying, hoping that her trembling legs would hold. *Breathe*, she reminded herself as another wave of nausea curled and crashed over her.

"First things first." She looked toward the market tents. When her balance had steadied, Xhea stepped cautiously from the alcove. She felt a tugging against her sternum as the tether stretched, then began dragging the ghost in her wake. The ghost girl gave a yelp of surprise, which Xhea ignored, instead tilting her head back so the quickening rain fell upon her upturned face. The clouds were just gray, but aircars wove among them, their shimmering exhaust like fine strands of copper wire strung across the sky.

She found a vendor who knew her and offered no more than a raised eyebrow at her less-than-sober state. With a chit, she purchased a few skewers off the grill—some sort of fatty meat, and a starchy, crunchy thing that might have been a potato, the taste of each buried beneath a thick layer of spice. Xhea hummed happily as she chewed.

"What . . ." the ghost said, then faltered into silence. A moment later, she tried again: "Why . . . why am I here?"

"That was the deal," Xhea said, turning to look at the ghost over her shoulder. The world spun at the movement. "Nothing personal, I assure you."

She turned down a side street, slipping between low apartments. Their ground levels had been reinforced or disguised to look abandoned: doors bricked or boarded over, windows clouded from untold years of dirt. Higher, the ruse had been abandoned. Warning chimes and fluttering prayer flags hung from balconies, while a line of laundry strung between two buildings was heavy with dripping clothes—all pinned too securely to be dislodged with a thrown rock.

"Deal?" the ghost asked. "I was just sleeping. And now . . ." The ghost looked down, apparently just realizing that she inhabited a space without gravity, hovering five feet from the ground and skimming forward without walking.

"Oh," said Xhea. "That. You're dead."

"I can't be," she whispered, peering over her crossed legs and watching the pavement speed by. "No. I'm just asleep."

Great, Xhea thought. *A talker.* She had seemed so quiet at first, so serene; Xhea had thought that she might dream away her death in silence. It would have made things so much easier. Perhaps this was why the man had wanted to get rid of her—a sense that an unseen presence was doing her best to talk his ear off.

Well, she had only committed to a day, perhaps two, and then she could let the tether go. The girl would catapult back to her original anchor and be out of Xhea's hair—unless, of course, the man wanted to pay her significantly more.

"I'm asleep," the ghost girl insisted. "Only asleep."

"Then this must be a very bad dream."

Xhea made her way through the Lower City core and out toward the edges where the buildings fell in slow surrender to the surrounding ruins. After a few more protests, largely ignored, the ghost fell into an uneasy silence. She made no attempt to propel herself forward, leaving Xhea to drag her by her tether like a rock on a string.

Just a City girl, Xhea thought, glancing back at the ghost. She'd probably spent the whole of her life in the Towers, never looking down, never considering what lay on the ground below or all the lives scratched out in the dirt and ruin. Then again, few even from the Lower City chose to leave the core; out in the ruins beyond, Xhea felt that she had the whole world to herself, a wide space that held only the memory of people and the echoes of her footsteps. Here the infrastructure was succumbing to rot and the slow erosion of rain and wind and time. Buildings sagged where they hadn't fallen entirely. Even the clearest streets were strewn with rubble, bits of lives—of a time—that even history had forgotten.

But here, too, it was beautiful. Shoots pushed up from between storm sewers and around the stagnant ponds that had once been basements, and the broken street was veined green from new leaves struggling through the cracks. Xhea looked from one small plant to the next, caught by their perfect green.

At last she came to her destination, a low building that from the outside seemed no different from its collapsing neighbors. Stepping between glass shards and exposed rebar, she made her careful way to the door. It hung from rusted hinges, leaving only a small gap for Xhea to squeeze through. She closed her eyes against the rain of paint flakes that fell from the old frame, then grabbed the tether and dragged the ghost in after her.

Inside, it was so bright she had to squint. Daylight poured in from every side, coming from nowhere and everywhere at once, as if she stood in the shade on a sunny day. Captured light, the owner called it: a spell that gathered sunlight on bright days and brought it inside, tamed to the flick of a switch. After days of rain and overcast skies, the effect was dazzling.

The building was a warehouse, clean and neatly kept, entirely filled with labeled shelves. But it was the structure itself that always took Xhea aback, for it was something that no one in the Lower City ever saw: a new structure, little older than Xhea herself, with straight walls and floors that did not dip or sag underfoot, its ceiling unstained. No reclaimed materials had gone into its construction, she knew, and she marveled at the cost. The exterior was an illusion, the owner had assured her, as if that was the start and end of it.

"Hello?" Xhea called into the warehouse's perfect quiet. "Wen, Brend, are you here?" As if Wen could be anywhere else.

After a moment, she heard the floor creak from the office on the floor above, and a voice called down, "Xhea? That you? I was just—" There was a scrape, a crash, and the voice added, "I, uh . . . just need a minute."

"Take your time," Xhea muttered. She wandered farther inside, running her fingers along the shelves' edges, peering at their contents: computers and hair dryers, old novels and magazines, beads and tins and glass bottles with their metal caps still attached. Just bits and pieces and odd finds, possessions lost or discarded in the fall of the city that had come before. Junk she'd once called them; artifacts, Wen had corrected.

But it was a living. While Xhea had only heard of a few with the knack of catching a glimpse of a ghost, and knew of no one else who could do what she did, the ghost-afflicted were not plentiful enough to keep her eating. There were hundreds of jobs in the Lower City, from hunters out in the badlands to builders and re-builders, charm twisters and makers and vendors of every kind—and none of them were suited to a girl with no magic at all.

The only gift her lack of power granted her was the ability to go below ground, down into the subway tunnels and buried shopping complexes that wove beneath the Lower City. Normal people couldn't stand going underground, feeling discomfort and even pain the deeper they traveled—feelings that left Xhea untouched. And underground was where the good junk—the artifacts, the treasures—could be found.

As she slid between the shelves, Xhea spotted familiar items that she'd brought to Wen over the years. Others had been sold—not to Lower City folk like her, but to City museums and stores and art collectors. A citizen himself, Wen had had access to people far beyond Xhea's reach, though he'd always kept his warehouse hidden away on the ground.

Wen waited at the table in the center of the warehouse and greeted her with his usual distracted smile. "Come, come, sit," the old man said, waving her closer and gesturing at the empty seat across from him. "Anything good today?"

"You tell me." Digging past the chits, she unload the week's treasures onto the table: a light bulb no larger than her thumb, a remote control, and a small gold frame with a photo trapped behind its cloudy glass. Wen peered at the items through the half-moon glasses perched on the end of his nose. The best came last: a working solar calculator. Wen exclaimed as Xhea's gentle touch brought the calculator to life; though its display showed only random lines, that it worked at all was miraculous.

Leaving Wen to his examination, Xhea kicked back in her chair, plucked a familiar tube from a nearby shelf, and placed it against her right eye. Colors sprang to life before her, blue and green tumbling across red and yellow, blurring into purple and orange and brown. The kaleidoscope hadn't been one of her finds; she would have never let it go.

Wen spared her a glance. "High again, are you?"

"Just got paid." She gave another twist and watched the fractal patterns dance. "I don't know how you got anything done with this thing around."

"After eighty-odd years, watching beads in a tube lost its fascination," Wen replied dryly.

Xhea felt a tug at her sternum and opened her left eye. The ghost had come forward to hover over the table, her skirt all but brushing the tabletop, and peered over her legs at the items spread before Wen.

"Hello there," Wen said, and looked up to meet the ghost's eyes.

The dead girl recoiled as if struck, flying to the far end of her tether with a look of pure panic. Xhea jerked forward as the tether yanked at her sternum. Her heels fell from the table's edge, the movement almost enough to send her tumbling to the floor. As Xhea flailed for balance, the world suddenly darkened: the colors vanished, replaced by shade and shadow, charcoal and gray.

She had done no more than gasp when the magic once more washed through her system, nausea hard on the heels of color. She looked at the ghost in shock. What had she done? For a moment, it had felt as if the bright magic had vanished—almost as if the ghost had disrupted it, or pulled it from Xhea through the tether. Yet ghosts were as devoid of magic as Xhea herself; while a few spells could affect ghosts, the dead couldn't wield any true power. Not magic, then. But what else could have affected her payment?

The ghost, trembling on the far end of her tether, clearly had no answers. She stared at Wen with wide eyes. "He can see me?" she whispered.

"So it seems," Xhea replied. The bright magic surged through her, and again she thought, *Breathe. Breathe.*

Wen looked away from the calculator, shaking his head. He pulled the half-moon glasses from his face and wiped the lenses on the edge of his shirt, seemingly without thought. "Xhea," he said at last, "you're callous with the souls in your care."

"No." She swallowed in an attempt to settle her stomach. "Just short on time."

"You mean impatient and disinclined to care."

Xhea shrugged and looked away, disguising her discomfort in a search for the kaleidoscope. She fished it from beneath the table and placed it before her eye. "Same thing."

Wen ignored her, turning to the ghost and showing her his empty hands. "I'm not going to hurt you," he said. "I couldn't, even if I wanted to."

The ghost stared, those wide blue eyes making her seem strangely young.

"What's her name?" Wen asked softly.

"I don't know." At his look, she added, "She's only been with me a couple of hours. And you know they don't all remember." Ghosts forgot much about their lives—whether through death or choice, she never quite knew. It turned some transactions into exercises in frustration.

Wen sighed at the beginnings of their familiar argument. "You think that's excuse enough? Must you be paid for kindness? You know—"

"Shai," the ghost said. They both turned to her in surprise. As if speaking had steadied her, she took a breath and pushed her hair from her face with a careful hand. "My name is Shai."

"Hello Shai," Wen said, a gentle smile lighting his face. "Welcome."

Whatever Shai might have replied was lost at the sound of a heavy tread on the stairs from the upstairs office. "Sorry about that," a younger man said, coming to stand by the table. "Still going through some of those old boxes."

"Hey, Brend," Xhea muttered. She reluctantly slid the kaleidoscope back onto its shelf. "Break anything important?"

Brend ignored her comment, instead walking around the table to look at the items she'd brought, careful not to touch

Xhea as he passed. Side-by-side with Wen, it was easy to see the resemblance between them: same round face and dark hair, same wide flare to their noses, same hunched stance as they looked over Xhea's offerings. Yet though he watched Brend, eyes riveted on the younger man's face, Wen made no move to greet his son.

When he'd inherited his father's business, Brend seemed to have kept it open out of a sense of loyalty—or perhaps, Xhea thought none too kindly, he just didn't know what to do with the masses of junk that his father had acquired and had not the heart to let it all crumble into ruin once more. Though he had skill as an antiques dealer and something of his father's eye for hidden value, Brend had little love for the trade itself. Xhea had often wondered what Brend had given up to maintain his father's business—and whether he resented his other finders as he seemed to resent her.

He examined the pieces quickly, turning each with a practiced hand and exclaiming over the functioning calculator. He was quick to give her an offer on the lot, too—one so low it went beyond insult into comedy.

"Brend, Brend," Xhea murmured, grabbing the kaleidoscope and returning her heels to the table's edge. "I just can't decide: are you trying to ruin your father's business, or just conning a young girl out of her dinner?"

"My father," Brend began, his expression strained.

"His father," Wen interjected, "says to offer something halfway decent or he's disowned."

Xhea grinned. "Little late," she told Wen, but passed the message along. Brend's next two offers were similarly ridiculous.

"Seven hundred for the calculator," Wen said as his son hemmed and hawed, saying something about falling market interest in certain items, which Xhea ignored. "Three hundred for the rest."

"Raw?"

"Chip-spelled," Wen countered. At her frown, he sighed dramatically and added, "And the kaleidoscope."

Xhea grinned. "Deal."

Brend's face darkened as Xhea conveyed the details of the bargain made without his participation. She suppressed a sigh; from his expression, it would be a few weeks before she could return with more items—and a few more years before he truly got used to dealing with her. Still, what choice did he have? She was the only conduit for his father's expertise.

Then again, years spent working with Wen hadn't made him like her, either. They only truly began to talk after his death and the loneliness that came with haunting. It was easier to condescend to her company when she was the only one who knew he was there.

Chapter Two

By the time Xhea emerged from the warehouse, payment chip in hand, afternoon had begun its surrender into evening. *Curse Brend anyway*, she thought, dithering over their deal and letting time slip away. Curse her for not noticing. Even she didn't dare be caught in the ruins when night fell.

Muttering beneath her breath, Xhea hurried back toward the Lower City.

Nearly as bad, she could feel a tightness across her forehead—discomfort that heralded the onset of a magic-induced headache. She could barely believe her payment was almost gone; nearly five hundred renai burned through in a single afternoon. She could remember when that much would have lasted days, the world bright with color and the pressure of the darkness within her held at bay.

She increased her pace to a light jog, the ghost trailing behind her like a strange banner.

From behind her came a voice: "I'm . . . dead?"

Oh, sweetness, Xhea thought. *Not again.*

"That's right," she said. She wouldn't make it back the way she'd come, she realized with a glance at the darkening sky; there wasn't time. She considered her options. She could take the highway overpass back to the core, avoiding the chaos on the ground, or she could divert, heading at an angle to the Lower City where she might connect with the subway line. Subway, she decided. Becoming stranded on the ruin of the elevated roadway after nightfall was a disaster beyond contemplation, and she disliked heights at the best of times.

"And the man," the ghost continued. "The one who could see me. He was dead too?"

"Right again."

"But where was his . . . his . . ." She gave up trying to find a suitable word and just tugged in frustration at the line of energy joining them.

"His tether? It's there—he's just bound to the whole warehouse." No such thing as an untethered ghost, and praise be for small mercies.

Above, the Towers glittered like jewels cast across darkening velvet, the shimmering veils of magic that surrounded them far brighter than the emerging stars. Xhea pushed herself into a run, trusting experience to keep her from turning an ankle on the rough roadway. These streets were deserted, but even closer to the core, in the buildings on the edge of the ruins where few Lower City dwellers dared live, the inhabitants would be all safely inside, doors locked and barred, curtains drawn against night's fall. Night—and the things that walked the streets when darkness came.

No, she thought, *not just things*. There were animals out in the badlands—dogs and raccoons and things that might once have been cats—all of which she knew more as meat than living things. Even plants struggled to grow in the core. But so close to the Lower City? The only creatures that moved through the ruins of the city that had come before were human.

Or had once been human.

Xhea had never seen them, the night walkers, and gave thanks that there were some horrors of dirt-bound life she'd been spared. Yet she had heard them: their slow footsteps and the sounds of their movement, fingers brushing against door handles and window panes; the pauses as if they were listening, always listening. She'd heard, too, what they did to those they caught outside, heard the pleas and the screams, and seen what little remained of those unlucky few come morning.

Xhea ran left, right, three blocks straight ahead and then down the sweeping curve of a street that eased to the west—it was routine now, a path she could follow with eyes closed. But familiarity made the journey no shorter. At last she reached a stretch of road blocked by a fallen building, the passage piled with decaying timber and twisted siding. She slowed not for the blockage but the grate in the sidewalk before it. Quickly she knelt, hooked her fingers through the rusty rungs, and heaved, struggling against seized hinges. Winter had been hard on more than her food stores, it seemed.

The grate lifted to reveal a square hole with metal rungs embedded in the side of the concrete, leading down. She let her legs dangle, turned back to reach for the tether—and froze.

For there, just behind the ghost, hovered an elevator. The device was no bigger than her palm, and held within it tightly coiled spells that could unfurl and wrap around a passenger to bear them aloft. She hadn't called it—had no way of calling it. She could only assume that it was sweeping the ruins for straggling City adventurers, come to wander and hike through the ruins as some crazy few were wont to do, and had found her instead.

As she watched, its status light flashed yellow, yellow, yellow . . . green, its indecision giving way to a grudging willingness to bear her aloft. Xhea stared in shock. Never before had an elevator so much as registered her existence, never mind offered to take her to the City, no matter how high she was on renai. With no magical signature, she had no way to prove that she was anything other than a living, breathing bit of furniture. But there it was.

She stared, breath caught, as the small device blinked impatiently. She had never been to a Tower, never even come close. Yet she dreamed of them: of walking through one of the great organic structures, or standing on a lacework balcony perched in the sky; of visiting the terraced gardens at the peak of the Central Spire and staring out at all the City stretched below.

Never mind how she'd get home again without bright magic to pay for the passage. No magic to pay for food or shelter or citizenship. They had no use for her above; and whatever gave her the ability to see and speak to ghosts, the darkness that tainted her vision and seemed to pool inside her like a black and silent lake, would be of no more use there than in the Lower City. She would only ever imagine what the world looked like from so high.

"Why now?" she whispered to it. After so many years of hoping and trying to reach the City, why would it only come to her when she knew too much to take the risk?

There were tears on her cheeks, and angrily she brushed them away.

Turning away, Xhea looked down into the darkness, and stretched with her toes until her feet hit the first rung. She pulled the grate closed above her as she descended into the subway service tunnel, leaving temptation to fade with the last glimmers of daylight.

The ghost's voice followed her into the darkness, soft and hesitant. "Where are we?"

"In the tunnels. It's not safe to be outside." *Not safe for me, anyway*, Xhea thought. There was little that could touch a ghost.

Blind, Xhea dropped the last few feet to track level. Her normal sight needed no light, and shapes were easy to discern when cast only in gray. Yet enough of her payment lingered that she saw only black. She fished a small flashlight out of her jacket—kept there for such occasions—and shone the beam around her. The tunnel was cool and damp, smelling of mildew. The only sound was a slow and distant dripping.

"Why didn't you take the elevator? It could have taken us home."

"This is my home," Xhea said, voice hard. She stalked down the tunnel, gravel crunching underfoot, swinging the light back and forth more quickly than was warranted. If she could have run and left the ghost behind then, she would have.

Wen's words returned to her: *You're callous with the souls in your care.* It wasn't the ghost's fault that she was here; probably wasn't her fault that she was dead, either. For all that Xhea scorned the dead girl for the soft life she'd lived, wouldn't she herself leap at the chance for that life? To live in a Tower; to never have to think about where she was going to find the next meal, or how to gather enough food to get her through the winter, or store and protect clean water, or keep herself warm.

Xhea forced herself to slow, then turned to meet the ghost's confused gaze. "I don't have any magic," she said. Voice steady, as if the admission brought no shame.

"But I thought—didn't my father transfer renai to you?"

Her father. Xhea pushed away that piece of information with a shake of her head—it was safer not to know. How could she explain that she just wanted the payment for the high, the way it lit her vision with color and eased the pressure of the darkness that seemed to coil deep within her? The money was useless to her, burning away to nothing.

"I meant, I don't have *any* magic. Not even a magical signature." She might have said that she didn't have a head for the shock in the ghost's reaction.

"But that's not possible," the dead girl—Shai—protested. "Everyone has magic. It's the power of *life*. No one has none."

Xhea spread her hands wide. "Yet here I am."

"No, you must be mistaken. Maybe you don't have enough magic to spare—maybe you don't know the spells—but *everyone* has a magical signature just by being alive."

"Everyone," agreed Xhea, "except me."

"Then . . . why did my father give you money?" The ghost's voice faltered, and her face, briefly so animated, fell again. "I don't understand what's happening. Who are you? Why am I here?"

"Ah." Xhea turned away. "The great questions in life." What could she possibly say? It had been a bad idea to even try. Just talking to the ghost made her feel weary.

Xhea had a small room just off the main tunnel, a maintenance space reached by a short flight of stairs. The door, unlocked, creaked open at her touch, and a quick sweep of the flashlight showed no disturbances. It was a crash space, little more, but dry and familiar for all that, with extra clothes, a collection of books and coins and trinkets too dirty or broken to be worth selling, and a pile of blankets in the corner as a bed.

She fell into the pile without pulling off her overstuffed jacket or rain-damp clothes. She burrowed into the blankets' softness and held the kaleidoscope against her chest for comfort. Her head felt as if it were caught in a tightening vice, and the headache's pounding promised worse to come before morning.

"I don't understand . . ." the ghost began again.

"Not now," Xhea said. Her payment was almost gone. There would be time enough to talk in the morning, discuss the mysteries of life, or the reality of her death, or whatever else the ghost wanted to ramble on about.

"It's just that . . . well, I—"

"Not. Now."

She turned the kaleidoscope over and over as she fell asleep, watching the colors fade and darken, blue and green and yellow.

Gray. Gray.

Black.

Hours later, the headache's promise had been made good. Xhea lay curled in a miserable ball in the midst of her blankets, sweating and trembling as she clutched her stomach. She wished she could blame the meat skewers, but coming down off a payment was like this sometimes, as if her body were trying to purge every last spark of magic.

Realizing she was about to be sick, Xhea rushed for her waste bucket and sat clutching it in the darkness. Her eyes still hadn't adjusted. The dark pressed in from all sides, making the room seem small and frightening. Beside her, the flashlight had grown strangely dim, as if seen through a bank of fog, and cast only a weak, flickering beam across the floor.

Xhea clutched her stomach as she heaved, gagging and choking on the taste of bile. Tears ran down her cheeks, hot and fast; her nose dripped, and sweat seemed to run from every pore as she was violently ill, again and again. Yet despite the taste, she heard no liquid hitting the bucket. She felt the tears run, and sweat; raised her hand to her face and felt only hot, dry skin.

Shaking, she fell back into her nest of blankets, lost to fevered dreams.

When Xhea woke sometime that felt like morning, the worst of the illness had passed. Her normal eyesight had returned, casting the room around her in shades of gray—good thing, as the flashlight appeared to have died entirely—and when she lifted her hands, she managed to keep them from shaking. Yet the strange feeling in the pit of her stomach remained, not nausea but a feeling so intense that she knew not what to name it if not pain.

She struggled out of the damp mess of her blankets, twisted and knotted from her long night. She fetched a bottle of rainwater from the side of the room, and sat sipping it in the hope it might ease the hurt. It was only as she finished the water, tipping back her head to drain the last drops, that she realized she was alone in the small room.

The ghost was gone.

Xhea's hands flew to her chest where she'd anchored the tether, even as she looked around—as if the ghost might have simply slipped behind the heap of spare clothes or hidden herself beneath the blankets. But the tether was still there, bonded to her breastbone and vibrating softly in time with her heartbeat. Carefully, she followed the length of slippery air with her fingertips. Close to her body it was as wide around as a clenched fist and as strong; yet it thinned quickly, so that at the extent of her arms' reach it was no wider around than a thread.

Had the ghost found some way to break the tether? Perhaps she'd fought the bond so hard that it snapped. In her state, it wasn't as if Xhea would have noticed. Except that the tether didn't seem to be broken, only thinned almost to non-existence.

Perhaps it was only stretched, the ghost girl wandering in the tunnels just beyond the room's concrete walls. Yet it hadn't allowed her such freedom the day before—she'd barely been able to get more than a body length from Xhea, and that only with effort. New ghosts, as this one seemed to be, rarely thought about walking through walls, too bound by the habits of their former lives.

Besides, what little tether remained didn't point outward, but *up*.

"Sweetness," Xhea said. "I need a cigarette."

Fine, she thought; if the tether wasn't broken, she could use it to drag the ghost back. She grasped her end of the line and hauled back; yet no matter how she pulled, Xhea remained alone.

"Blight it," she muttered, pacing. She rubbed sweaty palms on her thighs. There had to be some way to make the girl return—or say bye-bye to the promise of a few weeks' steady income.

If she couldn't pull the ghost back physically, perhaps there was some way to call her. What was her name? Xhea struggled to remember. *Callous indeed*, she thought.

"Shai?" she said at last, tentatively, and the name sounded right. Her voice echoed from the bare walls. Gods, if she had actually *lost* the ghost . . . She didn't know how to finish the thought.

Slowly, she built a mental picture of the ghost—no, she reminded herself, of *Shai*. Her youth. Her soft, hesitant way of speaking; her confusion. Pale hair and paler eyes. Her slender build and narrow hands; her plum-colored dress, seeming all the more expensive for its simplicity. Her fear. Her tentative questioning, answered curtly or turned aside. Her insistence that she was still alive.

With each detail, Xhea's mental image of the ghost intensified—as did the pain in her stomach. *Focus on Shai*, she told herself. *Just breathe.* But with a sudden lurch, she realized she was going to be sick. She grabbed the bucket.

Lips pressed tight against her stomach's renewed rebellion, it was her eyes that first betrayed her, leaking tears that felt cold against her cheek. Before she could wipe them away, they began to lift from her skin, up and away—tears that weren't water at all but something dark that curled and coiled in midair like smoke.

Xhea whimpered, and as her mouth opened more darkness rushed out, fast as breath. She watched as the darkness slipped from between her lips and up through the air. *Not good*, she thought, *not good, not good*—too shocked to manage anything more coherent.

As the darkness rose toward the ceiling, it began to twist together into a single line, almost like a finger pointing. No, she realized; it was following the line of the tether, up and out, in response to her call. Xhea was burning, freezing, as if she'd been dipped in alcohol and lit ablaze—and still the darkness poured from her, rising from her whole body as if from every pore, moving like fog, coiling up through the Lower City in search of the ghost.

Stranger still, Xhea could feel the darkness like a phantom limb. It was as if a part of her consciousness eased up through the reinforced concrete, steel, and tile of the subway tunnels, up through gravel and earth, up through asphalt and weeds, and higher still, questing into the air above. And oh, how she wished it would stop—wished she knew some way to lock the creeping fog back inside of her, in the depths of her belly where it had always slept. Not because it hurt, but because this terrible flowing darkness that rushed from her felt . . . good. Strange and frightening, but *right*. That was the most terrifying thing of all.

"*Shai!*" Xhea cried, and the ghost returned with an air-rending crack. She hung at the end of her tether, arms spread wide and head thrown back, hair flying around her face as if in a storm wind. Xhea staggered as the darkness contracted, condensing around them like a veil of night. As she watched, the strange smoke-like substance dissipated as if it were smoke in truth, vanishing into the air.

Xhea all but collapsed onto her nest of blankets, limp and exhausted, the clatter of the coins and charms in her hair the only sound in the suddenly silent room. She stared at the ghost, watching as Shai slowly curled in upon herself until she was as Xhea had first seen her: calm and serene, eyes closed and legs crossed beneath her, hands resting palm-up on her knees.

Xhea rose and crept, shaking, across the cold floor. She could only stand by holding the concrete wall, and even then her knees quivered, weak as a creature newly born.

"Shai?" Xhea whispered, and the ghost opened her eyes.

"I'm only dreaming." She sounded too heartbroken to cry.

Oh, would that this were a dream, Xhea thought; all of it a dream, and she would wake to simple darkness, none of it flowing from her like living smoke. She had always felt something dark inside her, a feeling she suppressed with the bright hit of payment, but she had likened it to absence—only a hole where magic should have been. Not this. Even now she felt it curl and coil within her like slow fog; felt the contentment, the satisfaction, that it left in its wake. Xhea shivered and wrapped her arms around herself.

"What did you do?" She didn't understand how the ghost had vanished or so suddenly returned, nor what she had done to bring her back—if the darkness had brought her back at all. She only knew that she had to do everything within her power to keep that darkness from overflowing again.

Shai didn't answer, only stared with pale eyes that gleamed silver. Xhea grabbed the tether and pulled until their faces were but a hand's width apart. Shai gasped and struggled to pull away, but Xhea held tight, fingernails digging into her own palm.

"Tell me," she said, voice low. "Tell me what you did, how you left this place. Tell me how—"

And stopped, caught breathless.

For it was only so close, face to face, with all the bright magic gone from her vision, that she saw it: a glint hidden deep within the pupil of Shai's eye. A single spark, white and fierce and pure. Xhea stared, thinking: *Just a reflection, just a flicker of light.*

Then it came again—a glint—and again, in the ghost's other eye. Xhea refocused her eyes to see the magic more clearly, and then there was no pretending, for Shai was alight with bright magic. And the dead had no magic—unless . . .

"No," Xhea whispered, a soft and useless denial. Only once had she seen a ghost that glimmered with magic—once—and she had sworn then that if it were in her power, she'd never witness, never allow, such a thing again.

She released her grip on the tether and began to search. She ran her hands through the air around the ghost, fingers outstretched, as Shai watched in perplexed silence. Xhea was careful never to touch the ghost. She knew that she could pass her hand right through Shai with little more than a chill against her skin, but still she shied away, as if her fingers might encounter warm flesh instead. But even focused on the most minute sensations against the skin and hair of her hands, Xhea almost missed it: the familiar slipperiness of a tether.

A second tether.

She followed the length, testing its strength, its boundaries, its shape. This tether was not joined to Shai's heart, as the first was, nor to her head as tethers often were, but to her body as a whole. As had happened but moments before, within a few feet of the ghost the tether narrowed to little more than a thread—and a ragged thread at that, damaged and fraying. There was something other than her father that bound the ghost to the living plane.

Still that voice whispered in Xhea's head: *No, no, no.*

Shai might be dead, but oh, it was easy to see now that she had magic. Here in the dark, with no bright magic affecting Xhea's vision, Shai was strangely alight, the tiny sparks growing brighter and more frequent as Xhea watched.

"Shai," Xhea said quietly, calmly, as if she were not holding back her fear with sheer will alone. "Did you return to your body?"

Shai's response seemed startled from her: "Yes."

"Did you mean to go there? Did you want to?"

The ghost shook her head. "I was here, with you, and then I was just . . . there. Trying to wake up."

Quieter still: "Did you open your eyes?"

"No. I tried, but I couldn't move, couldn't see at all. It was so cold and so dark and I *hurt* . . ."

No. Oh, please no. Yet still Shai glimmered.

What had Shai said the day before? The words came as if from very far away: *I'm asleep. Only asleep.*

Feeling the black fog coil contentedly through her, Xhea whispered, "Then this must be a very bad dream."

Chapter Three

Across the width of the small room and back again, Xhea paced, her hands twitching restlessly at her sides. The sound of her unsteady breath, her echoing footsteps, failed to fill the silence.

An hour or more remained before dawn, but there was no point in sleeping; no need even to try. The shakes from her ebbing adrenaline made it impossible to sit still. She wanted to run, to fight, to scream—anything to relieve the pressure that seemed to come from all sides, as if the walls were closing in. Anything to keep from thinking about Shai, those glints of bright magic, and the horror that they represented.

Anything to keep from thinking of that darkness.

"Okay," Xhea whispered, trying to think. "Okay, okay . . ." Except it wasn't. She would wear her boot soles to nothing pretending otherwise.

Fine, then: a distraction. She grabbed a crazed plastic basin from the corner and filled it with water from one of her reservoirs, pouring carefully to avoid disturbing the thick sludge that had settled in the bottom. She threw off her jacket and the sweaty shirt beneath, dropping each to the floor. Her hands shook as she wet a cleaning rag, and she watched waves flutter across the water's surface, each heavy with a weight of meaning that she could not translate. She lifted the rag and rung it out, fighting for calm. Suppressing the desire to scream.

It's just fear, she told herself. Uncertainty and adrenaline.

Felt the lie, and tasted it; closed her eyes and made herself breathe.

She washed her face and neck and arms, rivulets running down her chest and dripping from chin and elbows. The water was cold and it was just this, she told herself, that made her gasp. Only the chill that caught the breath in her throat and twisted it into a sob.

Xhea scrubbed until her skin felt raw and her fingers tingled from the cold, washing away the sweat—if not the memory of the shadow that lingered beneath. She stopped only when her shivers turned violent, then dressed in cleaner clothes. Her jacket came last, its weight a comfort across hunched shoulders.

"Xhea?" That quiet, hesitant voice.

Xhea didn't want to turn, didn't want to meet those strange pale eyes and all the unanswered questions in their depths. Even so, she could feel the ghost. She had always been aware of ghosts, sensing them as it seemed they sensed her; yet never before had she felt a ghost's presence like a bruise in midair. Though she willed it to stillness or oblivion, the darkness woken inside her reached for Shai, as if by yearning it could ease through the boundaries of her flesh toward the imbalance of a ghost lit with bright magic. Perhaps it could.

She should stand, she knew. Leave. Outside, this would soon be a morning like any other. On the edge of the Lower City core, small groups would gather: hunting parties with weapons and survival gear, planning their trips out to the badlands; scrounging teams going to search the ruins for anything usable; a few misguided souls with handfuls of seeds and fertilizer and more hope than sense. The rising sound of voices, the low roar of generators with their stinking plumes of dark smoke, the sizzle and smell of food frying. Breakfast.

It all seemed so far away.

Xhea turned to the ghost and found Shai watching from on high, legs curled beneath her, head cradled in one hand. There was no trace of her earlier pain and fear, only a slight wariness in the eyes Xhea knew to be blue. That was the thing with ghosts. They were terrified one moment, back to normal the next. Fears were strange and fickle when you no longer had a life to lose.

"Can you get down here?" Xhea asked. "You're cricking my neck something fierce."

"Can you put the knife away?"

Xhea glanced at her hand, surprised to find her fingers flipping the opened knife over and over in a familiar nervous gesture. There were no traces of blood on the blade, ghostly or otherwise. Years of obsessive polishing had worn the silver clean.

"It's not like I'm going to cut you," she said, thinking: *Probably. Not yet, anyway.*

"Still."

Xhea shrugged and folded the blade but kept the knife in hand, fingers restlessly rubbing the mother of pearl handle, its weight a comfort she little wished to banish to a pocket. Even closed, it held her attention. It was, she knew, the simplest answer to this problem; cutting the tether that tied her to Shai was the only sensible thing to do. What had she promised? A day, maybe two, and then they'd discuss more. Surely, after that night and all the distress the ghost had caused, she'd done work enough for the payment received.

Besides, the longer she kept Shai, the greater the chances that the ghost would be called again to her body, dragged back along the second tether and into the cold shell of flesh that had once been her own. If that happened, what would keep the strange darkness from rising again? Black tears and vomit, breath and sweat, wrenched out of her regardless of what she demanded or desired.

And that, right there, was the part of the problem that she couldn't cut away. The darkness, she called it—had always considered it such, if only in the part of her mind where fears and bad dreams lingered. Now that she had seen it, felt it ascendant, she knew it had another name and one far truer: magic. Magic unlike any she'd known or of which she'd heard tell. Magic dark and languid, like thick oil, like branching smoke.

Magic at last; her own magic. She choked back a bitter laugh. How long had she wished for magic, even the smallest glimmer? Her whole life, it seemed. She thought of the dark magic rushing uncontrolled from her throat and lips, leaking from her eyes and skin, and she shivered. Never had she imagined that having her wish granted could be so terrible, so horrifying or so cold.

"What are you thinking?" Shai asked softly, and Xhea looked up from her knife. The ghost had come to kneel beside her—or tried to, instead hovering a hand's width above the floor. She still had a lot to learn about being dead, but it wasn't a bad first try for a ghost so new.

That I'm afraid, Xhea thought, *and don't know what to do.* Instead she said, "Shai, how did you die?"

She expected the ghost's usual denial, but Shai just shook her head.

"Okay. What's the last thing you remember? Before you met me."

The answer came after a long pause. "I remember . . . the dark. A long time in the dark."

"What does that mean?"

Another pause, the silence stretching between them. "I don't know," Shai said, hesitant and unsure, as if Xhea might scold her for giving the wrong answer.

"Okay." Xhea sighed. "Don't worry about it." Shai wouldn't be the first ghost to forget her death, nor the first to not know quite how it happened. Death snuck up on people in a thousand ways, fast and slow and by surprise, and its inevitability made it no easier to accept.

Yet Shai seemed not to hear. "I remember . . ." she whispered, twisting her hands together. "I remember . . ." As if words might conjure the memories, bring them to the tips of teeth and tongue.

"I remember the dark, and I remember . . . hurting. But there are moments when the pain stops, and my father is there. Those times, he's with me." Perhaps she was remembering the first moments after her death—the moments when she left her body? If so, it seemed her dying had been a blessing; caught in the memory of her pain's ease Shai's face seemed alight, the faintest of smiles gracing her lips.

"But the rest of the time?" Xhea asked softly, thinking: *Careful, now. Careful.*

"All of me, my whole body. Hurting."

"Did someone do something to you? Hurt you?"

"No." Her denial was almost inaudible. Shai shook her head and squeezed her eyes shut. "No, it's . . . *me*."

"You hurt yourself?"

Shai's voice seemed to come from impossibly far away. "Only by living. By living and breathing, and the magic . . ." She shook her head again. Ghostly tears crept from the corners of her squeezed-tight eyes, sliding down her face to fall and vanish in midair. When she spoke again, the words were rushed and tinged with panic. "The magic . . . it's sick, wrong. Broken. It's all going wrong, all of it wrong—it's eating me from the inside out and I can't—I can't—*I can't stop it.*" With a cry, she buried her face in her hands.

Xhea could barely touch the ghost—was unsure what little comfort she could offer—and so she waited awkwardly, turning the knife over and over as she tried to make sense of Shai's explanation. Her mind circled the word "sick," fixated on it. Sick, wrong, broken—something eating her from the inside out. What could it be but an illness? Illness was rare in the Towers where the prevalence of magic brought health and long life, magic enough to keep sickness at bay, with spells to ease pain and cure disease. But their rarity did not mean fatal illnesses were impossible, and someone—her parents, most likely—might have been made all the more desperate for the unexpected nature of her death.

Question was, had they become desperate enough to resurrect her?

Oh, how she wanted to cut Shai's tether. Yet that would mean turning her back on what could only be an attempted resurrection—a horror Xhea had seen only once, and had sworn she'd do anything, everything, to keep from happening again.

She needed a cigarette. No, she needed a bit of bright magic to cast all this into memory, or the courage to cut the line that joined her to this cursed ghost, and had neither. She waited, rubbing the knife's smooth hilt, until Shai's cries quieted.

"Come on." Xhea forced herself to her feet. "I want to show you something."

After days of rain, the bare patch of ground that was the Lower City's only park resembled a lake dotted with islands of churned mud. Xhea grimaced at the sight. Above, the sky had yielded to a sluggish dawn, the heavy cloud cover hiding all but the lowest Towers, their shapes hulking shadows in the haze. No more rain, and praise be for such small mercies; but if the sun didn't come out soon, the few plants that managed to grow so close to the core would be drowned entirely.

Sighing, she picked her way across the expanse of mud, past the lone tree, and sat on a bench. Its ancient cast concrete supports were now spanned with boards from packing crates that creaked beneath her weight as she drew up her legs and wrapped her arms around her knees. After a moment, Shai attempted to sit beside her.

Only then did Xhea look at the building that loomed beyond the park's farthest edge like a tombstone marking a muddy plot. Orren: the Lower City's rotten tooth, jagged-edged and leaning. In the times before memory it had been an office building, sixty-five stories of gleaming black glass—a skyscraper in truth. Now it was called "skyscraper" only because it was one of the five tallest buildings left standing. Sometime during the fall of the city that had come before, Orren had been broken, nearly a full thirty stories toppled or ripped away, leaving the shortened building topped with jutting beams and broken concrete supports. Now only the buttons on its elevator banks stood as testament to its lost height.

Though the upper levels were still in the process of being reclaimed—Lower City code for "totally uninhabitable"—Orren's first twenty or more levels were in use, some packed almost to overflowing. As Xhea knew all too well. Usually she stayed as far from Orren as possible within the Lower City's boundaries, avoiding even the streets near its base as if she could feel its shadow heavy in the air like fog.

Xhea tugged on the ghost's tether to get her attention, and pointed. "See that? That's Orren."

"What . . . ?" Shai looked around slowly, as if unable to decide on which of the strange and incomprehensible things her gaze should rest.

"A skyscraper. It's about as close to a Tower as we get here on the ground." So much so that the five skyscrapers had names, mimicking those above—and a sad and sorry mimicry, at that. The airborne Towers were everything to their people: not just a home, but life and livelihood, business and family, community. Whatever spare magic citizens generated went into the Tower itself, fueling not only its ability to stay aloft but also its internal systems and spells, its businesses and industries, its coffers. In return those citizens lived in the communal glow of their Tower's magic, the gifts of health and happiness and long life inherent in every breath, every bite, every drop of captured rain.

The skyscrapers were just . . . buildings. Old and crumbling structures kept from collapse by years of hard work and, some said, the preserving effect of the City's magical runoff. Yet the power that resided in the Lower City—magical, political, and otherwise—belonged to one or other of the skyscrapers, as did most of its inhabitants. Only they had enough resources to garner attention from even the weakest Towers out on the City's fringes. Those few Towers that deigned to do business with the skyscrapers kept the Lower City alive: selling food and seeds, tools that worked, supplies to repair what little they had. And if the quality was but a fraction of that known to those in the City proper—well, who were they to complain?

"People live there?" Shai asked. She stared at Orren's crown of twisted girders.

"I lived there," Xhea said, and managed to keep her voice steady. "Once." It had been four years since her escape. At times it seemed but a moment ago, her fear little abated with the distance of time.

Joining Orren had been a mistake from the beginning. She'd known within days—hours—that she'd made the wrong choice. Had lain awake watching the snow swirl outside the window of the girls' dorm, wishing she'd chosen the very real possibility of freezing to death instead of the relative comfort of Orren's reclaimed glass and steel walls. But the indenture had been signed, and even the signature of a ten-year-old child was binding.

Orren's industry—for every skyscraper had one—was people. They could make it sound so safe, so promising, for it was only through a skyscraper that a Lower City dweller had even a chance at living in a Tower. Orren trained them; and while some few held respectable positions or learned skilled trades, most jobs were of the type that no City citizen would want, no matter how desperate. There were many uses that a young girl could be put to—yet Orren's recruiters had made a mistake when Xhea signed her contract: they hadn't touched her. Hadn't even tried.

She'd wondered since what might have happened had someone brushed her shoulder that fateful morning she signed away her life; how her future might have changed had someone tried to shake her hand and felt the crawling discomfort of her touch. The sensation had been described to her as an unending static shock, or pins-and-needles—even once as the ache of a new bruise. A localized version of the feeling that everyone else experienced underground.

"But . . ." Shai stared at Orren with her brows lowered. Mottled light shone dully from the skyscraper's metal and glass sides, darkened and pitted by the dirt of untold years. Xhea watched her judge the worth of those walls—even broken, even twisted— and deem them preferable to dank subway tunnels and forgotten shopping concourses.

"But . . . you don't live there anymore."

"No."

"Why?"

Xhea's quick reply caught in her throat. Oh, she didn't want to talk about this—didn't even want to think of it. Yet memories rose, and with them came fear. Xhea swallowed, choking on both. Remembering the only other ghost she'd ever seen who glowed and glimmered with magic when the light was right. Remembering his screams, and the whine of magic storage coils as they overloaded, flickered, and died. Remembering the feel of her knife, sticky with dark blood—and a man's soul.

"Something happened there," she managed. "Something very bad."

"And you just . . . left?"

Xhea nodded, wanting to laugh at the simplicity of that word. Left. As if anything could be so easy.

Again Shai frowned, looking from Orren to Xhea and back again. "It has to do with me, doesn't it? The thing that happened."

"Yes." She turned to Shai, shifting her eyes' focus to see the magic that imbued the ghost. It was stronger now, brighter: Shai seemed almost to glow. "I've seen a ghost like you before—a ghost who sparkled with magic. Someone had put spells on him. On his body, and . . . on his ghost."

"Spells?" Shai glanced down at her hands as if she too might see the magic that wove through her. "What were they supposed to do?"

"Bring him back to life."

It was a ludicrous idea, even in concept. No one—certainly no one in the Lower City—had enough magic to return life to the dead. Even with a skilled caster and assistance with the ghost, resurrection would require so much magic, so much power, as to be impossible. Magic to prepare the body, magic to prepare the ghost, magic to join the two and more to bind them. Magic to slow time's ravages and heal damage that the body could not. Magic to animate the flesh and tie it to the ghost's will: spells upon spells, one for every part of the body that needed to move; spells upon spells to animate every muscle in the face and mouth, lips and throat, required for even the most garbled of speech. Magic as fuel guzzled down: energy enough to make any person a force in the City. Energy enough to keep a Tower aloft.

Still, someone had tried—there, within those twisted walls. And she, gods save her, had helped.

"Heal him?" Shai asked. "But how could that be bad?"

Xhea shook her head, coins chiming, as if the memories and the emotions that swelled in their wake might be brushed away like flies. "Not heal him." She managed to keep her voice steady. "Force his spirit back into his dead body—and keep him there." Trap him, no matter how much he fought or screamed or cried.

No matter how much it hurt him, or how he pleaded. And what use were pleas that only Xhea could hear?

It was hard to think of those days; harder still to accept that she'd helped willingly, even eagerly. After a year of near uselessness within Orren, the debt of her indenture increasing as she struggled to earn her keep with menial chores, Xhea had confessed her ability to see ghosts. Then there had been work for her—and sudden interest from Orren's elite. They started with small jobs to prove her skills: speaking to a ghost, banishing another, changing tethers to a dizzying array of anchors. Only later did she realize that they'd been testing her for the one job they cared about.

They explained little of their goals, these men and women she'd known more by reputation than as living beings: the skyscraper's few casters, their magic strong enough—or so it was said—to have lived in the City proper but who chose to live in the Lower City like gods among mortals. Even with their power, preparations had taken weeks, spells woven from threads of magic, layered lines of will and intent that bound spirit and body both. Xhea had guided the casters to the ghost that she alone could see, and had steadied the ghost when he had struggled or shied away. The ghost had glimmered, then, as he moved: the spells' roots dug deep into his spirit, sparking as he fought to be free.

"But . . . why?"

"I don't know," Xhea whispered. "They didn't want to know something from him—they forbade me to speak to him. I thought he might have been someone important, but that's not how they treated him. I even thought that they might have been using him for his magic. They hooked him up to the skyscrapers' systems, as if he were a battery—maybe you can get more magic from a man when his body doesn't use it to live?" She shook her head. In all the time she'd thought about it, all the sleepless nights, the pieces had never quite fit.

"He was dead," Xhea said. "I mean, he had to have died for his ghost to be free—but they'd brought his body back. His heart was beating, lungs were breathing, but only because of the machines. Just looking at his body . . . you never would have thought something that broken, that ruined, could be alive."

Xhea stared at Orren, its dirty glass façade, and the empty floor near the top of the skyscraper's broken height where the attempted resurrection had occurred. Some days she had but to hear a sizzle of magic or smell flesh tinged with decay to return there. In memory she could see ghost and body both, each all but blinding from the layered spells that bound them. The machinery that forced the corpse to live had been nearly invisible in that harsh light. She saw too the shapes of the casters gathered around, pulling magic not from themselves but from massive storage coils, the type used by banks, drawing so hard on their energy that the coils whined in protest.

She'd been all but giddy in that room, high on spilled magic, vision dancing with color as often as not—and loving every moment of it.

The silence stretched. "What did they do?" Shai prompted.

Xhea swallowed. "There were four days of prep. On the fifth, they attempted the resurrection. For a while, everything seemed fine. The casters activated the spells—they were like magical lines, ropes almost, that bound the ghost to his body." Like tethers, she'd thought—a thousand tethers of bright magic, so thick that she could barely see for their light. "The spells drew the ghost down to his body. But when the two touched, the ghost . . . *screamed.*

"I've seen a lot of ghosts, and I've heard them scream before. Anger and frustration, hurt and denial and grief. But this—I'd never heard anything like it. It was the first time I'd ever heard a ghost in agony."

Shai's eyes widened. "What did you do?" she whispered.

Xhea laughed, quiet and bitter. "I screamed too. I told the casters to stop, told them they were hurting him. They didn't care. I tried to get to him, but . . . I was eleven years old. They held me back easily." She'd fought, but they were a child's struggles, a child's fists, and even her years on the streets had taught her no way to break free from a grown man willing to ignore the pain of touching her.

She continued. "One by one, the casters drained the storage coils dry—the coils, and then themselves. All that brightness going black. They pushed themselves right to the edge, first trembling and shaking as they tried to control the spells, and then just . . . falling. Then the spells began to fail, snapping and fraying.

"Through it all, the ghost kept screaming. On and on and on. He didn't need to breathe, and it was like the sound was being torn from him somehow, torn from his very self." She gestured helplessly, as if with hands alone she could shape how she'd felt at that moment, that powerless terror and revulsion and the terrible, terrible compassion. She'd been certain that she would be deafened by the ghost's anguish, unable to hear anything but the echoes of that sound.

"The spells worked," Xhea said. "For as long as they lasted. They bound the ghost to his body. But there wasn't nearly enough power to complete what they'd started. So he was stuck, half in his body, half out, fighting against the bonds and screaming."

Stop there, she told herself. Shai didn't need to know anything more. But the words seemed inevitable now, and the telling.

"As they fell, I freed myself. I took out my knife." Xhea closed her eyes. It was too hard, suddenly, to look at Orren; all that cracked and gleaming glass, too bright in the early morning light. Too bright for memories so dark.

"I tried to help him," she said, her voice little more than a whisper. "I tried. I ran to him with the knife and I started . . . cutting. But they were spells, not tethers, and they were so strong. Ropes and cords of magic. I had to use all the strength I had."

She took a deep breath, shuddering. "But there was nowhere to cut that didn't touch either his body or his ghost. And he was screaming and fighting to be free—and I was screaming too, cutting and flailing and nearly blind from so much magic."

"Did you hurt him?" Shai asked.

"Hurt him?" Xhea laughed bitterly. "I killed him."

"But . . ."

"He was already dead, I know. His body. It wasn't that." Even though blood had coated the blade and her hands, dark and thick and shining. Even though she'd slashed the failing ruin of his body, destroyed the plastic lines and wires that connected the body to the machines, shredded his clothes. No, not that.

"It was . . . him," Xhea managed. "His ghost. I cut him with the knife, sliced and shredded the ghost himself as surely as I had his body." When she had realized what was happening, she'd stumbled back, looking from the ravaged ghost and his hemorrhaging body to the bloody knife in her hand. She'd watched in horror as the ghost faded, slipping from existence like blood from a wound until only the echo of his screams remained.

"I killed him—his ghost, his soul, whatever you want to call it. That was the day I left Orren." Ignoring her contract, her debt, her fear, she'd run—and hadn't stopped running since.

Head bowed, trembling, Xhea tried to get control of herself. She'd never told that story to anyone. Never. One strange and frightening night, and she was baring her soul to some dead girl she'd just met? She hated remembering that time; she woke enough nights seeing what they—what she—had done without needing to conjure the images in daylight.

The silence stretched.

"You're shivering," Shai said.

Xhea nodded. What was there to say?

Opening her eyes, she turned to the ghost, and saw that Shai attempted what Xhea had not: she had raised a single hand to Xhea's shoulder in comfort. The touch of Shai's fingers was barely a touch—just a chill breath like a cool wind passing, the slightest hint of pressure. But the suddenness, the strangeness of the action almost made Xhea recoil. It was the first time anyone had touched her voluntarily for more years than she could remember. Stranger still was the feeling that followed: the desire to lean in to that touch, however insubstantial.

"You think that's what's happening to me," the ghost said. It wasn't, in the end, a question.

In silence Xhea looked at Shai's face, her pale eyes and narrow nose, the gentle sweep of her cheekbones. Shai looked nothing like him, the nameless ghost she had killed. Yet even were it not for the spirit that Xhea felt still stained her hands, she found that she did not want Shai to suffer. Despite her helplessness, her ghostly hands soft from a life of ease, Xhea knew that this girl had carried much in her short life. She looked at Xhea with not pity, not sympathy, but empathy. She, too, knew pain.

It would be easiest to cut the tether that joined them, that much seemed certain. Yet even as she reached for her silver blade, Xhea knew she could not. Even if she were wrong in her suspicions, even if Shai had never been hurt or used, she couldn't just let the ghost go to her fate. *Not alone*, she thought, *without any way to fight back*.

Not alone.

She took a deep breath. "Yes," Xhea said. Only that.

"Resurrection," Shai said slowly. She seemed to roll the word in her mouth as if feeling its shape with her tongue. "Yes. Yes, but . . ."

"But?"

"I think you're right. But there's . . . there's something . . ."

"Else?"

"Yes. No . . . I don't remember. It sounds right. Familiar, somehow." Each slow word sounded solid as a foundation newly laid. "Except . . . the one thing I know for certain is that I'm not dead. They wouldn't let me die."

Xhea's eyebrows rose. "How do you resurrect someone who's not dead?"

Shai didn't seem to hear. Instead, she stared at the City above them, the Towers moving in their slow dance-like battles for altitude. Xhea followed her gaze, but whatever Shai saw in the Towers' patterns was lost to her. They were only Towers, unreachable as stars.

Everyone died, whether others willed it or no. Xhea tried to imagine who Shai thought had the power to keep her from death—her family? Her Tower? Yet it was her father who had brought her to Xhea, separating the ghost from the body into which she would be forced to return. Perhaps, she thought slowly, that was why he had come to her: a last attempt to stop the resurrection.

"Well," Xhea said, "if you're not dead, you're certainly not alive, either. So what does that make you?"

The ghost turned to her, the silver of her eyes shadowed thundercloud gray, hazy like distant rain falling. She did not cry. She did not blink. Only whispered, "I don't know."

Xhea looked up again, following the near-invisible line of Shai's second tether toward the Towers, the most influential so far distant that they were no more than bright pinpoints, like stars radiant in daylight.

"That leaves me with two problems. When I left Orren, I swore I would never let anything like that happen again. Not ever—yet here you are." Xhea gestured to the great floating Towers, their sculptural shapes like spinning tops balanced on cloud. "But where's your body, Shai? And how can I possibly find it?"

"I don't know," Shai said softly. "I don't know why I can't remember."

Silence grew between them. At last Shai asked, "What's the second problem?"

Xhea snorted. "Breakfast."

Chapter Four

"No," the vendor said, and passed the chit back. It scraped across the surface of the wooden table he used as a counter, the sound nearly lost beneath the clamor of early morning bargaining.

"But—"

"It's empty," he said, turning away. "No."

Xhea swore. She wished the man had left the sandwich roll she'd ordered within reach; she'd have been gone long before he could maneuver his way out from the packing crate fortress of his stall.

"So much for breakfast," she muttered, weaving her way through the early morning crowd. "Your payment's for junk," she added to Shai over her shoulder. That had been the third stall she'd tried, using a different chit each time with identical results. Four days of food chits dead as stone, and her stomach empty besides. It was one thing to be bargained down; another thing entirely to be cheated. Lucky for Shai she'd already decided not to cut the tether.

Shai scrambled to keep up. "But didn't you use one of those yesterday?"

Xhea frowned, remembering the skewer. She couldn't have been so lucky as to choose the one chit that was actually imbued—or had the vendor simply not verified payment before handing over her meal? As if. But chits didn't just lose their magic. Shaking her head, she stuffed the dead chit back in her pocket. She still had the chip-spelled payment from Brend, but she couldn't access the chip's stored renai herself; she needed someone who could transfer the money—and would actually give her change. Xhea sighed.

There was a rhythm to the market and her movement through it, and she slipped into its patterns with the grace of long practice. She had to be careful here, where the press of bodies left little room for even one so slight as she. What space she might have earned by the discomfort of her touch was too quickly lost in the crowd's ebb and flow. Even the ever-present chime of the coins and charms bound into her hair was drowned beneath the sound of voices, the clatter of wares being stacked and arranged, and the roar of a generator burning yesterday's garbage for fuel.

She didn't so much look at the stalls and their varied wares as let them flow around her, all shade and shadow, hoping for inspiration. Xhea had felt the hair-fine tether that joined Shai to her body, its length taunt, its angle so steep that she shied from thinking on it. Shai's body was in one of the Towers, that much was clear. But getting there . . . ? Might as well seek to travel to the stars.

Xhea could not remember all the times she'd tried to reach the City, all the schemes and plans that had inevitably come to nothing. There had been enough that she'd begun to feel the weight of the accumulated failures; enough that she'd almost stopped dreaming of Towers. But if the dreams remained, she'd learned not to reach for them, lest she spend her whole life yearning for things forever beyond her grasp.

Except now she wasn't trying to make a life in the City, or in whatever Tower she found—only get there in time to stop the resurrection. And for that, perhaps all she needed was enough renai. Again she touched the pocket where she'd stashed the payment Brend had given her so reluctantly the night before, and grinned.

"Right," she said, and set off toward the market's far end, where smoke from the generator hung in a haze. Walking a path that repetition had carved into memory, she made her way through the stalls that surrounded the old mall in great, uneven rings. In theory, these stalls were temporary, the vendors too transient to earn a place in the true market held in the shelter of those ancient walls. Yet the "temporary" tents had been there so long that Xhea could remember nothing else in their place. So long as bribes were paid, there was little reason for Senn—the skyscraper that owned the ancient mall and all the surrounding buildings—to force out such a lucrative source of income.

At last Xhea came to a stall with its front displays overflowing with trays of twisted wire, carved discs, and bits of stone and wood. The proprietor moved through the cluttered interior gracefully, a whipcord thin woman with long beaded locks who ducked beneath bells and hanging ward chimes with an unthinking ease.

"Iya," Xhea called. Iya raised a distracted hand in acknowledgment and brought a carved charm to a customer, an older man dithering over his choices.

Iya was a charm twister, a common enough trade in the Lower City where few had the magical strength necessary to create an independent spell—but it was her artistry as much as skill that made Iya's charms so popular. All twisters made shapes to hold magic in a spell's pattern, asking wood or bone or wire to hold the spell shape that weak magic alone could not sustain; yet Iya's pieces had a certain grace that assured her steady business despite the mess of her storefront. Xhea herself had bartered for a few of Iya's charms; inert now, they were bound into her hair.

Even now, Iya was busy: the old man held most of her attention as he combed through a tray of medallions with single-minded intensity. The pieces in question glittered sluggishly, becoming lighter and darker without noticeable pattern; yet Shai made a sound of interest, floating down to peer at them around the man's piled packages. Xhea could only assume that the effect was more striking in color.

"Iya, any news?" Iya sent customers Xhea's way a few times a year, and was the closest thing she had to an ally in the market. They'd known each other for a long time—not, of course, that either mentioned their history. But today Iya shook her head, barely glancing away from her customer.

"Got time to do a transfer?" Xhea flashed the payment chip.

"Sorry," Iya said with a wave that could have as easily been apology as dismissal. Xhea nodded her thanks and continued, dragging a reluctant Shai behind.

Shared history or no, Iya rarely had much time for her. But being ignored served well enough, Xhea thought as she took a bite of the old man's sandwich roll. It was still fresh enough to be cold.

"Egg," she said to the ghost, gesturing at the roll she'd slipped from the man's shopping. "Not half bad." At the ghost's look she added, "Just be glad I don't have to feed you too." *And be glad*, she thought, *that finding food was so easy.* Xhea didn't want to know what Shai would say if she saw Xhea eat from the garbage—or worse.

Chewing, she looked at the chip in her hand. Finding someone else willing to transfer the magic was difficult, especially for anything less than half the renai. She flipped the chip over her fingers as she ran through the short list of individuals who had helped her with a transfer before, planning her next attempt. Idly, she unfocused her eyes, looking for the familiar glimmer of power beneath the plastic surface.

Not everyone could see raw magic, not spelled to be visible, but Xhea had been taught the trick of focusing her eyes just *so*, enabling her to see the energy even through solid objects. With practice, seeing lines of power had become almost second nature—not, of course, that she dared reveal the ability. Those able to see magic not of their own working, especially through plastic or flesh or stone, were the more powerful magic users: City folks, and high-powered ones at that. Even many of the strongest Lower City spell-casters lacked the talent. An ability to see spells would make most think her lack of magic a ruse, evidence to the contrary be blighted.

Yet as she stared at the chip, no curl of power lit her vision—not even a flicker. Dead, just like the food chits from Shai's father. One customer stiffing her was possible—but two in the same day? For all that he disliked her, Brend wouldn't cheat her; he needed her connection to his father, and the artifacts she brought, too much for that.

The dead chip in her hand said otherwise.

"You've got to be kidding me," she muttered. So much for that plan—and so much for eating well the rest of the week. She was back to emergency rations.

Okay, she told herself. Forget *how* she'd get to the City for a moment—time to focus on *where*. She pulled the still-staring Shai from the crowd and down a narrow side street, then felt for the second tether. The length was as fine as before, but easier to find now that she knew it was there. She followed it with her fingers as far as she could reach, then stood, arm outstretched to follow the tether. *Up*, she thought. *Up, up, and away.*

She turned toward the patch of sky at which she pointed.

"Well," she said to the ghost, staring southward, "I suppose that eliminates about half the City. Only a few hundred Towers left to go."

Shai looked from Xhea's pointing hand down to her own chest and back again. "You're following the . . . line? The tether?"

"Yeah. Except the blighted thing is too fine to see, and too short to give me more than a general direction."

"Could you use it to triangulate?"

Xhea blinked. "Could I use it to what?"

"Um . . . find the Tower by calculating the angles at known points along a line." Shai's hesitance made it almost sound like a question.

"I have no idea what you're talking about," Xhea said. Except . . .

She frowned, considering, and waved the ghost to silence. If she traveled across the Lower City, and saw how the angle of the tether changed, perhaps she could hone in on the right Tower—or at least reduce the possible Towers to a more reasonable number.

"Hey Shai," she said. "Can I interest you in a tour of the Lower City?"

Xhea hadn't truly meant to give a tour—but something about the ghost's attention, her shock and growing fascination with the

Lower City's decaying buildings and the people who sheltered within them, made Xhea's familiar haunts feel new. What did Shai see, she wondered. Did she only notice the ruin and decay, the ever-present scents of rust and mildew and damp, cold earth? Did she see how little sunlight reached the Lower City, the Towers like umbrellas that offered not shelter but shadow, the few plants stunted and withering in that shade?

Or could she see the beauty in the stadium arena's stained patchwork awnings as they underwent their spring repair? Did she feel the freedom of the wide, winding streets of skyscraper Farrow's territory? All those massive houses, their wide lawns dotted with little more than the stumps of trees burned for firewood. Then there was the warehouse district, where the gangs ran—the highway overpasses, like broken stumps of concrete rainbows—the abandoned gas stations and movie theatres and apartments, all crumbling in ways that made them seem like sculpture.

As they went, Xhea paused to check Shai's second tether, following the cobweb-thin line as it rose toward the City. Up, it pointed, and somewhere to the south; and as the afternoon passed, they began to narrow in on the location. Their target was not close to the Central Spire, the great golden needle around which the City slowly spun, but farther out toward the edges where Towers gave way to floating factories and growing platforms.

Perhaps Shai and her father weren't as well-off as she had first supposed.

As for potential transportation, Xhea could only think of one solution: the Edren skyscraper—and the eldest living son of the family that bore the Edren name—owed her a favor. Though Edren was not the most powerful of the Lower City skyscrapers, neither was it insignificant—nor, in truth, was the favor she was owed. It seemed a waste to spend it on a mere taxi ride. But what choice did she have?

She'd turned to check the ghost's tether again when Shai spasmed. They froze, each staring at the other. Shai tried to speak and jerked again, harder, as if she'd been struck by an invisible fist. They both cried out, Xhea in surprise and Shai in pain, as the ghost was thrown to the far end of her tether. The sudden pull made Xhea stumble forward and fall to her knees. The few people around them suddenly found other things to look at, other places to be. When Xhea managed to push herself up, they were all but alone in the street.

"Shai?" The ghost hung in midair, curled in upon herself and shaking as if from terrible cold. She didn't respond to Xhea's voice, only jerked at the end of her line. Xhea tried to grab the tether, but the line of energized air was drawn so tightly between them that its vibration felt akin to pain.

Shai suddenly stopped shivering and uncurled. Though her eyes stayed closed, her head lifted as if in response to a voice that Xhea couldn't hear. Slowly, she tilted her head back, and the magic within her shone bright enough to rival sunlight.

"Time to wake up," Shai whispered. She opened her eyes and was gone.

The tether's tension snapped like an elastic band, and Xhea tumbled back to the asphalt, still trying to grip the length of energized air. As before, the line thinned almost to nothing within reach of her hand—yet that length quivered as it swung through the air, questing like a compass needle toward the vanished ghost. Slowly it settled, pointing upward and out.

Xhea struggled to her feet, trying to gauge its direction. Toward the City, yes, but its angle was not as steep as she had imagined. She moved, trying to get a line of sight on the near-invisible tether joined to the centre of her chest. After one look at Xhea's flailing, a mother just leaving her building grabbed her child's hand and hurried back inside.

Had they started the resurrection? All too easily, Xhea could imagine Shai's screams as spells attempted to force her back into her body, the young ghost's form slipping into the nightmarish template Xhea's memory provided. Yet no matter how Xhea moved—running the length of the street and down another, crouching, climbing on garbage to change her angle—she could tell little more than she already knew: the Tower she sought was not overhead, but somewhere to the south. She started to run, trying to find a better way to read the direction the stronger tether provided, cursing with every step.

Cursing—until a sudden thickness in her throat stopped her voice and forward progress in an instant. "No," Xhea whispered, choking on the word, blinking back a sudden stinging in her eyes like too-cold tears.

Within her, the dark energy began once more to rise, flooding through her body, drawn after the ghost. She clutched her stomach, as if hands alone could hold back the force. Her lips burned with it, and her ears buzzed, as if the magic were trying to be heard, saying: *Set me free.*

Oh, how she wanted to. She remembered the high she'd felt upon releasing the darkness that morning; she'd never felt that right, that strong, that *whole*. It was a part of her, she knew, the part that she had always been missing—and she knew, just as clearly, that once freed it would work far beyond her control. Hurricanes and earthquakes, tidal waves and tornadoes: great forces pressed against the boundaries of her flesh and will, begging for release. Wanting to follow Shai.

That morning she had reached for the ghost—had seen Shai in her mind's eye and willed her to return—and that was all she'd needed to send the black energy pouring from her, vomit and sweat and tears. Now she tried to think of nothing but the asphalt before her strewn with bits of plastic and shards of broken glass, the narrow shoots of new weeds and the dried stems of last year's plants dried to nothing.

Nothing, she told herself. She felt nothing. For the strength the dark magic gave her, the beautiful peace, was a lie; only the pain was real, the hurt in her hands and knees and chest.

And still it rose.

"*No*," she said, not pleading—commanding. Slowly she dragged herself back, scraped palms and bruised knees against the rubble-strewn ground as she moved away from where Shai had been, away from the tether's pull and Tower that waited on the other end of the line. As if mere body lengths could make a difference. But the boundaries of her skin were far too small to contain such power. Tears ran, cold against her cheeks before rising in dark, languid spirals. She felt the magic in her throat pressing into her mouth, and could not restrain it.

No, she thought again, and made a choice. Not vomit, but breath: she exhaled, and a thick coil of dark rose from between her opened lips. Years of smoking made the gesture seem not frightening, but familiar. Known. Or almost so. Oh, Xhea thought, the lies one tells out of desperation. She released a shuddering breath stained dark, and didn't know if the sound she choked back was hysterical laughter or a sob.

She watched the darkness curl and coil as it made its way upward, moving to the dictates of a wind she could not feel. Moving, she realized, to coil around the thinned tether, rising as the tether rose—but not invisible and near-impossible to trace, but like an arrow formed of smoke, pointing to Shai's Tower.

Xhea pushed herself to her feet. She exhaled again and thought of Shai; felt the magic turn and almost pull her forward, as if the smoke of her magic rising were another arm, another hand, reaching. Up the darkness pointed, upward and onward toward the City's far fringes. Over the far ruins, toward the badlands. To know more, she'd have to get closer.

Harnessing the fear that set her heart to pounding, Xhea ran.

Beyond the Lower City core, the city that had come before showed its true age, the houses and shops and gas stations reduced to mounds of rubble. Though streets remained like arrow-straight corridors through the overgrowth, many were blocked with fallen buildings, had become sluggish rivers, or had suffered the collapse of the sewers beneath. Even the best made for difficult travel.

Xhea knew she should tread carefully, but there was no time. Running, she could do little more than avoid the biggest obstacles—a fallen bridge, the gaping hole of a basement—and pray that any accident was no worse than a turned ankle.

Yes, the magic seemed to say, rushing through her, drawing her on. She pushed herself too far, too fast, but felt no pain; only the joy of power let free. She paused just long enough to watch dark streamers of her breath rise, and shifted her direction. And if her drenching sweat didn't drip but lifted from her skin to stream behind her like fraying black ribbons, she could only pretend not to notice.

Yes, the magic said, and pulled her forward. Time had no meaning: there was only the thump of her feet against the uneven ground, her rough breathing, and the sun's slide toward evening.

Did an hour pass? Two? She didn't know, or care, until the last of her strength burned from her. Gasping, legs trembling, she stumbled to a stop. She swayed on unsteady feet, and neither the magic nor the fear of what might be happening to Shai was enough to push her forward again.

Xhea lowered herself to the curb, only now feeling the ache of her thirst, the empty pit of her stomach. Slowly, she looked around. She'd never come so far into the ruins. The crumbling buildings were no more than pieces: slumped structures shadowed with moss and mildew; a standing brick pillar that might have been a chimney; a car's rusted frame. The cool air was heavy with the smell of decay.

Though she had stopped, her magic continued to flow. She exhaled it with every panting breath and watched as it curled upward. She'd come far, but not far enough: the line of dark reached toward a cluster of Towers on the City's farthest fringes, though she couldn't tell which. But it was something; maybe it would be enough to help Shai.

Okay, she thought to the dark smoke of her breath. *Enough now. Stop.*

As easy as stopping the rain's fall.

Xhea remembered her earlier thought: hurricanes and earthquakes, tidal waves and tornadoes. Forces beyond her will or control. Worse, she felt as if the magic had started to take pieces of her with it as it left her body, her strength and power and ability for rational thought, burning them surely as any fire. The sense of rightness and unnatural calm that the magic bestowed warred with a sudden helpless panic.

She clenched her fists, ragged nails digging into her palms. Would that she had any normal magic, but a single renai in all her useless chits and chips, a bright spark to help her regain control. All she had was time, and pain, and fierce will. It took all three.

At last she sank back against the shattered curb and looked at her hands. The scabs had broken open and her palms were smeared black with blood. She dabbed the cuts with her pants' tattered hem until they stopped seeping, then rested her head on trembling arms. Pain brought clarity, but no comfort.

"What am I doing?" she whispered. "Oh, gods, what am I doing?"

Xhea didn't need to look up from the cradle of her arms to know that the Tower she sought was still impossibly far away, even its low altitude an unthinkable barrier. She had no renai, no allies, no plan. She was as she had always been: stranded on the ground, yearning for things out of reach. Even if she could reach the Tower, could find Shai and her body—what then? She had killed the last such ghost she'd tried to help, body and spirit both. In truth, there was nothing she could do to help Shai, no matter what memories the ghost's presence had stirred.

She had to cut the tether. Her fingers trembled as she touched the knife through the fabric of her jacket pocket, placing her hand over the folded blade as if pressing it to her heart. Felt the solid thud of her heartbeat and the tether's vibration. Closed her eyes and tried to breathe.

No, it wasn't just the desire to exorcise that ghost from her memory, the murder of his flesh and spirit, that drove her. There was something else—something deeper and more selfish. Xhea thought of Shai's hand on her shoulder. Was she so desperate, so lonely, that she would grab at any thread of kindness, however thin or tentatively offered?

Yes, the thought came, and she had not the strength to voice it.

When Shai returned with that same cracking sound, Xhea did not turn, did not rise, only pressed her hand harder to her chest as if she could ease the ache that had settled there. Before her the ground was black and gray, the cracked roadway darkened by the shadow of her bowed head and slumped shoulders. She stared at the image she cast—no face, no will, only a puppet to the sun's slow fall. Just the shape of a girl where no light fell.

She looked up to meet Shai's gaze, level with her own. In silence the ghost had descended, her luminous dress pooling around her as she attempted to sit on the curb. Shai waited, all the things that she didn't voice written in the lines of her face.

Xhea breathed deeply, and when she exhaled it was only air. "Are you okay?" she asked. Shai nodded slowly; the same nod that Xhea would have given. She was okay. Nothing more.

"Where are we?"

"The ruins." Whatever names these streets and neighborhoods had once borne were long since lost, and with them had vanished the need to know such places as anything other than ruin. "And your body," Xhea continued, "is somewhere up there."

Shai looked past Xhea's pointing hand toward the cluster of Towers hung low in the sky. They were small, their shapes static and poorly defensible. Shai frowned. "I don't know them. I don't remember being . . ." She turned away, frustration and sorrow warring across her features.

"But it's something," Xhea said. Some bit of hope, a direction to travel. Ignoring her muscles' protests, she forced herself to her feet and dug in her pockets until she found a bit of dried fruit, its surface caked with lint. Emergency rations—and never as fresh or as plentiful as she'd have liked. It had been a long winter, she thought as she shoved the piece into her mouth.

"Xhea?" Shai's voice was soft.

Xhea paused in her chewing, grimacing at the leather-hard stuff between her teeth. Not fruit, but some sort of jerky. Very old jerky.

"Yeah?" she managed around her mouthful.

"Thank you."

Xhea stopped. Turned. Shai was staring at her hands, fingers twisting nervously, but looked up to meet Xhea's eyes. "For doing this," she said, a gesture taking in the desolation around them, the cluster of Towers above. "For helping me."

Xhea's mouth was suddenly dry, and it had nothing to do with the jerky's salt. She tried to swallow; failed. Tried to speak, and failed at that too. At last she nodded and turned away.

The lengthening light was all the distraction she needed. "Come on," she said. "We've got to get back before dark." Straightening her shoulders, Xhea started for the distant huddle of structures of the Lower City, the ghost trailing silently after.

Chapter Five

By angling her approach to intersect with the Green Line subway, Xhea figured she could make it home—or at least to shelter—before sunset, even tired, hungry, and parched from her long run. Yet an hour into her walk home, a sound made her freeze mid-stride: a rustle of movement in dead weeds, a falling-rock rattle of shifting rubble. To her right stood the remains of a brick building, just a corner still standing, its window gaps like black eyes. To her left was a hill, only a protruding tangle of electrical wire betraying that it had been a building, not a burial mound.

Nothing should have been moving, she knew. Not yet, not before nightfall.

"What is it?" Shai asked. Xhea ignored her, attempting to pinpoint the sound. It had been close, but not immediately so; sound carried farther in the ruins. Ahead, she thought, and somewhat to her right—directly between her and the way home.

Again it came: a rustle, a scrape of stone on stone.

Xhea crept forward a single step. Then another step, and another—each placed with only a whisper of boot soles against the rocky asphalt. It took forever to reach the end of the brick wall that shielded her; forever again to gather the courage to peer around the corner.

She saw a stretch of empty road with collapsed houses to either side, the only movement the dust's slow twirl in the bands of light cast by the setting sun. One breath held in waiting, another—then a section of ground heaved. The piled edges of boards and asphalt slabs rose and shuddered, crumbled and fell away as something struggled to free itself from its burrow of stone and refuse.

It was not the movement that caused Xhea to recoil and press herself against the brick wall as if she could sink within the crumbling structure, but the sound. As the boards and piled soil lifted upward and the sunlight fell upon whatever lay beneath, there came a scream, high and sharp and inhuman. It echoed through the ruins long after the source had fallen quiet.

She'd seen no reaching hand, no glimpse of a face—yet Xhea knew that no mere animal struggled to free itself from that rubble. Certainty turned her bones to ice: it was a walker, one of the once-human things that stalked the Lower City's nighttime streets.

It shouldn't be out so early, Xhea thought, panicked. Sunlight burned their eyes, some said, or their skin; and perhaps, given the thing's scream, there was truth to that story. Yet common wisdom also held that the things spent their days burrowed beneath the ground out in the badlands, far from the Lower

City itself, and only drew near as darkness fell—and that, she could see all too clearly, was false.

Shai had followed her around the corner and back again, mirroring Xhea's caution if not her fear. Xhea braced for the questions that she didn't have time—nor could she risk the sound—to answer: who is that person, what happened to them, why are they there, buried, screaming? And even if she could speak, what could Xhea say but "I don't know"? No one knew where the walkers came from or what had made them the way they were.

Yet the ghost only whispered, "What can I do to help?"

The offer was a surprise. Xhea jerked to face her, charms clinking at the movement—and cringed, expecting the sound to draw the thing from cover, sunlight be blighted. After several long moments of silence, she opened her eyes; a few more, and she released her caught breath.

What could the ghost do? Xhea's mind spun; she barely knew what she could do, never mind what help Shai might be. If only she could run. If only there were a chance, however faint, that she could sprint to a subway entrance in time; if only her exhausted legs would let her make the attempt. She needed tunnels, concrete rooms with doors that could be locked or barred—a bomb shelter, an old bank safe, the highest floor of a building not yet fallen. And had none.

"I need to hide," she said softly, so softly. "Can you see . . . is there anywhere?" Shai nodded and pulled away, struggling against her tether's limits to search the nearby ruins.

Xhea forced herself to swallow, then pulled a length of folded cloth from a jacket pocket. Each movement slow and careful, she bound back her hair, wrapping the length with its charms tightly, and tying the whole thing into a knot at the back of her head. She couldn't let the sound of her hair give her away.

Shai returned a moment later. "I've found a place." Xhea pointed to the ground, questioning: a basement? Oh, to be underground, where it was dark and safe and nothing in the world could touch her. But Shai shook her head and pointed at the crumbling wall beside them. "It still has part of a floor above," she whispered. "There are enough gaps in the bricks that you could climb up."

At Xhea's look, she added, "There's nothing else, not as far as I could reach."

"Okay," Xhea whispered. "Lead me there."

She climbed as quickly as she could manage, attempting silence as she hauled herself up the crumbling brickwork. If she were to fall, she had to pray to break her neck. It would be faster than the death that thing would grant her.

Xhea made it to the top of the narrow platform and crawled across the triangle of rough flooring to the corner where she curled, pressing her shoulder blades against the walls and pulling her knees tight to her chest. Shai sat at her side, the magic inside her flickering at the edges of Xhea's vision. They looked out across a stretch of ruins, jutting girders and twisted lampposts where there might once have been trees. The walls of her shelter blocked most of the setting sun's light, casting darkness across the ground, black on gray.

As the shadows lengthened, the thing freed itself from its daytime shelter. Xhea heard it rise to its feet and slowly exhale as dirt and rubble clattered to the ground around it. In the Lower City streets, these once-human creatures never spoke, and this one seemed no exception. Yet she listened as it stumbled and began to walk, each step echoing through the ruins' silence; listened as its gait steadied and breathing slowed as the land grew dark.

Xhea trembled, not from weariness now, nor hunger, but fear. There was nowhere to run. No escape. Only the hope that on this tenuous perch she might pass the night unnoticed, with untold hours to wait until dawn.

She drew out her knife with shaking hands and extended the tiny blade. Where was her magic now? She had no darkness but that of sky and shadow; no curl of smoke, nor the sweet calm that swelled in its wake. When she breathed, there was only air; and the tears that trailed down her cheeks were just water, warm as blood.

Clutching her knife, she waited for the walker to see some scuff-mark she'd left in the dirt; to hear her breathing or the thud of her heart; to smell her, terrified and drenched with cold sweat. She'd heard people die at the hands of these things, distant screams and pleas that she'd tried to block out. Once she'd even found the bodies of two people caught outside when darkness fell. At least, she thought there had been two.

It seemed hours before the night walker moved away. Longer still before she could draw breath without shuddering.

It was cold now and the wind had picked up. In the distance, Xhea could just see the cluster of buildings that was the Lower City, huddled together as if for warmth. Lights flickered in the skyscrapers' upper windows, but whatever lamps still burned in the smaller structures were masked, rare glimmers creeping from around drawn curtains or windows boarded tight.

The City above showed no such fear. Xhea watched through a veil of tears as the Towers came alight. Within moments, every structure was haloed, twinkling as stars did, and brightening until they lit the whole sky on fire. As each Tower's shape was unique, so too was the energy displayed: in sheets and tendrils and waves, the power and status of every Tower was writ large across the heavens, brighter than any aurora. Xhea knew Towerlight for what it was: defensive spells and spell exhaust set alight, flagrant displays of power meant to show wealth and intimidate rivals. With spells that moved like living things, the Towers tested each other's defenses and guarded their own boundaries, their shimmering halos as much weapon as defense.

Brightest of all was the Central Spire. Vast beyond imagining, the great needle stretched like a luminous pillar set to pierce both the Lower City and the darkness above. It was gold, she knew; but even seen as silver and gray, it was beautiful. Beautiful and distant and so very cold.

It was probably the last thing she'd ever see, Xhea thought, and no matter how tightly she clenched her fists or curled her legs to her body, she could not stop shaking. Again she heard footsteps. More footsteps—two sets, three, more—all moving closer, all perfectly steady as if walking to the beat of an uncaring heart.

"Sweet gods," Xhea whispered. "There are more of them." How many hours until sunrise—eight? Nine? Without meaning to, she made a low sound in the back of her throat, almost a moan.

"Xhea?" Shai pressed close, ghostly hands against Xhea's right shoulder. Not real hands—for despite the girl she saw so clearly beside her, Xhea knew she was alone. Only empty stretches of nothing between her and safety, nothing and no one with her but the things that walked the ruins. Below her perch, the walkers circled as predators might, tracking the scent of their prey.

Her teeth chattered. She shoved the knuckle of her left thumb in her mouth and bit down hard, tasting dust and sweat.

"Xhea, please . . . look at me." Shai's hands were on her face, the touch cool and tingling. Xhea turned at the ghost's urging, silent. There was nothing she could say, nothing so important that she dared voice it.

Yet the very sight of Shai was enough to give her pause. Had she thought the ghost lit by mere glints and glimmers? Here, in darkness broken only by Towerlight, Shai was luminous. It seemed the Spire's light fell full across her face, shone from her hair, caught the shining folds of her dress. Even the hands pressed to Xhea's face felt . . . different. Like a ghost's hands, yes, but somehow more present—as if the bright magic bound to Shai's spirit gave her a physical presence, a strange radiance that brushed across Xhea's cheeks lightly as breath.

The ghost caught her gaze and held it. Fear etched her features, and Xhea imagined the expression a mirror of her own. Yet there was something in the set of her jaw, the faint creases between her eyebrows, that spoke of determination.

"I don't understand what's happening," Shai said, no louder than a whisper, but careful and steady. "I don't know what's wrong with those people and . . ." She shook her head. "I don't need to know. Not now."

The walkers gathered below, the crunch of their footsteps echoing. Shai's hands slid from Xhea's cheeks. Xhea felt where the ghost had touched her, as if the shape of Shai's fingers might still shimmer there in the darkness.

"I know you're out here because of me." Shai glanced down at her hands, glowing as if in moonlight, Towerlight. "And I can't do anything. Except I know what it's like to be afraid, like you are. I know how it feels to fear dying."

Not like this, Xhea wanted to say, hopelessly, angrily. *Oh, not like this*. She could hear them less than a stone's throw away. She could hear them breathing.

And yet . . . looking into the silver of Shai's eyes, Xhea reconsidered. She had but the fear of pain and suffering at a mindless thing's hands, and all the terrible moments that would come before death. Shai had not just feared pain, but felt it; she knew to fear suffering, for she had known it. And death? What could Xhea know of dying that a ghost did not?

"I remember that there were times . . ." Shai's voice seemed to catch, and she closed her eyes briefly. "Things got bad. But I also know that my father used to sit with me—hours at a time, hours upon hours. I think he used to stay even when I was asleep, just to be there when I woke. When the pain came, or when I was afraid, he would hold my hand and tell me stories. Sometimes it was bad enough that I couldn't understand him, couldn't even *think*—but I knew he was there. It was enough, somehow, to just hear his voice.

"Isn't it strange? There's so much I don't remember, but *that* I can't imagine forgetting."

Footsteps drew nearer, and nearer still, until Xhea realized that one of the walkers stood directly beneath her. Not daring to move, Xhea watched as Shai looked to the City then back down to meet her eyes.

"It's going to be a long night," Shai said, "but I think I can remember a story or two."

A moment passed before Xhea realized that it was an offer. She felt the hours before dawn stretch before them like a unbroken highway, and forced her head to nod.

Please. No sound: Xhea only mouthed the word, too-dry lips cracking.

"Okay," Shai said, and rested one hand palm-up on her knee. "So this was a long time ago, when I was just a child, and my parents took me to see the sky gardens in the Central Spire . . ."

It was impossible to forget where she was, or why. Yet something in the rise and fall of Shai's voice made Xhea think of a lullaby. It was not the words, but merely the speaking of them, that had the power to comfort. Listening to Shai's story, Xhea could almost pretend that she didn't see movement out in the darkness; that the sound of things creeping all around her was only the wind, or rubble shifting under its own weight, or her imagination.

Hours had passed before Xhea truly noticed the hand that Shai had reached toward her. Story after story the ghost had told, pulling tales from her gap-ridden memory—all without withdrawing that hand, or moving it from its place on her knee. Xhea remembered what Shai had said of her father: *When I was afraid, he used to hold my hand and tell me stories.*

Xhea's grip tightened on her knife's mother-of-pearl handle. She could only think of one person who had held her hand— one person who had even tried—and that had been a very long time ago. She felt immobilized, not knowing what to do with the gesture, or the strange and sudden wanting for such a thing: another's hand closed around her own. Distrusted the urge.

But what did it matter, for her fingers' tight grip seemed locked upon the knife. She was too tired, too bone-dead weary to gather the courage to reach across the small gap that separated them.

Yet it was there, an offering, and somehow that was enough.

The walkers moved off just before dawn, heading out to the badlands, leaving only a tense, echoing silence in their wake. Xhea tried to stifle her whimpers as she uncurled. Failed. Each movement hurt, muscles locked tight from fear and exertion and cold, and her swollen eyes burned with every blink. Yet morning brought gifts: the chill dew was just enough to ease her thirst, each bitter, metallic drop tasting as good as fresh rainwater; and the sun, when it rose, made her weak with relief.

Safe at last. She unbound her hair and let it tumble down her back in a ringing choir, then raised her face and arms as if the sun's pale light could wash her clean.

"Xhea," Shai murmured, and her voice sounded strange.

She felt she could dissolve in sunlight; felt its warmth enclose her, granting the freedom to breathe. Even years living underground hadn't purged her desire for sunlight—especially the rare moments when it shone unbroken by the Towers' shadows or cloud. Despite morning's chill, she pushed up her sleeves so the light could reach just a little more skin.

"Xhea," Shai said more urgently, and Xhea opened her eyes. Before them hovered the small, blinking shape of a City elevator.

After the long night, Xhea felt she'd lost her capacity for surprise. But she paused, staring at the palm-sized elevator and its flickering lights as one might look at a particularly difficult puzzle.

"Why's it here?" Xhea had tried to reach the City for years, only to be frustrated at every attempt. Yet now an elevator simply appeared—for the second time in three days. They'd done *nothing*—made no sound, no signal; she'd barely so much as breathed for hours.

She raised a hand and waved. No response. She made her gesture broader, as if trying to attract the attention of someone across a crowd, but the thing's lights only flickered, as if confused.

"It's blinking yellow, isn't it?"

"Yes," Shai said.

Yellow meant it was thinking. It wasn't denying her passage, yet neither was it offering. It seemed the thing hadn't quite decided whether she was human.

What was different? Could it sense her strange magic, newly risen? Yet her magic was calm, once more the dark lake she'd so long envisioned. Besides, she reasoned, an elevator couldn't have sensed her magic that first night, smothered as it had been by Shai's father's payment.

Struck by a sudden thought, she turned to the ghost in a clatter of charms. Maybe it wasn't reacting to her or her magic; perhaps it sensed Shai. She watched as the elevator seemed to tremble in its orbit, as if turning to face her, then Shai, then back again. Almost as if it saw a body with no magic, and magic . . .

". . . with no body. Shai, it can see you. Quick—do something."

Shai hesitated, looking at her hands and the glimmers of magic that ran through them, then waved her arms as Xhea had done. Again, the elevator blinked.

"Still yellow," Shai said.

"I think we're confusing it." Sweetness, she was so tired; just thinking felt exhausting as slogging through mud. Still her thoughts churned: a living body *and* bright magic. They had everything they needed for the elevator to whisk them away, only in separate forms. If only . . .

At the same moment, Shai extended her hand. "If we . . ." she said, and their eyes met.

"*Yes.*"

Xhea reached for Shai without thinking, as if she had not struggled in the attempt but hours before. With her hand above Shai's, the ghost seemed but a shadow that Xhea cast, a bright reflection shimmering in midair. The magic within Shai had grown strong enough that it pushed against Xhea, and for a brief moment they seemed to touch. Then they merged, fingers melding into a single hand.

Shai gasped, and Xhea barely kept from doing the same. It didn't hurt—not exactly. Not quite pins and needles, she thought, but ice and the ache of bruised muscles grown cold. As one, they lifted their joined hands and beckoned to the elevator, banishing the confusion from its wire-spelled mind. It blinked a pale gray that Xhea knew to be green, and descended.

Xhea's breath caught as the elevator brightened and broke open like a flower. Shai drew close as ribbons of light arced up and around them, surrounding them in a shimmering bubble. Xhea looked down, watching as the concrete of their shelter seemed to ripple as the spell lines joined beneath her feet.

"Oh sweetness," Xhea whispered, and they were rising.

Xhea had always been afraid of heights. Her bed in Orren had been next to the window, seventeen stories up. Cold in the winter, too bright during the day, beaded with moisture when it rained hard, it was the worst space in the girls' dorm. She used to lie curled with her eyes squeezed shut, trying to avoid even glimpsing the world stretched below.

Yet that distance had been contained by grimed windows and rusted girders. Now, with only ribbons of magic between her and a fall, Xhea's stomach dropped as quickly as the ground. Beneath her, she could suddenly see the whole of the ruined building in which she'd sheltered the night. Then more: the shapes of neighboring buildings and the gridwork of nameless streets that stretched in the cardinal directions, vanishing into the distance.

Instinctively she grabbed for a handhold, heart pounding with a sudden surge of adrenaline. She wasn't just afraid of heights, she realized in panic; she was afraid of falling.

"You won't fall," Shai said. "It's safe." Their hands were still linked, flesh and spirit entwined, and though her fingers were numb from the contact, Xhea did not pull away.

It was easier to breathe once they'd risen higher. The ground was so far it seemed unreal, like a picture beneath her feet, and the elevator's veil of light only added to the illusion. She stared at the Lower City below, fascinated, realizing that the scurrying specks were people. Stranger still, the whole of the Lower City was little more than a tiny patch of life in the wasteland of the city that had come before. Xhea had known the ancient city had been large, yet she could barely comprehend its vastness or the extent of its decay. Ruins stretched as far as she could see and beyond, crumbling into nothing.

Then she looked up.

She'd stared at the Towers' pointed underbellies her whole life, watching as they rose and fell, merged and reshaped in an incomprehensible political dance. Now a Tower loomed before her, so close she could almost touch it. Its grown metal flesh shimmered like sunlight across water, and Xhea imagined it to be water's blue, deep and hazed almost gray.

"We have to direct the elevator," Shai said.

She only knew that their destination lay south, and so they pointed southward, hand in hand. Xhea gasped as the elevator accelerated and merged into the line of aircars that zipped through the gaps separating the Towers. They rose and fell with the stream of traffic, moving between the massive airborne structures with the ease of breath. Briefly, she caught the bored expression on a fellow traveler's face as he sped by in an elevator of his own. Something bubbled up inside her, and it was only as she pressed the fingers of her free hand to her mouth that she realized it was laughter.

Focus, Xhea reminded herself, and none too soon; within moments, the elevator's swift passage brought them to the cluster of Towers she had identified from the ground. She'd thought them small, and though they were dwarfed by the central Towers, each was far larger than all of the skyscrapers combined. She craned upward just trying to catch a glimpse of the peaks of their top defensive spires.

"Do you recognize—?"

"No," Shai said, her voice gone hollow. "But I can feel it pulling."

"Your Tower?"

"My body."

Shai moved to point in the direction her second tether led and Xhea hurriedly mimicked the gesture. The elevator dove out of the aircar traffic at their command.

Their destination was a wide Tower, its central structure a misshapen orb like a blown-glass ornament gone wrong. Though it bore defensive spires on both top and bottom, even Xhea's untrained eye could see the obvious angles of attack another Tower might use, great sections of its bulk protected by neither spire nor spell.

Traffic thinned as they approached and circled toward the main landing bay. The Tower was dark—red, perhaps, or even brown— but as they neared, Xhea saw patches of discoloration along its side, and the air around it was almost still, undisturbed by spell exhaust. Xhea had seen Towers far younger and less damaged attacked and absorbed in a hostile takeover: materials, magic, and citizens alike physically absorbed by a more powerful Tower. Only location seemed to have spared this one a similar fate.

She glanced at Shai. From the cut of her dress to her bewilderment with the Lower City, everything about Shai spoke of close familiarity with luxury. Yet she had died here, in a Tower so old and poor that it risked falling from the sky.

Xhea blinked as they entered the Tower's shadowed landing bay. There was little to see: the gaping space held only a cluster of worn aircars parked to one side, while a row of poorly marked doors ran along the far wall, all closed. It felt like a parking garage—albeit larger, cleaner, and in better repair than the ones she knew.

The elevator set her down so gently that it was a moment before Xhea realized she could feel the floor. The spell peeled away as quickly as it had formed, the bright ribbons fluttering down around her and vanishing.

"I didn't pay," she said, watching the elevator swoop across the cavernous space and back into the sunshine. Not that she was complaining.

"Registers the signature," Shai whispered, staring blankly at an interior door. She released Xhea's hand and pressed her palm to her chest as if she might feel the echo of a living heart. "I don't . . ." she said. "I can't . . ."

"Can't what?" Xhea massaged her numbed fingers.

Shai closed her eyes, her face tightening in pain, and pressed her hands harder against her sternum, fingers splayed. No, Xhea realized; Shai was holding the place where the tether joined them, both hands flat as if to keep the tether from unraveling.

"Shai," she said. "What is it? What's happening?"

"I can't . . ." Shai was just loud enough to hear. "I can't stay." Slowly, slowly, she opened her eyes, lashes rising to reveal irises that gleamed silver. Their eyes met. "*Find me*," Shai said, and was gone.

Xhea braced as the tether snapped back against her chest. The free end swung as it sought the suddenly absent ghost, and—though thin—it was still tangible enough to handle. Xhea sighted off the tether's length; wherever Shai was being kept, it was on a higher floor than this. Magic stirred in the pit of her stomach—slow, but curious.

"*Not now*," she hissed.

She ran to a door in the far wall, but it was closed tight and sealed. No handle, only the blinking panel of a touchplate. She waved her hand before the plate and poked it a few times with her tingling fingers, wishing that enough bright magic remained from Shai's touch to garner a response. To come this close, and be stopped by a *door* . . .

In response to her frustration, Xhea's magic built like a storm beneath her breastbone and spread through her body, reaching after the ghost. It rose, curling smoke-like around her fingers and the touchplate.

"I said, *not* . . . oh." For at the brush of her magic, the spell controlling the door panel sputtered and died. She thought of the dead food chits, the inert payment from Brend—all kept in jacket pockets as her magic had run rampant that very first time.

"Oh," she said again.

With the latch spell gone, the pressure differential was just enough to open the door a crack. Putting her shoulder against the door and pushing, Xhea forced her way inside.

The curving hall that led from the landing bay was all but silent, only distant murmurs audible over the hiss of air from unseen vents. The overhead lights were cracked and flickering, and the air smelled like a room long closed. The floor was soft beneath her feet—not carpet, Xhea saw, but something growing and slightly damp that reminded her more of mold than moss.

Xhea wondered what she thought she'd find in an impoverished Tower. She could only think: *Not this*. If anything, this Tower seemed like the Lower City—a once-great place clothed only in the tatters of its former glory.

Her magic pulled toward the ghost, and the broken tether pointed, both saying: *Here. Close.* Xhea struggled to follow, hurrying down shadowed passages with dusty corners and failing light panels, all overgrown with moss. At last the tether pointed to a door, no different than countless others she had passed, and her stomach clenched in fear. *This is Shai*, she reminded herself. It was Shai who pulled her, Shai on the end of that line, Shai who had to struggle alone for every moment that Xhea delayed.

Even so, she paused just long enough to slip her silver knife from her pocket and open its blade.

Knife in hand, she knocked on the door.

Chapter Six

The door opened.

What had she been about to shout? *You can't do this to her.* Maybe, *I'm here to stop you.* Words she hadn't known she was readying until they died in her mouth unspoken.

Shai's father leaned heavily against the doorframe. His eyes moved from her face to the small blade in her hand and back again, no surprise in his expression. No anger. *At least*, she thought, staring back, *no new anger.* For beneath his evident exhaustion, she could see rage—an anger so constant it was ingrained in his every movement and breath, etched into the pinched lines of his face.

Xhea blinked, and clutched her knife.

What had she expected? Memory showed her: casters ringed around Shai's body, the air bright and buzzing with magic. Machinery, maybe; wires and storage coils. She'd expected shouting, and anger; she'd expected a crowd of powerful people, even here, on the City's farthest fringes.

She'd expected to fail. Strange, how easily she knew it now, how clearly the images came to her: being restrained and screaming, but fighting, always fighting, to free Shai. She hadn't expected a man who seemed not to have slept or shaved or eaten since she'd seen him last, his clothes rumpled and shoulders weighted by untold weariness. A man who stared at her unspeaking.

The silence grew to fill the space between them and expanded, like a great bubble where speech and movement died. It expanded into the empty room behind him and the hall to either side, compressing Xhea's chest until she felt that even breathing was an intrusion.

Still the magic urged her on, whispering: *Here. Here. Here.*

"I'm here . . ." she started hesitantly, only to be interrupted.

"I know," he said, his voice heavy. Such rage. Such exhaustion. "I know why you're here."

I don't, she thought. *Not anymore.*

He stood back and gestured for her to enter, then closed the door softly behind her. Xhea looked around the tiny apartment. Bare walls, bare floor: this, she realized, wasn't anyone's home. It smelled stuffy and faintly metallic, bringing a bitter taste to the back of her throat. Carefully, she folded her knife and slipped it into a pocket. This was not a resurrection—she knew that now with perfect certainty—but she was no closer to understanding.

"My daughter must have spoken to you, to tell you we were here."

"Yes," Xhea said. "I mean, we spoke, but she had problems remembering."

Shai's father ran his hand through his hair, then rubbed his eyes. "But you're here now. Please tell me that you know how to free her."

"Free her?" Xhea asked.

His expression darkened, then he shook his head. "It's easier, somehow, to think of it that way. Free. Release. Kill. It's all the same in the end. Just tell me you know what to do."

"But—" Xhea said and stopped, the words *She's already dead* caught between tongue and teeth. Instead she asked slowly, haltingly: "Where is she?"

She already knew the answer. Tether and magic alike pulled her, called to her.

Here. Here. Here.

But she was suddenly afraid, so afraid. She walked in the direction that Shai's father pointed: down a dark, narrow hall toward a single closed door at its end. Xhea kept her hand steady as she pushed the door open—but only just.

There in the bed lay the body they had sought. It lay still, dressed in a thin nightgown and draped with a white sheet, leaving only arms and face exposed, skin pale as any drowned corpse. Those arms were thin, and the shoulders, all so wasted that Xhea felt she could count the bones beneath. Pale hair spread across the pillow, surrounding a gaunt face—a nightmare's version of the one she had come to know.

No, Xhea thought. Not it: *her*. For the body's chest rose and fell in the slow and faltering rhythm of natural breath.

"Shai?" Xhea's breath caught in her throat.

It was only then that she realized that the room was unlit, curtains drawn tight over the narrow window on the far wall. It was Shai who lit the space: she glowed, her body laced with so many spells that her flesh was incandescent. The shadows shifted as she breathed. Looking at her, the shock wasn't that Shai was dying; only that someone so wasted could live at all.

Xhea walked to the bedside and knelt, and now nothing could stop her hands from trembling. "Shai," she whispered again, and Shai opened her eyes.

Xhea caught no more than a glimpse of pale irises before Shai's eyelids fluttered closed. Cracked lips parted. Shai's voice was faint and rough with pain, faltering as she struggled to say, "Hello, Xhea . . . I'm sorry for leaving."

"It's okay. I found you anyway."

"Yes," Shai said, the word a mere sigh. "Yes."

Carefully, Xhea examined Shai's body, shifting her focus to see the magic more clearly. There were spells there—the spells that she must have seen reflected in the ghost—so many, so layered and so bright that Xhea struggled to find meaning in them at all. But it was Shai herself, she realized, that shone with that dazzling light. Shai was filled with magic, pure and strong. It rose seemingly from nowhere, as if her very heart was a spring of power, and flooded through her. Overwhelmed her.

Magic was the energy of life, yes, but this life surged without control. It built upon itself, growing, multiplying: life without end. Mere blood and muscle and bone couldn't contain so much power. It raged through her, poured from her, and twisted her flesh as it went, leaving brightness and ruin in its wake.

Growth unchecked. Mutation. Cancer.

The spells she saw were not the resurrection spells she'd feared, but attempts to heal, and even they paled in comparison to Shai's power. There were spells to stem the growth of the tumors in her liver and her lungs, spells attacking the cancers that spread through her bones. There were more spells, spells upon spells, staunching bleeding and energizing her faltering heart, easing the pressure on failing organs, and repairing the damage that illness had wrought. But they were worn now, and failing.

And still that magic leaked from Shai, more magic, bright magic that because of its very nature said to body and tumors alike: *Live, grow.* What were spells against such raw power? The newest—the brightest—workings were for one purpose only: stopping Shai's pain.

Xhea pulled back, staring. Shai was rich beyond words, more powerful than Xhea could even dream—and it was killing her.

From the doorway, Shai's father said, "I cannot save her." Xhea glanced back, seeing again the heavy circles beneath his eyes, remembering his failing strength, his anger and exhaustion. At last she knew their cause.

Softly, despairing, he said, "I can't save her, and I can't find a way to let her die. I don't know what else to do."

"But why . . . ?"

At his expression, Xhea fell silent. Unfocusing her eyes once more, Xhea forced herself to look deeper still. The spells' fierce white was all but blinding; yet she persisted, and her vision adjusted. Still, many long moments passed before she began to see what anchored Shai's body to life and bound her spirit to that broken flesh. When at last she understood, she could but stare.

The spells that hid in the depths of Shai's body were old and infinitely stronger than those that fought her illness: that much was clear despite their seeming frailty. The individual spell lines were thin as threads, woven into intricate patterns the likes of which she'd never seen. Neither did this working shine as bright magic did, but had the dull gleam of tarnished mental. A true master wove these spells, Xhea knew. Only a magical genius could have created that pattern, the intricate steel-wire lace that bound Shai, body, magic and spirit.

A genius, but a dark one.

Some of the spells were akin to a resurrection spell, distinguished only by the skill, delicacy—and yes, beauty—with which they'd been wrought. She watched as magic flowed through the hair-fine shape: forcing life into dying cells, breath into a collapsing chest, blood through failing vessels. More and more, tapping into Shai's great wellspring of magical energy, pulling it from her body and taking it to places far beyond Xhea's sight or understanding. Together they bound Shai's spirit, forcing her to animate flesh too broken to live.

Had she feared Shai's resurrection? Instead someone had ensured she would never die. No matter her pain or suffering, regardless of what ravages illness inflicted, the lacework spells forced her to live.

"Who did this?" Xhea whispered.

Shai's ragged breathing was the only reply.

Xhea knew now what Shai's father had hoped to achieve by separating Shai's ghost from her body—not knowing of the tether that bound her; not seeing, as Xhea did, how deeply the spell was imbedded in her spirit. Xhea had begun to wonder if she might free Shai by simply cutting the second tether—and perhaps that would help enable her body to die. But something of Shai's spirit would die too, bound in that wirework lace, leaving her no more than a fraction of her true self. Leaving her, Xhea realized, as the person she had met, lost and disoriented, with a gap-ridden memory. If anything of her survived the separation at all.

This was not a problem she could cut away with her silver knife.

And yet . . .

Two days before, there would have been nothing more she could have done; but Shai's presence had changed so very much. Xhea felt her own magic, dark and newly woken, ease through her body at the thought. With it, she had unraveled spells, destroyed bright magic, at a touch. Why not this?

Xhea turned to Shai's father for permission.

"There is something I could try," she said slowly. "I don't know . . . I mean, I can't . . ."

"Try," he said. Only that.

He took a deep breath before coming into the room and kneeling at Shai's bedside. So carefully, he took one of her hands into his own, and gently stroked its back with a single trembling finger.

"Shai." Xhea called to the girl as she had the ghost. "Shai, look at me."

Shai gave a faint gasp, and her wasted body shuddered as she attempted to move. She was too weak to lift her head; but as Xhea called again, soft and insistent, she managed to open her eyes. They were glassy with fever, pupils wide within the pale rings of her irises, and Xhea knew that it wasn't her sight that made the blue of Shai's eyes look so empty or so gray.

"Shai," Xhea said again. "I'm going to try to help you. If you'll let me."

The darkness filled her, calm and slow. It did not reach for Shai, or test Xhea's tenuous control. It only waited.

"Dad?" Shai whispered.

"I'm here, baby." Again he stroked her hand, fingers trembling. "It's okay. It's almost over."

"Yes," Shai whispered. Her eyelids fluttered closed.

"That's my brave girl," her father said, his voice breaking. "My brave, brave girl."

Oh, would that Xhea were so brave. Yet her hands were steady, now, her breath even and slow. She stroked the hair from Shai's face, then leaned down and brushed her lips against Shai's fevered forehead. It did not hurt to touch her, nor did she feel a shock; there was only an intensity of feeling, as if that moment of contact echoed between them.

Xhea pulled back, the chime of the coins in her hair the only sound in the small room. Carefully, she placed one hand on Shai's stomach and the other on her chest above her heart. Shai's heat seemed to burn through her nightgown and the shroud of her sheet. Beneath, Xhea felt the shape of Shai's bones, the hard lumps of her tumors, and the tingle of bright magic so strong it thrummed like a live wire.

Dark magic rose at that touch, and Xhea let it come. It moved like a dark tide, easing through Xhea's body and down through her arms, pulled toward Shai's bright fire. *There*, Xhea told it, guiding it toward the healing spells; *there* and *there*. The magic turned at her command. One by one the spells began to fail, flicker and go dark, drowned beneath a tide of shadow; one by one they uncoiled, lines of magic releasing their hold on Shai's dying body, their power unraveling and spinning into nothing.

It should be harder, Xhea thought. There was no pain, no hesitation; only the flow of magic, slow and gentle as breath.

Time had no meaning. Deeper, she went, layer after layer of spells darkening to nothing as she worked. Soon only the wirework lace remained—and these spells, old and canny, resisted her magic. They had been designed to resist the bright surge of Shai's power, she realized; what was a little more magic against that constant onslaught?

But she did not need to destroy them; only weaken them. She guided her magic as if it were her silver blade, and attacked only the lacework's anchoring strands.

Xhea struggled with a single strand for what seemed like forever before it bent, blackened, and broke. The next snapped a little quicker, the next quicker still, as if the strength of the whole was compromised with the loss of each binding strand. One by one they parted beneath her onslaught, and as each broke she shuddered at the impact, feeling the spells' snapping recoil deep within her. Sweat beaded her forehead and her hands trembled with fatigue, but the sensations were distant things, ignored as easily as the rhythm of her heart.

At last she finished, and drew her hands away.

As Xhea watched, the great spring of magic at Shai's heart slowed. Shai took one long, shuddering breath, and another, and became still. Xhea waited, her own breath held, for an inhalation that never came.

The room slowly grew dark. It was silent now, peaceful as the depths of a deep lake and as dark. Shai was no longer bright with magic run rampant, nor dark from emptiness, but gray. Merely gray. Xhea touched the center of her own chest where the tether had joined them and felt only air.

"It's over," Shai's father whispered, faint and hollow and disbelieving. "I can't believe it's finally over." He pressed one hand to his mouth as if to hold back a sob.

He released Shai's unresisting fingers and slowly brushed her hair from her face, smoothing the sweaty tangles. He bowed his head to rest on the mattress beside Shai, eyes closed, fingers still caught in her hair.

"I'm so sorry, baby," he whispered. Tears ran down his face unchecked. "I'm so, so sorry."

He did not turn as Xhea stood. Her magic was gone now; she felt empty and shaky, struggling to rise on wooden legs. She wished she could reach for him; wished he would take her hand. More: she wished for Shai again, that presence at her side. But there was no ghost, no one from whom she could beg forgiveness.

Shai was gone.

Xhea stood at the Tower's peak and watched the sun set in tones of ash and rainwater. Spires stood in a circle around her, a bubble of spelled calm protecting her from the cold and wind of the open sky.

All that day she had wandered the nameless Tower, finding food, resting in corners, trying to sleep. Struggling to find the words to explain what she had done, or define how she felt, and failing at each.

For a long time, she had only eyes for the horizon. It was so straight. So vast. Below, the Lower City seemed but an aberration, the buildings and walls that defined her world so small as to be inconsequential. Xhea watched their shadows lengthen and stretch. So quickly it all fell away to nothing, emptiness and unfilled spaces, gentle hills where the ruins were worn to dust and rounded stone. But in the Towers spread across the sky around her, she could see the glow of life, the minutiae of lives being lived: all nature of magic, bright in her eyes.

In the darkness above the City, stars began to come out.

Part Two

Chapter Seven

Four days later, Xhea woke in the garden at the center of Tower Celleran and lifted her head from the pillow of her arms. She could hear no voices, see no people walking the curving paths so late at night; there was only the wind's soft rustle as it eased through the trees.

Trees, she thought, sleep and the wariness that came hard on the heels of waking doing little to dampen her wonder. Trees—actual trees—not the thin and stunted things she knew from the Lower City, with leaves like crumpled buds and twisted, brittle branches that littered the ground after a storm. Trees growing and vibrant and *alive*.

She looked up through the flowering bush beneath which she'd hidden for the night, attempting to see the wide branches of the nearest tree—and paused. The leaves just above her were curled and crisping, the pale flowers wilted. She glanced down.

Darkness spread around her like a stain. Not magic, as she'd feared the first time it had happened, but ash, fine and light as dust.

"Sweetness." She ran her fingers through the ash. "Not again."

It was all that was left of the soft moss that seemed to cover most Tower floors like an ever-present carpet. Shai was gone; there was no ghost lit with magic to call to Xhea's strange power. Yet still it flowed. Awake, she could restrain it with concentration and mental commands oft-repeated—though it lingered, a weight in her stomach, a presence calm and steady and strange. In sleep, her control vanished entirely, and she woke each day to ash and crumbling leaves, the ground blackened in the shape of her body.

At least she'd only killed leaves, she thought. This time.

She had wandered the City for four days, lost and alone—running, always running, from the memory of what had happened in that nondescript bedroom, the feel of that dark flood of power and the light fading from Shai's eyes. The night of Shai's death she'd hidden onboard a shipping transport to escape the unknown Tower, hugging herself against the chill of the altitude, invisible to the transport's onboard security sensors. Her destination hadn't mattered, so long as it was away. She shouldn't have left—not so quickly, without another word. At the least, she might have asked Shai's father for passage home. Yet once she'd gone, there had been no way back and no tether to lead her.

In the days that followed, she'd moved again and again, finding passage in luggage compartments and atop bulk transport containers, begging the indulgence of taxi passengers, and once even clinging—cold and terrified beyond words, eyes streaming in the fierce wind—to the outside rail of a bus. She'd found no way home, though life in the City was easier than it was below, if unfamiliar. Here, food was discarded as often as it was eaten. Bathrooms and shelter for the night were more challenging to find, if not prohibitively so. Only the thought of detection made her flee.

The City, even closer to the Central Spire, wasn't what she'd expected: it was larger and more chaotic, busier and louder and infinitely more beautiful. *Trees*, she thought again, and shook her head; trees and flowers and streams, markets and parks, restaurants and homes, a thousand homes, all just beyond her reach. Though it wasn't the homes she wanted now, so much as their baths. It had been too long since she'd bathed, she knew, and wrinkled her nose in distaste. Longer still since she'd done any laundry.

Now, the Tower seemed to sleep, a hush falling over the garden around her. Most of the space in the massive Towers was restricted to citizens and their guests, yet each had a public space where anyone might visit—including, it seemed, scraggly Lower City girls with a penchant for rummaging through the trash. Though Celleran wasn't a central Tower, it was rich enough, and displayed that wealth openly in the massive garden beneath its living heart—and the fountain at the garden's center.

She hadn't managed to steal any soap; water would have to do.

Xhea crawled from beneath the bush, curled leaves and limp petals raining in her wake, and began down a garden path, peering upward as she walked. Above her stretched the boughs of a massive tree, heavy with leaves, swaying softly in the garden's artificial wind. She took a deep breath and tasted fresh air; smelled only leaves and earth and flowers. No concrete to be seen, no broken asphalt, no fraying wire. No underlying scent of refuse or decay.

Soft light shone down from higher still—the source of so much vibrancy. Far overhead was the Tower's heart, the gathered magic of its citizens, their wealth and life force made into a physical shape that danced at Celleran's very core. Damped now, as if to mimic the moon's light. *How considerate*, Xhea thought.

The Towers' hearts fascinated her, and she'd spent whole evenings, curled and out of sight, staring upward. Each Tower's heart was unique, tones and patterns and the speed with which they moved varying greatly—a magical signature writ large. Celleran's heart moved slowly, its grays like shadow and stormcloud, its motion slow and calming. Mesmerizing. Yet even this was not enough to distract her from the notice displayed on the public information pillar at the side of the path.

A notice she'd seen countless times in every Tower, no matter how far she fled.

Missing. The word seemed to hover in midair, shining down on the surrounding flower beds, before being replaced by images: a girl staring outward, long hair tumbling over her shoulders. The same girl seen at a distance, walking forward, talking soundlessly to the camera. A young girl, healthy and whole. Smiling.

Shai.

Xhea had read the accompanying text so often that she had it memorized. MISSING: SHAI NALANI, FEMALE, AGED 17. LAST SEEN AT HER HOME IN ALLENAI TWO WEEKS BEFORE.

Allenai. Not some anonymous run-down Tower cast to the City's far edges, but a Tower so large and influential that even Xhea knew its name. Its proximity to the Central Spire marked Allenai's significance; its altitude established it as a force to be reckoned with in years to come. Upper class indeed.

She shook her head, coins chiming: there was no mention of Shai's father. Xhea could feel the layers of secrets and lies that surrounded Shai and her father both, and could only glimpse their edges.

Xhea watched the notice play again. She'd never known that person—someone smiling and happy and alive. That girl would never have talked to her, would never have had reason to. Something in her ached at the thought. Head bowed, she turned away.

The fountain stood in the center of a clearing, a multi-tiered cascade of water and light edged with glittering glass mosaics. The light of Celleran's heart played across the water's surface; yet it was not this that made the water glow, but the sparks of magic, pinpoint fractions of renai, that floated in the current. *No mere rainwater for City folks*, Xhea thought as she stepped to the fountain's edge. Here, even the water had more money than her.

She dropped her ashy jacket to the ground and peeled off her sweat-stiffened shirt in distaste. After kicking off her boots, she stepped into the fountain. The water was refreshing without feeling cold, and it swirled around her legs as if urging her deeper. She waded toward the center then sank to her knees and ducked her head beneath the cascading falls. Xhea ran her hands over her face and through her hair, trying to rinse away days of grime and sweat, before beginning to wash her shirt.

As she scrubbed, she fought against a growing pressure in her chest, an emptiness where a tether had once been, a strange heaviness in her heart and hands. *What's the matter with me*, she thought. Again she saw Shai's face, happy and smiling; again she watched that face transform, becoming gaunt and wasted by illness. Remembering that face, life slipping away. That strange, bright light of Shai's magic going dim; that bare room falling into shadow.

Xhea realized she was staring blankly at her shirt as it undulated on the water's surface. Flecks of magic glittered against the fabric like stars.

Stop it, she told herself. She didn't have time for weakness; not here, even in the dark and quiet—not when any moment some City citizen could walk into this clearing. Yet still she sat, staring.

As she watched, sparks of magic swirled through the water toward her. *Just like pennies*, she thought, feeling the weight of the ancient coins in her hair. Just as pretty. Just as useless. But these pennies, glittering sparks of renai, flowed against the current.

Xhea blinked and pulled back—but she was already too late. Instead of flowing over her with the water, a spark adhered itself to her forearm, and burned. She yelped and shook her hand, brushing madly at the spark. It didn't move, only flickered and died against her skin.

Then a second stuck to her hand, and a third to her cheek, each like a sharp pinprick. Xhea stood, water flowing from her in a wave—yet she was soaked, hair and pants and undershirt all glittering with bright magic. Magic that burned, each spark more painful than the last.

All through the water they flowed toward her, drawn like metal to a magnet. Drawn not to her, but the magic that hid beneath her skin, as constant and inexorable as a shadow. The sparks didn't last long, dying at her touch, but long enough. Even as Xhea struggled back toward the fountain's far edge and the dry ground beyond, she realized she was going numb. Her feet felt heavy as she sloshed through the water, and she slipped on the fountain's tiles, falling beneath the water's surface. Though she rolled to keep from choking, she couldn't keep the water—or its magic—out of her eyes. Her vision shimmered, and she saw glimpses of blue and gold amidst the gray: the fountain's swirling waters, aqua and pale cerulean, the sparks shining golden like pinpoints of sunlight.

She tried to struggle to her feet; slipped and stumbled and splashed back into the water.

"No," she whispered, lightheaded and suddenly afraid. Against the onslaught, her magic faded, receding to the depths of her self where it had lived for so long. Where she had forced it with magic such as this. The world around her was reborn in color and shadow.

Xhea sank into the water, curling in upon herself until the level reached her chin. Water washed over her, perfect blue and glittering in the dark. Her face was so wet that she never felt the tears as they began to flow, only noticed their warmth against her cheeks.

At last she voiced the thought that had followed her since she had released her magic—since she had, with conscious intent, asked it to strip the life from the only person she dared think a friend.

"Oh gods, what am I?"

A killer. A murderer. A monster. A freak.

A lost and frightened girl with no way home.

Her chest ached, grief constricting her breathing, and she clung to the empty fabric of her shirt as if it could ease the ache in her chest where a tether had once joined. Voice tight, she asked the empty air, "What have I done?"

In darkness, she looked up at the heart of the great Tower around her—a single Tower, when she was used to seeing them all, a landscape of moving structures of power and grace—and never before had she felt so small. So inconsequential.

So wrong.

Lost in her tears, Xhea thought herself alone until strong hands grabbed her by the arms. Hands that did not recoil, but tightened. She screamed and tried to pull away, but the hands held her fast and hauled her aloft, dripping and insensible, her toes barely touching the bottom of the fountain.

Fight back, instinct screamed. *Escape.* She kicked and twisted in her assailant's grip—or tried to. The attempt only made the dizziness and nausea from the bright magic to crest and crash over her, while she fought with numb fists. She was easily restrained.

Hard-earned lessons kicked in fast: if she could not fight, act sick. Not that she needed to pretend, Xhea thought, gagging.

"Come on, kid, stop messing around," a man's voice said. "Stand up." He shook her as if to punctuate the words, the movement making her head spin. Her foot slipped and she sunk back into the water until the man hauled her up once more.

Angrier now, he asked her questions: who was she, what was she doing here, why was she swimming half-naked in the fountain? Xhea whimpered. She stole a glance at his dark clothing, noting his muscled build, his gloved hands, and the unlikelihood of an escape from his grip. Security—but how?

Then she saw herself, covered with flaring, dying sparks of gold, and thought only: *oh.* A mental sigh. The Tower's security sweeps would never miss renai in the shape of a person, regardless of whether the magic bore a clear signature.

Xhea stayed limp as the security guard hauled her from the fountain, and it didn't take much to keep her earlier tears flowing. When he released her, muttering about the water soaking his shoes, she fell to her hands and knees, then let herself collapse between him and his partner.

"Come on." The guard nudged her with the toe of his waterlogged shoe. "Get up."

The partner swore, consulting a handheld device. "I'm not getting a signature. She's nearly too weak to register."

With those words, their attitude changed. The guard who had grabbed her now knelt at her side, supporting her head as he rolled her onto her back. Fingers felt her neck for a pulse and forehead for fever, the touch hot to her water-cooled skin.

"Hang in there, all right?" the guard murmured. "Help's coming."

Xhea lay with her eyes unfocused, staring upward as the Tower's heart shone like aurora, green and red and blue. Her mind raced: she didn't want to know what a medical team would do to her. But she couldn't escape while the guard held her; her only chance was to run while being transferred to the medics' care.

Yet even this vague plan derailed upon the medics' arrival. "Don't move," a woman said, and pressed something to Xhea's neck. Suddenly, Xhea did not have to feign difficulty responding; the blast of energy knocked her all but senseless.

It was a long moment before she regained true consciousness. *That wasn't renai*, Xhea realized, her mind swimming. Not money, raw or otherwise, but *magic*—pure bright magic, life force untainted and unshaped.

Sweetness and blight, she'd never be able to pay for that.

She felt as if she were floating, her body so strangely light she could barely feel it. She tried to wiggle her fingers and toes, and it was only when she forced her eyes open to see if they'd responded that she realized she was no longer by the fountain. She *was* floating, cushioned on a spell that followed the lead medic like a pet. They had already left the clearing, moving toward one of the elevator shafts that led up into the main part of the Tower.

"No," Xhea tried to say, "let me down," but what came from her mouth was a weak groan. The medic turned, then all Xhea could see were her eyes: eyes so green that they rivaled leaves;

eyes so transfixing that she could spend hours just studying their shift from emerald to jade, their faint accents of amber.

Xhea realized that the medic was speaking. She blinked and tried to pull her scattered thoughts together, while the world spun and glowed, everything beautiful and unsteady.

"Come on, stay with me. Do you feel any pain?"

"Dizzy," Xhea managed.

"Nothing hurts?"

She shook her head and shut her eyes, lost in euphoria and nausea.

"Vitals are strong," the medic said. "But she's barely absorbing the energy. Still no signature." Xhea was jostled as they guided the spell holding her into the elevator shaft. Even with her eyes closed, the light beyond the garden was blinding.

"Someone's drained the kid half-dry," a man's voice replied. "The paperwork on this one's going to be something." He sighed. "Give her another shot."

Once more Xhea felt something cold press against her neck, and that was all she remembered.

Xhea drifted, lost in vertigo's slow rock and turn. She floated bodiless in the clouds, the world drifting around her in a gentle wind, grays slipping lullaby-soft through the open hallways of her mind. Empty, she was content.

Forever later, she felt an edge of fear just sharp enough to pierce the haze: she didn't know where she was. It smelled wrong here, strange—too sweet with a sharpness beneath like cleaning solution. All she could hear was the slow hiss of air. Still the world held her gently and rocked her back and forth, back and forth.

No, she thought. *Focus. Focus.* As if mere repetition of the word could bring her scattered faculties into play or tame the bright magic that ran riot through her system. In silence she cursed magic, fountains, and the fools who thought it was pretty to combine the two.

Luck. As if.

She lay prone with her arms at her sides—that much she could tell. Something covered her—a sheet, she guessed, and blankets across her legs—though it wasn't only her disorientation that made the clean, soft fabric difficult to identify. She couldn't remember the last time she'd slept in a bed. Though she listened, she heard no scuff of feet or rustle of clothing, no breath but her own; and so slowly, cautiously, Xhea opened her eyes.

She recoiled from a blast of light and color. Blinking back tears, she tried again, glimpsing the room in snatches: the bed on which she lay, a door on the wall to her left, equipment beside and behind her. The walls were white—but, magic-dazzled, even the plainest stretch of wall was tinted: shadows edged with blue, touched with green; reflections casting shapes in pale cream and yellow and peach.

Hospital, she thought, or something like it. She'd never been in a medic's ward that smelled so little of illness or old blood. It was frightening to think what a place like this must cost; more frightening still to think what they might do when they learned that she could never, ever pay.

It was only when she could see without pain that Xhea noticed the man standing against the far wall. His unkempt hair was more gray than blond, and his green, hospital-issued pajamas hung from his gaunt frame. He watched her, the shadows beneath his eyes deep enough to fall into.

"You're in my bed," he said in a voice like old paper.

Xhea let her eyes flutter closed.

"Girl, don't pretend, I saw you're awake. You're not fooling anyone, hey?"

After a moment of strained silence, Xhea opened her eyes and attempted to shrug. Of everything in the room, she could look at the man without squinting. It didn't hurt to let her gaze rest on his wrinkled face, or study his jutting collarbones, his skin too thin over the bones.

"Sorry," she managed, the word slurred by her clumsy tongue. "I'd give it back, but I can't move."

"Heh. Figures." He dropped into the chair in the corner, studying her irritably. "Least you're talking to me," he said. "You know how many people just ignore me?"

Oh, sweetness save me, Xhea thought. But sure enough, she could just see it: an almost-invisible tether joining her visitor to the bed on which she lay.

"Figures," she muttered, echoing the man's sentiments.

More carefully now, Xhea looked around. To the right of her bed was a blank pane of glass, standing like a window to nowhere. It lit as she turned her head, graphs and diagrams springing to life across its surface. On a small table at the bedside rested a lamp, a touch panel that she guessed was a call button, and a glass of ice water. This last caught her attention, and she was suddenly aware of her raging thirst. She forced numb fingers to reach out, close around the glass, and pull it toward her. Her mouth quested for the straw.

Climbing into a fountain, Xhea decided, was a faster way to get drenched, but dumping glasses of water on her chest also worked nicely. She was grateful for the few mouthfuls she was able to swallow.

Okay, she thought, sagging back into her now-sodden sheets. *Escape. That shouldn't cause any problems.*

She turned to the medical equipment behind her. There was a small control panel from which a canopy of slender metal tines arced over her like the ribs of an antique umbrella. She watched as spells traveled along their lengths and the thin wires that ran between them, magic dancing over the strands. Most of the connecting wires led to a socket on the wall, yet one length curled down toward her. She followed the thin, plastic-wrapped strand, her numb fingers fumbling along its length until she found its end attached to her neck.

Her stomach roiled as she clutched the thin thing, tugging desperately to free it; but whatever held it to her skin—*oh please*, she thought, let it just be *on* her skin rather than *in* it—held fast.

"It's just for the monitor," Xhea whispered. Heartbeat and brain waves, blood pressure and the like—that was all. Or maybe it was an IV line like Lower City medics used—saline solution, pain meds, something. The thought of that line snaking through her veins was enough to make her pull at the wire until the skin on her neck burned.

Oh, how she hated feeling helpless.

"Say," she said to the old man, trying to sound calm. "You've been here a bit, right? Did you see where they put my clothes? Maybe my jacket?" A jacket that she sincerely hoped still held a knife in one of its many pockets.

"Sure," he said, gesturing to a boxlike storage compartment beneath the bedside table. She had to twist to see its front, the tiny latch and small touch panel. "Standard lock. If it's your stuff it'll open, hey?"

"Right," Xhea said. "Of course."

It was only a matter of reaching the panel. She glanced at her sodden pajama shirt and bedding, then down to her barely responsive hands. *Tough*, she told herself, and tried awkwardly to shift toward the edge of the bed.

A slight beep from above was the only warning. There was a flash as pure magical energy ran down the wire to her neck and into her body.

Ah, she thought as the world exploded in color and light. *This again.*

Dazzled and euphoric, Xhea slipped back into darkness.

"You're in my bed."

Xhea groaned. "I was unconscious," she protested—or tried to, the words slurred into incomprehensibility.

"Ah, I see you're awake." Another voice—a woman's voice—made Xhea force her eyes open, then wince at the assault of color. Her stomach churned—again. Still. *If this were a payment*, she thought, *I'd be loving this*. It wasn't much consolation.

The woman stood near the end of the bed, wearing neat scrubs and a look of professional concern. From the way the light seemed to glitter and dance around her, Xhea was fairly certain that this visitor was alive, though she checked for a tether just in case. The old man's ghost sat in his chair in the corner, sulking at the interruption.

"Are you feeling well enough to answer some questions?" the doctor asked. "The police would like to talk to you about what happened."

I can think of nothing I'd enjoy more, Xhea thought. But what she said was a slow, poorly enunciated, "Yes, okay."

When the police were brought in, Xhea kept her eyes closed to mere slits and allowed her tongue to be heavy and slow, so that she garbled even simple one-word answers. Even so, Xhea responded carefully to their patient questions, relying on vagueness, supposed memory loss, and outright lies to keep her anonymous.

No, she didn't remember anything. No, she couldn't tell them who had stripped her of life force and left her to die half-naked in a fountain. No, she didn't know who they could contact, nor the name of her Tower; she felt so strange—couldn't she sleep for a while longer, please? Oh, please. Surely she'd feel better soon.

Except that she didn't.

She received dose after dose of magic, and with each shot she seemed to wake less—to remember less—in the times between. She spoke to doctors, to nurses, to security—she didn't know quite who; their faces blended, one into the other, until she could not remember who'd she'd seen last or which of her visitors were still alive.

Places where people died were often thick with ghosts, and Celleran's hospital was no exception. The old man's ghost was waiting every time she opened her eyes, his greeting utterly predictable: "You're in my bed." Other ghosts visited as their tethers allowed, drawn to her presence. She tried to ignore them, but still they came: young ghosts and old, those that bore signs of their wounds or illnesses, and those that seemed whole and healthy and were nonetheless dead. Some of them spoke to her; some of them wept or cried or showed her the hurts that had killed them. After a while, she simply kept her eyes closed.

Still the magic pumped into her, beat after beat, breath after breath, until she felt she should glow with it, like Shai, radiant against the bed sheets. Until she felt like a ghost herself, bodiless yet tethered to this spot, this bed, this room.

I'm dying, she thought. The realization brought no fear.

Fight, she told herself. She could pull the wire from her neck, or try to reach the storage cupboard that held her knife . . .

If only the magic ebbed enough to let her care.

Perhaps it was better this way, she thought. At least she felt no hunger. At least there was no pain.

Shai came to her then. She stood at the end of Xhea's bed and shouted until Xhea forced her eyes open.

"Xhea," Shai said. "You have to wake up. You have to fight it."

Xhea looked at her, that long blonde hair, those so-blue eyes, and struggled to think what was wrong. Her hand lifted from her side—so heavy, so strangely light—its movements jerky as it came to rest on her chest.

"Gone," Xhea murmured. "Broken." She had done that. Done . . . something. Hadn't she? Why did she wish to apologize? The answer was slow in coming.

"Oh," she said, her voice a faint murmur. "You're dead."

Shai spoke slowly, shaping each word with care, and yet Xhea struggled to follow. ". . . get up. You have to get out—you can't let them find you." She made as if to grab Xhea's arm. "Understand? They're tracking . . ."

Something else bothered her. Xhea squinted at Shai, watching the fall of her pale hair against her shoulders, the way her skin looked almost transparent in this light. She watched Shai's lashes rise and fall over her perfect blue eyes as she blinked, the soft movements of pink lips as she spoke. Wasn't something missing, she wondered. Something . . . purple?

Her dress, she realized. Shai's plum dress with the full hem, the one that fluttered and flowed at her movements—gone. Instead Shai wore a plain eggplant shirt with embroidered vines at the neck and wrists, fitted pants, and a tailored vest arrayed with small pockets. Clothes that Xhea might have worn had she been able to afford them.

That's when Xhea understood. "Ah," she said slowly, interrupting Shai's increasingly frantic explanations. "I'm hallucinating."

"No, listen, Xhea—please! You have to—"

"I used to wonder, sometimes, what would happen if I got too much." Her voice was dreamlike and slow. "All the money in the world. Biggest job ever—a thousand renai, a million, all mine. All that light . . . color . . . power. Maybe I'd be normal." She laughed then, the sound slipping from her lips like dark liquid.

"Now I know. I'm just . . . nothing."

When the next dose of magic came, she did not fight it, only sighed and watched the world glimmer as it stole her away.

Chapter Eight

Clarity felt like the sun rising. Xhea blinked as she woke—truly woke, rather than struggling out of a magic-induced stupor. The world was still alight with color, but it no longer dazzled her, and her body, numb and clumsy, nevertheless moved as she willed.

A nurse stood at her bedside, adjusting the equipment above her head. Noticing Xhea's attention, he smiled broadly.

"How are you feeling?" he asked, all professional cheer.

"Okay. Tired." She tried to speak clearly. "What are you doing?"

"Just adjusting the drip. You're going to have a visitor, and we can't have your treatment interfering with his tests. Seems like it's been making you a little drowsy."

That was one way of putting it.

"So I won't be getting as much energy?"

"Don't worry," he said. "Once the specialist has completed his examination, we'll increase the dose again—or whatever he says will help you best recover." Again he smiled; the expression was not nearly as comforting as he seemed to think. He advised Xhea to rest—as if she could do much else—and said that they'd let her know when the specialist arrived.

But a cold knot had settled in her stomach. She wasn't certain what kind of specialist would be called for a case of suspected magical sapping, only knew that she never wanted to be examined by such a person. It wouldn't take long for a specialist to realize that her condition wasn't the result of an attack, but her version of normal. While she couldn't be certain of the reaction, her imagination provided her with any number of possibilities, ranging from unpleasant to deadly. If nothing else, there was the medical bill.

Then there was her dream of Shai. She remembered the intensity of the warning, if not the exact words. *Fight it*, Shai had said. *Get out of here. You can't let them find you.*

If only she could remember why.

It all brought her right back to the question of escape. Only now, she thought as she tried to curl her numbed fingers into a fist, she had perhaps an hour to make good her attempt.

"You're in my bed."

"Hello to you too," she muttered without looking up from her fingers. Make a fist, relax. Make a fist, relax. After a few dozen repetitions, the movement was no easier.

"Can't you see I'm an old man?" the ghost said. "I need rest, girl. Rest. Give a little precedence to your elders, hey?"

She shook out her hands and then tried to rub some feeling back into her arms. "I praise the wisdom your supreme age has surely granted you," she replied absently.

"Heh. Don't get snippy with me. I'm just asking to lie down in my own bed, that too much to ask?"

"Still can't move my legs, thanks."

Maybe recovering from a magical overdose was like a bad case of pins and needles—she just needed to convince the blood to return. No, not blood, she realized, and her head felt clear for the first time in days. Not blood, but magic—*her* magic, that energy dark and slow. When it filled her, she'd had the power to destroy the spells that kept Shai's body alive. Even when it had worked beyond her control, it had leeched the bright energy from living things, killed plants, unmade renai.

Yet this—to have her body and blood rage with bright magic— was the cure she'd stumbled on all unknowing, dosing herself with renai to keep the darkness down. She knew how to fight her magic, or at least subdue it; but calling it? That was beyond her. The one time she'd used it intentionally, the magic had already been drawn to Shai and the imbalance she represented—a living ghost, a dead girl filled with magic. She had felt the pull of Shai's presence, that ache like a bruise in midair.

Xhea looked at the old man sitting in the corner chair. He had no magic, nor its echo. And yet, as she stared, she felt . . . something. A trembling on the edge of her senses.

She frowned, concentrating. It was only with eyes closed that she truly felt it: a faint disturbance in the room's far corner—a chill like a cloud's passing, a hitch like breath held. The presence of a ghost. *Perhaps*, she thought. *Perhaps . . .*

"I'm sorry," she said. She tried to sound like she imagined a young City girl would: naïve and overconfident, perhaps a little embarrassed. "I didn't mean to be rude. I've just been feeling bad."

The ghost looked at her from under his eyebrows, forehead creasing as he considered her words. "It's all right," he said at last. "I get like that some days too."

"It's hard being in the hospital," she offered.

"Heh. You can say that again. Some days I can't remember my home, you know?"

Xhea had the feeling that if she were to ask him, he wouldn't be able to remember his home at all, the memories having vanished with his body. But she smiled, hoped she looked sympathetic, and asked, "Have you been here long?"

He nodded. "Good while, now, yeah. A good while."

"And you still don't have your own bed—I mean, your bed back? That's such a shame."

"Spoke to the nurses about it, but they don't even listen. Just act like they're too busy for the likes of me."

"Well, you do look pretty tired," she began, as if sounding out an idea, "and I'd move for you if I could, but I'm in pretty bad shape right now. But maybe . . . maybe I could let you rest here with me, just for a while." She tried not to shudder; tried to seem as if the thought of a strange, dead old man lying beside her was something she'd welcome.

"You'd really do that?" He was already limping to the bedside.

"Of course." *Just another ghost*, she told herself. *Think of it like any other job.*

As if she'd take a job like this.

He didn't attempt to touch her or the covers, only lowered himself onto the mattress, slipping through the metal railing without realizing it was there. Xhea shifted awkwardly, the coins in her hair clinking as she tried to make room. He sighed as he lay down, a slow exhalation that seemed to go on forever, and Xhea wondered if he might not bother to breathe again—might simply vanish, his purpose achieved with this brief moment of rest. Then his unneeded breath hissed in and he settled his head more comfortably on the pillow.

Xhea didn't speak, just let herself feel him there, the unmistakable chill of a ghost. She didn't touch him, though he was close enough that any movement might bring them into contact, face or shoulder or leg.

Yet even after a few long minutes spent face to face in silence, she felt little different. The colors hadn't dimmed, and as she opened and closed her hand, she knew her fist was as weak as before. Nothing stirred in the pit of her stomach. No sense of that dark stillness waiting to overflow. There wasn't even emptiness, just the bright magic, grinding nausea, and a bone-deep weariness that weighed her down as surely as if she'd been bound.

What had she expected? She'd dealt with ghosts countless times, bright with payment and without, and never had a ghost's mere proximity caused the dark magic to rise. Not before Shai.

It was only then that Xhea realized the old man was crying, ghostly tears slipping down his wrinkled cheeks and vanishing before they reached the pillow. There was no point in asking if he was all right. Instead, she whispered, "Why are you here?"

"I don't know." He shuddered with thin sobs. "I just want to go home."

What would she have done had this truly been a job? Used her knife, most likely; cut his tether to the world and released him to dissolve into air and memory. Yet her knife, locked but feet away, was far beyond her reach.

The darkness wasn't just going to come, she realized. So long rejected and buried under tides of bright power, it wasn't going to fight back. She'd never *wanted* it to fight back; just the opposite. Now, when it was needed, she didn't know how to call it.

Hesitantly, Xhea placed her hand against the old man's cheek. It hurt as her fingers passed through his flesh, suddenly not numb but burning, freezing. Still she persisted, cupping her hand as if she could touch him in truth, brush away his falling tears with a gesture. The pain helped focus her: it was a point of clarity in the midst of so much brightness.

She thought of stillness, of black that waited like the depths of a cold lake and the dark fog that crept from its surface. She was afraid—oh, she was so afraid of what she was, and terror curdled her empty stomach—and yet still she reached for calm and asked the darkness to come. If she had used words, she would have said only *yes*—affirmation and permission both.

This is what I am, she thought. The balance. The coin's other side.

This is who *I am: a bridge between darkness and light.*

And the magic flowed. It rose slowly at first, sluggishly. It felt cold, like a thin stream of melted ice rising through her, and where it met the bright energy Xhea burned, too hot and too cold. Still she called to it, welcomed it, and as the magic moved through her the brightness began to give way.

Against so much power, the thin stream of darkness held little sway. Yet she didn't need to flood her body with magic, merely encourage it to flow down her arm, pulse by pulse to the rhythm of her blood; allow it to swirl and coil through the flesh of her hand, and pool in her palm.

"What do you want?" she whispered. Not to know the answer; only to hear the words once more from his lips.

"Home," the ghost said, his voice tight with tears. "Just let me go home."

"Close your eyes." Xhea ran her magic-darkened fingers across his eyelids. "Think of home. Only of home."

Again she cupped her hand over his cheek, a mere breath of air between where her skin ended and his ghostly presence began. She said to the magic that rose so slowly inside her: *There. Him.*

Like mist rising, the dark energy seeped from her fingertips and lifted from the back of her hand, drifting down over the old man's face with impossible slowness, impossible gentleness. She watched as he took one sobbing breath and then another, drawing the darkness inside him each time. The magic wreathed him, coiling over his closed eyes, tracing the uneven lines of his brows. It drifted through the untamed chaos of his gray hair, and followed the tracks of his tears.

Slowly it spread, moving with that same languor over his whole body—over him, and through him. Part of Xhea's consciousness moved with it, following her magic's path. At last she moved her hand from the ghost's cheek to the center of his forehead where his tether was bound. She ran her hand through the line of energy tying him to the hospital, to the memories of sickness and to the bed upon which they lay. It parted at her gesture like smoke.

"You're free to go now," Xhea told him softly. "You've been discharged. You can go home."

"I can go home?" he whispered, and the tears on his face began to dry. He did not open his eyes, yet as Xhea watched, his face lit in a wide and joyful smile. The expression transformed him until it seemed he was not old, had not known loss or pain, had not caused it. Together, the ghost and the magic that had freed him dissipated, vanishing into the air until all that remained was the memory of that smile.

"Oh," Xhea said. She stared at the place where the ghost had lain, tears welling. It was this as much as dizziness that made her close her eyes.

A beep came from behind her; she jerked upright, but could not avoid the magic that surged down the wire into her neck. She cried out as the two magics, bright and dark, met within her. Her body spasmed, muscles cramping hard in reaction. She clenched her teeth and attempted to smother her whimpers, afraid of drawing the attention of the hospital staff—if her cry and falling energy levels hadn't already done so.

Fight it, she told herself, her words mirroring those of dream-Shai. Xhea's power had receded at the onslaught, and so she imagined mental hands, reached desperately inside herself, and pulled. Again the magic rose like dark water from a well—and again the monitor beeped, almost querulously, and the surge of bright energy slammed her back to the pillows.

It would be easier to just slip away, let oblivion close over her once more. But, Xhea thought, when had life ever been easy?

She grabbed the thin wire bound to her neck and pulled with all her strength. As the wire finally ripped free, it took with it the top layers of her skin. She felt the wound with clumsy fingers—but there was only a little blood and no hole, no needle left protruding.

Xhea sucked air through her teeth as the world seemed to tilt and sway. She wanted to lie back down; instead, she forced herself to slide down past the bed's side rail until her bare legs dangled over the side of the mattress. Only the sight of her numbed toes gave her pause: never before had her own skin looked *purple.*

It was only then that she realized the monitor was emitting a high whine of alarm, protesting its disconnection. *That,* Xhea thought, *is surely going to draw attention.* Without thinking, she raised a trembling hand, placed it against one of the monitor's reaching metal tines, and said, "*Shh.*"

Her magic was slow and sluggish, but it responded. Wisps of black reached from her fingers to twine around the metal structure. The alarm slowed, quavering and failing as the spells controlling it unraveled.

Xhea released her magic and it vanished into the air. She curled her hand into a tight fist: stronger already. Every breath felt steadier than the one before, and her thoughts felt clearer as the flood of bright energy drained from her flesh. As she watched, the blood on her fingertips from the wound on her neck seemed to flicker, crimson and black. Never had she been so glad for the promise of a world seen only in gray.

Hurry, she told herself. *Focus.* It was easy to slip into the strange haze caused by pain and disorientation, equally easy to lose herself in the contentment the dark magic evoked—too easy. She already heard voices calling from the far end of the hallway; running footsteps wouldn't be far behind.

Xhea slipped from the bed and crumpled to the floor, her weakened legs giving way beneath her. Gritting her teeth, she dragged herself to the storage container beneath the side table and placed her fingers against the lock touch panel. No flashes, no warning: it simply darkened to black.

"Of course," she said. "Lovely."

Ignoring the darkened panel, Xhea leaned on the latch until it gave way with a sullen crack. Inside, she found her clothing—properly washed, folded, and just a little closer to disintegrating. Her jacket was on top, the shape of her silver knife visible through the worn fabric. There was no time to undress; Xhea threw her clothes on over the pale green hospital shift, ignoring the way the fabric bunched and gathered beneath her shirt. She pushed her feet into her battered boots, not bothering to tie the laces, and forced herself to stand.

She stumbled into the bathroom, flicking on the light and turning the taps and shower on full before stepping out and slamming the door closed behind her. She pressed her hand against the touch panel until it too darkened, then tried the handle, grinning when it refused to do more than rattle. She slipped behind the door to her room and pulled it wide to hide her. The light and sound from the bathroom would only distract the hospital staff for a moment—but perhaps a moment would be all she needed.

A nurse entered the room, exclaiming over Xhea's empty bed and the damaged equipment. She went immediately to the bathroom door, knocking and calling out in a loud voice. With the nurse's back turned, Xhea slipped into the hall.

Head down, she told herself. She tried not to stumble, tried not to attract more attention than was necessary. She broke into an uneven run as she rounded the hall corner, the sound of her footsteps covered by the sound of the nurse attempting to break down the bathroom door.

Xhea ran down a long corridor, then another, choosing her route at random. She needed a plan, that much she knew, but she had no idea how a hospital was laid out, never mind the Tower as a whole—or how to escape it. Only when a familiar voice spoke did she stop, her momentary exhilaration vanishing.

"Not that way," Shai said.

Xhea turned. Shai stood behind her, looking as she had the night before: determined, yet afraid. As Xhea stared, Shai's blue eyes became silver, her clothing faded to black, and the golden tone slipped from her hair. Only gray now; familiar, unending gray.

Shai grabbed Xhea's hand. "Run," she said. "They've found us."

Chapter Nine

Living as she did in the streets of the Lower City, few things could spur Xhea to action as a warning to run. Yet the touch of the ghost's hand stopped her cold. She could feel Shai's fingers closing around her own—and if the sensation was different than that of flesh on flesh, it was wholly unlike the chill non-touch of a normal ghost.

Run, Shai had said. In the chaos of Xhea's half-formed thoughts, one took precedence: did she trust Shai? The answer came without hesitation, and perhaps that was the most surprising thing of all. *Yes*. So she nodded and, trying to hold the hand that wasn't quite there, ran after her.

As they rushed down the corridor, dodging a surprised medical technician, Xhea realized that she couldn't see Shai's tether. Surely it was only too faint for her to detect—for to what but Xhea herself could Shai be bound that would allow such freedom of movement?

You're here, Xhea wanted to say. Instead she asked, "How did you find me?"

"I could sort of . . . sense you," Shai said, running through a passing gurney and wincing. Their hall ended, opening into a wide atrium. "Figuring out how to get here was harder. Quick—through here." Shai passed through a wide door, which beeped as Xhea approached, apparently considering whether the approaching magic-poor object was a person. Xhea slammed into it with her shoulder, forcing it open. Holding her numbed arm and cursing, it was a few steps before she took in her surroundings.

Her first thought was that they'd somehow gone outside. She could see clouds and sky, and the light was sunlight. Xhea blinked as her eyes adjusted. They stood on the top of a set of shallow stairs that led down to . . . a road? Xhea blinked again, this time in confusion.

She remembered how Celleran had looked as she'd approached, hiding in the back of a transport container: a long, bottom-heavy shape, not unlike the bud of an unopened flower, around which spiraled a gleaming silver line. She'd thought the line mere decoration; now she gaped, realizing it wasn't ornamentation, but a highway.

Carefully, she stepped down toward the heavy flow of traffic before her, leaving the hospital behind. First came the pedestrians, a crowd thick as that in the market on its busiest mornings, walking in either direction. She caught sight of couples arm-in-arm, groups of friends chatting as they strolled, even children who flittered around their parents, arguing and laughing. Over their heads whizzed small bubbles of light: spells, messages, she knew not what else.

Next came the aircars, taxis, and elevators—things she had taken for granted out in the open air but had never imagined traveling within a Tower. Farthest out was a gleaming line of boxes and packages, pallets piled high, that swept by as if caught in a swift river of magic.

"This is the long way," Shai said, coming to stand at her shoulder, "but it's easier than trying to use the lifts."

"Easier to get lost in a crowd." Xhea slipped into the human traffic with the ease of long practice, arms pulled to her chest to avoid accidentally touching anyone. These people walked to different rhythms than those she knew from the Lower City; yet they were not so strange that she could not find her way.

Slowly, she told herself, curbing the need to run. Nothing stood out in a happy crowd like someone barreling by at high speed—and she stood out enough as it was. Besides, her rush of adrenaline was wearing off, and Xhea wasn't certain she could handle more than 200 floors worth of spiraling ramp—even downhill.

"Okay," she said under her breath. "Who are we running from?"

"My Tower, Allenai. At least, I think it's Allenai."

"You don't know? Or don't remember?"

Shai turned to face her, floating downhill. "No, I remember now. I remember everything."

"Just give me the highlights," Xhea said, struggling to slow her breathing.

"You were connected with my magical signature," Shai said, "and I'm officially missing. They have your image from the elevator that carried us up to that . . . that *place* where my body was."

"They think I kidnapped you?"

"No. They think that you may know where I am."

Fair enough, thought Xhea. *I do.*

"After I . . . died, I was bound to my father with one of those tethers. I was with him for a few days, and . . ." Shai looked away, eyes bright with tears. Suddenly Xhea didn't want to know what those days had been like for her, watching her father mourn.

"Anyway," the ghost managed, "I was with him until some people came. They wanted to know where I was and wouldn't listen when he tried to explain the arrangements he'd made for my body. There was an argument. They took him, and the tether just . . . snapped. I didn't know how to follow."

At this, Xhea's steps faltered; she knocked elbows with a random passer-by, who yelped at the contact. Xhea apologized, smiling her sweetest smile, and hurried away.

Tethers didn't just snap. They dissolved with their ghosts when that person's business in the living world was finished. While she'd learned to sever and reattach a tether using her knife, it wasn't the same as breaking the tether entirely. The only time she'd ever known a tether to snap was when the person to which the ghost was bound died.

Xhea suddenly felt weary in ways that had nothing to do with physical exhaustion. She didn't want to give Shai that news—yet, glancing at the ghost's expression, it seemed that Shai already knew.

"Xhea, they said that if he didn't know where I was, you would."

Right. So Allenai also appeared to have killed Shai's father, though whether as a consequence of hiding his daughter, her death, or something else entirely, Xhea didn't know. Being caught seemed less appealing with every moment. Yet the thing she couldn't comprehend was why there was such furor to track down Shai's ghost at all. Few people even admitted that ghosts existed. To hunt a ghost through the City—to kill in an attempt to find her—seemed beyond imaging.

"How do they know I'm here?"

"I recognized a man who talked to my father. I followed him and saw him meet with Celleran's security."

"They showed security the picture of me," Xhea said, heart sinking.

"No, they gave a signature print. Mine."

"But why . . . ?" Unless, Xhea realized, they assumed that Shai was still with her, and that enough magic still lingered in the ghost for Shai's signature to register. Did they not understand that Shai's magic had been an anomaly, the effect of a living ghost?

Not that any of that would matter, if she were found. How far had they descended? Two floors? Three? Each circuit seemed to take forever, the road's incline so shallow as to feel like level ground. And oh, she was tired. For all that the magic had brought her a brief rush, she suddenly felt her days of immobility—days she'd barely woken long enough to eat. Worse, the dark magic itself took a toll. She felt contentment in its wake, yes . . . but something deeper too. As if the dark smoke was her spirit burning.

"They were gaining permission to do a full sweep of the Tower," Shai said. "They'll be here within the hour—less, now."

That, Xhea thought, was her only bit of luck. Of the two groups looking for her in Celleran—the people from the hospital and the people from Allenai who had connected her with Shai's death—neither would exactly be looking for Xhea. One sought a girl who was desperately ill, while another had Celleran security searching blindly for a murder suspect with a stolen magical signature. That gave her less than an hour to get herself off this blighted corkscrew of a Tower before people who might recognize her arrived in force.

Xhea stopped dead in the middle of the road. Ignoring the sudden exclamations from the people around her—ignoring how she knew she would look, addressing the empty air—she turned to Shai and said, "I have a plan. Do you know the fastest way out of any building?"

Shai shook her head. "No, but Xhea—"

"Get thrown out."

"No!" Shai looked stricken. "You can't let them detain you."

"Detain?" Xhea glanced about, frowning. Celleran was far too clean to have anything like rocks strewn about its perfect roadway. She couldn't even spot a bit of garbage. Instead, she grabbed one of the coins from her hair and pulled it free, wincing. "Why would anyone detain Lower City scum like me? Eviction is so much easier."

She spun and hurled the coin out at the lines of aircar traffic. It seemed to glitter as it flipped through the air, bounced off the roof of a passing taxi, and ricocheted from a speeding pile of boxes. The impotent *ting* as it hit the ground was likely just her imagination.

Not, she thought, the effect she needed. She grabbed another coin, ripped it free from its tattered ribbon, and threw it.

The first coin had been nearly useless, but the second . . .

She watched as it sailed over the lanes of traffic before striking the Tower's magical barrier just beyond. At the point of impact, the spell that protected the roadway dissolved with a hissing, spitting noise. The dark-edged hole widened like a cigarette burn sizzling across paper, and a wild gust of wind swept across the crowd. People screamed as air was drawn out in a rush: perfect hairstyles were ripped into fluttering strands, papers and carelessly held sweaters flew airborne as if tossed, and the river-borne stream of objects was drawn hopelessly off course. Traffic swerved and collided, creating yet more destruction.

Xhea's eyes widened. She'd hoped to hit an aircar windshield, maybe cause a small accident; *this* was a little more unexpected. Though the fabric of the Tower's exterior protective spell was quickly repairing itself, the damage had already been done: almost everything on the road had come to a complete stop.

"Oh my," Xhea whispered. The wind caught her hair and set the charms to ringing. She couldn't help but smile, thinking: *This might actually work.* She only hoped that her strength held until the authorities arrived.

She caught bits of the confused babble.

"Honey, are you okay? We have to—"

"It was a hole in the field—an actual hole!"

"—couldn't have, I've seen the specs for that spell myself, and—"

Xhea turned, putting the grounded aircars and the healing hole in the exterior spell at her back, and looked into the gathered crowd. Confusion, fear, curiosity—and no little bit of anger. She latched on to this last, struggling to find words that would fuel their discontent.

"Oh, come on," she yelled, forcing all the scorn she could muster into her voice. She raised both arms in a broad gesture of disgust. "What's your problem? Crying over what—a few dropped packages? A dent in your fender? A two minute delay in your schedule? Whiners, the lot of you. You think this is bad? You think this is *damage*? Ha! This is nothing."

A few people turned toward her, seeking the source of the noise, but most turned away just as quickly. One or two shook their heads or pursed their lips in mild irritation before returning to their conversations, debating whose aircar caused which accident.

"Settle down, kid," someone called.

Come on, she thought. She needed to make enough of a disturbance that she'd be arrested and thrown out with few, if any, questions asked. If she'd snuck into the Lower City's inner market and made even half this much noise, she'd have been tossed in moments. Had been, many times.

"Xhea, don't do this," Shai begged. "We can still sneak out of here, no one would know—"

"You want to know who did this?" Xhea cried, louder, and her voice echoed. Shai covered her face, wincing. "Me! I just wish that I'd broken more—taught you brainless City drones what it's like to lose something."

The crowd turned toward her again, and this time voices fell silent—watching, listening, trying to understand how this small, strange girl had caused the hole.

Xhea caught sight of a woman on her knees, scrabbling after a bag of shopping she had dropped—too important, it seemed, for the parcel stream. An aircar had run it over, leaving only battered bits of what had once been a pair of shoes—if the strappy bits of glitter even deserved the name. The woman's face was stricken, fighting tears. Over *shoes*.

Not a child. Not food or clean water. Sweetness-blighted *shoes*.

"You don't understand what you have, do you?" Xhea said, and heard her voice twist, true pain coloring the words. "Not any of you. You've stopped seeing all the things you've been given. Gifts heaped on you for being born normal. Clothes, family, food. A place to sleep. People to love. You've stopped being grateful—if you ever were."

"Calm down," a voice said from nearby. "I understand that you're upset, but—"

Someone from the back of the crowd interrupted: "What do you want? The shirt off my back?"

"Yes!" Xhea cried. "Your shirt, your home, your *life*."

"Earn it," the unseen speaker called back.

A hand reached for her, coming to rest on her shoulder—then the unknown person yelped and recoiled.

Shai was there, too, trying to get her attention. "Xhea—Xhea, stop, you have to listen to me—"

But she couldn't stop. "Earn?" she yelled back. She was breathing hard now, and not just from running, not just from weakness. "*Earn?* You were born a citizen! Born with magic—renai—in your blood. What's there left for you to earn? You just can't stand the thought that you've had it easy—that all your little struggles are a whole lot of nothing."

It's just a show, she reminded herself. *A way out. They're supposed to be mad, not you.* But the anger felt like her magic: dark and fierce and not entirely under her control.

"What do you know? I've worked hard for what I have, and I—"

"Hard?" Xhea screamed back. "You don't even know the meaning of the word, you pampered, brainless—"

"Xhea, *stop*," Shai said, louder this time, trying to stand between Xhea and the crowd. "That's enough!" But Xhea didn't hear her; didn't even try. The words were already in her mouth, their bitter taste one she'd been born knowing.

"What's really your problem?" she yelled. "Don't like being called on what you are? You, who don't lift a finger to help anyone—who treat people from the Lower City like *garbage*. You and your precious City, you and your goddamn Towers."

She ripped another coin from her hair, and part of the braid with it; she felt no pain, only the beat of her anger and the rush of blood in her ears. She stared at them, that crowd of upset faces, milling witnesses, searching for the one who had shouted back. He could have been any of them, these nameless people who lived lives that she could never have.

She threw the coin blindly into the crowd. "What makes any of you so special?" she yelled, and her vision darkened not with magic but dizziness. It was too much, she was still too weak, but she couldn't stop. "Towers and gardens and hospitals? Sweetness-blighted fountains full of renai, you fools—*money*, when we have nothing. Nothing! What makes you worth this?"

To her left there was a commotion as the crowd made way for a vehicle to speed uphill. She barely noticed, only registering the presence of Tower security as they surrounded her.

"You're not better than me," Xhea screamed as gloved hands closed around her arms. Her legs gave way and she kicked, though whether to strike at her captors or regain her footing even she couldn't say. "You're not better than me!"

The crowd applauded as she was dragged away.

Xhea had been thrown out of more places than she could remember—for touching another person, for the state of her clothing, for her inability to bribe the thugs, for existing. Yet she, who'd been tossed out of the Lower City market in under thirty seconds one memorable summer evening, was unable to spur a response from the officers escorting her stronger than, "That's enough." As Shai predicted in a low tone, Xhea was placed in a holding room until she could "calm down"—and, apparently, until security had the time and manpower to devote to such a minor problem.

She'd made a fool of herself, and for nothing. No, worse than nothing, for now she was caged and at others' mercy. Again.

Xhea collapsed onto the chair in the center of the small room, covered her face with her hands, and closed her eyes. The sound of the door's lock engaging echoed in memory long after all else was silent. Shai settled onto the edge of the table, and even with her eyes closed Xhea could feel the ghost's presence like a pressure, an *awareness* in the space beside her. It seemed that, at least, hadn't changed with Shai's death.

"I didn't mean . . ." Xhea whispered, and let it trail away. She had tried; she could say that much, little good that it did her. It seemed that in Celleran, at least, procedure wasn't made to be ignored. How was she to know that security was so different here than in the Lower City?

Common sense, some part of her replied. Or she could have listened to Shai. Instead, tired and hungry, she was forced to wait in a hard plastic chair as the minutes crept by and her chance of evading Allenai's pursuit dwindled to nothing. There was no clock on the wall; she didn't need one. Every breath bore the weight of long seconds, counting away the last of her freedom.

Shai didn't speak, only waited in silence. It felt worse than any accusation.

An hour or more had passed before the door opened to admit a small, neatly-dressed man with a narrow rod held loosely in one hand. "Hello," he said. He placed the rod onto the table and settled into the chair across from her.

She looked from the nondescript length of metal up to the man's face and back again, her jaw tightening. *Not a cop*, Xhea thought. *Not security.* He looked too soft, too compact. Was that why he thought he needed a weapon? Did he expect her to believe that they beat adolescents here for minor crimes—or was he only playing to her fears? Unclenching her hands, Xhea exhaled and leaned back in her chair.

Ignoring her insolent look, he said, "I'm Jer Errison, your appointed negotiator. I'm afraid we don't have a name on file for you. Is there something you'd like to be called?"

"Not particularly."

"It might make this conversation go a little smoother." A wry edge colored his tone. "Give me something to call you instead of 'hey you.'"

Xhea shrugged, glancing away.

He nodded, acknowledging the refusal. "All right, then. To business." He spoke calmly. "I've heard that you caused a disruption on the thoroughfare this afternoon. Quite a bit of damage. You upset some people, too."

"That's one way of putting it."

"Was that your intention, then? Upsetting people?"

Shai spoke into the expectant silence. "Tell him you're sorry."

Xhea kept herself from turning toward the ghost, but only just. As it was, her surprise at the interruption made her startle, and she saw Jer Errison take note of her sudden discomfort. She couldn't shake her head; she had no way to express what she thought of that terrible idea—except plowing on as if she hadn't heard.

"I suppose—"

"No," Shai interrupted, her tone made sharp by anger. "We tried it your way, and now you're locked up and making things worse. It's my turn. Tell him you're sorry."

Xhea stared at the man's face, at his eyes, and grit her teeth until she could hear them grind together. What Shai was asking, she couldn't possibly—

"Xhea." Quieter this time, that sudden anger restrained. "Please."

Xhea whispered, "I . . . apologize." With the words, it felt as if all the fight drained out of her. Her shoulders slumped and her expression fell—her carefully crafted façade crumbling all around her, and nothing she did could call it back. She wanted to scream at Shai for ruining everything. She covered her face with her hands, feigning rubbing her tired eyes, as if hands alone could shield her from the shame of such weakness.

Jer leaned back slowly. "For?" he asked.

Xhea struggled with the words, their foreign shape—but again Shai was there, prompting. "Just say it. Explain what you did."

It was as if she had lost her voice; she could barely whisper. "For . . . damaging the spell. And for scaring those people, and breaking their things, and making them angry. I just threw something. I didn't know that it would cause such a problem, and then I was so upset, and I just . . . I'm sorry. I didn't know."

"You're from the Lower City, aren't you?" Now there was something gentle in his tone, a softness that lay beneath his surprise. Xhea found she was looking at her hands, her limp fingers curling like old leaves. She nodded.

"And how did you come to be here?"

Xhea glanced at Shai. "You're lost," the ghost prompted softly.

"It was an accident," Xhea whispered. "I never meant to be here. To stay. I've tried to get home, but I'm lost and everything I try . . ."

"You didn't mean to cause that damage."

Xhea shook her head, the movement doing nothing to hide her sudden flush. "I can't pay for it. I just want to go home."

"I know what you said this afternoon. I understand why you were upset." He picked up the rod from the table, but before she could tense, he used his fingers to draw it apart, expanding it into a wide rectangular shape. Not a weapon, Xhea saw, watching as a fine spell stretched between the thin spans, but a screen. It lit at his touch and he spun it toward her, allowing her to see a recording of her shouting at a crowd, the image dancing through the spell-strands. There was no sound; she didn't need it. She felt the words, as if they echoed through her.

"I could help you," he said. "I can't undo what you did, but there are ways to make amends. While you're here, you'd be given a room, three meals a day, a change of clothing."

Xhea realized that she was staring in bewilderment—but even her confusion couldn't hide her sudden eagerness. To have so much . . .

She allowed herself an instant of hope before crushing it. Beautiful as the City was, she didn't belong here. She didn't know the rules, didn't know how the rhythm of life's varying heartbeats in this vast landscape spread across the sky. Didn't know what to do with even the scraps of luxury she had been offered, or these strange, small kindnesses; could only imagine how each would twist and turn upon her when they learned who she was or what she had done. Even if she could make amends to Celleran, no place in the City would be safe for her—not with Allenai searching for her.

"Please," she said. Her voice trembled and cracked, and she felt so ashamed. "Please, just let me go home."

He tried for a while longer to convince her, outlining her options, before at last nodding and collapsing the screen. "If that's what you want," he said. If he sounded disappointed, Xhea imagined that he was also relieved.

He rose and gestured to the door. "This way."

She had expected an aircar ride, but instead he led her on foot down to one of the Tower's landing bays. The bay she knew from her arrival: a cavernous room with a wide opening protected by an opaque spell; collections of aircars parked one atop the other like toy blocks, while elevators hovered like flies. Jer raised a hand and an elevator rushed toward them.

"You're sure," he said, but the words were resigned.

Xhea nodded. She couldn't thank him; the words stuck in her mouth. She stood awkwardly until he activated the elevator and the bright ribbons arced up and around her. Shai slipped close as the spell enclosed them in a bubble of light and silence. They rose.

It was only as the elevator began to move and the boundary spell opened to let them through that Xhea saw what lay beyond: darkness.

Night.

"No!" she cried. She tried to force the elevator to reverse its course, but it moved inexorably forward. "No, please, not at night!" She thought of the night walkers roaming the Lower City streets, the torn bodies she'd discovered, the blood, and she screamed.

Yet the spell was designed to keep the sound of wind and traffic from buffeting its passenger; it silenced her cries. She twisted to see Jer Errison, but he hadn't stayed to watch her go. She only caught a glimpse of his retreating back as the elevator bore her out of Celleran and away.

Chapter Ten

The elevator fell surrounded by Towerlight, mercury and pewter, star-white and rainfall's gray; yet even the City's raw beauty couldn't distract Xhea from the approaching ground. Peering down through the ribbons of the elevator spell, she could just see the Lower City's huddled structures, glints of fires burning low on rooftops and electric light creeping around the edges of drawn shutters.

Only the skyscrapers let Xhea make sense of the shadowed roadways. They stood like squat sentinels in a wide, uneven ring: Senn, Edren, and Orren formed the circle's heavy base, while Farrow and Rown were spaced some distance apart. As if the ring were a target, the elevator fell arrow-true toward its center. Unless they'd dumped her in the ruins, Xhea couldn't think of a worse place to land. Within her temporary bubble of safety, she began to tremble.

The skyscrapers' core territories held little refuge to those not owing allegiance to one of the five, the glow of warmth and shelter glimpsed through their shielded windows a promise that their closed doors made a lie. All she needed was an open tunnel entrance—a subway station, a mall entry, a connecting passage—and knew them all blocked. Though few but Xhea herself could stand to travel the underground routes, that was threat enough for the skyscrapers, all of whom had connections to the underground mall in their lowest levels. Fearing attacks from rival skyscrapers, the likes of which had rocked the Lower City in a civil war just over a decade before, the remaining entrances and tunnels beneath were boarded over and barricaded.

She would have to run for blocks to find safety, run and pray—and she felt her fatigue like a weight of stone.

Shai hovered at Xhea's side, her anxiety accentuating her helplessness. Shai's eyes seemed brighter than Xhea remembered, though—sharper, as if true death had brought her an intensity denied in her former ghostly half-life. She watched everything as they fell.

For a moment they descended through the empty gap between the City and the ground, a stretch unbroken by Towerlight or traffic. Then the roofs were rushing toward them and Xhea reached out, unable to fight the feeling that she was falling to smash on the pavement below. She caught a glimpse of bright light behind the blur of Senn's black glass windows, the flicker of rooftops, tangles of strung wires, and then she was landing.

Her boots hit the street and the elevator dissolved, spell ribbons fluttering down around her as the elevator port sped back to the City. While the elevator had protected her from the fierce wind and noise of travel, so too had it shielded her from the night's chill. With the spell fizzling against the asphalt, she keenly felt the lack. Xhea peered around, orienting herself, and took a tentative step forward.

Yet it wasn't only the cold that made her shiver, but the sudden silence, the Lower City's absolute still. It seemed as if her breath were the loudest sound, quick and fearful gasps that even a closed mouth could not stifle; and when the wind came, rustling through the ancient corridors of concrete and steel, setting distant balcony charms to jangling, it only served to enhance the silence that lingered beneath.

It wasn't the silence she needed to fear, Xhea knew. But if the quiet was not her enemy, neither was it her friend; even the sound of the broken asphalt crunching beneath her boot-soles echoed, announcing her presence to anyone—anything—that knew to listen.

"Run," Shai whispered. Warning or encouragement, the word was the only spur Xhea needed to take flight. She knew these streets. Even panicked, she could navigate almost by instinct, memory providing the details that speed and darkness obscured: the blocked alleyway, the pothole deep enough to turn her ankle, the sagging line of charm flags that she had to duck beneath. She stumbled down the street that divided Edren from Orren and through the intersection where a single traffic light still hung, defying gravity and scavengers alike. The Lower City's smells were all but choking, drawn deep into her lungs with each panting breath. As she sped into an alley, all she noticed was the smell of refuse and urine, mud and putrefaction.

She'd run two steps before she saw the figure, and two more before she was able to bring herself to a skidding, pinwheeling stop.

A man stood before her, midway down the alley—and it was a man: she knew from his height and bulk, the way his shoulders seemed to fill the narrow space. He was still and silent in a way that she, gasping and shaking, couldn't hope to replicate. She stared, caught between the urge to beg for protection and her body's demand that she turn and run somewhere, anywhere, so long as it was *away*.

The man stepped forward—cautiously, like an uncertain animal—and Xhea noticed the hunch to his back and his head's lolling bow, lank hair hanging around his face and shoulders. Another step and he came into the thin pool of Towerlight that shone, faint as starlight, into the alley. He was dirty and naked, untold filth hanging in clumps from his body. *That*, she thought faintly, *explains the smell.*

He did not look at her—his eyes, she saw, were clouded milk-white—but Xhea could feel his attention, see the way he rolled his head slowly back and forth, nostrils flaring as he caught her scent. He inhaled, seeming to draw her essence deep into his belly. She knew that sound, had heard it countless times that long frozen night she'd spent in the ruins, trapped with only a ghost's voice for comfort. What hope remained turned to ice inside her.

Don't move, she thought. *Don't make a sound. Don't even breathe.*

Then Shai stepped forward, moving to stand in front of Xhea as if her incorporeal body were a shield. Xhea saw the ghost with a clarity with which she could not view the night walker, as if Shai were softly lit from all sides.

Xhea thought the gesture useless, yet at Shai's appearance the walker again stilled, his building tension changing as he shifted to view this new threat. He could see the ghost, that much seemed certain, wincing as if sight of her pained him; and yet when he inhaled, sniffing for her scent, he made a querulous sound, his head rocking on a neck that seemed too loose.

"Back away," Shai whispered without turning. She seemed as frightened as Xhea felt; her voice shook as she spoke. *He can't hurt* you, Xhea wanted to say, but she suddenly felt unsure.

Walking blindly, Xhea stepped back and back again, retreating from the alley. She crept around the corner until all she could see was a space between buildings that gaped like a dark mouth, and then she ran.

Fearing the sound of bare feet pounding after her, their movement a fast-paced metronome. Fearing the silence. The closest unbarred subway entrance seemed impossibly distant. There were people all around her in the low, barricaded buildings, behind those dark, blank windows. They would hear her scream if she were caught and killed. They would listen as she died—as she had listened, over the years, to others. Nothing to do, no way to help: caught on the wrong side of the walls, those on the nighttime streets were truly alone.

Senn was behind her, and Orren. By the time she reached Edren, the antique hotel with its towering addition, she didn't even try for quiet: her boots fell heavily upon the broken asphalt and she whimpered with every breath. The revolving door was locked tight and barricaded; the lower levels' embellished window frames held concrete blocks, not glass. Nothing to break—nothing, even, to pound against. She wanted to scream at Edren's darkened façade, reach her hand for the slivers of light she saw in the windows above.

Help me—oh please, help.

As if her words had been screamed in truth, there came a sound from the alley on Edren's far side, and a sudden beam of light shone from an opened door. Xhea changed course without thinking, barreling down the narrow passage and through the service entrance to the promise of safety just beyond—smack into a large man's chest.

A clothed, warm, breathing chest. The metal door closed with a bang that echoed down the bright hallway, and she almost collapsed in relief. Not thinking, she flung her arms around the unknown man, buried her face in his shirt, and wept.

He flinched but did not push her away. She recognized the way he tensed, the quiver that spoke of discomfort and the effort required to remain still as she clung to him. Later, she would be humiliated by her weakness; yet shuddering and gasping, she could not force her arms to release him.

"It's okay," he murmured, his voice a soft rumble that vibrated through his chest and against her cheek. "Stand down."

A moment passed before she understood the words; a moment more before she could raise her head to see the other man who stood before her, holding a length of shaped metal as one would wield weapon. Whatever it was, he lowered it slowly and with obvious reluctance.

"But—"

"I'll handle it. Return to your post."

The pause spoke louder than words. "Sir," he said at last, and turned.

Xhea swallowed and felt her face flush with embarrassment. She stepped back.

"It's okay," the man said again, and Xhea suddenly knew his voice and the rhythms of his speech—knew his face, that close-cropped hair, that dark skin. Lorn Edren, the eldest living son of the skyscraper's ruling family—and the man whose life she'd saved two years before.

Xhea took a deep breath. *Nothing happened*, she told herself. *You got away.* Yet her knees still quivered hard enough that she thought she might fall.

"You all right?" Lorn asked. Now that the guard had gone, his voice softened, the gentleness of his tone belying his hard exterior. She nodded shakily.

"You're lucky," he said. "What were you doing out there?"

"It wasn't by choice. It . . . it's a long story."

He stared down at her for a long moment. "With you," he said at last, "it would be."

Xhea shrugged; he wasn't wrong. "How did you know I was out there?"

"You tripped the perimeter spell. Lucky for you, I was supervising the watch."

Lucky indeed, Xhea thought, nodding. Slowly, she looked around. She stood in what had once been one of the hotel's back service corridors: pale paint flaked from breezeblock walls, the floor a river of cracked linoleum. Wires had been stapled along the hall, branching up the walls and through the ceiling. While some seemed to power the electric lights overhead, others had the telltale glimmer that spoke of magic.

It was the glimmer that made Xhea glance over her shoulder to where Shai usually stood, hovering one step behind like a shadow in midair, but she wasn't there. Xhea remembered the ghost staring at the blind man, the night walker, and that terrifying look in his milky eyes as he stared back. She turned back toward the door as if her attention would bring Shai to her; and yet it was only a door, flat black and dented, and the ghost did not appear.

"Don't worry," Lorn said, misunderstanding. "It's stronger than it looks." Xhea could only follow his lead down the corridor, steps dragging across the broken floor. Lorn still had a limp, Xhea saw, slight but present; a reminder of the accident that led to their first meeting. Farther from the entrance, she heard a distant, rhythmic thump, the bass throb of music filtering down through untold floors and the spaces between. Even if the Towers slept, she thought, perhaps the skyscrapers, huddled in the dark, never did.

Lorn led her to a room so small she assumed it had once been a maintenance closet. The space held only a cot with a thin blanket.

"Stay here," he said, ushering her inside. "No one will bother you." She heard the words he didn't speak: *No one will know you're here.*

"But," she protested softly. "The other man, won't he—"

"He won't say anything." Lorn's tone guaranteed it. "I'll come get you at dawn, okay?" She nodded before falling onto the cot, muscles trembling with fatigue and worry and the after-effects of fear. She thought again of Shai; but there was only darkness.

Xhea settled onto the cot, and pulled up the blanket. Her eyes closed seemingly of their own accord, and she lay there, thinking: *I'll sleep forever. I'll never sleep again.* Believing both to be true.

It was only a few moments before a faint light entered the room. Xhea didn't need to open her eyes; only smiled in relief and shifted position to make a space beside her. There was a pause, then she felt a familiar chill; imagined that the cot shifted with a weight not her own; felt a light pressure against her shoulder that might have been the shape of a hand.

"So." Shai's quiet voice came from somewhere near her ear. "That was your plan?" The ghost still sounded afraid, if unhurt; but also . . . happy.

"Yeah," Xhea managed. "Something like that."

A jolt of bright magic hit Xhea in the arm, knocking her from sleep and the cot with a cry. She rolled, tucking her limbs close, then sprung to her feet with the wall at her back. It wasn't elegant or well-executed, but served her purposes: she steadied in a crouch with her hands raised, ready to fight or run or scream. Yet the only thing before her in the tiny room was Shai, the shining ghost standing with one hand outstretched. She wore a shocked expression that could only mirror Xhea's own.

Xhea relaxed fractionally. "Did you see what it was?" she whispered. "Where did it go?" Her whole left arm felt strangely numb, though when she flexed her hand her fingers moved normally.

"I—" Shai whispered, her hand falling to her side. "I'm sorry, I didn't think . . ."

It took a moment for understanding to filter through Xhea's sleep-addled brain. "That was *you*? What, were you trying to kill me?" She stumbled back to the cot and cradled her arm against her chest, as if that might stop its throbbing. Both the numbness and the dissipating pain were familiar; almost like how she'd felt in the hospital between doses of pure magic. Only less severe, more localized. Only . . .

Shocked, Xhea looked up from her hand and met the ghost's eyes.

"You're *glowing*," she whispered. It was true: Shai looked as if she stood in moonlight, a soft light pale and without shadow, and it was not Xhea's vision that made the ghost look so bright. She had, she realized, seen the ghost's glow the night before—had looked for the light of Shai's presence without considering what that glow meant. Light glimmered in Shai's eyes and beneath her ghostly skin; it had lit Xhea's path through the darkness, a comfort when everything was black.

Throughout her ghostly half-life, Shai had glimmered with magic—and that light had grown stronger, brighter, with each passing day. Yet what Xhea saw now was not a reflection of spell-light or a mirror of the power that wove through her living body. It was magic in truth.

Xhea's hand tightened around her arm where the jolt had struck her. Not only was Shai filled with magic, but she could also use the power she held.

Shai's expression was unreadable. "Yes," she said.

"It wasn't just that you were alive. Wasn't just the spells in your body . . ."

"No." The single word bore a weight of weariness and sorrow.

Questions boiled up, too many and too varied for Xhea to make sense of them, even in her own mind. Somehow, the one that emerged was: "You have magic, and you used it to *zap me*?"

"I had to," Shai protested. "You were radiating."

"What?"

"That's what we call it with normal magic, anyway. Leaking energy unintentionally. But with you it wasn't light; it was more like you were . . . steaming. Breathing out smoke. It started to surround you like a cloud."

Xhea thought of all the mornings she had woken in one Tower or another to find the moss beneath her dead and black, flowers withering, bushes with leaves curled and crisping. *Radiating*, she thought; everything dying at her touch. She didn't know whether her sudden shiver was born of fear or excitement.

"Which was fine, really," Shai continued, "until the cloud started reaching for me. I really didn't want your magic to touch me. Not outside of your control."

Control. As if she had any of that. Yet, thinking of the ghost of the old man in her hospital bed, Xhea could only nod in agreement. She'd already killed Shai once, in body if not in spirit; she had little desire to finish the job.

"The . . . shock, or whatever—it was the only way to stop me?"

"You didn't wake when I called, and I was afraid to touch you, so . . ." Shai shrugged, looking uncomfortable. "It was just a little spark, I swear."

Which didn't explain why it had felt like being kicked in the shoulder. But—Xhea flexed her fingers—at least there seemed to be no lasting harm. As to how Shai could possibly possess the power to do what she had done . . .

There came a quick knock, then the door cracked open and Lorn peeked through the gap.

"It's dawn," he said simply. "I heard you were awake."

Looking at Lorn, Xhea felt a hot rush of embarrassment. While he might think little of her hysterics, the memory of the night before was enough to make her cringe. Yet he made no comment and did not question her speaking to an apparently empty room; the set of his shoulders said that he could feel Shai there, even if he could not see her. Those who had experienced a haunting knew the sensation—the feeling of a presence, a glimpse of blurred movement at the edges of their vision—and Lorn's expression said that he didn't want to know more.

Xhea used the offered bathroom, where she removed the hospital shift from beneath her clothes and lingered long enough to enjoy the running water, the plentiful soap, and the stack of clean towels. In the hall, Lorn offered her a twist of paper full of crackers for breakfast, which she accepted with barely concealed eagerness.

"Listen," she said at last. "Edren owed me a favor—"

"No," he said softly; it was still strange to hear that gentle tone in such a deep, rough voice. "Edren owes you a favor, yes, but so did I. For what you did for me, you're owed more than a night's shelter."

He glanced away and straightened, hiding that glimpse of softness. "Besides," he said, louder, all false cheer, "I just opened the door last night to check on a disruption to the perimeter spell, that's all. No one will say otherwise." He forced a smile, teeth bright in his dark face. "Now I'm going to check the perimeter spell again, and that means opening the back door, if you get my drift."

Xhea nodded, not inclined to argue. When he pushed the metal door open again on its heavy hinges, she slipped out into the street.

"Be careful," he called with a wave of his tattooed hand. Xhea waved once and the door slammed shut behind her.

The streets looked different in daylight. Though the overcast sky mimicked concrete, even that dull light leeched the menace from the roadway. The strange, looming shapes half-seen in her terror were revealed to be fire drums, scrap heaps, and other ordinary rubble. But thinking about her close call the night before made her uneasy, and Xhea hurried away from the nameless alley and the memory of the thing that had once been a man.

She managed not to pat her pockets until they were safely beyond range of Edren's security perimeter. Her jacket was stuffed with tiny bars of soap from the bathroom, and good quality soap at that—creamy, lightly scented bars wrapped in paper. Even after she traded most of it for meals, she would have enough to keep herself and her clothes clean for months. *There's a balance to everything*, she thought, eating a cracker with Shai at her side.

"Where are we heading?"

Xhea considered. "The market," she said. She could trade some soap or even the hospital shift for food before the crowds got too thick, and pick up the recent news. Perhaps she'd even find customers waiting for her return.

Shai nodded, looking around. "You know, I never thought I'd see this place again."

"Being back must be disappointing."

Shai made a sound that wasn't quite a laugh. "I'm happy to be anywhere."

Anywhere in the living world: the subtext reverberated between them. Xhea glanced at Shai, studying the subtleties of an expression that she couldn't quite read. She had so many questions that her mind felt blank—questions about Shai's magic, about what had happened in those days after her death, about Allenai and the pursuit that Shai had warned of the night before. She asked the first one that came to her lips.

"Why are you still here?"

Shai looked as if Xhea had slapped her.

Xhea grimaced. "No, sorry, I didn't mean *here*, with me—" She shook her head in frustration; not giving offense was so much work. "I just meant that I don't see your tether, so I don't know what's holding you to . . . life, this reality. Whatever. Here, stop a sec."

As she had done before, Xhea searched the air around the ghost with eyes half-closed, alert for even the narrowest thread of a tether. Yet though the air around Shai felt different—energized, almost, with a vibration akin to a tether's—she felt no line, no matter how thin.

"Huh." Xhea sat back on her heels and looked up at Shai. She'd never seen anything like it. Carefully she stood.

"When I was in Celleran," she asked, "how did you find me?"

Shai considered. "I just thought about you," she said at last. "Focused really hard on how much I needed to find you."

"Can you do it again?"

Shai closed her eyes, brow creasing. A moment passed, and another. There were more people in the road now, individuals emerging from the surrounding buildings in careful ones and twos, and Xhea began to feel conspicuous. She was about to tell Shai to stop when she felt it—*ping*, like the impact of a pin against her sternum. She looked down, and there, like a glimmering cobweb, was a tether.

"You make your own tethers," Xhea whispered, amazed.

Shai opened her eyes. "Is that strange?"

"Very. To have no tether . . ."

"What does it mean?"

Xhea shrugged. "A tether is what holds a ghost to the living world. But I interfered with yours before you actually died. Maybe that just means that, now, you have no unfinished business—only what you choose."

Shai made a noise that Xhea would have called a snort in someone less delicate. "No unfinished business? Too much, maybe." A pause, and then: "There was a moment when I was torn between everything. I didn't know where I belonged—with my father, trying to find my mother, doing my duty for Allenai, being here with you . . ." Her voice dropped as she spoke, as if the weight of all the possible responsibilities were dragging her slowly down.

"Why would you stay for *me*?"

"Probably the same reason that you helped me, in the end."

Payment, Xhea thought—then, *no*. Not at the end. Yet even she didn't want to put words to the tangled motive that had driven her into the ruins and to the City itself—didn't want to name what she felt kneeling at the dying girl's bedside as the spells flared and flickered to black.

"At first," Shai continued, "I was staying away from you. To protect you. I'd already caused you so much trouble."

"And now?"

"You can see me."

"I could always see you. What changed?"

Shai just stared at her, a single eyebrow raised, until Xhea turned away. It was true: what *hadn't* changed with Shai's death?

Xhea again felt the tether-like vibration surrounding the ghost. "Maybe it's not that you make your tethers," she said slowly, sounding out the thought, "but choose them. So many things are holding you here, pulling you in different directions, that you can only handle one at a time. You decide, and are bound." She pointed to the line that joined them as before; though even as she watched, the tether faded and vanished.

Shai smiled. "I guess that means I choose to be here."

Xhea stepped back to avoid being hit by a handcart overflowing with animal skins—poorly tanned, from the smell. "I think you're the first City girl to say that," she said, laughing.

Together they walked down a wide road that led to the Lower City's heart. It was so loud here, Xhea realized; how had she ever thought the mornings quiet? There were no silences, only lulls between waves of sound: footsteps and rickety wheels, voices calling and laughing and shouting, the roar of generators. Laundry and prayer flags flapped from long lines strung between buildings. Everything smelled of sweat and smoke, of dust and damp and sweet bread baking. She watched the crowd's movement as she approached the market, the bustle of vendors setting up displays, the luff of poorly tied awnings, the swirl of skirts, and wind charms' discordant chimes—more life on these battered streets than could be seen from on high.

Home, Xhea thought, and smiled.

Yet hard on the heels of that thought came a wave of uneasiness; something was different. She looked around more carefully, trying to identify the difference—the danger—that had alerted her instincts. Movement and people and things, faint rustling from shadows, a figure moving behind a boarded window—

There. In a stall at the edge of the market, an older man sitting on a sack of grain caught her eye. He was eating nuts, cracking their shells with blackened teeth. He did not look at her, but pointedly so, watching only from the corner of his eye. As she stared he turned aside and spat on the ground, spraying bits of phlegm and crunched shell.

That was it, she realized; she was being noticed. Not often, and not quickly, but she could no longer pass through the crowd unobserved. People glanced down as she slipped by, heads turned at the chime of the coins in her hair—and turned just as quickly away. Perhaps the attention was only the effect of her long absence, or sudden return. She wouldn't have been the first to vanish, never to reappear.

Trying to ignore the prickling on the back of her neck, Xhea made her way to Iya's stall. Iya rose from unpacking wares beneath her table, long locks swinging—and stiffened as she caught sight of Xhea's approach.

Xhea forgot all thoughts of bartering soap. "Something's wrong," she whispered to Shai. Still she pushed forward to the stall's front and placed her hands on the edge of the table. She stared at the trays of charms as if shopping, watching as the magic in each shape shifted restlessly against its bonds. Iya turned again, seemingly oblivious to Xhea's presence, and began to sort through a box just beneath the front table.

"Xhea," Iya murmured without looking up. "What are you doing here? It's not safe."

"What do you mean?"

"They're looking for you, child." Iya freed a long, twisted charm from the box, and hooked it to her stall's top bar. It hung limply, a curious thing of knotted rope and rough beads, trailing uneven fringe. "Days now they've been looking—asking questions too."

"Who has?"

Iya began sorting necklace charms on the counter without glancing up. "City folks. Real nice until you don't give them answers. One bought some charms from me—wind flutes. Said they were for his wife. You think they have balconies for those in the City?" Her long fingers turned one charm this way and that, settling its large glass bead where it lay in a band of daylight.

Allenai, Xhea thought, and felt cold.

"What did they want?"

"You, child. Or word of where you might be."

"Did you tell them anything?"

"Nothing that they hadn't heard a hundred times over."

Just the facts then: scrawny girl who lives underground. No magic, sees ghosts. Even that was more than she wanted her pursuers to know—not that she could do anything to keep such details from them. Iya may have been as cautious as she implied, but there would be those all too happy to tell what they knew, especially for a good price—and the Lower City definition of "good" would be bare sparks of renai for anyone from the City.

Xhea had to assume that her pursuers now knew everything: her entrances to the underground, the artifacts she scavenged, the places that she waited for customers—sweetness, her customers themselves. Even if her customers kept their mouths shut out of self-interest, her business would be in tatters for months.

"Iya, could you—"

"No." Iya sounded sad but firm. "Please, I don't want trouble. No more than this."

"But if—"

Iya looked up and met her eyes. "Xhea," she said slowly, clearly. "You should go now." Then quieter, lips barely moving, voice more imagined than heard: "They're here, looking for you. I've heard tell they've given Rown hunters your name. Hide while you still can."

Xhea realized she was gripping the display table so hard her knuckles were white, while around her the glittering charms began to flicker and go dark. *Control*, she thought, but didn't know what she was doing or how to stop the magic's seeping flow. She backed away.

"Thank you," she whispered. She wanted to shout at Iya—a child's reaction, she knew. There was risk in what the charm-seller had just done, with good City magic flowing for word of Xhea or her whereabouts.

"Shai," she whispered in sudden inspiration. "Keep an eye out for anyone watching or following." Shai nodded and rose, no longer mimicking a living girl's walk, but floating bubble-light into the air.

No running now, no matter that her heart sped at the thought of Rown's bounty hunters on her trail. Running would only attract attention. Instead, she drew her hair across her shoulder to quiet it, and kept her steps steady and even. Nothing to see, she said with eyes and hands and an easy gait. No problem here, no need to pay attention; just some girl on a quiet, confident, get-me-the-hell-out-of-here stroll.

Rown, she thought. *Oh, it would be Rown.* Orren might own a person's life with their carefully crafted indenture, but Rown knew how to possess someone, body, heart, and spirit. They took the addicts and wanderers, the hunters and little lost orphans, the gang rejects and crazies; they even took the scarred combatants rejected from Edren's arena, people with no skill or use but what they could carve from the world with fists and strength and speed. Rown took them, and bound them, and made them all whole—or the strange semblance of wholeness here, where no floor was without its worn board, no roof impervious to rain.

Once she'd considered joining their ranks, but the light in their eyes had scared her, that too-bright devotion to their skyscraper, its strange rituals, markings, and demands. Yet Xhea knew that if their pursuers had contracted Rown hunters, evasion would not be easy. More than a few Rown citizens were magic-weak; if the pay were high enough, they might just brave the discomfort and pain of moving underground to seek her. Going below was a risk, yes—but less, she figured, than remaining above. Even if they followed, there were levels upon levels of underground passages, most of which were marked only by her footprints in the dust. She'd smashed or removed the mall maps, every one.

She'd nearly made it out of the market and was angling toward the nearest open subway entrance when Shai returned.

"We're being followed. Two people, approaching from opposite sides of the market."

"How close?"

"One's halfway through the stalls, the other's farther back. They came out of the mall . . . building . . . thing."

Xhea snorted, but hurried her pace. Whoever had stationed a hunter inside the main market structure didn't know as much about her as they thought; she could count the number of times she'd managed to make her way into the inner market on her fingers. She slipped from the crowd into the ancient roadway and around the corner before breaking into a run, heading straight for the subway entrance.

She was nearly at the top of the rubble-strewn stairs when Shai cried out. "No—*stop!*"

Xhea skidded to a halt, arms wide for balance. "What—?"

Then she blinked, shifted her eyes' focus, and saw the huge spell that hovered a hand's length from her face. Xhea gasped and stepped back, staring. The spell was strangely beautiful, structured almost like an opened flower with long stamen that hung down to drift in an unfelt breeze. It was questing, but in a slow and sleepy way; its lines were dim, all but inert.

"It would activate if it touched you." Shai stared at the thing, reading the spell's lines of intent with an ease Xhea could only envy. Xhea squinted. The spell was so dim and finely woven that she struggled to make out its purpose—but what little she saw made her shrink back further. It reminded her of a spell rich hunters used to capture animals: something to catch and hold, leaving its prey helpless.

"It's a trap," Xhea whispered, shocked. "For me?"

"Yes," Shai said. Only that.

Xhea took a deep breath, spun, and ran in the opposite direction, leaving escape route and trap alike behind her. This was the only obvious tunnel entrance in the area—but far from the only entrance. Farther down the road was the boarded-over façade of an ancient bank, its plate glass windows long since stolen or smashed, the elaborate curlicues of its faux-pillared front worn away by years of wind and rain. Empty, now; abandoned for someplace with a more defensible exterior.

The nails had always been rusty; the boards were a random collection of wood and scrap metal, ill fitting even when newly placed. It wasn't difficult for Xhea to push a section aside and slip through a gap that would give a grown man pause. She didn't look behind her, only hoped that her disappearing boot heels hadn't been noticed by her pursuers—or any sharp-eyed passerby looking to earn a few extra renai.

It wasn't a difficult entrance, she thought as she picked herself up off the grimy, chipped marble floor of the bank's interior—but it wasn't a clean one, either. She grimaced at the new stains on her jacket's sleeves, and tried to brush the thick dust from her recently cleaned pants.

Shai hadn't attempted to slip through the gap, but walked directly though the boards and thick window frame. Arms wrapped around herself, she stared back at the layered materials through which she'd walked unscathed. "I don't know that I liked that," she said.

"You'll get used to it." Xhea gave a last, halfhearted brush at the dirt on her knees. "Cleaner than the alternative, anyway."

She made her way across the empty floor, then down a narrow escalator, metal treads clanking beneath her feet. There was little light in the underground complex, only the occasional mud-coated skylight allowing daylight to filter into the stillness beneath the roadways. The stores here were mostly empty, clothing racks and electronics displays just visible in the backs of the dark rooms. The mall's hallways split and split again, and Xhea chose her path without thinking; she'd traveled these routes more often than the streets above.

It wasn't until they'd walked for some minutes that Xhea found the mark she both sought and dreaded: there, amidst the crisscrossed tracks from years of her passage, was the shape of another's shoe. The tread was newer, clearer, and far larger than her familiar boot-scuffs.

"They've been here," she whispered. Even that slight sound seemed to echo. She crept closer, tentative, as if the mark might harm her. It was made by a man's shoe—and from the clear treads, she felt certain the shoe was no ill-fitting hand-me-down.

Turning, she spotted another mark, and another. The trail was uneven and scuffed, as if someone had stumbled half-drunk through these darkened passages. Yet their direction was clear: they came from the doors that she'd passed through on her last morning in the Lower City and made their stumbling way toward the nearest subway station. Suddenly, she knew with perfect clarity where that trail led, and what she would find upon her arrival.

She did not run; there was no need. Only an ache, the heavy weight of dread. She made her way to the subway station as if in a dream, ghosting by the empty toll-takers' booths and through a broken turnstile, Shai at her side. In silence she slipped down to track level and into the tunnel, the gravel laid between the rails crunching beneath her feet.

It was not deep here; this line, the Green Line, ran closest to the surface—even rising above the ground in one place out to the east. Shallow enough, perhaps, that some magic-weak hunter could walk these tracks, fortified by sheer will and the goal of some City-paid reward.

Between stations, she came to the subway maintenance room where she'd spent that long, terrible night when her magic had first risen. The metal door to the room, which she kept closed with a twist of wire, stood open, and the door's surface was dimpled as if from pounding. She crept closer. There, on the concrete stairs leading up from the train tunnel, were those too-large footsteps in the dirt.

"Why here?" she asked. The sense of invasion was overwhelming. "No one knows this place." Of everywhere she stayed in the warren of underground tunnels—the dozens of rooms and corners and hidden passages in which she kept a pillow, a tattered blanket, or the few things she dared name hers—why had those footsteps walked so unerringly here? No false turns, no backtracking.

"They're tracking me," Xhea whispered.

"No," Shai said. "They're tracking *me*."

"Your signature?"

Shai shrugged helplessly. "It's the only thing that makes sense. Look where they walked. You've gone everywhere underground, but they only walked the route that I followed with you."

Xhea crept up the stairs carefully, trying to leave no new footsteps. She pushed the door open with a toe and peered inside. Shai's faint light was the only illumination, but darkness didn't veil what had been done. Her blankets had been torn to ribbons and scattered, her bucket was overturned and cracked, and her water supply had been knocked over, bottles open to spill across the floor. Her novels—that small pile of carefully preserved books, their ancient pages darkened and crumbling and all the more valued for their frailty—had been scattered to lie in the wide puddle, wicking up water.

Xhea grit her teeth until they creaked. If she wanted to find safety below ground, she would have to go deeper than this. Down and down and down again to the levels where daylight never reached—the subway express tunnels, the storage halls, the third subterranean level of the shopping complex where few stairs led.

"I'm so sorry," Shai said, looking over Xhea's shoulder at the damage. "I didn't mean . . ."

But Xhea at last processed what Shai had said before, and knew it to be true: they were only searching the places where Shai's spirit had traveled before her death. "No," she whispered. "Oh, no." For there, scattered in the far corner, were beads and bits of glass, tiny gray shapes that she had once seen as yellow and blue, green and purple, tumbling over each other in ever-changing patterns. The kaleidoscope.

"Wen. They're going to go after Wen and Brend." The only people beyond Shai, living or dead, that she'd ever trusted with real information about her life. If anyone could betray her, it was Wen—but surely Shai's Tower had no way to talk to ordinary ghosts. Even so, she shuddered to think how many of her private conversations Brend had been present for, upstairs or across the warehouse, if not across the table from her, pretending not to hear. Brend knew far, far too much. The only question was, what bribes or threats—or how much pain—would it take to make him talk?

With an apology to her aching muscles, Xhea turned and ran for the exit.

Chapter Eleven

From the street, the warehouse appeared untouched—or no more ruined than its neighbors, artifice and spellwork mirroring their slow groundward sag. Xhea moved toward the entrance; hesitated, and drew back. She took a long, slow breath.

"What's done is done," she said to Shai, as if it were the ghost who needed reassurance. Xhea wouldn't admit to fear, but as she forced herself through the warehouse's disguised entrance, she dreaded what she'd find.

Inside, the light flickered from daylight to overcast evening and back again, as if heavy clouds sped across the sun at speeds unknown in the sky. The packed shelves looked untouched, familiar rows stretching in every direction; yet the daylight spell's irregular strobe made everything seem strange, the edged shadows taunting as Xhea crept through the maze of shelving.

Only at the warehouse's center did she find anything broken. Though the huge wooden table stood undisturbed, the papers and artifacts that had covered its surface were scattered across the floor. Wen knelt at the center of the mess, helplessly trying to pick up the pieces of a smashed teacup.

"Wen?" Xhea went to his side, kneeling as he did before the porcelain shards. He did not reply, did not so much as acknowledge her presence, only tried again to touch the cup's largest piece as if with infinite care and slowness his ghostly fingers might do anything but slide through unfeeling.

Xhea knew this cup; knew too the others that lay smashed in smaller pieces around him. They were artifacts, but not merely of the city that had come before. These cups, he had told her, were from an age even older than the ruins—an age beyond remembrance—and as such were of worth beyond measure. Looking at his expression, she had wondered if their true value was measured not in renai, but moments spent dreaming of the world long before the Fall, of lives and history they had no way to envision.

In the last weeks of Wen's life, when his death was foretold in every weakened gesture, every shallow breath, he had let her touch one of his six precious teacups. It had been the largest: a cup whose thick rim and chipped handle spoke both of inferior craftsmanship and rough handling in its centuries of existence. Even so, Xhea had known that Wen's placing it in her hands was a gesture. Perhaps of faith, or trust, or thanks; perhaps only preparing for the possibility that he might linger in this life, and she would become his only true companion. That he'd given it to her at all had almost made her weep, holding a thing worth more than she could ever be, and all the things it might symbolize.

She recognized them now: the pale blue cup's hair-fine brushstrokes of painted violets; the curlicued handle of the cup she knew to be red; a shard of gleaming rim that Wen had said was edged in real gold. Memory filled in color where vision gave her gray, cracks and shards and the powder between.

Wen knelt before a shard of porcelain so fine that light shone through it as if hindered by no more than a veil of smoke, a passing shadow. Again he reached for the shard, and again his fingers slipped through it as if he were the light, the smoke, the shadow.

"Wen," Xhea whispered again, and lifted the piece from the ground. His eyes rose then, following the shard in her hands before coming to rest on her face.

"It was an accident." His voice was as broken as the cups. He gestured toward the satin-lined box that had once held the cups in safety and now lay upturned on the floor, its lid gaping on torn ribbon hinges.

"What happened here?" Xhea spoke slowly, softly, to avoid startling him. "Where's Brend?"

Wen's gaze fell again to the shards, and an eternity seemed to pass in that false, flickering daylight before he spoke.

"I never thought I would see them broken." That quiet voice, those halting words. Xhea shivered to hear them; they were no part of the Wen she knew. "They were older than me," he said. "Older by far. I thought . . ." He shook his head. "What is it about beautiful things that makes you think they will last forever? It was just an accident, but now they're gone."

"If beauty lasted forever," Xhea murmured, "my friend Shai would have lived a very long time, and I will never die."

It was a poor joke, but just enough to make him blink. When he again met her eyes, some of the sorrow had left him.

The corner of his mouth twitched, and if it was not quite the beginnings of a smile, it was close enough.

"Ah, youth. Always so confident, always so wrong."

"Wen, what happencd here?"

"I don't know." He shook his head again. "Brend was . . . startled. Angry, even. He left in such a hurry, and didn't say where he was going. He doesn't, if you've been gone for a while."

"This was Brend?" She gestured to the mess.

"Yes." Wen seemed to see the rest of the destruction for the first time, ignoring the papers and food wrappers, and instead looking at the other artifacts damaged in their fall. "Yes, this was Brend," he said, and sighed. "Except . . . there might have been another man here too. Before."

"How much before?" Xhea realized the question's uselessness too late. A clear sense of time's passage was not a faculty Wen had retained in death.

Wen shrugged helplessly. "Before."

"Was he someone you knew? A business associate? An antique hunter?"

"No. He was tall—white haired, but not old enough to have earned it. He didn't even look at the artifacts, only stared at the ceiling and left."

Xhea peered upward, seeing nothing but the flat white of the ceiling and the harsh flicker of its light. "Did he break the daylight spell?"

Wen seemed to notice the failing light for the first time. "Brend must have used a lot of power before he left. Used it, or gathered it."

"Why?"

"I don't know, but my son is the only one who can take energy from my workings without damaging them. I keyed them to him before I . . . before."

"This isn't damaged?"

"Just weakened. It's reflecting things it shouldn't—nightfall, cloud cover."

Xhea watched the shadows flicker. If the spell wasn't damaged—if the destruction was due only to Brend pitching a fit or leaving in a hurry—then perhaps their pursuers hadn't managed to track Shai's signature all the way to the warehouse. She wished she believed it.

Wen rubbed his face as if to erase the lines etched there by his long years. With a last look at the broken teacups, he rose and turned away. "Will you help me clean?" he asked. "I can't stand to see them like that."

Xhea nodded and dropped the piece she held, wincing at its sharp edge. She stood—and staggered. The world flipped as if the warehouse were a snow globe and she the snow. She fell, shards crunching beneath her weight as she sagged to the floor. She couldn't stop her head's impact with the tile.

It was a long, dark moment before she could move, and even then she chose to remain still, grateful to lie prone while the world debated which way was up. There was a buzzing, mumbling sound. She forced an eyelid open to see the two ghosts hovering above her—in Shai's case, literally hovering.

"It's okay," Xhea murmured into the tangle of her hair. "I just fainted a little."

It wasn't an unfamiliar feeling, trying to gather the strength to rise after an unexpected collapse, but one she'd mostly managed to avoid the past few years—when she ate regularly. There had been that package of crackers from Lorn, water drunk greedily from the bathroom tap—and before that? She cast her mind further and further back and could not be certain of her last true meal.

But she did remember an awful lot of running.

Once she was able to push herself upright, she followed Wen's directions to a battered tin that Brend kept on a lower shelf. She helped herself to the cookies inside and was considering whether to drink or steal Brend's half-empty bottle of whiskey when a glint from the bottom of the tin caught her eye. It wasn't a coin, she found, turning it over in her hand, though it was about the same size and weight. One side was patterned with etching so fine the individual lines were all but invisible against the metal; the other bore only the symbol that she recognized as representing Eridian, Wen and Brend's home Tower.

Forget the whiskey, she thought as she slipped the token into a jacket pocket. This seemed far more valuable—and easier to carry.

"So," Wen said, "what brings you to my warehouse?" He looked from Xhea to Shai, who stood anxiously by the table, arms wrapped about her chest as if for warmth. Xhea watched as he took in Shai's changes from their last visit, clothes and stance and attitude.

Glossing over her trip to the City, Xhea explained the trouble she'd found waiting for her in the Lower City upon her return, and her fear that their pursuers might have done something to Wen, Brend, or their warehouse.

"They couldn't destroy this place," Wen said. "At least not legally. Brend's an Eridian citizen in good standing, as was I in my day. If anyone threatened or harassed him, my son would have legal recourse."

"I'm so happy for him," Xhea muttered, and bit down hard on an almond cookie. Of course, that didn't explain his rushed exit from the warehouse, either.

"But all this because—what? You didn't behave well in civilized society?"

"It's because of me," Shai said. "My Tower is trying to find me."

"Ah," Wen said, nodding. "Because you're their Radiant?"

Shai gaped. "But I—how did you—I didn't even . . ."

"Call it a hunch." Wen smiled, but the expression held little humor. "Your dress had the look of something you'd wear to a last binding."

"Yes."

"And your Tower?"

"Allenai."

Wen whistled. "Impressive. They would need you back, wouldn't they?"

Xhea spoke through a mouthful of cookie. "So which of you dead people wants to explain what you're talking about?"

Wen gestured Shai toward the table and they each took a seat, as if chairs could actually hold them. "Your friend here," he said, "is what we call a Radiant. Or she was, before her death."

"Never heard of it."

"I'm not surprised. No, calm down, child; it wasn't an insult. Even in the City, we tend not to speak of Radiants. Even most citizens don't know much about them, beyond that they exist."

"They're dangerous?"

"In a sense. But they aren't known mostly because they are protected. Highly guarded and highly prized."

"Right. But *what are they*?"

Shai leaned forward, eager to explain. "Magic is life force, right? Everyone has it—or, ah, at least that's what we're taught," she amended, frowning at the oddity that Xhea posed. Xhea shrugged; Shai wouldn't be the first stumped by her very existence—and that was before her dark energy had manifested.

The ghost continued. "When your body makes more than what you need just to stay alive, then that's power. You can trade it with others—transform it into renai—to buy things you need, or create spells to put the energy to work. If you only have enough to stay alive, then—"

"Then you end up in the Lower City, squabbling over scraps," Xhea said. The interruption made Shai hesitate, looking embarrassed. Xhea regretted her quick words.

"Some find work in the Towers still, Xhea," Wen said. Xhea ducked her head, almost grateful for the correction. *Well,* she thought, *there's a first for everything.*

"Right," Shai said. "And if your body naturally makes more magical energy—or if you earn a lot more through your work— you can do even larger spells. But when you're not using the energy, the excess goes into your Tower."

Or fills fountains, Xhea thought, *or is burned up in flashy light shows*; but this time she kept her mouth shut.

Wen added, "The more magic you make, the more valuable you are to your Tower, for just that reason." Xhea nodded. It was one of the reasons why top-tier magical workers were among the most sought-after citizens, wooed by Towers across the City.

"So a Radiant makes the most energy?" she guessed, remembering the harsh white light of Shai's magic as she died.

"A lot more," Wen said softly.

Xhea turned to Shai. "They're trying to capture your ghost because you're insanely rich?" She couldn't keep the incredulity from her voice. But she followed her train of thought, speaking again before either listener could refute her. "No," she said. "You're their *mint.*" The ancient word came readily to her lips, and she touched one of the coins caught in her hair, as if the feel of ancient money could make the concept more solid.

"Well . . ." Shai wrung her hands.

"Yes," Wen said. "Part mint, part power plant. Even with the thousands upon thousands of people living in every Tower—even with all their excess magical energy fueling that Tower's economy—there isn't enough power. Think about it, Xhea. Think about the magic needed to keep even one of those Towers aloft. And that doesn't even begin to touch the energy required for everyday tasks, or transportation—never mind huge energy expenditures like a takeover."

Xhea nodded. She'd seen takeovers, where two Towers merged their physical structures, energy, and population and became something entirely new. Most takeovers were slow and graceful, completed over weeks; hostile takeovers, in which one Tower attacked and absorbed another, were faster, more brutal—and much more fun to watch.

"Towers need Radiants. They're born rarely, and are never allowed to change their citizenship. But the human body isn't designed to hold that much energy. So much life force . . . the magic kills them in the end." To Shai he added, "That's what happened you, yes?"

Shai only hesitated a split second before agreeing, but that fractional pause was enough. Shai remembered exactly how she'd died. *And still*, Xhea thought, *she came back to me. With me. For me.*

Thinking of that day, Shai's broken body all but incandescent with magic and fever, Xhea clenched her hands into fists. At last, that bright spring of energy at Shai's core made sense: she had fueled the healing spells, even as her magic caused the damage that the spells attempted to repair. *All except the darker spells*, she thought, remembering that fine, complex spellwork that had reminded her of steel lace.

"There were spells on Shai," she said slowly, "to keep her from dying."

Shai startled at that, looking as if she wanted to capture Xhea's words and hide them away unsaid.

Wen made a thoughtful noise and leaned back in his chair. His chair, however, didn't lean with him, and Xhea watched as the chair back slid through his body until its uppermost rung appeared through the front of his chest.

"I wouldn't know about that, truthfully," he said. "I was an excellent spellcaster, but this wasn't my area of specialty. But it seems a sensible practice, does it not, to keep your Radiant from dying as long as possible?"

"But she's dead now."

"And glowing. I assume that's not normal for ghosts of your acquaintance?"

"No. But without a body, without a way to find her ghost—I mean, how would they harness . . ." Xhea's words fled as she thought: *Resurrection.* Hard on the heels of that thought came another: *Was that what Orren had been attempting, all those years ago?*

Wen raised an eyebrow. "No way to find her ghost? That explains why they wish to find you, does it not?"

"But would Shai actually be useful? I mean, the amount of magic produced by a ghost . . ."

"Look around," Wen said. "She's refueled the daylight spell as we talked."

Xhea blinked, realizing he was right. There were no flickers anymore, no moments of darkness like heavy clouds skidding across the sun; only light streaming in from all sides, as clear and bright as if they stood in a sunlit patio. As one, they turned to Shai.

"Um . . . you're welcome?" Shai offered, and tried to smile.

Xhea took an unfamiliar route into the ruins, picking her slow way through the broken streets. No use making it easy for their pursuers.

As she walked, her thoughts returned to her trashed hideaway in the subway tunnel. If Allenai knew that Shai's ghost was with her, why would they attempt to terrorize her? If they were trying to find Shai or Xhea, how did ruining one of her underground havens—or setting Rown's trained crazies after her—help attain that goal? If Allenai was as powerful as Shai implied, surely there were more effective ways to gain her assistance.

No, these people weren't stupid or impulsive. They wouldn't have sent thugs after her—at least not without reason. But it was that reason she failed to see.

Then again, maybe Allenai hadn't sent the hunters. If it were known that a Tower wanted her, other Lower City dwellers might attempt her capture in hope of a reward. But was that potential temptation enough to endure the pain of traveling underground? Xhea shook her head, wishing the pieces would fall into place. Wishing the cold knot in her stomach was only hunger.

"So," Xhea said, breaking the silence. "What was it about the spell keeping you alive that you didn't want Wen to hear?"

She didn't need to look at Shai to see her startle. The movement broke the rhythm of her false walk, and for a moment Shai slid helplessly through the air as if across ice. Xhea couldn't help but grin, and not even Shai's offended glare could chase the expression away.

"When I die, you're welcome to laugh at me too," Xhea offered. "I imagine it's hard getting used to being dead."

"It's almost too easy," Shai admitted, regaining her balance. "What's hard is remembering what it was like to be alive."

"You've only been dead—what, a little over a week? Were you outside your body for so long?"

"No." She made a sound that was almost a laugh, bitter and hard. "But I was dying for a very long time."

"Months?"

"Years."

They walked together in silence, the ruins quiet but for the rustle of the wind through new leaves and the crunch of Xhea's footsteps. At last Shai said, "Being dead is almost like being real again. Even if I'm only real to you, and to Wen."

"If you were suffering, why wouldn't they let you die?"

Shai sighed. "Power. Of course. It's all for the magic."

"And the spells binding you to your body?"

"My father tried to break them. I think he damaged them enough that I wasn't always trapped in myself, and yet . . ." She shook her head. "Kept alive, a Radiant's body can generate magic for a long time, even if the person is . . . like I was. Unable to stand, or eat, or even think. Caught on the edge of death."

"For years," Xhea said.

"Years upon years. They can block the pain, but . . ." Shai shrugged, a short, sharp gesture. "But that's only if the person— the spirit, I suppose—stays in the body. Without its spirit, a Radiant's body loses its ability to generate magic. The power slows, and within months the body is just . . . a body."

"Your father believed that if you were separated from your body, it would die without you. You'd be free." Free to die; free to fade away.

Shai nodded.

"But even if your ghost generates some magic, why do they need you if your body is dead?"

Shai said bleakly, "There are other bodies."

"Other—?"

"Other Radiants. Their spirits gone and their bodies kept alive until another can be found to fill it."

"But if only a few Radiants are born, and they bind your ghost to your body, then how—"

"It doesn't need to be a Radiant's spirit, though that's best. Any spirit is enough to keep the body generating magic. Fueling the Towers and their people."

"And if they only have a Radiant's ghost?"

Shai's face was grim. "The same, in reverse: any body will do."

She'd known possession was possible—but this was worse. The resurrection of a body with a ghost foreign to the flesh. A ghost forced there, trapped there, helpless. The thought was enough to turn Xhea's stomach.

Shai continued as if Xhea's reaction did not matter, could not matter. "If Allenai didn't have an empty body for me, they could buy one from an allied Tower for a price—even arrange to have a body . . . vacated. But there is one. A Radiant's body." She looked up at the City. "I knew him when I was a child. He used to tell me stories."

Xhea tried to imagine it: Shai bound to a body not her own—a man's body, the body of someone she had known. Hidden away in a Tower, broken and hurting and dying, endlessly dying, for years. Unable to escape. Bound so she couldn't even try.

"I won't let that happen," Xhea whispered, reaching for her knife as if to fend off those futures. There were worse things in the City than she knew, than she had ever dreamed.

"I will *not* let it happen," she vowed again. She knew she sounded savage, her voice harsh with anger, and did not care. Could not care. "Anything in my power, I will do it, Shai. *Anything*. I won't let them take you."

Shai simply looked at her, her face bright with the magic that built inside her, minute by minute, day by day. She reached out and touched the back of Xhea's knife hand with the tips of her fingers. But all she said was, "I know."

Chapter Twelve

They walked through the ruins without speaking. Xhea couldn't break the quiet, even had she found words to capture the sudden tightness in her chest. It had been a long time since she'd made a promise; longer still since she'd meant to keep one. Yet the feel of the words lingered in her mouth, dark like her magic, and heavy; and if those words had a taste, she only knew not to name it sweet.

In silence she asked herself: *What are you doing?* All she had needed—wanted, worked for—was to be safe. To have enough to eat and drink, a secure place to sleep, a way to care for herself when surrounded by those who cared for nothing. Now she was risking what little she had managed to earn—and for what?

Did she mourn the destruction of her safe haven, the ruin of mere things? She mocked herself for it. To keep this promise and protect the strange ghost that had fallen into her keeping, she was setting herself not only against one of the more powerful Towers, but the hidden workings of the City itself. How many Towers were there? They glittered across the sky, plentiful as stars; and if what Wen and Shai had told her was true, a Radiant—perhaps more than one, perhaps many more—was present in each. A dying person, or a dying body with a spirit trapped inside, bound to each structure. She could barely comprehend it.

Against all that, she was but one girl. One girl with strange magic that she didn't understand and barely controlled, no friends but a ghost, allies few enough to count on the fingers of one hand.

But I don't have to save everyone, Xhea thought. *Only one. This one.*

She would not abandon Shai to face this alone.

It was only then that Xhea realized where she was walking. At her feet, the road split. To her right the street continued uninterrupted; it would, she knew, take her to a crossroads that led quickly back to the Lower City, mere moments away. But to her left the ground sagged, sloping down and away. The depression was almost circular, and the surrounding buildings leaned in like broken teeth. Farther, she knew, there was no ground, no structures standing; everything had fallen in the collapse of the subway's Red Line tunnel. Sometimes, in dreams, she still heard that fall: the roar of asphalt, steel, and concrete losing the battle against gravity, the sound almost—almost— enough to obscure the screams.

But it was not that memory that made her want to turn and run, but all the ones that came before. Memories she would have called happy, if she had any right to the word.

She did not run, did not take the safe route home, but turned instead toward the destruction, careful of the asphalt's crumbling edge. Her feet had found and followed this path, once so familiar, without thought; and though the road had changed much in the intervening years, it still felt like returning home. Had she not walked on such treacherous ground, the thought would have made her close her eyes. As it was, it was all she could do to keep putting one foot in front of the other.

"What happened here?" Shai's eyes were wide as she took in the wide bowl of destruction. "An earthquake?"

It was easier to look at now, with the dust settled and the sharp edges of so many broken things dulled by years of rain and wind and snow. Easier, too, now that time had stolen the details of how the buildings had looked while standing, and the names of those who had lived in the fallen structures. Easier not to remember their faces.

"A subway tunnel collapsed." The Red Line tunnel—the deepest subway tunnel—had been flooded for as long as anyone remembered. Water always won in the end.

She skirted the disaster's edge, turned left onto a side street, and walked up the overgrown lane to a large rectangular building. The multi-paned windows were hazed dark with grime. It stood far enough from the collapse that the structure hadn't been threatened; a thrown stone would fall short of the crumbling edge. Even so, it was close. Too close.

There were seven steps to the building's front doors; she didn't need to count them. The doors were closed and locked, the large brass handles more solid than the wood in which they were mounted. Xhea did not kick out the lock as she would have in any other building, but reached into her tangled hair. There, braided to a thin cord and hidden against her neck, hung a brass key.

Her hands were steady as she freed the key; steady, too, as they fit the key in the lock and turned, struggling only briefly against its resistance.

"How do you—?" Shai began.

"I used to live here." Six years and a lifetime ago.

Xhea pushed the door open on protesting hinges and stepped cautiously inside. It was as she remembered, the circular entrance hall bare but for peeling paint and water damage near the ceiling, the floor's mosaic showing more gaps than tiles. The floor cracked and groaned beneath her as she crept toward the staircase, following a line of nails and the joist that ran beneath. The stairs were louder and visibly sagged, forcing her to step only on the treads' far edges and cling to the railing as she ascended.

It would have been safer to stay on the ground floor, but Xhea kept climbing, higher and higher as Shai watched and worried. It was not safety that kept her climbing but merely the memory of it, a feeling as misplaced as her naming this old building home.

On the top floor, all was as she'd left it. There was a short hall and four doors, all closed. A small mat of knotted rags lay before the final door, and though it was a rotted, ugly thing, her heart twisted at the sight. In six years, it seemed, no one had come to search these rooms or claim the possessions that she, and the others who had lived here, had inevitably left behind. This, more than the dust and damage, made her wary.

She unlocked the door and it opened slowly, noisily, its bottom scraping along the floor's unfinished boards. As she stepped inside, Xhea understood for the first time what people meant when they said they felt like they'd seen a ghost. As if the past, full of dreams and impossibilities and the shards of things that would never be, had come crashing down upon her, surrounding her with a presence that it seemed she could breathe, could taste, could feel in the sudden sting of tears in her eyes.

Oh, she had hated this place. Hated its openness, its echoing space that no screens or hanging fabric could ever properly divide; hated its foolish, lofty ceilings and exposed beams. Hated the way the huge windows sapped the warmth from the room, and gave only a view of crumbling ruins, the wide and empty horizon that the unfinished apartment seemed to mimic. The corner that was to have been a kitchen had always mocked them with the dead-end pipes that had promised a sink, the trailing wires and gaps in the countertops where no appliances would ever be installed. The metal barrel that had been their heat and oven both still stood in the center of the stained floor.

Yet there was the structure they'd called a loft: a silly cobbled-together platform where Xhea had often slept. She'd used sheets and blankets to make a tent there, a little cave in the midst of so much openness, where warmth and secrets could hide. There, on the sagging countertop, was her old mug, an antique blazoned with a logo that she'd never been able to read. Tiny things were still scattered in corners: rotted fabric that had once been clothing, an oil lamp, a hammerhead tied to a makeshift handle, a ball of twine.

And there, against the far wall, was the patchwork quilt that had served as bed and blanket both. So clearly, she remembered watching the needle flash in the lamplight as each of those stitches was painstakingly placed, binding together scraps of towels and cast-off clothes into a chaotic whole that Xhea had always found beautiful. It was into that quilt's warmth that she had fled on nights when they'd heard screams or worse from the streets below their windows; it was where she had curled when her nest of blankets was not enough to keep her warm.

In fear and cold, she had shivered—and found comfort and warmth near the slight body of the girl she had thought of as mother and sister, protector and best friend.

"Abelane," Xhea whispered to the empty room. "I've come home."

Throughout the afternoon, Xhea cleaned. She had never been much for neatness; her hidden rooms and corners were organized in a chaotic system of piles that made sense only to her—and sometimes not even then. Abelane had been Xhea's opposite in this as in so many other things, and Xhea knew that the older girl would've had a fit had she seen the apartment in its current state. Once Xhea would have laughed at the reaction, but now the thought was enough to make her seek the straw broom from its place in the corner.

The broom's bristles were mere stubble now, but it worked well enough when applied with force. Piles of dirt and dust and flaking paint undisturbed for years rose in great clouds, making Xhea cough and breathe through the edge of her shirt. She worked tirelessly, making pointless piles of dirt she had no way to pick up or throw out, dusting objects she had no desire to use or take with her, organizing old belongings best discarded entirely.

Over and over Shai called her name, asked her what was wrong, and Xhea found she couldn't answer. Words caught in her throat, thick with dust, and she could only turn away. At last, Shai retreated to the top rung of the loft's ladder and watched. Xhea kept her head down, pretending she didn't feel the weight of the ghost's stare, or all the questions unasked in silence.

Only when the sun vanished from beyond the grimy windows did Xhea sink to the ground against the far wall and place her head in her dirty hands. Blisters marked her palms and her arms ached from hours of unfamiliar motion, but she only felt them now, as if stopping had called the hurt forth. When twilight shrouded the apartment and veiled her naked expression, Xhea spoke.

"Abelane found me on the streets when I was a child," she said slowly, testing the words. "Four years old, five . . . something like that. She was just a child herself, younger than I am now, but she wanted to protect me anyway. Or maybe she just didn't want to be alone." Xhea shook her head; she'd never gathered the courage to ask.

"It was winter. She said that there were bruises around my wrists and ankles, as if I'd been tied and held, and my clothing was too thin for me to have been outside long. I . . . I don't remember any of it. She said it hurt when she first took my hand, as if I'd shocked her, and her hand was almost numb for an hour, but she took me home anyway."

Xhea glanced up. Shai now knelt on the floor before her, hands curled in her lap and face unreadable. She was not glowing, now; merely bright, as if lit by moonlight.

"That winter we were always moving. Finding a place to stay for a few days, then moving on. Always afraid. Always hiding.

"Later we found this place. The other rooms were already taken, but this one was unfinished and damaged. People had been using it for garbage. Took a long time to get it cleaned up." Even then it had been common to wake to the sound of waste bags hitting their door—bags that they'd had to drag downstairs themselves, lest they become trapped in their apartment by the pile.

"How long did you live here?" Shai asked softly.

"A little over three years. We were here until the collapse. Or . . . I was."

"Only you?"

"Only me," Xhea said. "In the end."

Those three years had seemed an eternity. There had been a time when she'd not known what to want if it was not this room, these unfinished walls, this blanket made from scraps. It was Lane who'd taught her to steal and to fight, how to find food and hide in places no one grown could go. She'd even taught Xhea to read and write, to see magic and understand the lines of intent in cast spells—though the learning process had evoked more swearing than gratitude. And yes, they had fought, the petty arguments of girls who were, in the end, only children with no one to help them, guide them, to watch them or to care.

But for those three years, she had not been alone. With Abelane always somewhere near, she'd almost forgotten what the word meant.

Until those last days before the collapse.

"Thing is, Lane was afraid of me—of what I was, or maybe what I wasn't—but she hid it well. Most of the time."

"Afraid that you had no magic?"

"Yes, that, but mostly that I could see ghosts. We fought about it. She used to say that I was lying to scare her." During one of their fights, Abelane had been the first one to say that there was something wrong with Xhea, a wrongness that could be felt by the merest brush of skin on skin.

Xhea shrugged. "Of course, later she was the one who helped turn my ability into a source of income. Not that too little renai was always a problem. Abelane had magic—she just didn't know how to use it. She didn't know many real spells, just . . . tricks." Ways to get vending machines to give extra, ways to create the sound of a voice where there was none, or coax fire from damp wood with a single match. "I've wondered whether she wasn't a runaway from the City. An ordinary girl fleeing something worse than this." She gestured at the bare room, its dirt and peeling paint.

Shai motioned for her to continue. "What happened?"

"I don't know," Xhea whispered. It was all she could do to force out the words, for here, in this place, the old hurt felt raw again, and speaking of such things was like casting salt atop the blood. "I woke one morning to find her gone. The door was locked, her blanket was folded, and Lane was just . . . gone.

"I waited all day, expecting her to return any minute with food or firewood. But she didn't, and when night fell, I knew that something was wrong. I was maybe nine years old, and hadn't spent more than a few hours without her. I didn't know what to do."

Xhea closed her eyes, remembering that night. She hadn't slept, cringing at every sound that might be a girl's scream or cry, no matter how distant. She had paced these floorboards until the downstairs neighbor pounded on his ceiling for her to stop, and then she'd just sat, hour after hour in the darkness, arms wrapped around her knees as she waited for dawn. Waited for Lane to come home.

But only the sun returned.

"The next day I searched," Xhea said. "Up and down streets and alleys, in the market, the skyscrapers, asking anyone and everyone I could find. No one had seen her.

"The day after that was the collapse."

Then, what was one more lost girl, one more child who might be dead, in the midst of so much chaos? Xhea was not the only one with hair and skin caked white with dust to cling to passersby and beg for word of a lost loved one.

"Was she in the collapse?" Shai asked.

Xhea smiled, a thin and bleak expression. "I don't know. I don't think so. Sometimes I used to hope that she was, just because it would mean that she hadn't abandoned me.

"I stayed for weeks anyway, sleeping here and combing the rubble in daylight. The ground used to shake and shudder—you could feel it, as if the bones of the world were moving beneath your feet. The other survivors left quickly, heading closer to the core, but I just couldn't." It had been too hard to care, scratching each day through the rubble until her hands bled and her muscles shook with exhaustion. Let the ground take her, if it would; she had no way to stop it anyway.

"I was the last one to leave."

Xhea turned to look at the mound of the quilt in the far corner, a dark shape that she could almost imagine was a girl lying curled for warmth. How old would Abelane be now—nineteen? Twenty? Yet she still saw a child. She didn't know how to imagine Lane as anything else.

"I kept looking for a long time," Xhea murmured, her eyes not leaving the quilt. "Watching the areas of the Lower City where we used to shop or steal, checking our hideaways. I never found anything. No one remembered seeing her after the collapse, or in the days just before."

Sometimes you have to leave someone behind, Xhea thought. *Sometimes you're the one that gets left.*

With Lane gone, so too was the life Xhea had known. Their friends and acquaintances were scattered across the Lower City, and those few that Xhea knew how to find spoke to her less and less without Lane's comforting presence between them. Already word of Xhea's strange talent had spread, and with it came fear—that same fear she'd seen born in Lane's eyes years before. Even those who still offered food or a moment of companionship turned distant when Xhea asked for a place to spend the night.

She'd done the rest of the work for them: walking away when they tried to speak to her, bowing her head as they passed as if she didn't recognize their faces, didn't hear them speak her name. Abandoning them before they too could leave her in slow ones and twos.

Sometimes she wondered what might have happened if someone had taken her in. She wouldn't have gone to Orren, desperate when winter's chill set in—yet maybe she wouldn't have ventured into the tunnels, either, and found she was untouched by the pain that all others felt beneath the ground. She remembered finding the tunnels: a whole world for her to explore and claim as her own; and if some nights she'd felt the press of earth above her head and remembered its terrible power, such thoughts only made her cautious, ensuring the respect that dark places deserved.

"I'm sorry," Shai said. "It doesn't change anything, but . . . I am sorry."

"I don't need your pity, Shai."

Shai just shook her head. "Why did you bring me here?"

Xhea wanted to protest that she hadn't brought Shai anywhere—that she hadn't even meant to come here herself. Yet she couldn't speak the lie; and she knew it to be such, even when voiced only in the depths of her mind.

"Because they can't take this from me," she said at last. "Your Tower. The City. Whoever's after us. They can't take it from me, because I lost it a long time ago."

She laughed, then—a choked and sputtering sound, but a laugh nonetheless, for she heard her own words and scorned herself for her blatant self-pity. Was glad, again, that the darkness hid her face, for she could feel the sudden flush burning to the tips of her ears.

"Oh, listen to me." She laughed again, for it was suddenly a choice of that or crying.

"Xhea," Shai said, and in that moment her voice was that of a patient older sister. "You're tired."

"When am I not?"

"When you're asleep."

Xhea sighed, a long exhalation that seemed to take with it the edge of her mirth and the bruise-like ache of disturbed hurts. There was no use protesting that she could not sleep now, not here, with memories and her words and the smell of dust heavy all around them—she could, and would. She slid down the wall to the ground, curling on a patch of floor made almost clean by her obsessive sweeping. After a long moment, she reached out and dragged the stinking quilt over her legs and shifted so that it dulled the press of her hip against the floor. Reluctance and weariness spoke in every movement.

"I'll be here," Shai said. Words so similar to ones Lane had uttered night after night, more comforting than any lullaby. In that moment Xhea wanted nothing more than to have again the strong tether that had joined Shai to her, and the security of knowing that there was nowhere she could go that the ghost could not follow.

Instead, Shai whispered, "Trust me." As if her words were tether enough.

And they were.

Shai woke her a few hours later, calling her name.

Xhea struggled to open her eyes; her eyelashes were gummed to her cheeks. "Am I doing it again?" she asked, words slurred. Her magic felt quiet—but she had no way of knowing what it did while she slept.

"Xhea," Shai said again, and her voice was strange. Distant. Xhea rubbed her eyes and saw the ghost's lit figure by the window, looking out. Her long, pale hair shone in the darkness. "You need to see this."

The window was the only part of the apartment Xhea hadn't cleaned, and she squinted as she approached the grimy panes, trying to see what had caught the ghost's eye. Though no one lived in this area anymore for fear of further collapses along the length of the Red Line subway, only a fool would assume that none ventured near. For a deserted building to suddenly have clean windows would draw attention—and the last thing she needed, Xhea thought irritably as she pushed tangled hair from her eyes, was more attention.

Outside, the full moon cast the ruined landscape in light bright enough to read by, while faint stars gleamed along the horizon. Above, Towerlight flickered and shifted like something alive, and though the intricacies of those shifting veils of power were lessened by distance, their colors lost to her vision, for a moment she could but stare.

"There," Shai said, her voice low. "Do you see?"

Xhea followed the ghost's cautious gesture, and froze. All but hidden in the shadows of the building across the road stood a figure.

"How long has she been there?" Xhea whispered. The gender was a guess, but something about the figure's slight stature and halo of tangled hair said "female." Still and unmoving, the stranger might have been a statue; Xhea wondered how long it would have taken to spot her if not for Shai.

"Since I looked out a few minutes ago. You were hard to wake."

"Gods, what's she doing out there?" Memory of her long night outside rose unbidden. Never again would she have anything less than four strong walls between her and the things that walked the night. Then again, if the woman was a hunter on their trail, four strong walls might not be enough. "I'm going to back away from the window. Tell me if she reacts."

"Xhea." Shai put out a hand to stop her. "She's already looking at us. When I called you, she was staring right at me."

Xhea went cold, a shiver running through her that had little to do with the spring chill. The figure was indeed staring upward: when she looked, Xhea could just see the glint of Towerlight in her eyes.

"She hasn't moved?"

"Not yet." Shai turned to her. "How does she know I'm here? Am I glowing brightly enough for anyone to see?"

"I don't know," Xhea said, soft as breath, as prayer.

Though Shai seemed bright to her, there was not so much magic in the ghost as to make Xhea wish to turn away. Magic, raw or spelled, was generally only visible to more powerful magic users; yet the most powerful magics were naturally in the visible spectrum—Towerlight most notably. She didn't think Shai was shining bright enough to be seen by the untrained eye—not yet, anyway.

Movement outside drew her attention. "Shai," she said, reaching for the ghost's hand. "There's another one."

She pointed. There was no use trying to hide the gesture, for the man's face was already lifted, staring at them as if he could see nothing else. As she watched, Xhea realized that he *couldn't* see anything else. His eyes were almost pure white.

"Is that . . . ?"

Xhea forced her reply past lips gone dry. "The walker we saw yesterday? Yes, I think so."

She knew that build, all wiry muscle and too-loose skin; recognized the strange questing movements of his head. Doubted, too, that there were many other naked blind men roaming the streets of the Lower City.

Shai gasped. "Xhea—"

"I know, I see him."

For coming from the opposite direction was another man, far older. He was clothed, but poorly: an oversized sweatshirt hung from his bent frame, its tattered edges reaching midway down his bare thighs, trailing threads. His hair was white in the moonlight, an electric shock of wiry strands that stood out from a balding pate and protruded in uncut tufts from his lip and chin. He, too, stared at them.

Xhea met his eyes, and it took all her strength and the paralysis borne of fear to keep from flinching. In his blank eyes she felt a danger as real and immediate as a drawn knife; as if he threatened her with a simple look, this distant figure, this bent ruin of a man, and her cringe was instinctive.

She was suddenly aware of the key's familiar presence at the base of her neck, hanging once more from its cord, and realized that she had not locked the door to the building. *Locks won't hold them back anyway*, Xhea thought. The was door all but rotted off its hinges. *If they want to get in, they can. They will.*

Still, she leapt from her place at the window, not caring as she scattered a pile of dust in her scramble to reach the apartment door and throw its bolt. Once across the room, she grabbed the broken hammer from the floor. The cool weight of the metal head was a comfort, even if it wobbled alarmingly on its handle.

Back at the window, she stilled, listening for any noise in the building, creaks or groans of an opening door, a foot moving across the floorboards, the smash of a breaking window. Outside, there had been no reaction to her movement. But they saw three walkers; who was to say that there weren't really four of them, or five? Crazy thoughts, Xhea knew; yet nothing about the three outside spoke of sanity.

"What do they want?" Shai's voice quivered.

Xhea didn't know, couldn't imagine. The night before, the wild, blind man had somehow seen Shai; and, if Shai was correct, the woman outside had seen the ghost at the window while Xhea still slept. There was no pretending that they were simply Lower City dwellers fallen on hard times; she knew what they were, even if she'd never had faces to put to the terrible sounds she'd heard at night or the metronome footsteps that circled in the dark.

In the end, silence was her only answer, and the only one Shai expected.

Time passed, stretching like a worn elastic band. After an hour or more of watching, Xhea's eyelids felt swollen and heavy. She sagged against the window ledge, wishing she could rest her aching knees without breaking her vigilance. And still the figures did not move or acknowledge each other, only stared upward, as unmoving as living creatures could be. It almost felt as if the walkers had become part of the landscape: a shadow cast by a fallen wall, a pillar in the road, a broken lamp-post anthropomorphized by distance and strange light. Then one would move or blink, the blind man's head turning as if he needed to catch their scents on a shifting wind, and a sudden surge of adrenaline would jolt her back to wakefulness, heartbeat thudding in her ears.

"Maybe," Xhea whispered, "we could throw something. Spur them into doing something."

"Do we really want them doing something?" Shai asked.

"No. I suppose not."

It was only as the far horizon lightened almost imperceptibly, black shading to a gray so deep that Xhea could barely discern the difference, that the three moved. As if this hint of dawn was a signal, as one they seemed to shake themselves; muscles held immobile for countless hours suddenly shrugged, twitched, and rolled about as if in slow-motion seizures. They did not look at each other, only turned to leave: the old man shambled the way he had come, hunched and shuffling, while the blind man stumbled around the corner of the building.

The woman moved last, and she alone had a gait that might blend into a crowd; yet still she moved cautiously, in a way that made Xhea think of someone picking their way over glass. She eased from the deep shadow that had veiled her, and the last of the Towerlight fell on her face. She was young and malnourished, her cheekbones and the tendons in her neck knife-sharp beneath her skin.

Yet she was as much a stranger as the two men. Nothing in her narrow, hawk-like features seemed familiar, and Xhea realized that some part of her had wondered if she hadn't found Abelane at last. It had been a child's dream, finding Lane—one she'd held close and secret through the passing years—and as the dawning light cast shadows across the strange woman's face, Xhea felt that dream break, crumble, and fade at last to nothing.

She watched long after the woman had made her way into the ruins. Even when she released the window ledge and slid down the wall to the floor, her leg muscles cramped and quivering— even when she let out her held breath and allowed her head to sag—Xhea thought, *I'll never sleep now. Not after this.*

But she could and, as the sun at last broke the far horizon, did.

Come true morning, Xhea could barely turn her neck, and she had to hit her legs with her fists to release their cramps. *Take it slow*, she told herself; yet the sun was in her eyes, and she wanted nothing more than to be gone from this place and its hauntings of flesh and memory.

She could not forget this small apartment, its crumbling walls and the remains of a life she no longer lived; nor would she be able to blot this night from her mind, or anything it might portend. But she would try. Broken as it was, she missed her life in the Lower City, the familiarity of her routine, and the comfort of her tunnels.

Besides, she thought, trying to hide her grimace as forced herself to stand, she was out of food. Again.

Xhea limped to the door. "Time to go."

Shai slipped past her into the hall like a breath of chilled air. One hand on the doorframe, Xhea spared a last glance at the room that had been her home for more than three years. She knew that in her absence, the dust would again settle, coating the floors and counters, her mug and the quilt, with its fuzzy layer of gray. The grime would build on the windows until little more than the glow of sunlight passed through; or the panes would crack or break, damaged by a bird, a shift in the structure, a thrown stone.

When she left the first time, she hadn't been able to speak at all, fear and grief stealing her voice and leaving only the taste of tears. Now she spoke a final whispered word softened by something that felt almost like forgiveness.

"Goodbye."

She closed the door behind her, and left it as she should have six years before.

Unlocked.

Chapter Thirteen

"And another thing," said the old woman's ghost. "Those *rags* on his feet. Those are not socks. It has been *years* since they resembled socks." Her white bun had loosened and now flopped about her head with every emphatic gesture.

The old man seated on a nearby crate threw his hands in the air and rolled his eyes dramatically. "Here we go. I can already see it coming."

"Your socks," Xhea said. "Your wife feels that they are . . . past their prime."

"Oh, I'll bet she does."

"You think I like having to look at his toes poking through those things? Let me tell you, that's the worst thing about being dead—never listens when I tell him to get his feet off the coffee table or put on a perfectly good pair of slippers. You tell him to go down to Erikson's shop and get some of those hand-knit socks. Now that's quality."

Xhea turned to the husband, and he waved a dismissive hand. "If she's talking about the socks from Erikson's, I don't want to hear it. Damn itchy things—lumpy too. You ever have to wear lumpy socks, girl? They bunch up in your shoes something fierce, they do, and you limp around like you're walking on stones. Erikson socks. I'll be dead first."

The woman's ghost snorted. "He will if he spends another winter in those shreds he calls socks. Cheap old man."

Xhea cheerfully conveyed this message, snort and all. Before he could reply, a small chime sounded from the old man's watch to announce the end of the hour for which he'd paid.

"Well," he said and blinked, then pushed back his shoulders as if trying to settle himself in his body, in this place; again seeing only Xhea and not the specter of his wife that he knew was so near, and untouchable. "Well. I suppose that anything else will have to wait until another time." Xhea had never tried to cut them off, and yet the old man kept the appointments to the hour they had agreed upon, not a second more.

At the sound, his wife had stilled. Slowly, she unbound the last of her bun, letting snow-white hair tumble down her back before coiling it again and securing it at the base of her neck with a worn hair stick. Always the same gestures, easy motions that reflected habit rather than thought. Her voice was low and her eyes never left her husband's face as she said, "Tell him that I love him. Tell him that I'll wait for him, however long he has."

"Your wife said—" Xhea began, and was waved to silence.

"I know what she said. Silly harpy." He turned away as he spoke, hiding his face, and Xhea ignored the hand he lifted to wipe his eyes.

Since the woman's death just over two years before, they had come to Xhea once a month to argue with her as their intermediary. Not that they needed her once their arguments got going. She had never questioned their desire to continue bickering long after death should have made such mundane considerations moot—and not because she was paid for her part in the arguments, though that didn't hurt. No, it was the tether between them, strong and wider around than her arm, that joined them heart to heart.

The man rose from his crate, nodded farewell to Xhea, and turned away. His wife walked beside him, her groundless steps falling perfectly in time to his, their hands but a breath apart.

"All clear," Shai said. She descended from her lookout perch atop the corner of the roof, and stared speculatively after the couple. "I don't know whether it makes me happy or sad to see them like that."

Xhea shrugged and glanced into the lunch bag that the man had provided for her services. She needed food, but it felt anticlimactic to complete a job and still see the world cast in gray. Yet the sparks of magic that Shai used to help her regain control of her power—and the memory of her reaction to bright magic in the hospital—had forced Xhea to seek other payment. The rise of her own magic, it seemed, had changed her, and she could only try not to yearn for that old rush or the brilliance with which bright magic had painted her vision.

If anything, it seemed that her customers—those few she'd managed to find—appreciated the change. The old man had always paid her fairly, but this time, amidst the carefully wrapped sandwich rolls that she'd requested, she found a few extras: a hardboiled egg, a stick of dried fruit, and sugar cookies in a twist of thin paper. The wife's additions, Xhea had no doubt, the husband guided in his choices even in her absence.

She took a hasty bite of one of the sandwich rolls before heading toward the alley's opposite end and peering cautiously around the corner. "No hunters?" she asked Shai. "No sign of our pale-haired friend?"

"Nothing yet," Shai confirmed.

While they'd managed to evade capture largely due to Xhea's knowledge of the Lower City streets and ability to travel deep underground, it was only Shai's sentry work that allowed them some small measure of freedom. Even their near-escapes had cost her only bruises. But Xhea had hoped that the pursuit would die off after a few days—a week at the most. Instead, they faced more hunters, more money offered for Xhea's detainment—and now, something new.

The last few days Shai and Xhea had both caught sight of a City man on their trail. He never followed so closely that they could say that he was trailing them—yet he was never far enough away that either discounted the idea. He never ran, never seemed to be looking for anyone at all; just walked, careful and slow, without letting so much as a puddle soil the hem of his pants or an errant breeze muss his white-blonde hair. But he asked about her, let it be known that he had a job for which he required Xhea's services—a good job, a paying job.

Xhea didn't know what made her more nervous: the thought that this was yet another Allenai ploy, or the possibility that she was carefully evading the most potentially lucrative job available.

The road was clear. Xhea kept her pace to a quick walk to avoid unnecessary attention, but still heads turned, and she grimaced in irritation. If this continued, she'd have to consider a radical change in hairstyle to just get down the street.

When they reached the subway exit that they'd used that morning, Xhea didn't need Shai's warning to come to an early stop.

"Be careful, it's—"

"I know, I see it." She cautiously stepped closer. Dormant, the entrapment spell was difficult to see, its hanging tendrils all but invisible in the shadow of the subway's entrance stair. It was a more complex spell than the first few she'd seen, more finely woven and with only a faint glimmer revealing its presence, though its shape had become familiar enough that she didn't need to read its purpose. "This makes—what? Seven in the past few days?"

"Eight," Shai said, descending to stand at her side. "Don't forget the one by the market."

Even Xhea had to admit, they were clever creations. With no signature to which to key them, the spells had been designed to activate upon touching a living person who lacked bright magic—meaning that most Lower City dwellers could pass the spells by without harm while Xhea alone would be caught. She and Shai found them all across the Lower City, mainly outside subway entrances and in the doorways and niches that were Xhea's known loitering spots. *Clever*, she thought, *but blighted annoying*.

While Shai examined the spell, Xhea crouched to peer at the stones that were arranged beneath it in a wide X. Such markings, like the spells themselves, had become familiar. She didn't always find stones: once there had been a scrap of fabric held down by a piece of rounded glass; another time she'd found the cracked plastic casings of two antique ballpoint pens forming an arrow that pointed to the spell.

She frowned as she looked at the stones. If she were as magic-poor as she seemed and unable to see the dormant spells, this might have been her only warning. Difficult as it was to admit, someone was trying to protect her. The thought troubled her almost as much as the spells.

Carefully, she picked up a stone and turned it over in her hand, its worn edges cool against her skin. There was nothing distinctive about it, yet she studied it as if she might feel the hand that had held it before her or know its intent. *Why this*, she thought to her unknown ally. *Why now?*

"Xhea," Shai said. "You're radiating."

Xhea opened her eyes, not knowing when she had closed them, and looked at her hand. Was she angry? Afraid? She would have said no; yet her own power made lie of the unspoken words, curling about her fingers like ink in midair.

The easiest way to be rid of the entrapment spells was to blast them with her magic, Xhea thought, watching the black power. A torrent of dark, and the spells would unravel. If only their destruction wouldn't cause more trouble than their absence was worth; the last thing she wanted was to let her enemies, potential or otherwise, to know of her strange power or its effects.

"Do the breathing exercises," Shai said. "Like I showed you."

Xhea grimaced, but nodded and tried to calm her thoughts. Shai had run her through various breathing exercises in an effort to help her curb her rising power; but keeping the exercises straight—and doing them right—was proving more of a challenge. There were patterns to help her enter a state of relaxation, patterns to clear her thoughts and focus her mind, patterns to increase awareness of her power, and patterns to make that awareness grow dim. On and on. Xhea could only imagine the trial and error hyperventilation that had gone into their development.

Slowly she drew in a deep breath and held it as she counted, then exhaled in a thin stream, doubling her earlier count. Again, slower this time, and again, slower still. The curl of dark began to dissipate. How was it, she wondered as she drew another deep breath, that the power could come to her entirely unheeded, and yet its sudden absence felt like loss?

"You're doing really well," Shai said. "You got control faster than last time. And I didn't need to shock you."

"Small mercies." Xhea tried to ignore the unspoken fact that she was radiating more, not less, with each passing day, no matter how quickly the exercises helped her regain control. It was terrifying, when she let herself think of it at all. Instead, she dropped the stone and rose. "Come on, we can try the next station."

Yet as they walked, all she could think of was her hand wreathed in black—and with so little provocation. Anxious, she fumbled in her pockets until she found an old cigarette and a match with which to light it. The rush of smoke as she inhaled— true smoke, pale and acrid—was like a balm, far more calming than any breathing exercises.

"Is this normal?" she asked Shai at last, gesturing with her cigarette as if movement could encompass the tangle of her thoughts. "What's happening to me, I mean. My magic."

Shai tilted her head, considering. "Probably not for someone with no control. But basic energy management is taught at a young age, when the power isn't so strong."

"So has no one else had their power manifest this late?"

"Your magic didn't suddenly appear. You just stopped poisoning yourself." Shai glanced at the cigarette. "Or mostly stopped, anyway," she muttered. Xhea blew smoke through the ghost's midsection in reply.

"If we work on the theory that bright magic is the opposite of yours, then being paid was helping keep your power suppressed. Did you ever call on your magic before?"

"Never." She had run to find whatever source of bright magic she could at the slightest hint that the darkness inside her was stirring, burning it away like fog in the morning sun.

"So you didn't just stop keeping it suppressed. You started using it, too. You opened a door that you can't close again."

Xhea nodded. "'Course," she said, "we don't really know anything about any of this. It could be poisoning me, couldn't it? Killing me just as surely as I kill everything around me."

Shai shrugged in unconscious mimic of Xhea's own gesture. "True enough."

"Don't try to soften the blow or anything."

They walked in silence for a time before Xhea was able to put the question that had been bothering her into words. "But . . . you believe I can learn to control this, right? Really control it. I'm not . . ."—and oh, she cringed to say it aloud—"not like you, am I?"

It was a long moment before Shai replied. "I think you'll be strong. And I think it'll be a while before you know your full strength—or what to do with it. But you can't become what I am."

"You were always . . . Radiant?"

Shai nodded, and softly she replied, "Always." An untold depth in that single word. She added, "It's not a disease, you know. My magic. It's not something to fear."

"But it killed you. It made your people want to *enslave* you. How is that okay?"

Shai smiled, and it was a strange smile; a smile that Xhea did not know how to read. "It doesn't need to be okay," the ghost said. "It just is. Yes, the magic killed me, but it also made me. It shaped me and I shaped it, like water and a stream bed. It killed me . . . but Xhea, when I was alive I did some glorious things."

Shai looked at the City far above, sunlight bright on her face. In that moment Xhea wished that she could see color, for it seemed that more than mere light played across the ghost's features, and all the languid brilliance of the Towers' aurora gleamed in her eyes.

Xhea stopped as they rounded the next corner. The subway entrance that had been safe but hours before was now marked with an entrapment spell that hovered by the crumbling stairs, reaching with near-invisible arms. Yet it wasn't the spell that stopped her, but the man crouched beneath it. Neat and perfectly coiffed, the pale-haired City man reached to place a stone beneath the spell, completing the tell-tale X.

He was her unknown ally?

No, she realized, watching him. He wasn't placing the stone— he was removing it. She had time for the realization, nothing more, for the man sat back on his heels and turned as if he'd heard her silence, felt her stillness. Their eyes met, and for a moment the air seemed to vibrate between them.

"Hello," he called, and the strange tension between them snapped. He brushed his hands on his pants and stood, the entrapment spell's dormant tendrils drifting over his hair and shoulders like long fingers.

"Hello," Xhea replied. She dropped the remains of her cigarette and ground it out, using the motion to disguise her quick scan of the area. No one else was paying attention to either her or the man—that she could see. Not that it meant a blighted thing.

Behind her, Shai faded back, putting the building's crumbling corner between her and the stranger. They'd yet to ascertain how easily a citizen could see the ghost by her radiant magic, and this didn't seem like a terribly good time to find out.

"Escape routes," Xhea murmured. "Quick."

The man stepped forward, and the heel of his shoe clicked on the broken pavement, a sharp, decisive sound. "You must be Xhea," he said. "I've been looking for you."

"So I've heard."

His hands stayed loose at his side, no movement betraying the beginnings of a spell or a weapon concealed in a pocket—not that his sharply tailored outfit would allow something so crass. Yet there was something about him that set all her mental alarms to ringing—and the last thing she wanted was to find out why.

She took a step backward, and he raised a hand to stop her. "Wait." Another moment, and he raised the other hand, showing her his palms. "I'm not here to accost you," he said. "Just give you an offer. You don't like it, you can walk away, no problem."

Run, Xhea thought, even as her mouth said, "What kind of offer?"

"I'm looking to hire you on a short-term contract—an estimated three weeks in duration."

Three weeks was short term? Xhea swallowed her exclamation. "Why?" she managed.

"I'll be honest," he said, lowering his hands. "We can afford you. The extent of the service we require—the extent of the haunting—would result in a truly exorbitant price if we went to anyone else. We could provide you with whatever payment you needed—more than you could imagine—and not break our budget. A mutually profitable arrangement, yes?"

"No," Xhea said, trying to hide her shock at his reply. "Or, yes, but—that wasn't what I meant." Her mind spun. There were others like her? Where—and why had she never heard of them? The next thought followed hard on the heels of the first: if there were others who could see ghosts, did they also have her strange dark magic? She forced that line of thinking aside. "I meant why do you need my help."

"Ah, yes. Like I said, it's rather an extensive haunting and . . . a complicated situation."

"You need an exorcism? Of the whole Tower?"

"That's one solution, and certainly what some are hoping for. But you're the expert; perhaps you'd be able to recommend a different solution."

"For this contract, I'd have to live in your Tower?"

"We'd provide meals and accommodations, yes. Unless, of course, you'd be more comfortable making your own arrangements, in which case we would be happy to provide you with daily transportation."

"Your Tower's not Allenai, is it?"

"Allenai?" The man's pale brows raised in evident confusion. "No. Why?"

Xhea shrugged. "Not important. How much are you offering?"

The sum he named was so astronomical that Xhea could barely process it. She stood, staring—knowing she was staring, slack-jawed and stupid, and unable to do anything about it.

"I've heard that you can't process the energy directly," he continued as she gaped, "so we could make arrangements for you to be paid an equal amount in goods and services, or hold some of the funds for you to draw on as needed, or—well, I'm sure we could find a satisfactory arrangement."

"I need . . ." Xhea choked on the words. "I need . . ."

"To think about it," he replied. "Yes, of course. But here, let me give you this." He reached slowly and carefully into his pocket, and drew forth what Xhea took to be a small metallic chit. A coin? No, she saw as he raised his hand toward her, the metal disc laid flat on his palm. It was more like the token that she'd stolen from Brend's private food storage, the metal inscribed with a detailed pattern that was almost like a spell.

"Use this to contact me—I'm known as Derren. We can even arrange for you to have a tour, understand the details of the situation, before you—"

Xhea stepped forward, reaching for the offered disc. Somewhere behind her, Shai cried out. "Xhea, on your right!"

There was a yell—a harsh, inarticulate sound—

The pale-haired man, Derren, shouted, "*No*, not now!"

A man struck Xhea on her right shoulder, sending her sprawling into the road. She hit the ground hard and tried to roll; cried out as the weight of the man hit her moments later, impacting against her chest and legs. Whoever hit her cried out as well, a sharp sound of pain as their bodies connected, and he flinched away.

"Grab her," someone was shouting. "Blight it, just grab her!"

"Not like that," another voice said—a familiar voice, though she couldn't place the speaker. "I told you—"

Xhea pushed herself away, and fought to gain her feet, but the impact had rattled her, knocked the breath from her chest and set her head to spinning. She stood, stumbled, and almost fell again. Where were her attackers? One on the ground, voices behind her shouting. Which way was the subway entrance?

"Xhea," Shai called again, closer this time. "This way—toward my voice."

She stumbled forward, gasping for air. Caught sight of Derren being held by a hunter, his perfect hair in sudden disarray. His offered token was on the ground, light glinting from its etched patterns, but there was no time to grab it. Shai was like a beacon before her, the ghost's light calling her onward.

"That's it. Now duck under the spell."

Xhea dropped and rolled, feeling each of the stones of the warning X dig into her side. Suddenly she was at the lip of the stairway and rolling down, the broken tile of the stair treads sharp against her shoulders and hip and back. She caught herself after a few stairs, whimpered, and made her way down the rest. Gates barred the subway entrance, but they were old and rusting, and she'd unlocked the chain that bound them years before, only leaving it for show. Yanking away the chain, she pushed the gates open and forced herself through the narrow gap into the cold and shadow beyond.

"I'm sorry," Shai said, glowing like a candle in the darkness. Xhea struggled to catch her breath. "I was distracted—I should have seen them coming, they just . . ."

"It's okay." With tentative fingertips, she cataloged her new hurts, countless bruises on her arms and legs and side. "We're both idiots."

Not now, Derren had said. Not "Stop," not "What are you doing?"

Not now—as if only the timing had been wrong. Of course his offer had been too good to be true. Hope did such terrible things to one's sense.

She heard shouting from beyond the gate and then the crunch of heavy footsteps on the stairs. With a grimace, Xhea made her way into the subway station to stand in the shadows past the turnstiles, watching. Waiting. Listening to the footsteps grow nearer. A voice murmured but there was no reply, only the crunch of a second set of feet. *Oh yes*, she thought. She knew that voice. Knew, too, who had trashed her maintenance room in the Green Line tunnel, and used that knowledge to harden her expression and heart alike.

"Business," she reminded herself in a whisper, watching the shadows the approaching figures cast. "It was only ever about business."

A man arrived first: lanky and sandy-haired, Torrence looked like some City kid gone slumming and enjoying every moment of his temporary fall from grace. Equal parts charm and businessman, with one part knife-you-in-the-back, that was Torrence. Yet his easy smile was nowhere in sight as he straightened and squinted, searching for Xhea in the gloom.

His partner followed a moment later—slower, more carefully, and in perfect silence. She was short, barely reaching Torrence's shoulder, with a hard face and a build of pure whipcord muscle. Daye had none of Torrence's charm or easy manner, and was as likely to knife you in the throat as the back. You knew exactly where you stood with Daye—on perpetually uneasy ground—and for that reason she and Xhea had always gotten along.

"How are they following?" Shai moved restlessly like a flame in midair.

Xhea had no fear that either would see the shining ghost; both were so magic-poor that their signatures barely registered. They had turned their joint weaknesses into a business, stealing, collecting, hunting, and going places few others in the Lower City could. The jobs that had required them to go too deep underground they had outsourced to Xhea.

She shook her head in response to Shai's question. This station might be deeper than some—but it was far from truly underground. Yet she knew, too, the pair's normal preparations for venturing underground included both meditation and drugs, a mix that allowed them to endure the pain. She doubted that their quick pursuit had allowed for any such planning.

At the movement, the coins in her hair clinked softly. Daye stiffened and turned, her eyes meeting Xhea's in the near-darkness.

"Ah," Torrence said. "There you are, darlin'. And here I thought you went sneaking off rather than waiting for us."

He knew not to call her darling, or sweetie, or the thousand other names he used to mock his marks—they'd agreed on that their very first job together. He was just trying to goad her, annoying rat that he was; and the thought was almost enough to make Xhea grin, despite everything.

"Now why would I do that?" she replied, casual and slow. "Seems like such fun to be dragged away to—hmm, which Tower hired you again?"

"Tsk, tsk. You know the rules, doll, and you know how this is going to go. Nothing personal, you understand—all past favors aside, et cetera, et cetera." He waved a hand airily. "We have a job to do here, and it's best for all of us if you don't make that any harder than it needs to be."

His voice was steady, Xhea gave him that, but sweat already beaded his forehead. She watched as a droplet trickled down his cheek, glinting in the faint daylight from above. He tried to smile—that easy, habitual gesture—but it soured, lips twisting into a pained expression.

Oh yes, she thought. *I know how this is going to go.*

"I wouldn't dream of making your life harder," she said. "Business is business." But she did not move, the turnstiles and the expanse of dirty floor between them as solid as any wall.

"Right, that's a girl." Torrence swallowed, his Adam's apple bobbing in his throat. "Now what I want you to do . . ." He paused and swallowed again, then raised a hand to wipe the sweat from his brow. His fingers shook. He stared at his hand, turning it over in disbelief before suddenly balling it into a fist and shoving it into his pocket, out of sight.

Too late, she thought. From the glance that Daye spared him, she wasn't the only one.

He tried again, slower: "What I want you to do is . . . is to step forward . . ." His voice caught, and his hand flew to his stomach. His arms were shaking now, and his knees. With his free hand, he reached for the wall to keep from falling.

"What's happening to him?" Shai asked.

"Just watch."

"I . . . I can't . . ." he said, before doubling over and retching. He trembled like a junkie in withdrawal as he reached for stair rail to haul himself upward, nearly falling as his stomach doubled him over again. Xhea listened to his fumbling, staggering steps recede.

Daye was stronger. She always had been.

Daye grit her teeth and stepped forward. Xhea didn't say anything; she didn't have to. Just stood, calm and casual, watching with feigned indifference as the woman attempted to approach. If Daye came within five feet of her, Xhea would be down the stairs to the platform and gone—they both knew it. That didn't stop Daye from forcing herself closer, just to prove that she could.

Step by careful step, the woman approached. Sweat broke out across her face, and her hands shook, and she took another heavy step, and another. By the time she made it to the turnstiles, it was all she could do to hold one with shaking hands and stare at Xhea unblinking. She would go no farther.

In silence, Xhea nodded—a low nod, almost a bow. When she rose, their eyes met one last time, and then Xhea turned and walked down to the subway platform, Shai at her back. Her only farewell was the sound of her footsteps, echoing into the darkness.

Chapter Fourteen

"Again," Shai said.

Xhea looked down at her hands, held cupped before her, and grimaced. *Focus*, she told herself, willing the magic to come. She remembered how it felt as it rose through her, slow and calm and powerful; she remembered too how it looked, lifting from her skin like steam from a hot stone.

Her hands remained stubbornly empty.

She glanced at Shai across the cracked food court table. "It's too early for this, Shai," she said. The ghost simply waited, face impassive, until Xhea sighed and looked back to her hands.

The key to controlling her magic, Shai had patiently explained—time and time again—was owning the power. Magic wasn't an entity of its own; it was a part of her, and it reacted to her thoughts and emotions and needs. Gaining control was only a matter of practice and time.

Theoretically.

Of course, after three solid days of nothing but practice, Xhea was about ready to abandon the whole thing. Shai insisted that Xhea was improving. Then again, it would have been difficult for her to become more incompetent.

She'd remained hidden underground since the disastrous near-meeting with Derren. Her pursuers had systematically blocked, booby-trapped, or set watchers around every single entrance in the Lower City core, and while she could simply use one of the tunnel entrances out in the ruins, alleviating her own boredom didn't seem worth the risk. Her food stores were running low, but not dangerously so, and it had rained enough to keep her water stores nearly full. And while she'd heard Torrence and Daye enter the underground more than once, their foreign footsteps loud in her normally quiet haunts, neither could delve deep enough to threaten her, not now that she knew they were coming.

So she stayed in the lowest levels—the food courts and parking garages, the maintenance shafts and back hallways—attempted to smother her frustration, and practiced under Shai's ever-patient eye. Xhea wasn't sure how she would have stayed sane without the ghost; though it would be nice, she thought, to wake up once—just *once*—without Shai zapping her. Of course, it would have been nicer to perform the tedious repetitions in sunlight, breathing air that didn't smell like ancient concrete and countless years of dust. It would be nicer to *understand* who these people were and what they wanted of her, rather than being forced to be a pawn in a—

And there it was: a wisp of dark rising from the palm of her right hand. It's not that the magic didn't respond to her; it only ever needed a spark of anger to rise.

Carefully now, she directed the power, trying to contain the swirling wisps in the bowl of her hands, willing it to become the simple sphere that Shai had asked of her. Yet it seemed to slip from her mental grasp, the magic turning and twisting not in response to her will, but evading it.

At last she let out an explosive breath and shook her tingling hands.

"Not bad," Shai said as the darkness dissipated. "You lasted eleven seconds that time."

"Eleven whole seconds."

"Nearly twelve."

Xhea snorted. "Oh joy."

She was massaging her hands in preparation for the next attempt when she heard a scuff like a heavy door opening, and then another sound, louder. Xhea tensed and looked to the escalators that led to the mall's main level, listening.

"Did you hear that?" she whispered.

"Hear what?"

"I thought I heard a voice. Calling."

"I didn't—"

The voice came again, louder this time: "Hello?" A woman's voice, faint and echoing.

"It's just past dawn," Xhea said softly. She rose from her seat, practice forgotten. "Almost no one's out yet." It would take half an hour or more for the streets to fill, safety assured as daylight chased away the last of night's shadows. Whoever approached did so with caution, not wanting to be seen; and even her voice was hushed by more than the distance between them.

Again the woman called, closer this time: "Please. Is anyone there?"

Xhea swore and backed toward the service hall that led behind the vacant fast food counters and away. Shai did not move. She hovered as if caught in midair, her face gone paler than death, the fingers of a single hand pressed to her lips.

"Come on," Xhea urged.

But Shai only said, "No."

"You're staying? Why?"

Shai turned away from the escalator and met Xhea's eyes; her silver-pale irises looked almost white with the magic shining behind them. Because of the light, it took Xhea a moment to realize that the ghost's eyes glistened with tears; a moment more to believe she was truly crying. After all that had happened—even Shai's death—this was the first time Xhea had seen her weep.

"Xhea," Shai said. "That's my mother."

Surrounded by dust-coated countertops, cash registers, and faded photos of greasy food, Xhea listened as Shai's mother called again. Hearing the echoes, she knew that the woman was near the external doors on the floor above, only one long flight of escalator steps away.

"Is anyone there?"

This time Xhea answered: "Yes, I'm here."

For a moment, silence was the only reply. "Can you come out where I can see you?" the woman asked at last.

Xhea moved from the shadows to the base of the escalator where a band of early morning light fell, and looked up at the woman standing just inside the dirty glass doors. Her pale hair was cut to curl and kiss the line of her jaw, and small earrings hung from each earlobe, their sparkle brighter than mere diamonds. Her outfit was simple, pants and a tailored blouse, though even at a distance Xhea could tell that the fabric was far finer than anything she'd known.

Discomfort was written in every line of the woman's body, from the set of her shoulders to the way she held her hands as if fighting to keep them from fists. As Xhea watched, those hands began to shake, and a rivulet of sweat tricked down from her forehead—and she hadn't even begun to walk below ground. The spells that had guarded the door were gone; brushed away, Xhea could only assume, as easily as she might brush away an errant lock of hair.

Shai's mother took a few slow breaths before speaking again. "I'm looking for Xhea. Is that you?"

"Yes."

"You can be a difficult person to find."

"Intentionally, these days."

"Is that so?"

Xhea inclined her head, using the movement to hide her glance back at Shai. The ghost had remained in the shadows, out of her mother's line of sight. Xhea caught a glimpse of Shai's expression. Shai stared at her mother with such naked pain, such hurt and sorrow and longing, that Xhea briefly wished she could take the ghost's hand or curl an arm around her shoulder. Yet it wasn't Xhea from whom Shai wished comfort, and Xhea bit her lip as she turned away.

"Would you mind coming closer?" Shai's mother called, her voice echoing. Xhea could only hope that Torrence and Daye had not yet entered the complex this morning. "It's a little difficult, shouting down to you like this."

"Rather not, thanks. It's safer for me here."

"Safer?"

"Big set of stairs between me and you. I like that sort of distance until I know why you've come."

"Even though I could just walk down the stairs?"

"I think you'd find that more unpleasant than expected."

A pause. "Is that a threat?"

"Simple fact. Citizens don't like to go below ground level. It's rather painful, I'm told—but you're welcome to give it a try."

"I'll take your word for it." She cleared her throat. "I'm sorry, I haven't introduced myself."

"I know who you are, Ms. Nalani," Xhea said. "Though I can't say I know why you're here."

"Councilwoman Nalani," the woman said with a hint of a smile, "but yes." She had the same smile as her daughter, Xhea saw, a slight upturn of her lips that spoke both of soft humor and sorrow.

Councilwoman? Xhea raised an eyebrow. Shai shrugged and bowed her head—apology if not explanation—and Xhea could not help but wonder what other secrets the ghost had hidden, or how much more of Shai's strange past she would have to encounter by surprise.

Each Tower was run differently; Xhea had never quite managed to grasp the intricacies of the political structures that governed each—nor wanted to. Yet she knew that each had a Council, a controlling body that was government, economic control, and judicial system wrapped into one, accountable only to the Tower's citizens and the Central Spire. If Shai's mother was on Allenai's Council, she was not only in a position of great power and influence—if Wen were to be believed, she also helped rule one of the most prominent bodies in the City.

And she stood at the top of a dusty mall escalator with her shoes caked in mud.

"As for why I'm here," Councilwoman Nalani continued, "I thought you would know that better than I."

"Did you?"

"Please, child," she said, and if her tone was patronizing, it spoke equally of grief and exhaustion. "Don't play games with me."

Abruptly, Xhea remembered that despite all that had happened, this was a woman whose daughter had just died. She would never hear her daughter's voice again, nor feel her touch; could only mourn the child she would never see grow to adulthood. She hadn't even been there for her daughter's passing. Sometimes it was too easy to forget the pain that death brought.

Yet what did she expect Xhea to say? *Ah yes, you must be here about the ghost of your magical daughter, the one whose ghost is hiding behind me.* Or perhaps: *You must have come about the traps laid for me—or is it the attempted kidnapping that you'd like to discuss?*

Instead, Xhea simply replied, "Nor you with me. Speak plainly, or I'm leaving."

"I could find you again if you ran. Track you down."

"That doesn't sound like much of a way to gain my cooperation, and I doubt I'd make it so easy," Xhea said. "Still, your choice."

The Councilwoman hesitated, then sighed and briefly closed her eyes. "I'm sorry. I just . . . this isn't going how I wanted."

"And what did you want?"

"I thought that I'd find you, and I could take you for breakfast, and we could . . . talk. Just talk. Much has happened, and it seems that you might be the only one with certain answers."

"A talk over breakfast. How civilized." At the Councilwoman's look, Xhea hastened to add, "Not that I'm complaining. It's just that no one's made quite that offer before."

"Then you accept?"

Xhea hesitated. "Only breakfast? You're not going to try to take me anywhere, capture me, anything like that?"

"Capture you?" Councilwoman Nalani sounded surprised, even shocked. "No, I promise, only breakfast. I don't mean you any harm. I won't let anything happen to you while you're with me." She spoke with her hands spread, palms upward. She was a politician, Xhea knew, and lying was in her job description. Still, she sounded sincere.

"I just wonder if I can trust you."

Again, that smile, lips wreathed in sorrow. Softly Shai's mother said, "I wonder the same thing."

Into the silence, Shai said, "She can be a hard woman, my mother, but she's never broken her word."

"Okay." Xhea sighed. "I'll make the leap of faith for both of us." All of us, she mentally amended, sparing a glance at Shai.

"You'll come out?"

Xhea nodded. "I hope I don't regret this," she whispered.

She thought she'd spoken softly enough that only Shai would hear, but the Councilwoman replied, "I hope that I don't, either."

More than her promise, it was that brief admission of reluctance that compelled Xhea to climb the ancient escalator and walk out into the early morning sunlight. At last, it was a reaction that she recognized.

Councilwoman Nalani gestured down the dirty street with a perfectly manicured hand. "Shall we?" she said. Side by side they walked, Shai trailing silently behind.

Councilwoman Nalani led her toward the skyscrapers and the well-preserved shops in the center of their uneven protective ring. Here, there were areas where the roads and buildings were mostly uncracked, the sidewalks smooth, the stone façades posing little threat to those passing below. Coming to these few blocks felt like stepping into another world, a city almost frightening in the way it brought the ancient to life; and it was this, as much as the silvery presence of Orren behind her, that made the back of Xhea's neck crawl.

It felt strange to walk here unhurried, with another at her side— not spirit but flesh and blood. Strange to hear the sound of shoes on asphalt, high heels echoing, falling in time to Xhea's own. Their breaths puffed in the chill, early morning air: two clouds of white, rising. The strangeness asked for her silence, and willingly she gave it, not mentally mocking the imitations of riches in the stores that they passed, not scoping out the few people on the street for the dangers they might pose—not wishing or hoping or thinking of things that could have been—but walking. Simply walking.

They came to a restaurant, its entrance marked by a slim sign. A string of bells on the door announced their presence; the narrow flight of stairs leading upward creaked beneath their weight. The woman waiting at the top greeted them, hung up the Councilwoman's coat, and led them to a small table made private by a folding wooden screen. The server poured tea into small cups and promised to return with food.

Xhea blew the steam from her cup, staring at the tea to avoid meeting the Councilwoman's eyes. She could just see Shai, who hovered at the window behind her mother's back with her arms crossed tightly across her chest. With each moment, the expanse of table seemed wider, the presence and unspoken expectations of both mother and daughter pressing down until Xhea struggled to breathe. She took a swallow of the scalding tea just to break the tension.

By the time she'd finished choking, the server had returned with a towel-covered basket and a tray with small dishes, tiny spoon handles protruding from beneath their lids. At the Councilwoman's gesture, Xhea drew back the top layer of the towel to find baked goods—crumbly-topped muffins and puffy buns filled with sweet bean, scones and rolls—fresh and steaming, hot to the touch. She took a few almost at random, intoxicated by the smell alone, then peeked inside the dishes, finding berry jam, lime marmalade, butter, and honey. She slathered a muffin with butter and jam and began stuffing it into her mouth.

She'd never tasted anything so good.

Halfway through the muffin, she looked up, met the Councilwoman's eyes, and momentarily forgot to chew. Shai's mother had broken open a scone that now lay untouched on the plate before her. Hands folded on the tabletop, she watched Xhea eat. She looked so much like Shai, Xhea realized then. They had different hair and a different nose, but something in the line of her cheekbones and curve of her jaw, maybe something in the cast of her eyes, was so similar that not even the creases of age and weariness could disguise their kinship. Xhea kept herself from looking from mother to ghost, but only just.

She swallowed, and Councilwoman Nalani smiled sadly. "You're hungry," she said.

Xhea shrugged. "Of course." She couldn't be embarrassed by hunger. She was again reaching for her muffin when she understood the Councilwoman's expression. Xhea folded her hands on the table in purposeful mimic and stared back.

"Don't pity me," she said, voice hard.

"Pity you?"

"I'm not starving. I don't *need* this." She pushed away her plate. The Councilwoman sighed. "Relax, child. I didn't say you did." "Don't lie to me, either."

Anger stirred in the Councilwoman's expression. "The truth, then. It's not just you. I pity all of you here, living in dirt and ruin, no way to make yourselves anything more, anything *better*."

She shook her head, and Xhea saw the tears she tried to blink back. "I'm sorry. I shouldn't have said that. I don't . . ." She looked at her untouched scone as if it held answers. "I feel the weight of my privilege, these days. My responsibilities." As if that were explanation enough—and perhaps it was.

Xhea pulled her plate back and took a bite of her muffin. Reached out, and picked another from the basket.

"Are you not hungry?" she asked, as if their conversation were only beginning.

"No. Not even a little." Councilwoman Nalani looked down at her scone, sighed, and slowly spread butter over its surface. She watched the butter melt, then bit and chewed as if it were a chore.

"She doesn't eat when she's stressed," Shai whispered. "Or when she's upset. I had to remind her. Bring her meals in her study."

"You haven't been eating."

"Of course I haven't. My daughter is dead." Then, slower but no less bitter: "But then, you know that, don't you?" It took Xhea a moment to realize that it was a real question; a moment more before she nodded.

"Can you tell me how you know?"

Xhea raised her eyebrows. She suppressed a desire to say, "Are you asking if I killed her?" That, she knew with cold certainty, was not a subject she wished to broach with the Councilwoman. Not ever.

"I'm not blaming you for anything," Councilwoman Nalani continued. "I'm just trying to understand. My daughter is gone and I'm just trying . . ." She took a deep breath.

"I see ghosts." Only that.

"That's what I heard." The Councilwoman failed to hide her skepticism. "But that's also what I don't understand. If the reports I've received are true, then my husband sought you *before* Shai's death. Now why would he do that?"

"Perhaps," Xhea said softly, "you should ask him."

"I would if I could. He hasn't been seen since we found Shai's body."

Xhea tried to hide her confusion in yet another morning pastry. Was she lying? All too clearly, Xhea recalled Shai's saying that people had taken her father away, and that the tether between them had snapped. She'd assumed he had been taken and killed by Allenai—but if that were the case, would not the Councilwoman have known?

"In my experience," Xhea said slowly, "a person's spirit can leave their body before the moment of death, especially if the death is slow or prolonged, as I believe your daughter's was."

"There were spells on Shai to prevent that from happening."

"Were there also spells keeping her from dying?"

"Well, yes, but—"

"And she's dead. So who am I to say what happened?"

"But you admit that you saw her ghost. Shai's ghost."

"Yes."

"And spoke with her."

"Yes," Xhea said, not liking where this was going.

"When did you see her last?"

"I . . . can't quite say."

"Can't? Or won't?"

Xhea shrugged and turned to the window. Yet now she could see Shai, curled awkwardly against the window ledge, misery writ large in her expression.

"You need to understand, my daughter isn't just dead. She was abducted."

Shai froze. Xhea gestured to her beneath the table, and yet Shai pretended not to see, pretended that there was no reason to turn away. Nothing to explain, nothing to apologize for.

Not missing, not hidden—abducted. *This is what she would not tell me*, Xhea thought, and mentally cursed Shai, her ghostly memory, and her stream of lies by omission.

The anger would come later, Xhea knew. Now, she said only, "Abducted?"

"By her father."

"Why would he do that?"

"We had a disagreement, he and I, over Shai's future. I believe that he felt he had no other choice." Simple words, stripped of emotion.

Xhea thought of those bare rooms where she'd found Shai dying: a spare and ramshackle place, no furniture that wasn't for Shai's survival or comfort. A temporary location—a place for her father to hide them both until he could find a way to let her die.

"Xhea," the Councilwoman said. "Xhea, please. She was more than just my daughter. You don't know what her loss means, not just to me, but to all of Allenai."

"She was your Radiant."

The word brought the Councilwoman up short. Her expression changed in that instant, her grief masked quickly and fiercely, vulnerability vanishing. "You know what that means." The words were both question and statement, spoken in a politician's even tones.

Xhea shrugged again, aware of how very little she knew, her ignorance almost a physical pain. "I know some. I know that she generated far more magical energy than even the best casters. That the Towers run on the magic generated by Shai and others like her."

Councilwoman Nalani nodded. "Put simply, Shai's death has moved Allenai into a position of instability, politically and financially, and there are those who seek to profit from that instability."

Orren, Xhea wanted to say—but how could an earthbound skyscraper possibly threaten one of the City's most powerful Towers? Instead, remembering Brend's sudden panic, the smashed teacups and the lighting spell damage in his haste, she took a stab in the dark: "Eridian?"

The Councilwoman became still. "How did you hear that name?"

Got it in one, Xhea thought. Beside her Shai whispered, "No. Oh, no." She placed her head in her glowing hands. Xhea had to strain to hear her next words: "They loaned against me."

She didn't know how to respond to Shai's comment or ask what she meant. Instead of answering the Councilwoman, Xhea fished in her jacket's breast pocket. There, beside her knife, she found the metal token that she'd taken from Brend's food stash. She placed it with its sigil facing upward and pushed it across the tabletop with a finger.

Councilwoman Nalani made no move to touch it; she looked from the token, lying in the shadow of the honey dish, back to Xhea's face. "You're working for them," she said.

"No. You asked how I knew the name. An acquaintance is a citizen, nothing more."

"An 'acquaintance,' as you say, would never give you this."

"I never said he did." Xhea wondered, suddenly, what she'd stolen. She slipped the token back into her pocket.

The Councilwoman paused, considering. "Perhaps," she said slowly, "it would be in your best interests to avoid this particular acquaintance for a while. Especially if he knows of your . . . ability."

Again, the skepticism.

There were so many questions she wanted to ask, yet it was the skepticism that caught her. Slowly, Xhea took a third muffin, which she ate as she buttered a biscuit. "You were asking about your daughter's ghost," she said. "So why does it sound like you don't believe in ghosts at all?"

The Councilwoman smiled thinly. "It's not ghosts that I disbelieve, only you and your abilities. Forgive me," she said in a tone that was anything but apologetic, "but saying that you can see ghosts strikes me as an effective way for you to earn a living. Given so few options."

"I'm not a fraud." Xhea shrugged. "I don't need your approval."

"Be that as it may."

"You believe my talent's fictional, and yet you believe in ghosts?"

"With your talent, I have only your word that it's true." She took a sip of tea. "But ghosts? It's not uncommon for spirits of the more magically inclined to remain behind. An echo of their power, perhaps. I have even seen evidence of a Radiant's spirit who remained for a time in this world after his body died."

You mean you've seen a ghost forced to resurrect and inhabit a body foreign to them, Xhea thought, and was surprised at the force of the anger she felt rising. She hid her reaction in another sip of tea.

But with the anger came magic, dark and curling, swelling on the tide of emotion. *Not now*, she thought. She pulled her hands from her teacup and shoved them beneath the table to hide the smoke-like wisps that drifted from her fingertips.

"Evidence?" she asked in a tight, uneven voice.

The Councilwoman waved the question away and leaned forward, catching and holding Xhea's gaze. "Please," she said. "I'm looking for my daughter's ghost—not just for me, but for the safety and security of my whole Tower. You understand, I wasn't with Shai when she died. I had no idea where she was—and her ghost, if she did stay in this world, is lost to me."

Beneath the table, Xhea's energy flowed. She dared not look down, only imagined the spreading mist of darkness wreathing the legs of her chair, growing like a thunderhead. She expected Shai to notice and readied herself for that now-familiar shock; but the ghost seemed unaware, and still the power rose.

"Tell me why you want her back." As if she had the power to command. As if forcing a confession of her intended enslavement of her daughter's ghost would somehow give Xhea a power—a right—that she did not currently wield.

"Allenai—"

"Yes," Xhea said through teeth. The magic surged. "But tell me *why*."

"Why does it matter to you?" the Councilwoman countered, her anger growing to mirror Xhea's own. "I've asked about you— all you worry about is getting paid. You don't care. You didn't even know her."

Xhea leaned forward until her face was but a few hands' span from the Councilwoman's, clenching her fists not to stop the magic but to feel the sharp pain of her nails in her palms—an anchor. "And I'd need to know her to give a shit? Oh, no, I'd just look at some grief-stricken father and the ghost of his daughter and say, 'What's it worth to me?' Why would I *care* about some fearful, hesitant dead girl? Why would I *care* about someone caught in the agony of perpetually dying?" She resisted the impulse to spit, but only just. It wasn't only the anger; the taste of the truth that lay beneath her savage denials was strong and bitter.

"No," Xhea said, her voice becoming harsh, "I'm just the selfish

Lower City trash that cares for nothing but herself. I only care that since your husband came to me with your daughter's ghost, I have been arrested, detained, harassed, and nearly captured. My home has been ransacked. My property has been destroyed. Traps have been laid for me in the blighted *streets*, and anyone who'd ever so much as given me a polite word has been told to stay away from me, or else."

Xhea wanted to strike out, just to ease the frustration; yet her magic felt like storm waves riding her blood, and didn't dare raise her hands above the table. *Shut it down*, she thought.

The Councilwoman blinked and sat back. "You're not lying," she said in the voice of someone just waking. "You really did see her. My daughter." Xhea watched as possibilities were born in the Councilwoman's eyes, watched scenarios play out lightning-fast in the shift of her expression, and quailed at the thought of their import.

She saw her sudden, dawning value in the look the Councilwoman gave her across their breakfast table, and fear traced a cold line down her back.

This, she realized, was what it was to be seen by someone not of the Lower City, not of a skyscraper or the ruined downtown streets, but of power. To have one's value judged and measured; to see one's price—muffins and tea, clean clothes and a place to sit—reflected in the narrowing of eyes, the glimpse of an edge of a smile. It was an expression she'd seen only once before, and that on the face of the man in Orren who'd first had her work with ghosts.

"You can help me," Councilwoman Nalani said, "and Xhea, I can help you. Even beyond finding Shai, yours is a talent that Allenai could dearly use."

"That's what I'm afraid of," Xhea muttered, suddenly feeling like the unmannered adolescent that the Councilwoman took her for.

"Yes." Councilwoman Nalani sipped her tea. "Perhaps your future—and the opportunities and rewards Allenai might offer— is something to discuss another time. For now, tell me when you last saw my daughter. A week ago? A few days?"

"You have no proof I've seen her at all. You're just making assumptions," Xhea said, but she felt both denial and misdirection fall flat. She looked at her hands and saw no wreathing magic, no cloud of dark—only hands, soft and shadowed in the morning's pale light.

"Yes, I am." In Councilwoman Nalani's suddenly calm and measured tones Xhea heard not the grieving mother or the politician out of her depth, but something far more dangerous. "Let me make a few more. I know that my daughter's spirit was freed from her body before her death, and that you at the very least saw her."

"You can't prove that."

"I can. I have a recording from an elevator activated with my daughter's signature that shows you were the only passenger, and that the elevator took you to the Tower where my daughter's body was found. So I assume that you have also seen my daughter *since* her death—in the days after my husband came to you for help, and after your interesting trip to the City—else you would have simply denied it. I also assume that you know more than you would have me believe, as your lines of questioning would otherwise be of little value."

This time when the Councilwoman leaned forward, steepling her hands on the table, Xhea fought the urge to recoil. "You know why I need her back," she said, a low murmur laced with steel. "And you know where she is."

"She can go where she pleases." Xhea regretted the words as

they slipped out.

"Ah. So you have seen her."

"Yeah," she admitted, then attempted to divert the conversation. "But since the last time someone tried to trap me, we've been—" For a moment, she could only close her eyes.

"*We*," Councilwoman Nalani said, repeating the word softly. "Tell me. Is she here?"

"I can't—" But her mouth was so dry, her saliva vanishing with her words.

"Xhea, I will ask you this once: give my daughter back."

"She's not mine to give, Councilwoman," Xhea replied. It sounded nowhere near as confident as she had intended.

The silence stretched between them. Xhea dared not so much as glance at the ghost, still hovering in the window behind her mother's right shoulder; yet she could see Shai's distress, the fretful twisting of her hands as she looked from Xhea to her mother.

"Don't you understand what it would mean?" Xhea cried at last. "What it would do to her?"

The Councilwoman sighed, an untold weight in that breath. "Of course I understand, child. I know more of Radiants than but a handful of people in the City. I know what it is we ask of them, and the pain their gifts exact. I've known since Shai was born what her talent would mean for her, how it would shape her life, and her death—and yes, everything after."

Again Xhea's anger surged, and her fear, but they felt weak compared to the sudden force emanating from the woman before her, a power that seemed but a glimmer away from becoming visible. And oh, in that presence she felt so small. So inconsequential.

"But how could you—how *can* you ask this of her? A lifetime spent trapped and dying . . ."

"How could I not ask it, Xhea?" Softly, so softly. "It's how the City is run—don't you see? On the strength—the magic—of its people, and yes, some must give far more than others ever can. I try to ensure that her power isn't wasted or spent frivolously, but I cannot change the workings of our society, child. Not even for the one person I love more than anything else in this world."

The Councilwoman shook her head. "I cannot ask for what I would not give. When a Radiant is born, I, as part of the Council, ask the parents to give that child to the good of the Tower. I ask that child to learn and grow and dedicate themselves to Allenai— and yes, to die and keep on giving, should that be their fate." Her eyes were fierce, shining. "How can I ask—how can I *take*—what I would not myself willingly sacrifice?"

"Your daughter."

"Shai," she said, shuddered, and burst into tears.

Xhea could but stare, helpless at the sight of this woman who hid her crumpling expression behind a manicured hand. As if caught in a dream, Shai rose from her perch on the window ledge and moved toward her mother. She reached to cup her mother's face in her hand, as if in this small way she could make her presence known. As she touched her mother's tear-stained cheek, Councilwoman Nalani looked up, eyes wide and almost frightened.

"Shai?" she whispered. And again, her voice cracking, "Shai?"

"She's not . . ." Xhea began, but her voice failed her. She could not lie. Had not the will to, nor the desire.

Shai's mother turned toward her daughter's ghost, guided by the sense of her presence or a glimpse of her light—Xhea knew not which. "Shai, if you can hear me, please, *please*, remember what you promised. I know you're scared, baby. I know. But you won't be alone, okay? I'll be there for you, always. Right beside you."

Hand outstretched toward her mother, Shai bowed her head. Her long, pale hair fell forward like a shimmering curtain, shielding her face. In that moment Xhea could not fathom the ghost's expression, only knew it was one that she dared not see.

And so they remained, in stillness and perfect quiet, until the waitress returned to refill their tea.

Chapter Fifteen

Outside the restaurant, it was all Xhea could do to keep from fleeing. Instead, she slipped around the corner and stood with her back against the brick wall, breathing hard. Her hands shook.

Councilwoman Nalani had let Xhea rise from her seat and escape with only the barest thanks for the meal; she'd made no move to follow. There had been nothing left to say—or, rather, too much, and no words with which to shape them.

Xhea felt drained. The day stretched before her, hour after hour of uncertainty and nowhere she'd feel safe. She peered around the corner and down the length of the street, and couldn't see anyone watching for her, or waiting. *Even so*, she thought wearily. She pulled out her scarf and covered her hair, then shrugged off her jacket and tucked it into a rough bundle beneath her arm.

Sweetness, she was tired of running.

She took a deep breath and slipped out into the street. "Come on," she said over her shoulder.

Shai made no move to follow, just stared at the restaurant window as if lost in the grip of some terrible dream. Xhea followed her gaze, but couldn't see past the pale curtains. Perhaps the Councilwoman was still there, looking blankly at the flat surface of her cooling tea, her crumbled breakfast uneaten on her plate; perhaps she stood there, looking down, seeking the daughter that stood seeking her.

"Shai?" Xhea's voice caught.

Remember what you promised, Councilwoman Nalani had said.

She's not coming, Xhea thought; and at that realization, it felt like something was breaking inside her—something new and fragile and of unspeakable worth, breaking in her chest, breaking with every moment that Shai stood silent and unmoving.

"You're thinking of staying, aren't you? Shai?" Staying, Xhea said; but what she meant was, *You're leaving me.* It hurt, that realization—and oh, she knew this wound, knew its shape as well as any scar written in flesh.

"No."

Xhea blinked, staring.

"I should stay." Shai's voice was flat. "I promised. I'm just not strong enough."

"But—"

"Be quiet. I don't want to hear it."

"I was just—"

"Don't. Say. Anything." The ghost glanced toward her, long hair veiling all but a glimpse of one furious, glistening eye. "Just . . . go. Go."

Xhea forced herself to walk away, head down and jacket clutched to her side. After a long moment Shai followed, a bright shadow in her wake.

Xhea stared up the long metal ladder, hands trembling, her full stomach souring by the minute.

"Why did I think this was a good idea?" she asked. Shai didn't reply.

Xhea grasped the ladder's sides; flakes of rust crumbled at her touch. Gathering her courage, she hauled herself up to get her feet on the bottom-most rung, nearly at shoulder height. She climbed with eyes closed, not daring to open them until it was time to scramble over the lip of the roof and collapse on the surface, panting.

The roof surface was flat and damp with old puddles, strewn with rocks and random litter, but safe—or seemingly so. Xhea had never run the roofs, never even wanted to try. When the one gang who had checked her out learned of her fear of heights, even that little interest dried up. Not, she thought, that Lower City buildings were exactly *high*. It just felt that way.

It was also the last place that anyone would think to look for her. So long as she kept herself disguised and out of the way of the rooftop traffic and commerce, she figured she could pass most of the day unnoticed.

Ignoring Shai, she crept to the edge and peered over, swallowing hard. Below, a group of children were playing a game that involved balls hung from long strings at the end of sticks, which one whirled and whacked into opponents at somewhat alarming speeds. Nearby, a large group of parents scrubbed clothes in the local fountain-turned-laundry-basin. No pursuers that she could see; no glimpse of the pale-haired man, Derren, either.

Xhea slumped back and ran her hands over her face. At last, Shai settled grudgingly to the rooftop beside her, more than an arm's span away. She could barely meet Xhea's eyes, all fury and loss and sorrow.

"So," Xhea said at last, the tension between them stretched to breaking. Even now she struggled for calm, holding back the anger—and the magic—that pressed just beneath the surface. "What your mother said. Were you planning on telling me any of that stuff? Or were you just going to let me fumble around like an idiot trying to figure it out until we were captured?"

"You act like this is about you." Shai glared at the roof's edge as if it were the source of her problems. "I was never supposed to talk to *anyone* about this 'stuff.' Most people think that Radiants just become reclusive later in life." Her laugh was bitter and edged. "You think being dead suddenly makes discussing this *easy*?"

"No—but it makes it necessary."

Shai shrugged.

"Fine," Xhea said. "Don't be sorry. But can you at least stop shutting me out? It's not helping, and it's blighted frustrating."

After a long moment, Shai nodded. Xhea figured it was the best she was going to get. She doubted Shai had been told off much in her short life; doubted, too, that she'd needed the correction. Shai had had a perfect, sheltered existence, with an unnatural burden and an early expiration date.

"What did you mean when you said they borrowed against you?"

"It's . . ." Shai shook her head. "Complicated. I'm not an economist, Xhea."

"Oh, and I am. Besides, you're a walking mint. Closest thing I'm going to get to an economist around here."

"Fair." Shai glanced up as if for inspiration. "Okay. So, Allenai is one of the most influential Towers in the City—close to the Central Spire, high altitude, everything. It takes a lot of magic to attain and then keep that kind of status and standard of living—yeah?"

Xhea nodded.

"I was the first Radiant born to an Allenai citizen in almost four decades. The Tower was . . . stretched. Working to capacity. Maybe the situation was even worse than I knew—my parents, the Council, didn't tell me much. As a child, I wasn't generating anywhere the kind of power that an adult Radiant would. My capacity was growing as I aged, but I still wasn't at my full potential. Not what the Tower required."

"So if you'd been kept alive, you would have generated even more magic in a few years."

"Yes. The Council would have assumed there would be excess magic when I was older, and so they must have loaned the magic from another Tower in the meantime."

"Just one?" Xhea scoffed. "Only a fool would borrow from only one source."

"One, ten, a hundred—I don't know. It's just business. In a few years, I would have generated enough to exceed the expenditures—there would have been enough to repay the loans without difficulty. Now that's impossible."

"And that's a problem because . . . ?"

"Because," Shai snapped, "without me, Allenai has no way to repay that debt. They gambled against my generating capacity and *lost*. They're going to have to pull funding from projects, take more magic from ordinary citizens—I don't know what else—all to pay back Eridian, and whoever else they borrowed from. And if Eridian managed to consolidate Allenai's debt and become the primary lender, they can take *everything*." At Xhea's silence, Shai turned to her, frustrated anger sharpening the lines of her face. "Don't you understand? It means the Tower's going to fall. Lose status, lose position, lose power—everything Allenai's managed to attain. Gone. Because of me."

"You didn't plan on getting sick," Xhea reasoned. "Or dying."

"No, but I knew it'd happen sometime. But instead of doing what I'd *sworn* to do for the good of my people—I ran. Sweetness save me, I ran." Her voice broke, and she looked away.

When she spoke again, it was but a whisper: "I'm still running."

Xhea sighed and peeked over the edge: by the laundry basin, the children gathered around a boy with his hand clutched to his eye, ball and stick forgotten. Each of the kids' hands glimmered with unspelled magic as they reached for the hurt boy, offering little flickers of power to soothe and comfort and heal. She turned away.

"If you're looking for someone to change your mind," Xhea said, "you've come to the wrong place. I think it's rot, all of it. To give your life, your death, everything—and for what? Politics? Power? Blighted *status*?" She shook her head. "I've spent my life desperate for the privilege you were born to. Once I would have said I'd give anything to achieve it, so when I say that it's not worth that kind of sacrifice, for you or for anyone, believe it.

"*It's not worth it*, Shai. Nothing is."

"You don't understand," Shai mumbled.

"No, I don't. Not even a little."

Xhea tilted her head to look at the gray of the cloud-dotted sky and the rounded shapes of the Towers' underbellies dominating the expanse. From directly below, the graceful structures seemed flatter, their defensive spires all but invisible against their bulk. Yet something of their magnificence remained: they glimmered in the sunlight, all shades of silvery-gray that Xhea knew to be violet and amber, red and gold and green.

"Look up. Look at them."

Grudgingly, Shai complied. "I've seen the City before."

"Just watch."

For a long moment the only movement was the flicker of elevators and aircars, the shimmering haze of spell exhaust. Then in the space directly above them, a wide Tower rose as if it were a sail that had caught the wind. A moment later, a needle-slender Tower eased to the side and sank with the grace of a dancer taking her final bow. Brief stillness, and then again: a Tower rising, turning, tilting; another falling, shifting; until soon it seemed that not a moment passed when the City above did not change, Towers moving as if they were the blood and breath of some great beast stretched out across the sky—heart beating, chest expanding and falling, closed eyes shifting in slumber. Alive.

Xhea said, "Maybe up close you don't notice it, but Towers are always falling, always rising. Fortunes made and lost, goals achieved, lives ruined. Little shifts of magic and status, horizon to horizon.

"But look," she said, and swept her arm as if to encompass everything that surrounded them: the crumbling rooftops, peaks and flats and every one leaking; the cluster of people around the old concrete fountain below; the dark and soapy sludge in the gutters. The smell and noise, both so constant that they faded from notice. "You're in the Lower City now, and here the Towers are far beyond our grasp."

"Yes," Shai said after a moment of sullen thought. "But we're not beyond theirs."

Xhea looked away first. "True enough."

Crouched behind the decorative roof edge of an abandoned building, Xhea shifted to peer down at her latest stalker. No matter how many times she glanced over, the drop still stole her breath.

"What's he waiting for?" she muttered. A few more minutes and the sun would be down.

"You," Shai replied from the shadows.

Xhea had chosen a more distant tunnel entrance, with a route into the underground complex through an ancient hotel lobby and down a narrow, unmarked escalator. But it was not this that made it her target, but the fact that it already had two spells glimmering outside the hotel's doors, making it an unlikely location for further surveillance. Yet she had returned to find a man crouched by the doors. She'd thought he'd leave long before dusk and had been proven frighteningly wrong.

From the corner of her eye, she saw Shai shrug—an action that had become familiar over the long afternoon. Xhea's attempts to distract her had failed; and even her clumsy control of her dark magic, which flared and fluctuated with her own increasingly poor mood, didn't earn Xhea more than a glance.

Ignoring the ghost, Xhea had spent the afternoon curled behind a chimney, hidden, uncomfortable, and lost in thought. No matter how she'd turned their problems over in her mind, it was clear she was out of her depth. She could run, and she could hide—but for how much longer? Sooner or later, she would slip up. A trap would catch her, or one of the hunters, or a run of bad luck would leave her with no food or water or options beyond turning herself in. In the end, none of it would help Shai.

Though it had galled her to admit it, she needed help. The time had come to call in her favor from Edren.

Yet there was no way easy way for her to reach the skyscraper. The streets were watched, and though running the roofs was supposed to be a quick way to travel through the Lower City, Xhea couldn't even stomach the thought of traversing the rickety bridges and knotted ropes strung between buildings as so many others did with ease. Her only hope, she'd decided, was to return to the tunnels and try to find a way past Edren's basement barricade. After all, it had been years since the last battle between skyscrapers—surely they'd relaxed their security.

After that, sunset couldn't come fast enough.

Yet for all her hours spent wishing the sun from the sky, as twilight fell she wished she could stay its course. Surely the man would leave soon; neither of them wanted to be out when darkness came. Xhea shifted, boots grinding against the crumbled brick that scattered the rooftop, and resisted the urge to stretch her legs. *Just a moment more*, she told herself. The lengthening shadows mocked her words.

"What's he doing?" Xhea whispered, watching the man and trying to see what his hunched body shielded. "It's almost like . . ." A glittering light rose from the man's hands to hang in midair, and Xhea swore vehemently enough that Shai looked up.

"Weaving spells," she spat. "This entire time, he was just weaving more spells."

Three now guarded her supposedly safe entrance. The original two followed the pattern that she'd come to know so well, tentacles and all. The new spell was a softly glowing sphere, set some distance apart.

His work finished, the man—City man, spell-weaver, enemy-at-large—rose, dusted his pants, and set off down the street.

Xhea waited a moment before lifting her head above the roof edge. Caution told her to wait long enough for him to round the corner, or catch an elevator—but there was no time.

"Sweetness save me." Xhea gestured to Shai and crept to the rusted fire escape. She made her clumsy way down, her eyes only open enough to let her see her next handhold. Back on real ground, she hurried across the street, and ducked under the faint tendrils of one of the old entrapment spells. The new spell was more difficult to avoid, but not impossible; by pressing herself to the hotel's brick wall and inching along, she made it up to the doors without coming within an arm's span of the hovering sphere. Though locked, the doors' once-shatterproof glass had long since been pounded to powder; faint remnants glittered underfoot.

Shai spoke as Xhea crouched to duck inside. "This one . . . I think it's keyed to me."

Xhea turned back to find the ghost peering warily at the sphere. "How can you tell?"

"This section." Shai pointed at spell lines at the thing's core. "That's my signature. Or . . . almost."

"That's rather more efficient," Xhea replied cautiously. After all, no one really wanted Xhea, only the ghost in her possession. If they had found a way to capture Shai herself, a spell that trapped not flesh but spirit . . .

Turning, Xhea caught sight of the warning placed beneath the original entrapment spell closest to the door. Not an X of stones this time, but an object: an ancient solar-powered calculator, its screen still intact. Her breath caught. Carefully, she crept toward it and knelt, hesitant to touch it.

"I sold this to Wen," she whispered. "To Brend. He wouldn't . . ."

Even without his father's skill for the antique trade, Brend wouldn't have lost an object of such value, wouldn't have discarded it. Had he sold it? She thought again of the disarray she'd found in the warehouse, precious artifacts smashed and the daylight spell flickering, and wondered for the first time whether Brend was all right.

Distracted by the thought, Xhea stood. There was a flash as the entrapment spell activated. She gasped, twisted, and tried to turn away—all too late. The spell's light was the last thing she saw as a tendril fell across her face and caught fast.

Xhea barely stifled her scream. The magic burned, then froze, the sensations fierce along her cheekbone and across her left eye. She staggered back and tried to pull away, but the tendril held her effortlessly. Her struggles only allowed other tendrils to catch her hands and arms, and grasp at her sides. Every tendril burned, even through her clothing and hair—the pain from the magic so sharp she felt dizzy with it, disoriented. She wondered if she was going to pass out.

Each tendril found its hold—and began to rise. Xhea screamed then, unable to quell her panic as her boots left the ground. With her single unaffected eye, she caught sight of Shai's horrified expression. The ghost reached for her, shouting something that Xhea couldn't understand over the ringing in her ears.

"Make it let go!" Xhea cried. She reached for Shai's hand as if that ghostly flesh could keep her earthbound. Tears, hot and furious, leaked from Xhea's eyes—and as the tears slipped down her cheeks, she felt the tendril's grip on her face ease. She saw a wisp of something dark pass in front of her unbound eye, soft and sinuous as smoke.

The thought came, falling in perfect time to the words shaped by Shai's lips: *Magic. Dark magic.*

The thought was a call, a need, and it came, a rush of black power. As if it were air, she cried with the force of it, screaming as it left her lips; as if it were sweat and tears, it poured from her, a liquid antidote to the pain's fire. Around her, the tendrils' light flickered and seemed almost to flinch, their edges darkening as they curled in upon themselves. Face, arms, legs, torso—their tightly woven grip loosened, and Xhea fell to the ground.

She landed hard on her right knee and tumbled into a boneless heap, the air forced from her lungs on impact. Her scream was no more than a choked cry; she could only grasp weakly at her knee with trembling hands as she struggled to inhale.

It was a long moment before she could breathe, and air did little to dissipate the pain. She grit her teeth, trying not to whimper, and rolled over. The last of the spell hovered between her and the Towers' growing light, flailing and twisting in on itself as it died. She took a long, slow breath, and another.

"Magic," Xhea mumbled, road grit clinging to her swelling, bloodied lip. "Keep forgetting about that."

A paler light, Shai sank until she knelt at Xhea's side. Xhea welcomed the chill of the ghost's touch as Shai tried helplessly to check for breaks, or slow the sluggish bleeding of the cuts on Xhea's cheek and palms. There was no sign of Shai's introverted guilt and hurt, or the closed expression that had become so familiar over the course of the afternoon.

A moment of hesitation, then the ghost offered softly, "That looked like it hurt."

Xhea laughed, cringing as the movement hurt her ribs, but managed her reply. "A good observation."

Shai smiled.

"Come on." Xhea slowly got to her feet. Her knee hurt—oh, how it hurt—but it would hold her weight, if barely. She covered her aching, dazzled eye with her palm, and limped to the doors. "The night's not getting any younger."

Chapter Sixteen

Xhea made her slow way into the tunnels. Even half-blind from the entrapment spell and stumbling from the pain in her swelling knee, she tried to hurry. Though she doubted her pursuers could investigate at night, having triggered a spell would help narrow their search. Her only escape was to go deeper than anyone could follow, and in this end of town her only choice was the Red Line tunnel. She followed the rails downhill.

All too quickly the spring-like warmth gave way to a damp, aching cold that settled into her bruised limbs. A nearby storage cache yielded an emergency blanket and a few bland ration sticks; she wrapped herself in the former and chewed mechanically on the latter as she descended. The scrape of her boots against the gravel rail bed echoed the length of the tunnel.

Only when she could hear the lap of water against the concrete walls did she stop. The only thing farther down the tunnel was the collapse, the fallen tunnel walls and the floodwaters that had brought them down, ringed now by years of heavy mud and sediment. Safe enough for one night, she supposed. There was a service room nearby filled with scrap metal where she'd planned to sleep, but now she didn't think her injuries would make the shelter worth the pain of entrance. Though the smell of rot and mildew was choking, Xhea lowered herself to the ground by the tracks and leaned back against the cold wall.

Wrapped in the crinkling blanket, she pressed her hands to the sides of her knee and hissed in pain.

"It's not supposed to do that," Shai said. "An entrapment spell, I mean. It's not meant to be painful."

"Guess I'm just lucky. Lucky, lucky me." Xhea raised her pant leg to look at her knee, blinking and squinting to see past the dazzled after-images still painted across her vision. Already the flesh was mottled dark with spider-like tracings of broken blood vessels patterning the kneecap.

"That'll be a good one," she said, her voice loud in the tunnel's silence. "You'll have to tell me what colors it turns. Purple, for sure."

"I'm sorry," Shai said, seemingly transfixed by the dawning bruise.

Xhea shrugged. "Wasn't your fault."

"If I wasn't here—"

"Then I'd be here all alone, and what's the good in that?" Xhea sighed at the ghost's expression. "Look, Shai, I don't like this any more than you do. But I can take a little pain—especially if it means that we may get out of this eventually."

Xhea shifted, trying to settle down, and winced at the movement. *Of all nights,* she thought, *I could have chosen a better one to sleep on gravel.*

"Regardless, we should be safe for now."

"I'll keep watch." Shai rested against the tunnel's opposite wall, her soft glow the only light. Xhea should have needed neither glow nor reassurance, yet at the ghost's words something inside her relaxed nonetheless. It didn't ease the pain or soften the gravel beneath her—but it was enough to let her sleep.

Xhea wasn't sure what woke her first: Shai's hand against her shoulder, or the sound that echoed softly from the tunnel's concrete walls. She froze, her wide eyes the only sign of awareness.

For the space of a few long breaths, there was only silence. Only water dripping from the tunnel roof—only something shifting, crumbling, in the old infrastructure. Just as she was about to move, she heard it again: a splash, followed by the slow sloshing sound of a person walking through water. Someone was approaching—not from the Lower City, but from the tunnel's broken end.

Xhea turned toward the noise, resting her cheek against gravel as she stared into the black. Afterimages still clouded her vision. She could just make out the empty light fixtures along the ceiling like a row of gaping mouths and the dark, dull gray of the old subway tracks. Farther, she caught a flicker of Shai's light reflecting across the water as a small wave broke, thick with mud and oil. Cursing the tendril that had fallen across her face, Xhea covered her injured eye. Only then could she see it: a hunched figure, black against the darkness, head down as it crept forward.

Fear coiled through her, cold and hard.

"We have to go," Xhea said almost inaudibly and no less urgent for her caution. Shai nodded, staring down the tunnel with one hand pressed to her lips.

Xhea pushed herself to sitting, wincing at the pain in her knee and hip and shoulder. Instinct hammered her, shouting *go, go, go* in surges of adrenaline and that fierce, bitter fear.

Just as strong was the need for silence. It wasn't the gravel that gave her pause, but the emergency blanket that she'd so carefully wrapped around herself for warmth. And oh, it was warm— she lay sweating beneath it—and near impossible to move with anything resembling quiet.

Just like opening a ration bar, she thought, and peeled back the silver foil blanket in a single sweep. The sound was like a shout in the quiet tunnel. She caught her breath, waiting—then the figure in the water splashed forward. Another step, and another, in her direction.

Xhea kicked her feet free of the blanket's trailing end, heedless of the tear she caused. She could salvage it later—if she had a later. Because as the figure came closer, she knew she'd seen this man before. A dirty sweatshirt hung loose around his distended belly and thin, bony legs, the shirt's tattered hem trailing through the water. His white hair was wild about his face, matted clumps standing in clear disregard of gravity's dictates.

She didn't spare him more than a glance as he sloshed through the water toward them—didn't dare take the time. Knew, too, that if she could better focus her aching eyes, she'd see his unblinking stare fixed on her face, as it had been in the street outside her old apartment in the ruins.

Had she thought she would be safe here, at the edge of where the city that had come before succumbed to time and decay? She knew the hole caused by the Red Line's collapse as she knew her own self; felt the echoes of its fall in sleep and dream. Had it seemed safe, sheltering in the deep where the tunnel gaped wide, an empty space open to the distant night sky? She'd been a fool.

Safe, yes, from City folks, true and Lower alike; normal people in whom magic flowed as certainly as blood. But the things, the *creatures* that walked the ruins' midnight streets were not people, no matter who or what they might have once been. The walkers didn't come into the tunnels normally—too complicated a shelter to reach, with nothing they wanted hiding in the depths. And yet she'd stationed herself and Shai close to a hole that the walkers could climb through, knowing that the radiance of the ghost's magic or her own drew them like flies to spilled sugar.

"Go, go, go." The words fell from her lips in thoughtless time to her heart's hammering. She pushed herself up, heedless of her skinned hands and bruised shoulder—only to cry out as she tried to stand. Her knee wouldn't hold. The pain she'd ignored now redoubled, the joint aggravated by walking and stiffened from hours on the hard ground.

Again she tried and fell back as her knee buckled beneath her with a searing pain. She touched it: swollen to nearly double its size and hot even through the thick fabric of her pants.

Beside her, Shai held out a hand in useless gesture. "Come on." Xhea tried only to hear the encouragement in Shai's voice, not the growing panic. "Come on, try again."

The pain only worsened with each attempt. At last Xhea grit her teeth and scrambled across the gravel on her hands and single knee, dragging her leg behind her—and crying out as the movement jarred her knee, again and again. Behind her, the walker's footsteps came faster as it reached shallower water, drawing nearer more quickly than she could crawl.

Just get to the service room, she thought. The door was warped in its frame, but surely she could jam it closed until the walker was chased away by dawn.

As the splashing grew louder, Shai starcd over Xhea's head, transfixed by the sight of the approaching walker. Xhea dared not turn, fighting panic. How far was she from the service room? Another fifty feet down the line, at least, just before the last branch in the tunnel. She whimpered as a rock ground into her good kneecap, and forced herself to crawl faster, knowing it wouldn't be fast enough.

The thing had come to eat her, and how kind of her to tenderize herself with a good gravel pounding. *Lovely loose joints*, she thought darkly, horribly. *Freshly bruised and delicious.*

"Xhea," Shai whispered, her voice gone faint.

"I know," she managed. "I'm trying."

"There's another one."

A second set of splashing footsteps had joined the first—and these sounded as if they were made by something larger. Like the first, this thing didn't run, but walked, steadily drawing nearer.

She had to stand, she realized, regardless of the pain. Xhea scrambled across the tunnel to where pipes and electrical wires ran along the wall. Untouched since the Fall, the wires were thick with grime and dust, their plastic casing crumbling at her touch. Heedless of her bloodied palms, she grabbed hold of the wires and pulled until she managed to get her good leg beneath her. *Hopping is faster than crawling*, she thought. But she did one better: grabbing on to the wall, she forced herself into something like a stumbling, limping run.

Until she heard the sound of gravel crunching from the dark tunnel before her. Xhea clutched a rusted pipe for balance, and tried to keep moving.

"Shai—there's someone ahead. Can you—"

"I'll check." The ghost hurried into the darkness. As Shai rounded the corner, the glow of her pale luminance vanished, and Xhea struggled to see. From her good eye she saw the gray shapes of gravel and rail lines, distance markers painted on the wall. Her magic-dazzled eye showed only black.

A moment later, Shai's voice echoed back: "It's another one!" Before Xhea could reply, the ghost added, "More than one."

"Before the service room?"

"Yes." A single, hopeless word.

At that Xhea stopped, still clinging to the wires for support, and turned to face the two figures that approached from the tunnel's flooded end. Though both now walked dripping across dry gravel, she still heard splashing footsteps: there were more of them in the darkness.

Of course, Xhea thought. *Of course.* She sagged against the crumbling tunnel wall.

"Be careful." Xhea's voice was thin against the sound of countless feet walking, none of them hers. "Remember, they can see you." Somehow. The only other living things who could see ghosts as she could were blank-eyed, starving mockeries of people, less human than the ghosts themselves.

"Wait," Shai said. "He's . . ." Her voice trailed away.

Xhea stared at the approaching walkers. Two she recognized from the streets above: the old man in his fraying sweatshirt and the young woman lost in her oversized clothes. The others were unfamiliar—but their eyes, their fixed and staring eyes, watched her as if nothing else existed in the world.

Xhea drew her knife, long practice allowing her to open the blade with a single hand. The short blade would be all but useless, but it was better than facing them empty-handed. Except these were not normal people, their flesh as devoid of bright magic as that of corpses; perhaps the blade—and her magic, imbued into the silver through years resting in a pocket by her heart—might work against these things as it did against ghosts.

Or perhaps raw magic would be her only defense. Could her magic kill? Shai had died at her touch, though perhaps that had only been from the destruction of the bright spells that kept her alive so long. Weapon or not, Xhea wanted the strength the magic brought her, its calm. She ignored the breathing exercises she'd practiced; control was not what she needed now, at least not the clumsy control that was the only thing she could bring to bear. No, she needed energy, raw force. There was no anger to fuel it now; that was gone, burned from her so fully that she couldn't even stir its ashes. Only fear was left, cold and hard, smelling like sweat and tasting like bile, and it was enough. It had to be enough.

Had magic already been seeping from her, blood and sweat and tears? It must have been, for it responded to her call with ease, calming her heart and the rush of her breath. The bruise-like pain from the entrapment spell eased, and she blinked as her vision returned. Wires in one hand, knife in the other, Xhea pushed away from the wall and let her good leg take her weight. The magic curled around her hands and the sheen of the darkened blade, rising from her lips to wreath her head with every breath. *Steady now*, she thought.

Still the walkers approached, steps neither hurried nor slowed, merely constant, relentless, as if each walked in time to an unheard metronome. The closest ones dripped, their sodden clothes streaming muddy water, their bare skin smeared with things she could smell but not identify.

Xhea shook her head and the charms in her hair chimed and clattered in the tunnel's unnatural quiet. "Don't come any closer," she said.

If they understood her, they gave no sign, only walked until they were within a few easy paces of her. Then they shifted until they stood shoulder-to-shoulder around her, blocking the tunnel in an uneven arc.

The light brightened as Shai returned. The walkers swiveled toward Shai as one, and their pupils contracted at the ghost's radiance. Xhea expected to see Shai hurrying toward her but saw only the ghost's back: step by careful step in midair, Shai stumbled backward, her eyes never leaving the figures that approached from the tunnel's opposite end.

"No," Shai whispered. She stepped back and back again, her voice anguished. "No, no, no . . ." A litany of useless denial.

"Shai." Xhea looked from one blank face to the next. Dark magic poured from her now, falling from her in a slow cascade and spreading in an ever-widening pool about her feet. "I don't know if they can touch you, but if they can't . . . you should run."

"No," the ghost said. "No, no . . ." The words were a continuation, not a response, as if Xhea hadn't spoken.

She tried again, eyeing the human-shaped creatures that stared back with unblinking eyes. "There are too many, Shai. I can't stop them. You don't . . . you don't want to see what they're going to do." She rather wished she could skip that part herself. She swallowed, choking back something that felt like a whimper.

"Please," Xhea managed. "Please, Shai, just get out of here while you can."

Oh, so noble, she mocked herself silently, and just as silently told that part of herself to shut up and die.

Shai turned to her, crying. Each teardrop shone as it traced a path down her cheek and fell glittering to the rocks below. She ran the last few steps that separated them and, heedless of Xhea's magic and knife, grabbed her arm. Xhea cringed at the touch, thinking of what her magic might do to the ghost—yet Shai seemed not to notice, her eyes intent on Xhea's face as she tried speak through her panicked gasping: "It's—it's—my da—"

It took a moment for Xhea to grasp Shai's meaning. She looked toward the walkers that had followed Shai down the tunnel and now joined their brethren in the large, uneven half-circle, effectively blocking all escape. Even without Shai's cry, she would have seen him: the middle-aged paunch, the faint thinning of the hairline, that face that she'd never seen looking unwearied. He was cleaner than those around him—his clothes sodden and dirtied, yes, but clearly new to such treatment. It was Shai's father.

Or, rather, what was left of him. Whatever Xhea might have said to him, this City man who had begged her to kill his daughter, died in her mouth unspoken; for his eyes were blank as stones and fixed unblinkingly on hers.

"Oh, sweetness and blight," she said, and yearned stupidly, desperately, for a cigarette.

She banished the thought as the gaunt old man in his dripping sweatshirt stepped forward, blocking her view of Shai's father. He walked slowly, no hesitance in the movement, no caution. Only mindless determination.

"Stay back," Xhea said. She turned the knife to let Shai's light flash from the blade in vain hope that a sharp edge would give the thing pause. *Oh, please stay back*, she begged in silence, the thought so desperate as to be a prayer to absent gods.

It was not only fear of stabbing the man that made her reluctant to strike. For if Shai's father was among their number, the walkers could not simply be things, twisted human remains dredged up and out of the ruins. They, like him, might have once been people—real people, with lives and loves and the glitter of magic flowing through them.

There were so very many. She tried to count, eyes darting from one to the next: was it six from the flooded end—or seven? Five from the tunnel's other end. Her hand trembled. How could she kill so many? How could she even kill one?

Would that she saw light in the old man's eyes, or purpose, or understanding. He reached for her, curled fingers grasping, as Xhea cringed back against the wall. "Stay back," she said again, "I'm warning you." No theatrics now, no threats of movement— only the feel of the knife handle, slippery with her sweat, as she tightened her grip.

His hands closed around her shoulders, his skinny fingers as strong as rusted vice grips and as hard to pry away. He squeezed and did not stop, fingers digging into the already bruised joints single-mindedly, his hold pinning her upper arms to her sides. Xhea cried out in fear and pain and for courage as she struggled to raise the knife. She stabbed him in the only place she could reach: the muscle of his upper arm.

She felt the blade tear through the sodden fabric of his sweatshirt and the resistance as it parted flesh and muscle until it scraped against bone. She twisted the blade and blood flowed, trickling over the handle and her hand, and dribbling to the gravel below. He did not waver, did not so much as flinch, only held her, those iron-hard fingers of withered flesh and bone digging into her shoulders until she gasped.

So close, Xhea could see his storm-dark eyes, the whites veined and bloody. He breathed across her face, and she smelled only dryness, as if his insides were filled with salt and sand, desiccated flesh and ashy paper.

Beside her, Shai grabbed at the walker, clawing at his eyes and the sagging flesh of his throat. He flinched from her touch, but little more; Shai's ghostly hands passed through him unhindered. She cried out in frustration as he held Xhea ever tighter.

"Xhea!" Shai cried, and fought harder.

There was no fighting him, Xhea knew, though she writhed and bit at his hands all the same. Even when she kicked him, even when the nails of her free hand ripped open the skin of his cheek, he did not falter. Would not falter. She stabbed him again, wherever his crushing grip allowed her arm to move: his shoulder, his forearm, even a nick that opened the flesh along his bony ribs through a hole in his shirt, to no effect.

Still he stared as he pulled her toward him as if closeness was the only message he had, eyes tainted with neither sorrow nor pain, hope nor denial—yet neither were they blank. There was no person inside this flesh, Xhea saw; he was—if such a thing existed—the opposite of a ghost, flesh without inhabitant, life without memory or magic. But not, she thought, without purpose.

What did he want? She could barely imagine: life again? Magic? The power of thought or speech or recollection? Whatever he wanted, how could she possibly grant it?

For a moment the old man's lips parted, and the flesh between his brows creased with more than age. His fingers curled tighter—not, she thought, to cause pain, though she wept from it nonetheless, but as if he wished to press understanding into her flesh even if he had to tear holes in her to do so. There was something, *something*—but, a blank page of a man, he seemed not to know it himself, only trembled with its echoes.

If only she could comprehend the fractured remnants of the thought that seemed lost inside his head—some way to understand the driving need that she saw in him, this living ruin, before he killed her. Because he would, she knew; she felt it with a certainty as intense as the pain of his hands on her shoulders. Her struggles only brought that death closer as his grip tightened and the intensity of his need deepened.

"What do you want?" she cried, the sound low and hoarse with fear and pain and something that felt almost like terrible sympathy. With her words, the dark smoke of her magic slipped from between her lips to drift into the space between them. It hung there, curling in the currents of their movement, before he inhaled and breathed deeply of its darkness.

Briefly, the pressure of his grip loosened. For but a moment his face seemed to ease, weathered lines softening. He was not so old, Xhea saw; only hurting and starved and stripped of everything he had once been.

There was no fighting him, Xhea thought again, because he was not there to fight. He bore no message but death—his or hers, and each was its own kind of understanding. And death? Death she did not fear. She had stared into its face, into its echoes and memory, for as long as she could recall. It was only dying—the pain and suffering—that made her afraid.

She exhaled again, mouth pursed as if to blow a kiss, until dark coils of magic swam before her like a veil. She wept from the pain of his grip, and the magic flowed with her tears; it seeped darkly from the small wounds on her arms where his ragged nails had dug through fabric into flesh.

She watched the magic enter him, and he shuddered at the touch. *Oh,* she thought, *how did I ever think of this power as anything but death?*

Xhea stopped fighting and pulled him closer. Knife forgotten in the flesh of his arm, she gripped his shoulders in both hands and pulled, drawing them together like strange and stilted dancers. She breathed his breath of ash and paper, as he breathed deeply of hers, and he shuddered from the touch of it, from the taste. Sweet and bitter, rainwater and apples, a scent like the beginnings of decay and the promise of rain on the horizon.

She released the magic and it flowed through her like blood, pulsing down her arms, slipping through her fingers, and into his body. His grip on her shoulders eased.

She was afraid—oh, she was so afraid—and yet she wasn't, as if her magic and this slow death were enough to take her to a place beyond fear and hurting, a trance where nothing else existed but the two of them. She watched the darkness sink into him; watched his shoulders go slack, his fingers loosening and falling away; watched his breathing slow.

Watched herself kill him, and felt as if it were right.

He sagged into her arms. For all his strength, the wiry hardness of his limbs and the knife-sharp edges of his face, he was so light. She might have held him if not for her injuries. Instead they fell together, a slow collapse of hurting limbs tumbling to the tunnel's gravel bed, and landed with his face somehow still held in the cradle of her arms, staring upward.

So light, she thought again, eyes tracing the dirtied mats of his hair, the sweaty hollow of his throat. As if he were not flesh and blood but dried leaves and emptiness. Even his relentless determination was fading, his intensity dimming with his life, and though no true awareness came into his face, she saw something in him like an abandoned child's weakness. Something that looked almost like loss.

"It's okay," she whispered, holding him to her. He calmed at the sound of her voice, though she doubted he understood. *No spirit anymore*, she thought. No ghost bound in this flesh to be released at her hand; no magic to flicker and fade. They had been taken from him already, leaving only this dying, crumbling shell.

Yet at the last that shell of a man opened his mouth, cracked lips bleeding as they struggled to shape his faltering breath. He made a noise that almost sounded like "I . . . I . . ." though whether he meant to speak in truth or was merely caught in his body's dying memory, she did not know. Would never know. For his eyelids flickered and fell, and his weak and struggling mouth became still. His body was suddenly a slack weight in her arms and across her lap.

For a long moment Xhea did not move, her eyes half-lidded, lost in the final moments of her trance. Then she took a long, shuddering breath and the world crashed back upon her, pain in her shoulders and legs and knee, and a cold and creeping shiver that she could only take to be the after-effects of adrenaline—or the beginnings of shock. She looked up, and gasped.

Shai stood above, quietly radiant and hovering a full foot from the ground, staring with a look that Xhea could not read. Behind the ghost, all the other mindless creatures, broken shells and murderous husks of people, stood in their ragged half-circle, watching with mindless intent. They had watched everything, she realized. Could they even understand the death of one of their kind? Would such a thing even matter? The corpse pinned her legs to the ground, and light though he was Xhea could not easily push the body aside.

She had killed a night walker, yes, and with a gentleness she'd never imagined; yet it had left her adrift. The magic still moved through her, slow and contented, but she did not know if she had the strength to take on a second, never mind a tenth or eleventh.

There was no need. She saw no signal, no word or nod, but the creatures turned as one and began to walk away. Their movements slow and steady, they walked in a ragged line toward the flooded end of the tunnel and the gaping hole beyond.

Shai watched her father go with them, her face a study in despair. She raised a hand toward the shell that had once held the person she'd loved, but only that; and even that movement she quickly hid, curling her hand into a fist and turning away. Within moments they had gone beyond reach of Shai's soft glow; a moment more and not even Xhea's keen eyes could pick their shapes from the darkness. She listened as their splashing steps receded, becoming faint echoes and then only memory.

Mission accomplished, Xhea thought in a haze of confusion and pain. *Message delivered.* She looked down at the body in her arms, thinking of death and consequences. After a moment, she drew her blade from the old man's shoulder and wiped away the worst of the blood. Then slowly, gingerly, she rolled his body from her lap.

"Why?" Shai whispered into the silence.

There was too much to say; Xhea only shook her head.

Chapter Seventeen

Confused and hurting, Xhea woke sometime in the indeterminable dark from dreams that she couldn't—didn't want to—remember. She clenched her jaw to keep from whimpering. *Just a dream*, she thought, pushing away the image of her vomiting magic the same inky-dark as spilled blood.

Just a dream.

She saw a faint glow through her eyelids, and sagged against the concrete floor, taking a long, shuddering breath to slow her heartbeat. For all her years living underground, there was comfort in waking to that glimmer of light. Knowing that, even here, hurt and battered and down at the depth of all things, she was not alone.

"Morning," Xhea managed. She brushed away the crust of tears cried in sleep. "Is it morning? Do you know?" Her inner clock, usually infallible, was confused by the rough night. But

Shai, seeming to perch on piled rubble on the other side of the closet-sized room, only stared at her hands.

After rolling the old man's body aside, Xhea had wanted nothing more than to collapse and sleep, but had managed to drag herself the rest of the way to the service room. The room was in poor repair and overflowing with scrap metal, but she had forced the twisted door nearly closed and cleared a small patch for herself on the floor—heroic efforts both. A very subdued Shai had promised to watch over her.

Now Xhea sat up, stifling a groan. If it wasn't morning already, it would be by the time she managed to drag her aching self to anywhere near ground level. Everything hurt—*everything*—and she'd have allowed herself more sleep had not her empty stomach and full bladder joined in the aching.

"At least I wasn't eaten," she muttered. Always an upside.

It wasn't until she managed to stand—a slow process involving much swearing and the generous assistance of both the wall and a stack of spooled wire—that Xhea truly looked at Shai.

"Shai," she began, and faltered. For what could she ask? What's wrong? What *wasn't* wrong? And yet what, in the space of mere hours, could have so changed the ghost? *No*, she thought: what had taken her friend from her?

Shai's dark shirt with its embroidered vine patterns at neck and wrist was gone; so too were the pants that Xhea had so envied. In their place, the ghost wore a dress that was all too familiar: an expensive swirl of glimmering gray fabric that Xhea knew to be the color of a fresh plum. It cascaded over Shai's slim body, hanging loosely over legs that were tucked beneath her. She wasn't sitting on the heavy spools of wire, as Xhea had assumed, but rather floating before them in midair.

Shai looked up, and her eyes . . .

Could she call them dead, the eyes that now met her own? Yet Shai was as dead as she had been in all the days past, and never had Xhea seen the ghost look so empty or so hollow.

So hopeless.

Xhea had almost forgotten her, this girl—a ghost she had thought so helpless as to be worth her time only if she were paid for it. Yet that girl stared back from the now-familiar planes of her friend's face, and her hands, soft and untried, lay palm up as if in supplication.

"Shai," Xhea said again, in shock, in plea, and knew she had no words to follow.

"I don't want you to die," the ghost whispered at last. "Not you too."

"I'm not going to die."

Shai continued as if Xhea hadn't spoken. "The longer I'm here, the worse it's going to get. Your evading capture this long has just been an inconvenience."

"I'm good at being inconvenient."

"Look at what they did to him, Xhea. My father. Because he tried to help me."

Xhea thought of that slack face, those unseeing eyes, the monotonous rhythm of his breath and steps—then shook her head to force the image away. She did not know what had been done to him, or how, or why.

Shai continued in that quiet, helpless voice. "It's my fault, Xhea. He's dead because of me—worse than dead—and it's all my fault."

"Even if you leave now . . ." Xhea said, the words halting. Because that's what lay between them, unspoken to this moment: Shai's leaving. Already Xhea could feel Shai's coming absence as if it were a physical thing, a force that pressed on her chest. She forced herself to continue: "Even if you leave now, they won't stop coming for me. They know about me now—they know what I can do. You think that abandoning me is going to change that?"

"You won't be their priority. You know how to run—how to defend yourself. You can find ways to stay safe. But the longer I evade them, the more people I endanger—if not you, then my mother, or, or . . . anyone else. No one should suffer because of me."

"You're *dead*. Allenai should let you go in peace, not bind you to some other body for years just to make money."

"I have a responsibility," Shai replied quietly, hopelessly, and gestured to her dress as if its mere presence was the only explanation needed. What had Wen said about it? That it was something one would wear to a last binding. A ceremony, she guessed. But why promise to give yourself to a Tower when they would take what they wanted, willing or no?

"I have a responsibility, and all this has happened because I ignored it. How many people have to die, Xhea, before I admit that I can't ever escape? I can't think of anything else I can do. This is the only way I know how to make it stop." Shai looked up, then shook her head and turned away again. "I don't expect you to understand."

"What's there to understand? Responsibility? You're just afraid." Xhea heard the vicious edge come into her voice, and felt helpless to stop it. "You're giving in. For the first time you're finding out that the decisions you make *matter*, and it scares you. So you're just giving up—giving *in*, as if none of it ever mattered—as if nothing we did mattered at all. You're making your father's sacrifice worthless. You're just going to go home and let them use you like they always have."

Shai just shook her head, not meeting Xhea's eyes. "Yes, I am afraid. But this is the only choice left to me. I'm sorry. I'm so, so sorry."

The finality in her voice hit Xhea like a rock to the gut. "Shai, I—"

"Goodbye, Xhea. I'm glad I met you." Shai rose and turned away. She moved toward the service room door with steps that slid across air, her pale hair shining.

"Shai, *no*—"

Then she was through the door's surface and gone. The tiny room with its tangles of metal scrap and debris, its single gaping girl, was plunged into perfect darkness.

"No," Xhea whispered. "No, no, *no*—"

She struggled to keep her balance, rushing to the door, metal scraps catching on her pant legs and slicing at her hands as she reached out for balance. She adjusted quickly to the darkness, seeing in a way that had nothing to do with her eyes. The twisted door had taken many long minutes to coax closed, bit by careful bit toward its frame; yet now she grasped its edge with both aching hands and pulled it open in a series of hard, fast jerks, the corroded hinges squealing. She struggled out the gap, hopped forward on her good leg, and all but fell down the steps to track level.

At last she stood, clutching the remains of the metal railing, and searched the long stretch of tunnel around her. To her right, toward the flooded end, the faintest wash of gray was just visible beyond the tunnel's curve—but it was pale enough to be the first hint of daylight from the hole from the collapse, not the glow of a Radiant ghost's magic.

To her left there was only darkness, the rails' sweeping arc, and rough gravel underfoot. No flicker of light; no final words echoing back to disturb the silence. Xhea stared at that emptiness. The long, slow climb to the surface stretched before her, and every part of her felt bruised and battered, scabbed wounds torn open and bleeding—not least of all her heart.

"Please," she begged. "Please don't leave me."

But she was alone.

Part Three

Chapter Eighteen

If she could have, Xhea would have run after Shai, would have checked every room and passage in the underground complex in the hope she could stop the ghost and make her change her mind. But she could not run—wouldn't for months, if she understood the fiery pain that ripped through her right knee with every limping step—and the swelling made bending the joint all but impossible.

"I'd be easy to catch now," she said between panting breaths. "Too bad there's no one down here to find me."

She'd always talked to herself; the sound of her own voice had been a comfort in many dark places. Yet now she heard only her voice's echoes, not filling the tunnel's cavernous space but emphasizing it, and the emptiness when she fell silent was worse.

Still she staggered on, clutching at the dirty pipes strapped to the tunnel wall, counting her steps and cursing under her breath, because anything was better than weeping. Too slow, too late: her unspoken accusations reverberated around her. She'd said too little, she'd said too much; she should have talked to Shai about her father before collapsing into sleep; she should have begged her to stay.

She pushed herself onward, inching her way up the incline—and for what? Did she truly believe that she would find Shai—that the ghost might return as quickly as she had left? As if anything awaited her beyond empty days of searching. This was a road she'd walked before, and she knew where it led.

Admit it, she thought savagely. This was just like when Abelane had left her—and "left" was the right word, the one she'd never dared say, even to herself. Lane hadn't been killed or kidnapped, hadn't been captured or stolen away. She had *left*, simply gone, leaving Xhea behind.

The only difference was that Shai had stayed long enough to say goodbye.

Reaching the subway station took two hours; it only felt like more. By the time she pulled herself onto the platform, Xhea wanted nothing more than to collapse to the ground and sob. Which, of course, would do precisely nothing except delay her, and so she continued, eyes leaking tears, hissing in pain at every step.

Soon, she could not walk at all, could not even manage the awkward limp-and-drag of her earlier passage. Her knee had swollen to twice its size, straining against the fabric of her pant leg, and throbbed with every movement. So Xhea sat, legs stretched before her, and pulled herself backward across the filthy floor.

She winced when she thought of what this would do to her pants, then clung to the thought as a distraction from the pain. *So many stains*, she thought. So many rips and tears, and where would she find a needle?

Such mundane concerns got her down a long service corridor, across a hall, and then up the narrow escalator that led to the hotel lobby. The charms in her hair clanked with every heave, tread by tread, almost loud enough to smother the sounds of her whimpers.

At the top, she dragged herself toward the shattered doors, following her own day-old tracks through the dirt. Outside, the world was the gray of fishing weights and galvanized nails. Early morning, and a foggy morning besides. She couldn't have slept more than an hour or two.

She knew that the ghost was not outside. There was no shimmer that spoke of Shai's magic—only the light of a single entrapment spell. Even through the cracked glass of the hotel's front windows, she could see that the sphere that Shai had said was keyed to her own signature was missing.

Xhea took a long shuddering breath. That spell had been the ghost's ticket home. Shai was truly gone.

Xhea crawled out through the broken doors and sagged on the hotel's front step, her breath ragged. At last she raised her head. It took a long moment to notice the hunched figure on the sidewalk, the last remaining spell shining above him—longer still to connect his unshaven face with the man she knew.

"Brend?"

Brend stared, surprise yielding to concern as his eyes moved from her dirty clothing to the dried blood on her hands and arms, and the awkward wreck of her leg. Mist swirled, seeming to enclose them in a veil of gray. Still, her mind reeled: *Brend* had been helping set the traps? But no—as he turned, she saw what lay behind him: small white rocks forming an X on the pavement.

X marks the spot, she thought in a daze. X for her name. She remembered the calculator left the night before, and all the other bits and pieces sure to catch her attention. Warning her away.

"They haven't got you yet," Brend said. His mouth moved, forming an expression that was all but foreign to his face: a real smile.

"Sweetness," Xhea breathed, prayer and curse in one, and was suddenly glad that she was crippled. If she could have run, she would have thrown herself into Brend's arms, and sobbed until she had no more tears left. Just for the touch of someone who knew her name; someone who cared enough to smile when he saw that that she lived.

It was just as well. She could imagine the pained look on his face, or his reaction to her touch. Wen she could have trusted, even before his death, but Brend . . . Even the knowledge that he had been trying to help her didn't ease her natural reaction: hide your weakness.

Xhea forced herself to lean back, feigning a casual pose, and brushed idly at the dirt on her pants. Given the level of filth, the gesture seemed flippant enough to be a joke. It was a mockery of her usual self, but it would serve as mask enough.

Brend remained crouched with his hands where she could see them, a small rock held loosely within the cage of his fingers. "Are you all right?" he asked quietly.

She met his eyes, a dark gray ringed by shadows, and struggled for words. The weariness written across his face was as unfamiliar as the look of his patchy, unshaven chin. *If only he would smile again*, she thought. How she longed to see his familiar mask of false cheer. There was no safety in his concern, and she struggled to rebuild a façade to hide behind.

"Had a bit of a rough night," Xhea said and shrugged. She hoped he hadn't heard the hitch in her voice or seen her wince at the movement of her bruised shoulders. From his expression, he missed neither.

"A bit? You're bleeding."

Xhea lifted a hand to her scraped cheeks, tentatively touched her nose, licked furtively at her lips but tasted no salt. Brend watched her unthinkingly catalog her hurts, until she realized what she was doing and abruptly stilled.

Tired and hurt and it's making you stupid, she thought, hard and fierce, and it didn't make any of it any better. Brend gestured at her hands, now curled against her pant legs, jagged fingernails whirring against the fabric. She turned them over to find the palms ripped raw and bloody, leaving little patches of blood on her thighs.

"Huh," she said. Blood gathered in the tracery of lines across her palms, darkening the creases in some unreadable fortune. "Would you look at that."

"What did they do to you?"

They? Answers piled on top of one another—they came on us in the tunnels, and we had no way to run—they stalked me and followed me and tried to trap me—they left me, both of them— until she didn't know how to speak, how to untangle one thought from another and have the words make sense.

"Xhea? I've tried—"

She struggled to follow his meaning, as Brend struggled to find words. He'd tried to tell her about the spells, he meant—the people tracking her and Shai. She looked at the one remaining spell, staring at it as if the magic held answers, then back down to Brend. Who was watching her. Who had watched her look directly at the spell—which should have been invisible to her, weak and magic-less creature that everyone thought her to be.

"Tired and hurt and *stupid*," she whispered, too low for any ears but her own. She would have fled, if she could: away from Brend's piercing look, his growing suspicion; away from the spell in its glimmering slumber; away from all of it. But there was no away. Not anymore.

"Well," Brend said. The stone fell from his fingers. "I see I've been wasting my time."

"No," she said. "No."

"But you can see it, can't you? The spell."

A moment of frozen stillness, then Xhea nodded and looked down at her bloody hands, all strength gone with the movement. The long-kept secret was in the open, hovering like a spell waiting to trigger and just as dangerous.

Brend swore, but without any real anger. "I can barely see them," he said.

"I've always . . ." She shook her head again, but the words refused to be spoken, sticking in her throat in a lump. Instead she asked, "You were trying . . . to protect me?"

Save me, she thought, plea and realization in one. *He was trying to save me.*

Brend nodded. "Little good that it did." His mouth twisted. "I don't know enough to diffuse the spells, or change them." As his father would have.

"But . . . why? Why are you doing this?" She hated how pain and barely suppressed tears made her sound foolish and weak. Little lost girl, weeping on the steps. "You don't even like me."

"No." This time he almost did smile, and if the humor in his expression was bitter, it was no less true. "But what does that matter?"

"Then why?"

"Without you, I wouldn't have my father's business." A pause, then quieter: "I wouldn't have my father."

"You paid me."

He shrugged, the movement so like her habitual gesture that for one crazy moment she wanted to laugh. Hysteria; she choked it back.

"Still," Brend said, as if it were explanation enough. "I'd help more, if I could, but they're watching Dad's warehouse in case you return, making my life miserable. They turned the daylight spell into a giant camera—did you realize? I managed to change it back, but . . ." Again, he shrugged. "Nearly destroyed it in the attempt."

He glanced up at the sky. The world around them was the featureless gray of slate and ashes: cool and overcast, the Towers and most of the Lower City lost in heavy mist.

It was only then, staring at his profile, that Xhea realized: Eridian. Brend had warned her about spells he could barely see—and yet the warnings had appeared nearly as quickly as the spells, no matter what strange corner of the Lower City they'd been placed, nor how well they'd been hidden. He had some way of knowing how and where her enemies were trying to capture her and Shai . . . which meant that the entrapment spells had not been placed by Allenai's agents at all.

For Brend was a citizen of Eridian.

Xhea looked to the empty spot where a shimmering sphere had hovered, keyed to Shai's signature—the spell that Shai had used to return home mere hours before. Except it wouldn't have taken her home. Blindly committed to fulfilling her responsibilities to protect those few she loved, Shai had instead handed herself to Allenai's enemy.

And there wasn't a blighted thing Xhea could do about it.

Brend sighed, the sound just enough to draw Xhea back from her despairing thoughts. "I have to go," he said, dusting his pants and moving carefully away. Xhea watched emotions flicker across his face like shadows: happy to leave, reluctant to leave her behind. Watched, too, as he weighed his options and found them too few and all inadequate. She knew the feeling. "But if there's anything . . ."

If only he could rescue a ghost for her—though for all she knew, it was already too late. If only he could heal her, or turn back time.

She was about to shake her head, wave him away with dismissive assurances of her safety, when she reconsidered. "Do you have a bandage?"

Brend thought, then pulled off his jacket and the shirt beneath. These, like all his clothes, were good quality, though now hopelessly wrinkled. With a couple of sudden pulls and the sound of threads snapping, he tore both sleeves from his shirt, which he tossed to her before dressing again.

Xhea carefully picked up the ripped fabric, as if the sleeves might somehow vanish. Softly, she said, "Thank you." Brend nodded once and was gone, the sound of his footsteps muffled in the misty morning air.

She had never imagined that he would risk so much for her. It was foolish, then, to feel a pang at the sight of him vanishing into the fog, to ache at the sound of his steps receding. But with him gone, there was no need to posture—if the need had ever been there at all. Xhea sagged, her poor show of strength vanishing in the space of a breath. She shuddered with a sudden chill.

The fabric was smooth in her hands, almost slippery. She had not Brend's strength, but with the help of her teeth, she managed to rip the sleeves into a few long strips. She raised her pant leg, gasping and whimpering as the bottom hem scraped over the swollen joint. Her knee was burning hot, lumpy and discolored. Xhea swallowed, wanting to look away.

"It'll be okay," she lied.

She bound the joint, giving it whatever stability mere fabric might offer, her fingers leaving smears of dirt and blood. A fingernail bent backward as she struggled to tighten her poor knots and she hissed, more in frustration than from the small hurt.

All she needed was someone to help. Just a finger placed *so*. A bit of cloth to wipe clean her face. A hand to help her stand. And no one to give any.

Oh, to be grateful for torn shirtsleeves. For stones and scraps left as ambiguous warnings. For the veil of fog; for a sky not yet releasing its rain; for a bit of cold ground on which to rest. Were these her blessings? She could not count them as such. She mocked herself as a little girl, lost and alone, yet knew in truth she was all these things, had always been such. Would always be.

For even if she was valued, was known, was even cared for, it could only be for a moment, brief and fleeting. There was always— would always be—something greater than her, more important. More worthy of time or attention. Something, someone, worth being loved.

As she would never be.

Stop it, she thought, savagely, viciously, as if vehemence could force the emotion back, could dry the tears that spilled down her cheeks or ease her wracking sobs. *Stop it, stop it*, she cursed in silence, for she could not speak, could not rise; and the only sounds in the cool morning air were those of her crying.

Faint and muffled, a sound came from somewhere nearby. Xhea took a slow breath, calming the last of her sobs; after many long minutes, she had little left to cry.

What had it been? A whir? A whine? She could not tell; the mist curled in upon the sound, deadening all but a whisper. Probably just an ordinary noise—a hungry child, a bit of debris falling from a crumbling rooftop.

Still, she thought. Still.

She lifted her head and looked around, each movement an effort. There was no one on the broken sidewalk before her, nor on the road. She saw no movement in the mist but its own slow swirls and eddies, pushed by a subtle wind.

She knew she should run, scramble away and hide, drag her bruised and hurting self back inside the shell of the hotel's front lobby, ignoring the pain—just in case. She felt a quiver of alarm, an echo of her usual wariness, but it too seemed dulled; whatever fear now stirred within her seemed distant, close enough to see but too far to touch. It was as if the fog had seeped into her, deadening her emotions, slowing her thoughts. She imagined the mist creeping down her limbs into fingers and toes, leaving only cool and quiet in its wake, a soft and numbing chill.

Xhea stared at her hands and the patches of skin washed clean by tears. She opened and closed her fingers, feeling them as something apart from herself: the gritty, bloody skin; the tired, aching joints; the black-sliver moons of dirt beneath the fingernails. So easy to lose herself in details.

Again the sound came, louder this time. She jerked her head back from where it had sagged, and forced her eyes open, not knowing when she had closed them. But there was no one there, not even a stray Lower City dweller wandering the early-morning streets. Nothing, nothing, nothing. Yet as she gazed around something made her afraid as mere sounds had not, the dregs of adrenaline stirring in her blood. Something was different. Something had changed.

She felt so tired, so leaden.

Again the sound, louder and longer: *whirr-thump.* Then a sound like hot metal cooling: *tick . . . tick . . . tick.*

Her gaze fell upon Brend's almost-completed X of pale stones, undisturbed on the pavement. *Ah*, she thought, understanding coming in a slow and heavy wave: where the spell had hovered, there was only air. Not triggered, she knew. Recalled. Dissolved.

As if it were no longer needed.

The sound was coming closer, she realized. And there was a smell . . . the strangest sweet smell . . . honey and burning plastic . . .

She tried to think, fighting the desire to place her head on her arms and rest. Only rest.

Closer, she repeated. A sound coming closer, and nothing around her. Nothing before her but empty air. Almost as if . . .

Xhea looked up, but it was already far too late to run.

Little more than a body-length above her hovered a battered aircar, the air twisting and shimmering with its exhaust. From its open doors hung three people, all but their eyes hidden by medical masks. Two held between them a simple net, ready to unfurl, while the third held a canister from which seeped a haze of sweet-smelling drug. The haze cascaded down and over her, tranquilizing her, and she'd thought it nothing but fog.

Xhea tried to stand, to roll, to crawl back toward the hotel, and for nothing. There was no need for the net; she saw the same realization in those watching faces. She sagged to one side, suddenly too heavy, too loose, to keep her body upright. Her shoulder hit the concrete steps, her head not too far behind, and she felt a strange and horrible twist in her damaged right knee.

But the pain, when it came, was muffled, as if she were wrapped in invisible cotton wool. Nothing could reach her, not pain nor help nor light.

In the darkness behind her eyelids, she cried as hands lifted her up—lost, insensible tears—but they were tears of gratitude. *No pain*, she thought in her haze. No need to struggle. No need to fight.

No more.

In that darkness, unresisting, they raised her up and took her away.

Chapter Nineteen

Xhea licked her lips with a tongue that felt like sandpaper. Her mouth tasted of sour fruit, and her head felt as if it had been pounded with a sharp rock. She tried to sit up. Failed. Tried to muster the energy to care, and failed at that too.

She remembered someone putting a needle in her thigh. Remembered the sound of conversation around her, senseless words rising and falling like waves. *Hospital* was her first thought, but no: while she lay in bed with instruments and bandages arrayed on a table beside her, the table had rusty folding metal legs, and the bed was just a cot with a pillow so worn it was barely there.

Definitely not a hospital, she thought, looking around. The room was massive, echoing, and stripped bare. There was no carpet, only adhesive stains left on the concrete to mark its absence, and the ceiling tiles had been removed, exposing wires and plumbing made fuzzy from decades of undisturbed dust.

Before her, there was a wall of featureless gray light—windows, she realized. One full corner of the room was made from glass that looked out into a bank of day-bright cloud. She'd never been in this room, but there was something familiar about the space nonetheless. Something in the air whispering through the ancient vents, filtered by cloth and magic but still smelling of crumbling drywall and unwashed doors stained with greasy handprints, of floor after floor of leaking pipes and corroded wiring.

It had never been a good skyscraper, never a prosperous one, for all that it still stood. She looked around and the building itself seemed to mock her, whispering, "Welcome home."

Orren.

She could have laughed, voice edged with hysteria. She could have spit. The one thing she would not do was cry. Not here. Not ever again.

Instead, she took stock. She wore her shirt and jacket, but her pants had been cut away. Her bare legs, skinny and pale after the long winter, looked almost fragile. Anger stirred at the sight of the ruined pants in a heap on the floor; even dirty and torn, they were *hers*. A replacement pair was folded over the back of a nearby chair, seemingly unworn, with large pockets down each leg. She eyed them: they wouldn't just fit, but fit well. She scowled.

Better that than to let eyes and mind alike linger on her knee. Her rough bandages had been unbound and lay across the sheet like a gift's discarded wrapping. Her skin tingled as if from phantom touches, but little more; from mid-thigh down, her right leg was numb. Even without the pain, there was something about the knee that looked—that felt—wrong. She turned aside.

At the movement, a figure stepped into her peripheral vision. She glanced at the boy, for boy he was—no nurse this, no doctor with clever tools and healing spells. He had an adult's size, but his open expression and the downy stubble across his chin made him seem little older than Xhea herself.

Without speaking, he helped her sit, then tried to prop her up with another flat pillow. He handed her a blanket, which she used to cover her legs, and a cup of water. His hands were gentle, impersonal, even kind; yet Xhea found herself tensing, ready to cringe or run. As if either were an option.

"You don't remember me, do you?" the boy asked. He dragged the plastic chair to her bedside and sat.

If it had been easier to speak, she would have simply said "No"—and how appropriate, for her first word in this place to be a flat denial. But once she looked, there was something familiar about him. Xhea realized that he had been the one holding the fog canister. She recognized his eyes with their upturned lashes; the soft, dark curls of his hair.

"What was that?" she croaked. "The drug." Sweetness, her head hurt.

"Nothing to worry about, really. Just an airborne sedative—a nice mild one." He blushed at her incredulous look, the deepening color barely noticeable through his skin's natural dark.

"I'm sorry," he said at last. "I thought it'd be easier than the net."

"Easier?" That was one word for it. "It would have been easier to just *leave me alone.*"

Instead of replying, he moved the edge of the blanket and probed her wounded knee, hissing softly at that first touch. It was strange to watch someone touch her; stranger still to feel none of it, not even the whisper of skin on skin.

She watched his face. His forehead creased and the skin around his eyes tightened, lips pursing, and knew that more than concentration wrote such lines. Yet he did not recoil or pull back, almost as if he knew what it was to touch her.

"You really don't remember me, do you?" He smiled sadly.

But that smile stirred a memory buried deep with all the things she tried never to recall. Xhea stared a moment, considering. Imagining those eyes, that softly curling hair, on someone much smaller. A child who had always looked young, with thin limbs and a face that seemed gaunt no matter how much he ate. A quiet child who had been as ostracized from the other boys in the dorm as surely as Xhea had been from the girls—though less content with such treatment. Had they been friends? Aching from the loss of Abelane, she'd had no friends; yet if she'd had a companion in that year, someone familiar enough to almost be safe, it would have been him.

She remembered, too, the night of her escape. After the failed resurrection, the skyscraper had been in chaos. Orren's magically supported systems had failed at the spell overload, everything from lights and elevators to security on the fritz, all hands scrambling to restore power before another skyscraper took advantage of the disarray. Xhea had no plan, only the sudden conviction that this was her one chance to run.

With evening already darkening the sky, she'd slipped from her dorm with only her knife and jacket. As she'd crept away, she caught sight of dark eyes watching her, two glints in the shadows. She'd frozen before she realized that it wasn't Orren security, only the quiet boy who never seemed to grow. He'd peered through open crack of the door to the boys' dorm, one hand clutching the doorframe.

"Are you coming?" she had whispered, suddenly thinking that maybe she could save him, if no one else.

After a long moment, he had mutely shaken his head. She'd shrugged and slipped out to make good her escape, only looking back once. In the years that followed, she'd tried not to think of him. Pretended she didn't remember those dark eyes, watching her as she ran.

Sometimes you have to leave someone behind.

Yet now that she looked, she could see the child's echo in the young man before her, the quiet boy grown tall and strong. Wondered, too, who he would have become had he followed her that night; what he might have meant to her.

"Lin," she said, the name rising like the memory of a dream. "You grew."

Lin laughed. "Rather a lot, actually. I've been going through clothes like you wouldn't believe."

Nice to have that option, Xhea thought.

He pulled his hands from her knee and surreptitiously massaged his fingers. She caught a glimpse of the gray that tinged his fingers and knuckles—blue, perhaps, as if from cold. She couldn't remember anyone who had touched her for so long.

At least no one living.

"Your kneecap is isn't broken," Lin said, "but there's ligament damage." His gaze flickered to her face, gauging her reaction. "It's pretty bad."

"Define bad."

"Unless you give me permission to perform a healing, it's not going to heal at all. Not well, anyway."

"A healing. At what price?"

"That's not for me to decide. I have another five years until I earn out my contract." He was still indentured, in other words, for the time, food, and magic the skyscraper had spent to raise him. Orren would name the cost for his services.

"Xhea," he said, then hesitated, as if tasting her name. "Xhea, without treatment, you won't be able to walk again. Even braced, the joint won't properly support your weight. At best, you'll have to use crutches for the rest of your life."

She shook her head. "There must be some other way."

"In the before-times, there was surgery for things like this." Lin shrugged, almost apologetically. "I don't suppose you know any surgeons."

Xhea closed her eyes. "Is that why you're here? So they can trap me with a healing I can never pay for?" Indenture herself again—though in truth, she'd never worked off her earlier debt.

"I'm here because I asked to be. I'm apprenticed to Orren's top medic, you know. Only two more years until I'm fully certified." Lin radiated pride, and Xhea was impressed despite herself; it meant a lot of work for one with so little magical talent. He added softly, "And I remember you. I've heard stories about you these last few years. I want to help."

He spoke truly, she thought. Yet it was a truth that hid as much as it told.

"They're watching us, aren't they?" she murmured. "A camera, a spell—maybe just a couple little holes in the wall back there, huh? They're watching us, and you're just here to try and gain my trust." A familiar person who had never hurt her, kind hands offering help and healing. An attractive face on someone nearly as young as she.

I don't trust your gifts, she thought to the unseen watchers. *I don't trust your gifts, and I don't believe in coincidence.*

Lin waited silently.

She knew it would be near impossible to get another medic to so much as touch her, never mind perform a healing, even if she had anything to offer in payment. Maimed and crippled people were not uncommon in the Lower City; yet she knew what such a fate would mean to her. She was just hanging on as it was, scrounging for artifacts and talking to ghosts, living in the tunnels beneath the Lower City. What little of that could she still do, unable to walk—never mind run or leap or climb? It was a death sentence, little more; one that would be served in seasons of struggle and pain, the slow waste of starvation.

Could Orren's price be any worse?

Yes, she thought with cold certainty. Yes.

Still Xhea whispered, "You have my permission." For as awful as their price might be, it alone gave her a chance—for herself, and for Shai.

Lin nodded. All he said was, "Keep still. This may feel uncomfortable."

It was only as Lin reached out that she allowed herself to think what the healing would entail. Oh, for braces and bandages, use of the instruments on the folding table. Anything but magic.

He touched her, fingers cupping the swollen joint, and his weak power flowed through his hands—a bare trickle compared to Shai's unthinking light. Yet Xhea gasped nonetheless, and bit down on her lip, feeling pain that the injection did nothing to touch. She couldn't show discomfort or pain—and it was only pain, familiar now as rain in the spring. Let them think her high, her gasp that of an addict reunited with her drug.

Don't let them know what magic does to you now. Over and over, she thought it, a slow mantra. *They can't ever know.*

"Do you need more painkillers?" Lin asked.

She shook her head, managing to say, "It just feels a little funny." He accepted the lie.

Yet every moment that Lin poured magic into her knee, shaping and binding and fixing, Xhea felt worse. Her stomach roiled, and her eyes stung as she saw sparks of color: lightning-quick glimpses of dusty red wire, the off-white sheets, the pinkish golden-brown of Lin's flushed cheek.

They can't ever know, she repeated, fighting down bile. For whatever the price of her healing, whatever they wanted of her, if Orren knew of the dark magic they would never let her go. Death or indenture or bargaining chip in a game of power too large for her to comprehend, she did not know; only feared it, a slow and certain terror.

At last Lin straightened, taking his hands from her knee. "There," he said, confident for all that his hands trembled, fingers bleached of blood. He fumbled for bandages as Xhea looked at her knee. It seemed no different. *Let it be worth it*, she thought, and sat still as he wrapped the bandages.

"Lin." Even whispering, her voice shook. "Can you get me out of here?"

He went still for a moment, only that. Didn't look up or meet her eyes, only paused, shoulders tense, before resuming his careful bandaging. The silence between them grew and expanded until it was almost tangible.

"Are you feeling any better?" Lin asked as if she'd never spoken.

Her leg was still numb. She only imagined the sting and ache of the spells now woven thread-fine through her knee; it was only fear and the after-effects of sedation that made her feel sickly and slow. Lin wasn't trying to hurt or trap her, she reminded herself; he was a pawn, just as she was. Not a friend or an ally. It was foolish to forget that.

Yet she was angry with him all the same.

For all the magic and healing, none of it even touched the real hurt, the absence and the anger and the fear that laced it all. She'd had a friend, an ally, and lost her—driven her away, failed to keep her safe.

What's happening to you? she thought to Shai. *What is Eridian doing to you?*

Xhea looked toward the window and the featureless expanse of pale gray cloud, looking at nothing at all. "Not really," she said, voice cold. "But we can pretend."

Lin returned after dawn the next morning, the gray beyond the windows heralding a day dull as old iron. The day before had seemed endless, the night worse still. Xhea had sworn she'd never spend another minute within Orren's steel and concrete walls— had sworn, too, that she'd protect Shai from those who wished to use her. Such vows were only as good as the one who made them, and she felt her broken promises' sharp edges in heart and hands.

Lin smiled as he set a tray piled high with food and medical equipment onto the table at her bedside. Addled by pain pills, Xhea almost smiled back. She stopped, and pressed her lips into a thin line.

Lin seemed not to notice, talking cheerfully as he unwound the bandages. His eyes unfocused as he concentrated on the workings of the joint, mapped out by the magic he'd laid beneath, and he made a sound of surprise and confusion. He placed his hands on her knee, fingers already lit with magic. Xhea jerked back, despite his gentleness—as did Lin, forgetting to brace for her touch. *A little warning would have been nice,* she thought, all anger and acid, struggling against her suddenly roiling stomach. But when he pulled his hands away, she said only, "What was that?"

"Sorry." Lin rubbed the back of his neck in a poor attempt to cover his discomfort. "It was just a spell reinforcement."

"Something else to add to my debt, huh?" There was no hiding her irritation now.

He looked at her in surprise. "What? No! I mean, the spell had just . . . weakened. I thought I'd set it better than that, but . . ." He shrugged awkwardly, and laughed. "All part of the learning process, right?"

I bet it weakened, Xhea thought. She'd done her best to keep calm, but her control of her magic was as thin as her patience. She had little doubt that she'd all but ruined Lin's work overnight.

Lin took her silence as recrimination and made an apologetic gesture. "Is that what you're angry about? I'll cover it, all right? My mistake, so I'll pay. No worries. And here, look, I brought you breakfast." He smiled again and uncovered the tray.

She looked at the offered breakfast: a grilled sandwich roll oozing melted cheese, a sprig of fresh grapes, and a steaming cup of tea. *Nothing whets the appetite like the taste of bile*, she thought, swallowing.

Xhea picked at her grapes while Lin applied a new bandage and then attached a brace, immobilizing her knee. The brace was hard plastic with wide fabric bands that buckled around her leg. On either side of her knee there was a hinging mechanism, which Lin locked in place. The fraying straps were pale from age, and the hinged plastic spars were scratched and gouged. Xhea wondered how many others had worn it, staining it dark with their sweat.

"How long until I can walk again?"

"Wait at least a few days before you put any weight on it. Take it slowly."

"Especially considering the glitches in the healing process so far."

Lin blushed and looked away. "Right."

Quieter, she said, "You know that they're using you, right? Using you to trap me and hold me here."

"I don't know what you're talking about."

"They need me, Lin. They need what I can do, and if they can push me into debt—"

Lin grabbed his things and stood, leaving only the tray with her barely-touched breakfast. "I'll be back to check on you later, okay?" he said, not meeting her eyes, and hurried away. The sound of the door's closing reverberated through the bare room. Xhea listened: his footsteps receded, then an elevator door opened and closed. She counted the seconds in silence.

After two full minutes she pushed the breakfast tray away and untangled her legs from the blanket. Yet the twinge in her knee at even that much movement made her reconsider standing. After clumsily turning in the cot, Xhea managed to shift herself into the chair. It was still warm.

She glanced at the pants waiting by the bedside. *Later*, she thought, ignoring her goosebumps. Heating, it seemed, was too good for a guest of her stature—or Orren's re-engineers had yet to find a way to force air to the ruins of the upper floors. Neither would have surprised her.

When no one came to force her back to bed, Xhea began to push the chair across the floor with her good leg. It was a slow and frustrating process, the chair's metal feet squealing against the concrete, but she reached the door and rattled the handle. It was, of course, locked.

She pulled a tool from her jacket pocket. Slim with a pointed end, she had no idea what Lin might have used it for; she hadn't asked before she'd slipped it from the table and hidden it beneath her leg until he left. The door had no visible locking mechanism, but, squinting, she could just see a deadbolt between the door's edge and its frame. Slipping her stolen probe into the doorframe, Xhea began the careful work of earning her freedom.

The tool finally snapped an hour later, even surgical steel giving up in the face of the strongest deadbolt in the known universe. Xhea dropped the broken handle in disgust, watching as it rolled to the center of the room and lay there, as useless as she.

She turned to stare at the bare expanse of wall beside her and the dimple in its center that might be a hole or a hidden camera or nothing at all. "I hope you're finding this funny," she said, and began the slow work of pushing herself back to the cot.

Despite Lin's promise to return, Xhea remained alone. The hours passed in slow tedium. It was only when she searched her pockets for distraction that she realized her last cigarettes were gone, along with her matches, any length of string long enough to be useful— and her knife. Of course they would take her weapons. They had no idea what it meant to her—nor would they care. Still she seethed.

Xhea's only distraction was her knee itself. By unfocusing her eyes and squinting, she could see past flesh and bone to the shimmering lines of Lin's spell. Threads of energy wove through the joint, differences in brightness, density, and tone indicating hidden meanings at which she could only guess. She was no expert, but it seemed to be good work.

Good, and fading. Despite Lin's reinforcement, she could see flickers in the lines' vibration, fraying ends, and bit her lip at the sight. For all her bravado, Lin's warning echoed. Though she feared Orren and a lifetime of servitude within its ancient walls, she could not imagine how she'd survive if she could not walk at all. She focused on her power until it felt like a small, hard stone lodged beneath her breastbone.

Evening had come before she was disturbed again. The door opened and a short woman stood in the frame, neat and plainly dressed with her dark hair pulled back and a clipboard in her hands. A small light hovered above her right shoulder, dispelling the room's shadowed gloom. Xhea blinked, her eyes watering in the sudden light. She'd imagined what might happen if Orren recaptured her, but never had she thought that she'd be relegated to some late-shift administrative lackey.

Well, that's one way of putting me in my place.

The woman crossed the floor to Xhea's bedside, the heels of her sensible shoes ticking against the bare concrete. She settled in the plastic chair, adjusted her skirt, and began to review the notes on her clipboard, the words scrolling by at a flick of her pen—all without so much as a glance at Xhea.

Hello to you too, Xhea thought in the silence. But what she said was, "You're here because of what I said to Lin." She knew she'd run a risk trying to talk to him about how he was being used, or why Orren wanted her.

"What you did or did not say to your medical care provider is of no consequence in this conversation." The woman flicked her pen, and more text flew by.

"Then what is?"

A pause, then the woman looked up, the slow lift of her gaze as full of meaning as the eyebrow quirk that accompanied the movement. "The past, Xhea," she said. "Not to mention your current situation."

"You're here to try to indenture me."

"Try?" The woman smiled slightly, a humorless expression. "I'm afraid that was long since done. You signed yourself into Orren's keeping—" a brief glance at the clipboard "—more than five years ago. It is merely time to repay that debt."

Xhea snorted and crossed her arms across her chest, hoping the woman thought her shivers were due merely to cold. "As if the few measly renai you spent on me are worth this hassle to collect."

That smile again, dry and thin as old bones. "Shall I introduce you to the concept of 'interest'?"

"Sorry, try again—I'm not buying it. The pittance I owe isn't worth the trouble you've taken to abduct me."

"Perhaps you are unaware, but your account also shows that you bear partial responsibility for the destruction of two medium-capacity storage coils—a cost that is indeed worth the effort."

Xhea gaped. The storage coils? She thought of the failed resurrection attempt, her hands and knife slick with blood, a man's soul ripping at her touch—and they wanted to charge her for their blighted *storage coils?* A thought surfaced: better that than charge her with murder. A body's death, a soul's death— nothing could repay that debt.

The woman continued, oblivious. "We acknowledge that you bear only partial fault for that particular . . . incident, and have adjusted the totals accordingly. For the storage coils, feeding and housing you during your period of residency, and the cost of attempting to collect on that debt to date, you owe an estimated fifteen years of service."

Xhea choked. "*Fifteen—*"

"Now that total is based on an assumed productivity value from manual labor. Additional—or, say, more specialized—contributions would speed your repayment considerably." The woman seemed only then to notice Xhea's reaction. She frowned. "We gave you years, Xhea, to return on your own terms. You knew you had a debt to repay, and you chose to ignore it. Chose, too, to dodge the messengers we sent to request your return using rather less forceful methods."

"Messengers? Try thugs."

Again, that slow lift of her eyebrow. "You still have an overactive imagination, I see. The fact remains that the nature of your return was, if not at your choosing, at least a direct consequence of your actions."

"And now you're holding me captive."

"With that leg, I hardly think you'd want to be up and walking."

"That makes it okay to lock me in here?"

"If you were on the ground floor or in an unlocked room, would you run away again?" Xhea's silence was answer enough. "Exactly. You'd be gone, and your debt would remain unpaid. We are merely taking appropriate precautions."

"This isn't about my debt." Xhea tried to keep her voice firm and forceful, and failed utterly. "You wanted to *use* me! You still do!"

"Use you? Like Lin is used, when he heals? As a chef is used, when cooking your meals? You act as if we're hurting you, giving you a bed and shelter, work to do that plays to your talents—and doesn't involve scrabbling in the ruins for scraps. It's clear you haven't eaten regularly since you left here; you're all muscle and bone, Xhea. You've barely grown."

Xhea shook her head, the defiant rattle of charms speaking where she had no words—for the woman was not wrong. "It's my choice," she managed. "You never asked what I wanted."

A thin smile. "Children rarely want what's best for them. But if you were unhappy, you need have only said so. We could have arranged for a transfer to another skyscraper—found you another home, and worked out the debt later."

"As if you would have let me go." Orren, giving one of their land-bound rivals a potentially useful asset, merely because she was unhappy? Never. And if they told no one of her ability to see ghosts, what use would another skyscraper have for her, lacking even the poorest magic? Besides, one only needed to look at her during those long months to know she was unhappy; it had been written in every move, every gesture, the sullen silences that she'd never really lost.

"Did you even ask?"

Xhea stared. Ask? Surely, the woman had lost her mind.

The woman shook her head, and when she spoke her voice was weary and frustrated. "Of course not. Because it's easier to see yourself as the victim. Exiled and taken advantage of—isn't that it?" She sighed. "Child, the world is not out to get you. Orren has done nothing but care for you when you were hurt and in trouble. We have fed and clothed and housed you, now and for more than a year in the past—and yet you find it awful that we would ask you to contribute in turn. Is it too much to ask that you earn what you receive?"

A slow flush climbed Xhea's cheeks unbidden. The woman was trying to mess with her head—but it didn't change that grain of truth, nor the way it burned to hear it spoken. Even with her face radiating heat, Xhea raised her chin, clenched her jaw, and stared.

"You want me to believe," Xhea said, teeth clenched against the words, "that this has nothing to do with Allenai and their missing ghost. Nothing to do with Eridian. It's just coincidence that you wanted me back at the same time they sent hunters after me."

The woman capped her pen with an air of finality. "Child," she said, "I have no idea what you're talking about. But if we have indeed spared you from a fate at the hands of the City proper, then perhaps you should be more grateful. After all, all *we* want of you is a bit of your time."

With that she stood and made her way to the door, the hovering light following obediently. One hand on the handle, she turned back only long enough to add, "And Xhea?" She gestured to the breakfast dishes at the bedside. "That's the last free meal. The next you have to earn."

Or starve. The words resonated, unspoken.

The door closed with a thud, and there was a click as the lock engaged. Xhea sagged back on her cot and closed her eyes against the return of darkness.

Earn. As if she didn't understand the value of food, warmth, and security. As if she didn't know what it was to scratch and scrabble and steal, to carve such things from nothing with will and hands alone. She pulled the thin blanket to her chin, cot creaking beneath her. Orren wanted something from her that had nothing to do with her debt, that much she knew sure as breathing. Yet it didn't make a single thing the woman had said untrue.

Fifteen years, Xhea thought, and stared at the ceiling in silence.

Chapter Twenty

Night had fallen, Towerlight patterning the sky beyond the windows, when Xhea heard a scratch at the door. She stiffened, vulnerable on her cot in the middle of the empty room, a thin blanket her only defense. The sound came again: a scratch, then the handle rattled and the door opened just wide enough to admit Lin. He crept across the floor like a nervous, first-time thief, and crouched by her bed.

"I'm sorry," he whispered. "They wouldn't allow me to come any earlier."

"Wouldn't allow?"

Lin shook his head. "Doesn't matter—I'm here now. How's your knee?" He reached out, visibly bracing for her touch. *Fifteen years*, Xhea thought and drew back.

"It's fine," she said.

Lin stared, eyes unfocused, then shook his head. "No, it's not—it's weakening again. I'm so sorry, my work usually isn't like this . . ." Again he reached, and again Xhea pulled away, wrapping the blanket tighter around her legs.

He hesitated. "I know this is uncomfortable, but with a couple more days of treatment you'll be walking again."

"I can't afford a couple more days of treatment."

"I told you, I'll pay—"

"And what will I owe you?"

Lin looked shocked, then shook his head in swift denial. "It's not like that," he stammered.

"Then what is it like, Lin? Tell me. Why are they using you to get at me?"

"Using—? No one's—I mean . . ."

Xhea leaned forward, the cot creaking beneath her. "Haven't you asked what they want from me? Why they're holding me here?" She gestured around the ruined room, the bare structure and the unbroken expanse of glass. "Ever wonder why you're the only one they've let see me? Why you're the only one *allowed*?"

"I—"

She'd rolled that question over and over as the long hours passed, knowing the answer. If she had a weakness here, it was Lin, the one person she'd almost trusted during her long, lonely year within these walls. But sometimes you have to leave someone behind.

Xhea made her voice cold. "I don't want you here. Not now, not ever again—get it?"

"If this is about how I wouldn't—how I can't help you—"

She cut him off. "I know Orren," she said, low and angry, "and I know that it holds no safety, no warmth. No friendship that isn't bought and paid for. They control everything here and nothing that happens is ever a coincidence."

"Not even your escape?" Lin's voice was thin, brittle and breaking. His eyes, too, betrayed him: for all his newfound size, he was so young.

She looked down at her hands and smiled, the lift of her lips like a knife's slow curve. "Not even that," she whispered, and knew it to be true. She didn't look up when Lin rose, only saw the stiffness of his back, the hunch of shoulders drawn tight with anger.

He paused at the door to look back, staring as he had on that night years before. "You know, Xhea," he said, "you're going to run out of people willing to try to be your friend, and then what're you going to do?"

She did not say anything, could not, and this time he was the one who walked away. It wasn't until the door was long shut, his footsteps vanished into silence, that she wished to speak. Words lodged like stones in her throat: hard and cold, and as useless.

"Wait," she wanted to say. Or, "I'm sorry." Or even just, "Talk to me." As if she deserved to be forgiven. So long alone in the dark tunnels and rarely had she wished for the sound of another voice, living or dead, as she did in that moment.

She didn't know how to speak such words; only how to choke them back, how to twist and turn them until they hurt not in speaking, but in hearing. Words like rocks thrown. She thought of the line of Lin's shoulders, the flat mask of Shai's face, and knew she used her weapons well: once and again, she had drawn blood.

Wasn't that what she'd wanted? She felt an ache that had nothing to do with her injuries, and knew it was the only thing she had rightfully earned in days. The dirty dishes beside her should glimmer with the renai they represented, each morsel a mark in the tally of her debt. The ancient cot was Orren's too, and its thin mattress and blanket. If she didn't deserve friendship and had already taxed Orren's so-called charity, let her take nothing more of either.

The pants, though—those were hers. Replacement for the ones they'd cut away.

She pushed herself to the cot's edge and used the plastic chair to lower herself to the floor, leaving the blanket behind. The process was slow and painful, though her gasps were barely audible over the cot's squealing springs. She wished she could crawl; instead she slowly dragged herself across the floor. Her new pants were soon mottled gray with dust and chips of broken concrete, and she shivered—from cold, from fear, she knew not which.

At last Xhea collapsed in the corner to where the two walls of windows met. She who had run tirelessly through the Lower City now lay panting, exhausted and unable to catch her breath. She looked at her trembling hands, the skin marred with near-black smears of blood, her myriad scrapes reopened. Behind her, the marks led like deepening footsteps from the cot to her corner in an uneven, stuttering trail.

Pillowing one arm beneath her, she curled up and tucked her good leg toward her body for warmth. Still she trembled; the floor pulled the heat from her body like wax through a wick. She didn't let herself think of the blanket she'd left behind; she'd been colder, and for far less reason.

Ignoring her familiar fear, Xhea peered out the window. Down and down and down she looked: the shops and homes that huddled near the skyscraper's base looked like toy blocks, dirty and damaged from too much use. Above, glimmering Towers and the shifting veils of their light obscured most of the sky. The Central Spire was somewhere overhead and behind her, and no amount of craning let her see more than a reflection of its glow: shadows cast slantwise, glints in window glass.

She could identify only a few of the countless Towers scattered above her; their constant movement and transformations made most unrecognizable. But there, its deep hues almost lost against the darkening sky, was Allenai. She could just see its shape, long and needle-like, its center swelling with its central living platforms. Shai had said it was maroon, and yet the energy it exuded was far brighter, swirling and shifting until the Tower was all but lost inside the veils of its own power.

I'm sorry, she thought to the distant Tower. Everything had gone wrong, it seemed. She had lost everything, as had Shai and Allenai, despite their intentions. If the Tower and its leadership were not innocent, neither were they guilty of all the crimes for which she'd blamed them. She looked away, searching.

There: her eyes lit upon a Tower shaped like a stack of widening plates impaled on a single long spear, a shining gray that she thought to be green. It was no longer as Wen had described it to her; its shape was narrower, and its widest platform bristled with defensive spires like a crown of swords. Though still low in the sky, it was now positioned directly below Allenai, close enough to the City's center that a streak of the Spire's light shone along its mirrored sides.

Eridian.

For them she had no thoughts, no words. There was only the ache that had settled deep inside her when Shai had left and not eased a moment since. Xhea closed her eyes. The ending was inevitable, she thought, however slow it might be to play out. It wouldn't help her to watch as Eridian glowed brighter as it absorbed Shai's stolen power; began to shift and transform into a more aggressive shape to prepare for its battle upward; began to rise.

Wouldn't help her, and wouldn't help Shai. But what else could she do? So she lay on the cold floor, shivering and alone, and waited.

A spark jolted her from her doze, forcing back the dark.

"Okay, okay," Xhea muttered, struggling to regain control of her magic. "Shai, I'm—"

The words died, and the thought.

Like a rush of blood, magic flowed harder on the heels of her sudden remembrance: awareness of the cold floor beneath her, the chill radiating from the windows by her side. She clamped down, hard and fast, the magic's sudden constraint almost a physical pain in her chest. She ran through the first control exercise Shai had taught her, and the second, feeling the magic's pressure ease, if not her heart's pounding. Xhea took a long, shuddering breath and opened her eyes.

There was no ghost watching over her; just the room, filled only by weight of silence. Wisps of smoke-like black slid along the floor, fading until the only darkness she cast was shadow. She glanced at the indentation in the far wall through which she thought her captors might be watching. Perhaps she had caught her magic before it had entered the visible spectrum. Perhaps her captors wouldn't recognize the strange, seeping dark as magic at all. Thin hopes, and little worth clinging to.

Xhea absently rubbed the spot in the center of her chest where she'd imagined the spark. Beyond the windows, Towerlight crawled across the sky like violent aurora. Though only hours had passed since sunset, the scene she saw was subtly different, Towers moving in their constant dance. Only two truly seemed unchanged—the only two that she cared about.

Xhea frowned and pushed herself to sitting, one hand still pressed to the center of her chest. There was something . . . *off* about the scene: Eridian's stillness, Allenai's frozen position, both poised as if waiting. Waiting—but for what? Perhaps Allenai didn't know of Shai's capture. They might still be searching the City and Lower streets alike for sign of the Radiant, a whisper of her signature, or word of the girl who could see ghosts.

"Too late." Xhea stared up through the glass.

Then the jolt came again, a spark of magic that struck her sternum through her protective hand. With fumbling fingers, Xhea opened her jacket and pulled at her shirt's neckline until she could see it: not a mark or burn, but an almost invisible flicker against her skin. Not bright magic, as she had expected— yet neither did it bear her taint. She touched the spot with cold, tentative fingertips and felt a hair-fine line of smoothness, as if the air had been oiled. There was a quiver of reaction at her touch, like the vibration of a guitar string softly played.

A tether.

Faint and flickering but *there*, the tether led sharply up beyond the barrier of window glass and across the unthinkable distance to the City above. It tugged at her, calling, as if she might traverse that empty stretch of open air by desire alone.

"Shai?" she whispered.

As if in response, her magic again stirred, reaching for the ghost. It struggled in time to the tether's flickers, as if both she and Shai were fish caught on the opposite ends of the same line. She touched that thin line and seemed for a moment to hear Shai's voice, screaming.

Shai needed her. Xhea looked about in sudden desperation, but the change in circumstance did nothing to fill the room around her, bringing no tools or assistance, no ready means of escape. Nor did the sudden pounding of her heart do anything to ease her hurts, strengthen her aching knee or make it able to bear her weight.

"Think," she whispered, feeling every quiver of the tether's fading pull. She would pace if she could, try to clear the fog from her brain, shake off the hurt and lethargy that weighed her down. "Think, think, think."

It was crazy to think she might still help Shai—she couldn't defend herself against Orren, never mind a Tower that she had no way of reaching. She couldn't even get out of this cursed room. Couldn't walk.

You're all alone, child, she heard, words spoken softly in the Orren woman's pitiless tones. *All alone, hurt, and falling to pieces.*

All alone . . .

It was this place, Xhea realized. It was as if pieces of her younger, shattered self had entered Orren's very walls, its air and pitted glass, its decaying concrete bones. Here she had tried to keep her mouth shut, to keep herself still, obedient—*helpless*—to avoid rejection. She had listened to the howl of the snow-heavy wind outside during the long winter nights and known that she was but a misstep away from dying in that snow, cries unheard—or worse, ignored.

Yet she had faced that wind and cold, faced abandonment and starvation and worse, and she'd survived. She'd escaped Orren before, eluded their pursuit for years. She was not that helpless girl anymore.

So why, she asked herself, *are you still cowering in the corner?*

Xhea took a steadying breath, then pushed herself upright and brushed the worst of the dust and grime from her clothes and hair with trembling hands. *Not afraid*, she thought, tasting the lie. She touched the dark window and the glass against her palm was cold, as if winter lurked beyond the pane. With outstretched hands braced against both windows, and the trembling efforts of a single leg, she managed to stand.

Somehow, standing, the distance from the top of Orren to the ground seemed even farther. The reach to the City proper was impossible. Yet still the tether tugged: a flutter like insect wings above her pounding heart.

Shai *needed* her.

To the voice that still murmured, *helpless, trapped, all alone*, she said, "So what?" Her voice, thin and shaking, echoed in the empty room. She repeated it, louder: "So what?"

Yes, she was trapped, and yes, she was alone. But she looked down at her hands and the slow swirl of shadow that wreathed her fingers at her call, and knew that one thing she would never be again was helpless.

She went to work.

The deadbolt on the door was strong, Xhea thought, remembering the shorn-off medical probe. But she also recalled one of Abelane's old lessons: the easiest way to escape is rarely through the guarded door. Neither could she try the window; even if she dared break the glass, it was too far to climb, and her leg would never allow the attempt. Too far to fall.

Pushing herself in the chair with her good leg, Xhea peered down the wall's length, looking for ripples in the drywall, screw holes, inconsistencies. Everything around her was dirtied and water-stained, damaged by years of rot and exposure that Orren's increasing power had done little to repair. Yet this wall, stained though it was, was whole but for its single seeming peephole; and drywall, she knew, rarely stood long in the rain. New, then, and likely poorly made. There was no reason to waste valuable building materials in an area where they would soon succumb to the elements.

Making a fist, Xhea tapped on the wall. A deadened thump greeted her touch. She shifted her chair and rapped again; a little farther, and again. With taps and knocks, she mapped the structure beneath. Wood in places, still strong and unyielding at her touch; metal in others, thin strips that rattled like aluminum within the wall's housing, their tension maintained by little more than strapping and screws.

Near the wall's far end, she found a place between wood and metal both that was wider than her shoulders and seemed to have no bracing pieces between. She tsked at Orren's builders, then lowered herself to the floor and placed her foot against the wall. Without a horizontal fire-stop, a fire could use the inside of the wall like a chimney. That, and it left enough give for even a small, injured girl to kick out the wall.

Xhea grinned, and proceeded to do just that.

After she'd dragged herself through the hole she'd made and shaken the drywall dust from her hair, Xhea looked around. This side was as empty as her room had been—more, lacking furniture entirely. She peered along the wall, but where she had expected to see cameras, there was nothing. Had they truly not been watching? She shook her head. The only real difference on this side of the wall was the bank of elevators, their metal doors reflecting her face as a moon-like gleam in the dark.

She dragged herself to the elevators, only noticing the call button when she lay sprawled before the doors. *Of course*, she thought. Orren had once been taller, but whatever had sheered away the top of the building, leaving a ragged stump and exposed iron bars stabbing skyward, had also taken the top of the elevator shafts. The lifts that moved now through the darkened shafts were driven more by magic than by wires and pulleys. The call button, just beyond her reach, wanted not the press of her finger but her magical signature.

Perhaps it was just as well, given her magic's unpredictability; her presence alone might be enough to damage the elevator's spells. She hadn't wanted to fall out the window, and couldn't imagine that the drop would be much improved from inside a metal box.

Stairs, then. The stairway door was a mess of peeling paint; the dirty sign, hanging above it from a single limp wire, read: exit. *Let's hope so*, Xhea thought.

She didn't know what made her pause, turning back to the elevator doors. There was no sound from the shaft behind, no shimmer of spell exhaust, no vibration of motion. Yet her eyes narrowed. She was tired of being afraid. Now it was someone else's turn.

With hands and magic alike, Xhea reached toward the doors and the complex spells she knew lay beyond. Dark magic, black magic: a seeping fog, a roiling smoke. It rose to fill her: a pressure behind her eyes like hot tears; a tingling in her fingertips that asked for release. She granted it.

As the magic reached out, Xhea felt the spell-reinforced cables beyond as clearly as if she held them in her hands. A moment, and it became clear that the elevator cars were still, sleeping with the rest of the skyscraper. The spell on the call button died first, sparking and sizzling as it unraveled; then spells on the cables, the cars themselves, and the electronics that had given the magic its shape. Her magic flowed from floor to floor, burning plastic and twisting circuit boards in its wake.

A thread of true smoke drifted from between the closed doors, the only sign of the damage she'd wrought beyond. It had only taken a moment—seconds at best. And in that moment the taste and smell of her magic was all around—lightning and rain-wet pavement, burnt sugar and winter-deep night. She wanted more: for one wild second she yearned to follow through on the threat inherent in that small gesture, to release the darkness on the skyscraper and see, freed, what havoc she could wreak. Set the building afire, just to watch it burn.

"Focus," she whispered, as Shai had so many times before.

That dark part of herself simply vowed: soon.

Her elation died when she saw the stairs. Somewhere above the stairwell was exposed to open air; a chill wind swept down through the black, murmuring and sighing around bare corners. Untold years of rain and snow had washed water and worse down the stairs, leaving the treads worn, thick puddles of standing water lingering where foot traffic had worn hollows, mildew blooming in every corner.

"This," she murmured, "is not going to be fun."

By the time the treads below her were merely damp, Xhea had lost count of the number of flights she'd descended, sitting and lowering herself down one stair at a time. No matter: she'd be able to count every step from the bruises that now patterned her backside.

Some few floors below was a level that was clearly under construction. The door to the stairwell stood propped open with a heavy can, airing out paint fumes. Xhea paused, struggling to catch her breath, and peered inside. The entire floor was empty, stripped of whatever walls and furnishings had once filled it, leaving only bare concrete and reinforced pillars. Building materials were stacked nearby: some seemed newly purchased from City sources, but most bore the look of material reclaimed from the ruins. It was in one of these latter piles that she spied a length of heavy plumbing pipe—no flimsy copper this, but good iron, its surface textured as much from age as from casting.

It was a little too weighty to be a good crutch, and tall enough to almost reach her shoulder, but it was too good a find to ignore. With the pipe and the rickety banister taking most of her weight, she managed to make her way downward, step by careful step.

And still too slowly. The tether, always weak and thin, seemed to falter, and Xhea could only wonder whether it was about to vanish entirely. Her mind spun images of Shai's torment, each more awful than the last. The attempted resurrection she remembered, performed within these cold walls, was surely but a crude and doomed version of Eridian's method, but her imagination was far too willing to extrapolate.

"Hurry," she whispered, and pushed onward.

When at last she reached the main level, she all but crumpled to the floor. Her good leg was so fatigued that it trembled, and she felt as if she'd been beating herself with the iron pipe rather than carrying it. Still, she managed to stay standing—and was glad of it when she heard the footsteps approach from the other side of the stairwell door.

So much for everyone being asleep, Xhea thought.

First through the door were a pair of men: security, wearing black clothing and laden tool belts. Their keys jangled as they walked, and Xhea blinked at a memory: back in the dorms, the sound of the guards' tool belts had given warning to anyone with half an ear and the patience to listen. Not that she was one to talk, Xhea thought, holding her head still to keep her charms silent.

It was a moment before they noticed her, barely illuminated by the light from the hall. "Hey," one said, clearly taking her for a resident. "Shouldn't you be—"

The third person through the door was familiar indeed. She bore no clipboard, wore no neat outfit or twisted-back bun; instead, she seemed to have been roused from sleep, her knee-length robe covering very little in the way of pajamas, her hair pillow-mussed. Still, the woman walked briskly, her thin slippers striking the bare ground as precisely as the neat shoes she'd worn earlier.

She was speaking as she came through the door that a guard held open. "We'll need to enact emergency transport procedures Seven A through N, until such time as—" She stopped. "Well," she said slowly. "Xhea. This is a surprise."

A surprise? Xhea glanced from the woman to the guards and back. They hadn't been after her? No, she realized: they'd been dealing with the broken elevators. Catching her mid-escape had merely been coincidence. Score one against vengeful destruction.

"I don't recommend you get any closer," Xhea said to the security men. There was no fear in their expressions, no surprise, just irritation at this girl blocking the way with her little metal pipe.

Xhea loosened her grip on her magic. The guards did not react to the sudden rush of dark from her skin, the pooling shadow at her feet; stupid as sticks she judged them both, and all but blind to magic. Not so the woman. She stiffened at the sight, as one might when suddenly faced with an unknown danger.

Xhea smiled thinly at the reaction. "I don't recommend you get any closer," she repeated.

"I see," the woman said, her voice gone quiet. She raised a hand, gesturing for the confused guards to fall back against the stairwell wall. She was no simple administrator, Xhea realized, no matter what she might feign.

She studied Xhea, as if she were a specimen beneath glass. Her eyes followed the darkness that drifted up and swirled around Xhea's head like aimless smoke and pooled beneath her like living shadow. Details, details: from her white-knuckled grip on the plumbing pipe to the damp, mildew patches that now marred her pants, Xhea had no doubt that there was nothing about her that this woman missed.

At last the woman said, "You're leaving, then?" Her face was hard, but there was only faint disappointment in her tone, as if Xhea were a guest insisting on leaving a party early.

"Looks that way."

"But Xhea," she murmured, "our business here is not done."

"No need to bill me for the elevators." Xhea gestured for the woman to stand aside; what little patience she'd possessed had vanished a few dozen flights of stairs ago. "Just add 'em to my tab."

The woman's eyebrow twitched at the word "elevators." She hadn't known that was Xhea's work, then. *Cleverness on top of cleverness*, Xhea thought, and grit her teeth.

"Lovely chatting with you again," she ground out, "but I really must be going."

"Let us escort you, then."

"No need."

"Oh, but I insist." The woman stood aside and gestured to the vacant doorway and the dimly lit hall beyond.

Xhea tightened her grip on her pipe, and inched past them into the hall. *Faster*, she thought; she couldn't just creep away. She tried to step forward and gasped at the searing pain, stumbling and all but falling. Half-blinded, she clung to the pipe. Yet even through the tears, she saw the sudden rush of motion toward her.

"Get back," she cried, throwing out her left hand, fingers stretched wide. Only the woman saw the rush of darkness that all but eclipsed the gesture, but it was enough: she grabbed the security guard closest to her, stopping his lunge toward Xhea just in time.

Steady, Xhea thought, trying to slow the sudden pounding of her heart and rein in the darkness. Perhaps a single touch of her magic wouldn't have killed the man—but she didn't know.

"Please," she said, ignoring her voice's sudden quiver. "Just stay back."

Even half-healed, her knee could not bear her full weight; yet she refused to pull herself along the floor again like a child still learning to walk—not now, not with witnesses. If the leg would not bear her, she'd simply drag it behind her.

Easier said than done. Her progress was slower and more painful than she imagined, each hopping step jarring her swollen knee even within its protective brace. Xhea was soaked with sweat before she'd traveled more than ten feet, and the hall stretched out before her. She heard the whisper of the woman's slippers pacing slowly behind her, the security guards' heavy treads, and envied them their ease of movement.

They can't just let me walk out of here, Xhea thought. There was something she was missing.

The answer, when it came, was so soft she almost missed it: a slight clink like metal on metal. Xhea hesitated, mere steps from where the hall turned toward the left and led to the skyscraper's front lobby. Something about the sound . . .

The jangle of keys, she realized. She leaned on her pipe, not needing to feign fatigue, and looked carefully ahead. There: a shadow shifted across the threadbare carpet. She wasn't being escorted; they were leading her into an ambush.

Xhea let the pipe and wall hold her weight, and slapped her free hand flat against the drywall beside her. Flecks of paint fell in a whispering rain. Her awareness followed her magic through the wall to the workings beneath. As in Edren, great bundles of wires ran through the walls—a physical structure to shape and hold the spells that ran the skyscraper. She mapped their paths in a second, then her eyes flew open and she stared down the woman and the guards at her sides.

"I will not," Xhea said, speaking slowly and forcefully for all that her voice trembled, "let you hold me here any longer."

"Child, I wasn't . . ."

"The guards around the corner. Tell them to stand down."

A lift of that perfect eyebrow. "Or?"

"Tell me," Xhea said. "What spells do you have running within these walls? Security, lighting, communications, information flow . . . ? Let me walk out of here unhindered, or they're all gone."

"Xhea, do you really think that—"

"Do you really think I'm bluffing? It took me seconds to destroy the elevator—if that. I could unravel in an instant what it's taken Orren decades to build, you know I could. *And I'd enjoy it.*"

The woman's mouth thinned into a hard, flat line.

"Let me go," Xhea said, forcing her voice to be soft. Let her think it a plea. "Just let me go."

The moment stretched, aching. "As you wish," the woman said. "For now."

At her nod, the guards stepped back. Others moved too, and only then did Xhea realize how many witnesses had gathered. She took a firmer grip on her pipe and forced herself forward again, step by agonizing step. As she went, doors opened behind her. No fancy rooms these, not in a service hall of the skyscraper's ground level, yet they were occupied nonetheless. Light streamed from opened doors, and people began to peek out, curious, cautious. In the way.

There was a whisper of silken fabric as the woman gestured the witnesses back. Xhea could feel their eyes on her, heard their motion as she passed—footsteps, more footsteps, whispers and murmured questions, all following behind.

Sweetness save me, she thought. *I'm leading a parade.*

Down the hall and through the doors into the skyscraper's battered front vestibule, chipped faux marble and stained mirror glass. The gap where a revolving door had once stood had been boarded over, only a soft breath of night air slipping in through the nail holes. The doors to either side had been bolted and barred, chains wrapped around the handles.

Almost there. The lie was so bold it was laughable.

A babble rose behind her when Xhea gestured for the doors to be unbarred.

"It's dark, she can't—"

"Surely she doesn't mean—"

"She'll be killed!"

Somehow the thought of again facing the night walkers held little fear. She stood stoically, face as blank as she could manage, while one of the security men fumbled at his belt for the correct keys.

"Xhea," a voice said. Lin. For him alone she turned.

He stood just a step from the small crowd, hands raised, palms out and empty. He stared, his jutting Adam's apple bobbing wildly as he swallowed. "The brace," he said. "If you turn the adjustment screws on the side, you can keep it from bending."

Xhea nodded. It took a moment to do as he said, fumbling for the screws through the fabric of her pants. At last she felt the brace harden: not magic, but a stiffening of the material itself, the kind of mechanical genius that marked the inventions of the before-times. Tentatively, she shifted her weight onto her injured leg. It hurt—oh sweetness and blight, did it hurt—but it held.

Lin almost smiled at the sight, something like pride warring with the fear in his expression. Xhea wanted to speak, but the simple words died on her lips. *Thank you.* Instead she nodded as she turned away.

Outside the air was cool enough to make her shiver, but it was a chill that spoke of early mornings and dawning light, the swirl of air through the Lower City's crumbling structures. She stepped away from Orren—stumbled, staggered. It took a few hurting steps, near-falling, before she found her stride. Then the rhythm of her makeshift cane striking the asphalt reverberated with a sound like a bell, singing in perfect time to her breathing.

"I'm coming," Xhea whispered. She clung to the tether like a lifeline, face streaked with pained tears. "Hang in there Shai, I'm coming."

She walked without turning back, cloud-tattered darkness swirling all around her.

Chapter Twenty-One

"One," Xhea panted. She dragged herself forward a single step, hopped to regain her precarious balance, and leaned heavily on her length of pipe. A breath and then she swung the pipe forward, shifted her weight, and pushed forward again.

"Two."

Only three more steps until she could pause for breath. Then five more steps. Then five more.

Edren was only a few blocks from Orren, and little had troubled her path but cracks and stones, yet that short walk had already taken an hour or more. Her legs hurt, and her knee; she had expected no less. It was the pain in her bruised shoulder and hands that took her aback, the muscles exhausted and trembling from use of her makeshift cane; that, and the sharp ache in her palms, unused to bearing so much of her weight. The rust stains on her hands were a deep enough gray that she almost mistook them for blood.

"Three," she said, and dragged herself forward. "Four."

On the next swing her pipe struck a curb and Xhea looked up in slow surprise. Edren stood before her, the bulk of the antique hotel dominating the block. She leaned on the pipe, and watched the long shadows shift across Edren's decorative façade as dawn broke on the far horizon.

No back-alley entrance, this; she'd come to the former hotel's front doors. Four thick pillars supported an overhang that was easily two stories overhead, and decorative lions stood guard beside massive doors with handles of upswept brass. At least she thought they'd once been lions. The creatures' faces were pitted and smashed away, as were their claws, leaving only hulking pale shapes with edges smoothed by the touch of countless hands. Neither had Edren escaped time's ravages: the pillars were cracked and stained, the windows were boarded or bricked, and those elegant brass handles were tarnished black. Yet in that soft light, Xhea could almost imagine it as it must have once been, a thick carpet unfurled down its wide front steps, uniformed doormen waiting to usher guests inside.

Forget them, Xhea thought, carpet and doormen both—she'd settle for a sentry coming to see what she wanted. The curb and shallow flight of stairs between her and those doors felt like a barricade, complete with armed guards. It would be better if she went around back, as quietly and unobtrusively as possible. Yet her legs shook, and her arms; she did not know that she could make it so far. Did not know if Shai had the time left for her to make the effort.

The only other option seemed to be to lower herself to the ground and drag herself to the door, step by uncomfortable step. Except—no. She knew that Edren set watchers, human and spelled alike; knew that she had to be watched, even now. What attention would knocking earn her that she didn't already have, emerging as she had from the pre-dawn darkness to stand unmoving in the road before the skyscraper? No, they knew she was here. What she needed was to provoke a reaction.

Xhea took a deep breath to steady herself. *Help*, she wanted to cry, *please help*—and could let nothing of that weakness to show. *Stand up*, she told herself. She shifted her weight to her good leg and relaxed her aching arm, moving her grip to hold the pipe as if it were a weapon rather than a cane. She pushed her shoulders back and shook out her hair, letting the charms chime freely.

She was not exhausted; she was not hurt or desperate or afraid; she was not moments from collapsing. *Believe the lie*, she thought, and smiled.

"Edren!" Xhea's voice was loud and steady, and the echoes circled like a flock of birds. "I've come to speak to Lorn Edren. We have business to discuss."

There was no response, not that she'd expected any. No, all she wanted was for the on-guard duty to watch her—and know who to run and tell when things became interesting.

And *interesting* was most definitely her goal.

She drew a long, deep breath and held it, focusing. When she exhaled, it was as if releasing a long drag on a cigarette—and her breath stained the air black. *More*, she thought to it, urging it on, and the magic surged forth, rushing out of her hard and fast. She felt a chill as the power left her, but gripped her makeshift cane all the harder and maintained the flow. She held on until it seemed the magic was a dark presence above her: no raincloud, this; no puff like smoke; but a deep ache of black, a spreading patch of night.

Black enough that it had to have entered the visual spectrum, even for the most magic-poor watcher. No point in hiding—not when Orren already knew this little secret of hers.

Now for the hard part, Xhea thought. As if the cloud of magic was her hand, an extension of herself, she willed the magic to move. Shai had shown her how to do this, but in miniature: dark little flows of power caught between her palms made to turn slow circles or form a shape. And as Shai had always said, it was one thing to work magic when caught in a rush of emotion; another thing entirely to use it with thought and precision and control. It was much, much harder. But Shai was there, her tether an anchor, the memory of her voice a guide. Desperation, it seemed, was the best motivation of all.

Xhea willed the magic to form a wide ring and spin, and though she struggled with the power she could feel it moving faster and faster, until it spun dizzily above her head. Then she broke the ring into a spiral and sent it curling inward and down, and tipped her head back to meet it. Opening her mouth, she inhaled sharply.

Sweetness save me, she thought as the magic rushed back into her, hot and cold and like a shock of sugar to the blood. *Oh sweetness, don't choke.*

Her hand shook where she gripped her pipe, and she shuddered—but made herself stare straight at Edren. She waited.

A minute passed, and another. A nervous sheen of sweat broke out across her skin. In the distance she could hear movement: people leaving their houses, vendors beginning to set up outside the market walls. If they didn't answer soon there would be witnesses, something she wanted as little as Lorn would want their arrangement publicly known.

Perhaps it wasn't too late to go around the back doors—but no, of course it was. It was two days too late, Shai in her enemies' hands all the while.

Still Xhea waited.

There was one other thing she could try, though it meant breaking a sworn promise. There was a story she could tell, a secret, and she already knew how the telling would begin: *Once upon a time there were two brothers who both lay dying: one from a terrible wound, and one from an illness with no known cause . . .*

With every word she would make an enemy of Lorn. He would honor the favor he owed her, but no more, and his enmity would turn all of Edren against her. She knew it—and yet still she drew breath to speak the words.

The door cracked open. A young man slipped out, tall like a light-starved tree, a lock and chain still held in his hands. He jumped and scrambled out of the way as the door opened again and Lorn stepped through, still buttoning his shirt. In all the tattoos that patterned his dark chest, it was the one above his heart that held her attention: a single name in bold cursive writing, *Addis*.

Xhea fought the urge to swallow.

Lorn came down the steps, his expression blank, his feet bare. His limp was more pronounced than she remembered; his leg stiffened, perhaps, from sleep. "Xhea," he said, looking down at her. His rough voice was perfectly calm, perfectly polite, and it chilled her to the core. "Would you care to explain yourself?"

Xhea glanced down at her boots, wishing it was only fatigue that made her turn away. "You owe me a favor, and I've come to collect. I need—I'd like to ask of you two things."

"I owe you only one favor." The hard, naked simplicity of the words told her just how angry he was.

"Both are small," she hastened to add. "First, I'd like to send a message to the City. Paper and pen is fine, any method of delivery so long as it's fast." An easy task. Lorn took a slow breath, as if to steady himself—as if to keep his large hands from curling into fists. At last he nodded, and Xhea continued. "Second, I'd like you to call me an elevator and provide the fare to take me to a central Tower." A moment's work, and a few renai. Surely he would not refuse.

Yet Lorn just watched her, expression stiff, a faint crease between his dark brows.

"Look," Xhea said. "There's no catch. Just deliver a message, call me a lift, and all debts between us are clear."

Some of the anger went out of him, at that. He shook his head, frustrated. "Why this, Xhea? Why now?"

"I need . . . it's just . . ." Xhea fumbled over her words. "I don't know how to explain."

"Try."

Again she looked to her feet, their ragged nails and cold, discolored flesh. Favor or no, she realized that Lorn was as likely to send her away as to help. She swayed slightly; she was so tired. She had to trust him, she realized, trust him as he had trusted her.

"They stole someone," she said at last. "A Tower. They stole someone—a friend—that they had no right to take. I'm the only one who can help her."

"A . . . ghost?"

Xhea nodded and met his eyes. "A bright ghost," she said, gambling. "A ghost that shone."

A change came into Lorn's face, though she couldn't read the expression that swept across his features as fast and fierce as a storm wind—and was as quickly gone.

"And what you did before?" Lorn moved his hand in a circle above his head, mimicking her ring of darkness. "What am I to think of that?"

Xhea shrugged, uncomfortable. "I needed to get your attention."

"So you threatened me?"

"What? No! I—" Xhea clamped her jaw shut. He knew something about her power, she realized—as had the woman in Orren—and she needed that knowledge. Wished she knew the right questions, or had the time in which to ask them. "I didn't mean it that way," she whispered.

Lorn studied her. "You don't understand, do you? You don't understand what you did."

Xhea shook her head, the slightest fraction of movements.

"A blade to my throat," he said quietly. "A bomb. Those might have been lesser threats."

"I didn't mean it that way," she whispered.

"Okay," he said finally. "I'll help you save your friend. But when you return, we should have a talk, you and I."

She met his gaze, those dark eyes so steady.

"Yes," Xhea said softly. "I think I'd like that."

To the voice that still whispered, *all alone*, she thought: *I might be alone, but that doesn't mean I won't have help.*

Her message was a simple thing, no more than a few lines, and

Xhea knew that she should have agonized over each one, tested the weight of each word. No time. Instead she strove for clarity in wording and penmanship both, and trusted the rest to fate.

After her message was whisked away, Xhea ran through her breathing exercises, resisting the urge to rush. Even a stray wisp of magic might disrupt the elevator, and she shuddered to think of the fall. She visualized in time to her breath: a door swinging shut; a hand curling into a fist; a flower, petals closing. With her emotions running high, her magic was slow to contract. She struggled, at last feeling the power clot beneath her breastbone into a weight like stone.

When the elevator that Lorn had called arrived, whirring quietly, Xhea opened her eyes. "I'm ready," she said.

Lorn flicked a small sphere of renai toward her—just enough magic to get her to Eridian. Xhea expected a shock, expected pain, and braced herself for both. It wasn't enough. She cried out as the magic struck her, and cringed so violently that she lost her balance. She fell hard, barely avoiding landing on her injured knee, and the iron pipe clanged to the ground beside her. The bright magic *burned*, running through her veins like fire. All she could hear was her heart, pounding too hard, too fast, its rhythm frantic.

Xhea struggled to draw breath, gasping as her muscles twitched and shuddered. *Keep control*, she told herself—but where was the control in this? She struggled to see, trying to focus on her hands splayed on the dirty pavement. She struggled to rise. Lorn called to her, but she couldn't understand him, nor could she shape a reply. Color came in brief, harsh flashes, each a knife's point to her eyes. She saw her new pants, not black but muddy green—the brown of Lorn's skin, the amber flecks in his eyes—the pipe's rust and its residue on her hands, orange like a sunset, orange and brown and a strange flaking red, and it hurt, oh sweetness save her, it *hurt*.

Lorn had already paid the elevator and now, hovering above her, it opened like a flower. Its spell-strands fell around her, glowing liquid gold—gray—gold. Again she tried to push herself off the ground, but her head was spinning, spinning. Xhea grabbed for her pipe, thinking, *I'll stand when I get there.*

Yet as the elevator strands closed around her, one fell across her bad leg. It sizzled as it touched her, then flickered and died, gold burning to ash. *No*, she thought, and looked up. Another strand fell across her leg instead of trying to hold her, as if her leg was a lifeless thing, undetectable.

Then the elevator collapsed all around her, the strands sliding across the backs of her hands, her upturned face, their brilliant light turned harsh and cold. She heard its noises, the protests of a machine struggling against its destruction, the whirr of its engines as it tried to pull away. Xhea tried to speak, tried to scream, but the world was spinning, or she was spinning against the hard ground, and she was going to be sick, and nothing came out of her mouth at all.

Then: black.

Blind, she thought. No room left for panic or shock.

She lay on the ground, the pavement cold beneath her cheek. Slowly the light crept back to her eyes, bringing with it dimension and shape, the perfect arc of a stone-gray sky and only Towers' shadowed bellies above her. It took a long time to focus; the world swam before her, smeared and uncertain, until any hint of color faded. The elevator was gone, destroyed, she knew not which. With a quivering hand, Xhea wiped away her tears.

"That," Xhea whispered, "didn't go so well." She pushed herself to sitting, palms against the ground as if to keep the world still. She looked at one arm, then the other—at both hands, pressed hard to the crumbling road. She wished no showy display of power, and yet a shadow-gray mist surrounded her, clinging like scent or sorrow. She tried to push it down, to pull it back, to smother it with will and anger and fear, and it did nothing but move gently, drifting as if in a slow current.

She had called the magic to her, allowed it to flow, and now it would not stop. Xhea looked at the growing darkness around her, felt a seeping chill, and could only think: *I'm bleeding.* She wished she could sink into the ground, or walk away; wished she could fly to her destination and be done with it. Wished, too, that the shadowy people she could just see through Edren's upper windows would stop gaping. *Show's over,* she thought. *Move along.*

Time for Plan B. *Oops,* she thought fuzzily. *Forgot to make a Plan B.*

"Hey, kid," Lorn said, loudly. Slow footsteps and he was beside her. Then in a softer voice, unguarded: "Looks like you could use a bit more help."

Xhea licked her lower lip, tasting blood. "Looks that way, yeah."

Lorn held out his hand, and she took it without thinking. He jerked at the shock of her touch and pulled away, shaking his hand as if in pain—and stopped when he saw her expression. He steeled himself, and offered his hand again. Carefully, he pulled her to her feet and held on until she could steady herself with the pipe; and if both of their hands went numb, neither deigned to mention it.

"You still need to get to the City?" he asked.

Xhea stared upward, thinking desperately. She felt for the

hair-fine tether that still pulled her and nodded mutely.

"Wait here—I'll have someone bring a car around." At her expression, Lorn added, "But don't get any ideas. I'm driving."

Xhea fit in the trunk. Barely. It was the farthest they could get her from the aircar's engine and the storage coil that fueled it without towing her off the back with a rope—an idea that Lorn had rejected out of hand. He dropped the passenger seat to allow her braced leg to protrude forward, makeshift cane at her side, and with a little contortion she could just see out the windshield.

Lorn had chosen the oldest, most mechanical of the aircars in his collection. Even so, it was small and sleek, with glossy paint and an engine so quiet she could barely detect its soft whir. Xhea tried to touch as little of the car as she could as she curled into its trunk, running through every exercise she could remember to stay calm and keep her energy in check. She'd never been particularly good with nerves.

"Speed might be good," she said as Lorn flared the engine to life.

Knowing this favor pushed the limits of even Lorn's sense of fairness, Xhea had paid him in her only trustworthy coin: information. She'd told him what she could of Allenai and Eridian's struggle while a guard brought the car down from the garage on Edren's roof. She cared little for politics but knew that there was an advantage to be gained by major shifts in Towers' positions—even for a skyscraper like Edren. From the spark in Lorn's eyes as he'd listened, he agreed.

Xhea's stomach twisted as the aircar rose—magic or motion or nerves, she didn't know. Didn't matter. A detached voice provided Lorn with instructions from somewhere within the dashboard: *"Entrance to ascension lane accepted. Course correction for sector*

7-B-Rising accepted. Please maintain your current speed."

"Hang on, Shai," she whispered. The tether flickered.

They climbed steadily through the gap between the ground and the lowest Towers. Xhea strained and twisted but could see little but empty sky. *This is going to work*, she told herself. The thought did nothing to ease her curdled stomach.

It wasn't until they were entering the City proper, the lowest Towers' defensive spires filling the windshield, that the car began to shudder. There were only small movements at first, like a nervous hand's quiver; yet the shaking grew more violent with each passing moment. The engine whined, and their upward progress slowed. A warning light flashed on, and another.

"*Please maintain recommended speed*," said the dashboard.

Lorn corrected, calming their flight path—only to swear as the car shuddered and swerved as if hit. The engine's steady whir sputtered, then rose in volume as if the car were growling. Xhea grabbed for the sides of the trunk, then pulled her hands away just as quickly.

"What happened?" she called over the rising sound of the engine.

"Just a few shorts in the spell." Lorn's hands flew across the controls. "Nothing that we can't—"

This time the aircar didn't just shudder but dropped, falling like a stone before catching itself and climbing again. Xhea swallowed, feeling as if her stomach had become lodged in her throat. The sputtering grew louder. Lorn swore and fought with the wheel.

"*Please maintain recommended speed*."

"Now?"

"We've got a partial drive failure," he said shortly, "and the left rear braking thruster's offline." There was a sharp pop from somewhere near Xhea's head. Lorn glanced at the displays and added, "That was the taillights."

"Oh." Xhea pressed her lips shut and focused on her breathing.

The ride grew progressively rougher as they entered the City's proper traffic lanes, the car rattling and sputtering as Lorn forced it upward. It seemed a small eternity before Lorn announced that they were on approach to Eridian's main landing bay, the relief in his voice audible even over the growing clamor. Peering forward, Xhea could just see the wide shape of the bay's closed doors in the side of Eridian's middle tier, a cone of hovering lights blinking to direct traffic safely inward.

"*Approach denied*," the dash said in its polite, pseudo-female voice. "*Please re-enter main traffic lanes, and resume minimum accepted speed.*"

"Approach denied?" Xhea said incredulously. "They can *do* that?"

"Coming around," Lorn said, and directed the car in a tight, wobbling—and, from the screeching alarms, highly illegal—circle, and made the approach again, only to be rejected with the same message. He swore. "They've got the Tower in lockdown—no traffic in or out."

Xhea shifted to peer out at the closed landing bay doors. "So how do we get in?"

"We don't." The car shuddered violently, their speed slowing further, eliciting yet more protests from the dashboard. "I'm sorry," Lorn said, his voice tense, "but the car can't take much more of this. I have to take it back down."

"No!" Xhea cried. Not now—not when she was so close. Eridian gleamed, seeming to fill every window in turn as Lorn struggled to bring the aircar around to re-enter the main traffic lane.

Lorn glanced over his shoulder at her, face creased in frustration and, she realized, no little fear. "There's nothing I can do," he said. "We can't get in without a passkey, and this car is crashing." The car shuddered and jerked until its very panels rattled, while the engine's unsteady whine rose to a scream.

Crashing? Xhea thought. *Sweetness save us.*

The second thought followed hard on its heels: a passkey. She fumbled desperately in her jacket's top pocket.

"Lorn!" Xhea had to yell to be heard over the engine and the racket of the car's slow self-destruction. "What about this?" She held out the token she'd stolen from the warehouse. Eridian's etched symbol gleamed in the early morning sunlight.

"Where did you . . . ?" Lorn released the controls just long enough to reach back and grab the token from her hand, then jam it into a thin slot in the dash. "Never mind. Just pray it works."

He brought the car around a final time, and Xhea saw that even if the landing bay doors opened they'd barely clear the lower lip. "Come on," she whispered. "Come on."

"*Approach—approach denied,*" the dashboard stuttered. "*Please—main traffic—Please re-enter main traffic lanes—*"

"No." Xhea couldn't hear the sound of her own voice over the engine. She'd been so sure . . . Eridian vanished behind her as Lorn turned the car, struggling to guide it toward the ground in what seemed to be a wide, uneven spiral.

"*And resume accepted—resume—resume—Please re-enter—*"

Xhea shook her head as if to free her thoughts from the noise. It didn't make sense that Brend would have a broken passkey to his own Tower. He spent as little time in the Lower City as he could, coming to the ground only to accept new items or to prepare shipments . . . She gasped.

"Lorn!" she shouted, but the engine drowned out the sound. They were descending, their hard-won altitude escaping like sand through open fingers. She tried again, screaming over the engine and the sound of rattling, breaking metal. "Lorn—the key, it's for the shipping bay."

"What?" he called.

"The *shipping bay!*" She pointed desperately at Eridian as they came around again. She couldn't hear Lorn's reply, only a snatch of something that sounded like "bad idea," and then they banked hard to the left. The aircar seemed to slip sideways as they turned, their flight turned into a barely controlled fall. A moment later, Xhea caught sight of another, smaller entrance near the bottom of Eridian's lowest tier, all but hidden by the downward spike of a defensive spire. As Lorn tried to direct them toward the closed doors, the car began to shake so violently that Xhea's teeth rattled.

"*Approach—*" The speakers were failing, the voice rising and falling in an ear-splitting warble. "*Approach—please maintain— approach accepted—decrease speed—*"

"It's opening," Lorn called, and Xhea could just see it over his shoulder, a widening gap in the shipping bay door rushing toward them like an oncoming fist. "Brace for impact!"

Xhea curled into a ball, struggling against her knee brace and the iron bar. She wrapped her hands around her head, felt her magic flare around her like living shadow—and the aircar's remaining spells died. The screaming engine went silent, and they fell.

For an instant, her ears ringing, there was nothing but that terrible silence. Then the car hit something hard with a crunch, ricocheted upward, and they rolled. End over end the aircar tumbled, Xhea thrown around inside like a rag in a storm. She might have screamed—but everything was screaming, everything was light and noise and the impact of too-soft flesh against wall and door and window—

They slid to a stop.

Xhea lay in an aching, tumbled heap, with her arms still wrapped tightly around her head. She tasted blood. Around her, the ruins of the car gave a slow *tick-tick-tick* as the overstressed metal cooled.

Dazed, she reached out and fumbled at the trunk latch. It gave with a weak pop, and the trunk lifted a bare inch to admit a beam of light. Slowly, she pushed the trunk open and dragged herself onto the smooth floor of Eridian's shipping bay. Her pipe clattered to the ground behind her.

"Lorn?" she attempted, and coughed. The air stank of spell exhaust, too-hot metal, and burned plastic. The aircar was a ruin, its smooth lines and perfect paint replaced by a tangled wreck that only hinted at its original shape. Fractured glass fell from its windows like stars.

"Lorn," she said again, licking blood from her split lip, and the driver's side door creaked open. Carefully, Lorn pulled himself from the wreckage. Seeing him there, Xhea laughed. The sound was horrible and unsteady, punctuated by chattering teeth, and she had no idea what could possibly be funny. Lorn was untouched but for a slight cut on his temple from which ran a single rivulet of blood. *He had restraints*, she thought, and laughed helplessly.

Lorn knelt at her side. "Are you okay?" he asked. "Can you stand?"

Xhea grabbed the pipe, squeezing her trembling fingers until her knuckles went bloodless. Slowly, carefully, she stood, using the pipe and the ruined aircar to help support her weight. Her good leg trembled. Her bad knee throbbed with every beat of her heart, while countless small hurts patterned her arms and legs and back, some seeping blood. *No, not okay*, she thought. But she was in Eridian, and standing, and it would take more than just pain to keep her from Shai.

She felt for the tether; it pulled sharply upward, near vertical, and she tilted her head to follow its rise. Above, she could see no ceiling, no equipment, no movement—only the shipping bay's walls vanishing into shadow. Arrayed around them were boxes and stacked crates, the hulking lumps of wrapped shipments ringing the walls. All still and silent. No workers in sight, no sound but their breathing and metallic ticks as the aircar's wreckage settled.

"No stairs," she murmured. Of course not: this was the City proper, after all. Whatever spells the workers used to access this bay—whatever spells they used to transport goods to various parts of the Tower—were useless to her.

Lorn frowned at the weariness in her voice. "No, but there's always a backup system." He began a slow sweep of the shipping bay. "You don't imagine that they do *everything* by magic, right?"

Xhea blinked, and kept her mouth shut.

"Ah, here we are." He pushed aside a stack of crates that floated on a cushion of air, revealing a rickety lift attached to a mess of pulleys and wires. Lorn dusted off the controls. "In you get. Come on, the faster you can get wherever you need to go, the faster I can get out of here."

Xhea stepped onto the platform and clung to the narrow rail, trying to ignore the way the whole contraption twisted and groaned under even her slight weight. She turned back to Lorn. "But you . . . Your car . . . I mean, I didn't . . ."

"We'll worry about that later," he said. "For now, go find your friend." He pressed his fingers to his chest where she'd seen the tattoo of his brother's name. Then he flicked a switch and the lift's mechanical motor roared to life. She rose.

Chapter Twenty-Two

The lift ground to a halt at the entrance to a hall that was better lit than the shipping bay, but just as empty. Xhea stepped carefully from the metal platform to solid ground, then peered up and down the hall: even Towers, it seemed, had service corridors. She didn't know why the revelation was surprising.

The tether pointed and she attempted to follow, limping forward to the pipe's loud accompaniment. She expected to find someone at every turn, yet there was only silence, as if all of Eridian waited with breath held. The tether led her forward, forward and up, and she wound her way through the maze of back halls shaking with the after-effects of adrenaline. Yet it seemed she had to backtrack as often as she moved forward, peeking out into what could only be shopping areas and restaurants and sculpture gardens, all empty, before turning and trying again.

Her mind whirled as she calculated the time since the message had left her hands and risen for delivery: how long, how long?

She wanted to run to Shai as fast as feet could carry her, turn all her fear and fury to speed while there was still some hope of saving the ghost. Yet she also wanted to curl away, small and unnoticed—for who was she to stand against a Tower? Caught between the two instincts she quivered, breathing through opened lips and a mouth gone dry as sun-baked bone. The Tower's silence echoed.

There would be no running, she knew. There was nowhere to hide. Her hand shook as she raised it to the center of her chest, feeling for the thread that connected her to Shai. *So thin,* she thought, holding to that taunt line. So fine, and fraying. Her pain and fear did not matter—not her knee, not the scrapes and bruises from the crash, not any of it. For she remembered the sound of Shai's voiceless scream, and in that memory she found the strength to keep moving.

"I'm coming," she whispered and walked on, leaving ash-black footprints in her wake. Thinking: *Hang on, Shai. Hang on.*

At last the corridor split and she followed the widest pathway, climbing a ramp up and in toward what felt like the Tower's center. She rounded a darkened corner, hearing a sound like rustling, or soft wind . . .

Breath.

People.

The sound of hundreds of people breathing at once.

It took mere seconds for her eyes to become accustomed to the dark. Here was the garden she had expected, the huge space at the Tower's core filled with trees and flowers and wandering pathways. Above, the energy of Eridian's living heart pulsed like a miniature flaring sun—though even that great power, like the rest of the Tower, seemed somehow muted, its glow dimmed, its movements slow.

In its light she could clearly see the crowd spread before her—and crowd it was. They sat on the ground and ringed the trees so that all Xhea could see were countless bowed heads in every direction, men and women, young and old—still, silent, breathing. The people of Eridian all had their eyes closed and their hands pressed to the floor or walls or decorative pillars, planted against the sides of fountains or the wide curves of the abstract sculptures which dotted the garden. Yet it was their expressions that caught her: each wore a look of focus so intense it seemed akin to pain. Every face she could see had creased brows and tight lips, foreheads bright with sweat, as if they felt the same hurt, the same urgency, the same need.

She stared, and at last saw the faint glimmer around each of their hands, brief pulses of power that vanished as quickly as they appeared, absorbed into the surfaces that they touched so intently. They were feeding the Tower, Xhea realized. With every beat of their hearts, every breath and thought, the life within their very cells was sent into Eridian.

She stepped forward, and one by one they opened their eyes.

In her plan—if she even had the right to use the word for such a tangled mess of half-conceived ideas—she had assumed she could follow Shai's tether to where the ghost was being held, slipping through the Tower's morning crowds as she did the Lower City market: if not unobtrusively, then at least largely ignored. Yet while few in the Lower City could see her magic, magical talent was the rule above. The gift that made Lorn's family powerful enough to reign as the Lower City's elite was commonplace in the City proper—average, if not weak.

So she stood before the gathered citizens of Eridian veiled by the swirling darkness she no longer knew how to dispel, and they stared. Seeing her—seeing her magic. The ground died at her feet, a spreading pool of black; and they stared.

Xhea stared back, looking from one face to another, settling nowhere. *Say something*, she thought. *Say anything*—anything to break the terrible weight of silence, the pressure of their eyes upon her.

There came a whisper from the crowd to her right and she turned. By a lift tube stood a familiar pale-haired man. As she watched, bright sparks flowed between his fingers, weaving a spell faster than Xhea had ever before seen. She just had time to recognize the shape of a message spell before it lifted from his hands, up and away, vanishing in the light of the Tower's heart above.

"Derren," Xhea said, thinking: *no*, not when she'd come so close. Derren met her eyes and smiled.

"Now this is an unexpected surprise."

"Yes," Xhea said, mind spinning. "I've . . . I've come to take you up on your offer. Am I too late?"

She braced for his reaction, expecting more than the slow raise of a single pale eyebrow. "That's why you've come?" he asked.

"Of course." Xhea spread her arms, holding tight to her pipe. "Why else?"

Oh, why else indeed? Yet if she could not sneak in unaware, or storm the gates, why not walk in invited? A mental clock ticked in time to her heartbeat, to the tether's stuttering pull, Shai's silent cry.

Derren smiled thinly. "Such an unexpected surprise." He started to gesture across the crowded garden when a returning message drew his attention. "Ah, here we are." He beckoned it forward, and the spell unfurled to settle, petal-soft, across his face before dissolving. Derren paused, and gave her a considering look.

"Tell me—the ghosts in your care. Do they matter to you?"

"Matter?" She could feel the question's hidden weight and took a leap of faith, hoping that he knew enough of her reputation to believe her answer. "What can they matter? They're dead."

"And the ghost you had with you when last we met. What was she to you?"

Xhea grimaced. "I'd say a payment, but a missed opportunity is more like it. Couple of bidders interested in claiming that one, then she up and vanishes. A year's income, gone." Yet even as she spoke, her mind reeled: he'd seen Shai's glow. He'd *known* she was there. Who was this man?

"Why?" she asked. "What's it matter?"

"That's not for me to say." He gestured to the lift. "After you. We can discuss the details of our arrangement on the way."

As he came to stand beside her, she made a gesture of her own, smoke-like ribbons trailing from her fingers as she raised her hand. "I think not," she said, keeping her tone casual and vaguely threatening. Better that than: sorry, no can do, this stuff's entirely out of my control.

"As you wish," he said, clearly humoring her. "After me."

He stepped into the empty air of the tube. With a rush of light, a platform formed beneath his feet, the glimmering spellwork as steady as the floor. He extended both hands and his magic flowed. There were no movements of his fingers, no whispered words, and yet Xhea watched as spells seemed to write themselves in midair, complex patterns writhing and joining too fast for her to read, almost too fast to follow. The lines twined around the lift spells beneath him, amplifying and reinforcing the platform. Xhea had never seen a working like it—and he did it without hesitation, seemingly without thought.

"Now, please," Derren said, all politeness and steel, and Xhea entered the tube at his side.

The platform shuddered at her slight weight, and she was all but blinded by the sudden surge of Derren's magic. In the twisting spell lines, Xhea glimpsed patterns that spoke of strength and stability and endurance—could feel their sudden heat through her boots. The magic cascading from her eroded the spells holding them aloft; yet as fast as the spell-lines sputtered and died, Derren's magic mended what she ruined so unthinkingly.

The spells shuddered again and they rose. Xhea couldn't bear to watch the ground drop away and so she looked up. The lift tube around her was so tall that she couldn't see its top, branching in countless directions like a great tree. Floors rushed by, allowing her glimpses of gently curving halls and wide chambers, children's play areas, gardens and dining halls and open pools. All dim now, empty and waiting.

She thought, *I never could have done this alone. Never.* But what she said was, "Let's talk payment."

Derren spared her a sideways glance. "Without knowing the nature of the job?"

Clumsy. She tried to recover. "You said that's not for you to say—but you're clearly able to make me an offer. Considering how fast we're going, I'm guessing it's important." She shrugged. "I want to know how much 'important' is worth to you. Or, rather, to me."

The lift tube around them branched, and branched again. She didn't see how Derren guided them along one route rather than another; yet, unerringly, they moved toward the Tower's core. The tether joining her to Shai strengthened with every passing second. Light began to shimmer through the tube's frosted length: Eridian's heart, she realized. The Tower's living magic pulsed just beyond her reach. She clasped her hands together, white-knuckled, sweating.

"I offered you renai before—but there are other options, should that not be to your liking. A life like this, for example." Derren gestured at the walls with a hand streaming magic.

"I can't live in a Tower," Xhea said, all scorn and haloed darkness. Thinking: *especially not this one.*

"Clearly. Yet you could have enough to eat and drink. Clothes to keep you warm in winter. A place to live that isn't leaking or rotting or buried underground. And you would be safe. You would have protection from a source that no one in the Lower City would dare cross."

It took Xhea a moment to find her voice. "You're offering me—what, Eridian's patronage? For one job?"

"One or more—that's for you to decide."

Then Xhea heard Shai screaming.

At first the sound was barely audible over the wind of their passage and the sizzle of the spells beneath them fading, dying and being reborn. The sound grew as they approached until it took effort for Xhea not cover her ears with her hands. The tether had given her only the resonance of a scream, echoing breathless and undying.

The sound was far worse.

Whatever she might have replied—whatever Derren might have made of her reaction—was lost on their arrival. The lift shuddered to a stop, open to a room that was as large, if not larger, than the garden below. No trees, here, no bushes or statues. Nothing to hide what was happening.

"Oh sweetness," Xhea whispered. "Sweetness and blight."

They were directly above Eridian's heart. Power rose through a glass-clear floor in great shimmering arcs, like flares lifting from the surface of an uncertain sun. The chamber was huge, echoing, but everything seemed to be made from crystal: wherever she looked, bright facets reflected the light—the magic—and amplified it until the very air vibrated. It felt like a physical force, pushing against her like heavy hands, choking her, stealing breath and strength alike. Glimpses of color shimmered across Xhea's vision, blurring the world around her, and she felt a surge of fear. Yet fear was a defense in itself: the instinctive swirl of dark energy it conjured was just enough to keep the power from swamping her.

Xhea stood frozen until Derren pulled her from the lift tube and she stumbled, barely catching her unsteady weight with the length of pipe. It was her only motion; she could but stare, wide-eyed and incapacitated by shock.

There were no storage coils here, no makeshift medical bed with tubes and wires. But it was the same. She'd sworn never again—those whispered words sometimes all that lulled her trembling self to sleep, alone in the darkness—and yet here it was, a nightmare reborn in light. Her fingers quivered as if to reach for the silver knife that Orren had taken from her—though whether to grab it or throw it away, she did not know.

A body lay prone in the center of the room on an edged and gleaming platform carved of glass. A young woman: eyes open, lips parted, dark hair spread about her face in a mussed tangle, trim body covered with a sheet. She might have been tall had she stood, but Xhea knew at a glance that this girl would never stand again. Though she breathed and her dark eyes jerked as if caught in dreams, her spirit had been torn from her body. It was Shai who now gave the flesh what little life it possessed—Shai who was stuck, half absorbed by the body and fighting wildly to be free. In this room of magic and reflections, her light was the brightest of all.

Never again. The echoes of the silent words mocked her, and she could have wept. Could have screamed, her voice a living echo of Shai's. Would have run to her, but Derren had hold of her shoulders, his grip firm despite the discomfort—the pain—of her touch.

"Easy now," he said.

So she only turned to them, the others in the room, two of whom were moving toward her. She knew she had to pretend at this crucial moment, and could not. They were speaking to her, their lips moving as one reached out a hand in greeting, and she heard none of it. There was only a scream that went on and on and on—a sound of pain unending, voiced by one long past the need for breath.

"You can't do this," she said. Faint and barely voiced—but somehow the sound reached Shai. The ghost's desperate struggles did not cease, but changed: Shai reached blindly for Xhea, her one free hand outstretched and grasping, and when she screamed it was Xhea's name.

Do something, Xhea thought in desperation. But with Shai's scream broken, she heard other sounds: the murmur of slow chants, whispers from the casters that ringed the platform; a few words from the people before her, "—so glad you could—"; and a whimper, soft and yearning.

Ignoring the two before her, Xhea stepped forward, pushing one aside with a touch of her bare hand against his exposed arm, ignoring the jolt. She moved slowly, not toward the platform but circling it, and Derren let her do that much, his hands on her shoulders as if he guided her steps, the near-contact of their bodies buzzing and numbing her skin. Far enough to see that the room held not one ghost, but two.

A young woman's ghost sat curled on the floor, hugging her knees as if to ward against cold. The tether that had held her spirit to her body had been severed—and not cleanly, as Xhea's knife might have done, but mangled to the point of breaking. The tattered edges still reached from the center of the ghost's chest and quested toward the body on the platform, until it looked like the young woman bled heart's blood into the air—a ghost's blood, not dark but cloudy-white.

Where the tether's fraying ends touched the myriad spells that dragged Shai into the young woman's body, they tangled, spitting and sparking. Shai's struggles only worsened the twisted mess, her wild flares of magic destroying some spell lines but reinforcing others, and only drawing the tether further into the hopeless tangle of magic.

"*Xhea!*" Shai screamed. Her body arched as she was drawn down into the waiting flesh just a little bit more. Another scream and she struggled back up, tearing at the spells that bound her as one might tear out their own hair.

Xhea stared. Had she thought that she could keep playing along, acting as if this were but a job while she tried to get close enough to Shai to free her? Impossible, now.

"You can't do this," Xhea said again, and this time her voice was hard and cold. She turned. "I'm going to stop you."

Chapter Twenty-Three

"Child," said a man before her—the one who seemed in charge of this ruin of a spellcasting. "Please. I don't think you understand." He smiled, and though the expression creased the skin around his mouth into well-worn lines, it did nothing to ease the bruise-like shadows beneath his eyes.

He was not kind, that much Xhea knew. She jerked her shoulders to throw off Derren's hands. It was all she could do not ball her hands into fists—little threat to the gathered officials and spellcasters, the least of whom was easily half again her size.

"You see the problem," Derren said. "Why we need your help."

"What I see—" she started, only to have his hands return to her shoulders and clamp down. Caution—or threat?

She did see their problem—but not, she thought, the one he meant. Where Orren's attempted resurrection had been botched by ineptitude and a critical lack of magic, here neither would have been a concern.

No, the difference was that Shai had fought. Perhaps that ghost that Xhea had met so long ago—a hesitant spirit, passive and afraid—would have undergone this process without struggle, slipping into the stolen flesh with no one to hear her cries. But that girl was dead as surely as her body. The ghost that bucked and twisted, screaming as she fought against her bonds, wore dark clothes: a jacket with many pockets, laced boots good for running or kicking or making a stand. This girl had had her father taken from her, only to be faced with his spiritless body; she'd had her sacrifice turned into abduction; and she had, in all likelihood, watched these people sever a young woman's spirit so that they might have use of her flesh.

To the man before her she said, "No, *you* don't understand. You're torturing her."

When she made to step forward, Derren's hands clenched like vices against her shoulders—but at a gesture from the man, he released her and stepped away. Still he loomed behind her.

"Xhea," said the man. "Your name is Xhea, is it not? I'm afraid you've misunderstood. This is a routine procedure. We're not torturing anyone. And yes, we're asking for your assistance—but this is only a minor delay, I assure you."

Perhaps this was a routine procedure. But something about the scene—maybe the stress written in their faces, the sweaty exhaustion of the working casters, or the obvious disarray—spoke of more than routine gone wrong. It was, she thought, very much like Orren's attempt all those years ago, if vastly different in scale—as if they were trying to re-create something they didn't quite understand. Yes, the power of Radiants, both living and spirit, were harnessed daily by every Tower in the City, that much Shai had told her; but not, she thought, like this. So what was missing?

"You're torturing *them*," Xhea said as if he hadn't spoken. "Shai and that girl whose body you've stolen."

"We haven't stolen anything." An edge of exasperation crept into his voice. "The body you see is that of a girl who was in an accident more than a year ago. She's brain dead, child—has been for months. There was nothing we could do."

"I can see her," Xhea hissed. "I can see her ghost right there on the floor, weeping and struggling to get back to her body. *I can see what you did to her.*"

The man—a politician, he had to be a politician with that neat clothing and a face that could look kind while speaking only misdirection and lies—glanced at the woman who stood beside him, his hands lifting fractionally to suggest a shrug. The woman turned to meet Xhea's eyes, and Xhea knew that she was no politician: there was too much frustration in the set of her mouth and crease of her eyebrows, too much anger in those eyes, too much weariness in her hand as she pushed a stray strand of hair from her face.

"Normal people don't have ghosts," she said shortly. Spellcaster, Xhea named her, and likely the one managing the details of this disaster; she wondered how many of the spells dragging at Shai had been cast by this woman's slim fingers. "Only those with very powerful magic remain—and even then it's not a person, only the shape of their power."

Xhea shook her head, the denial causing a clatter of charms. "I can see them," she repeated, each word sharp. "And they are not just reflections of power, either of them."

Idiots, Xhea named them in silence, clenching her jaw until her teeth creaked. Morons and idiots all, to think that the Radiant's glow was a ghost—to believe that only a Radiant spirit could form a ghost at all, no matter the evidence to the contrary.

They would have chosen someone with strong magic to be Shai's vessel—but even so, the young woman's ghost was but a ghost, no glitter of bright magic to her form. Xhea looked from face to face, from the politicians before her to the three spellcasters who ringed the platform, trying fruitlessly to untangle the spells that bound Shai to the living body. Yet none could see the ghosts or their tethers, regardless of the strength of their power—so what did they see? A shuddering body and a bright magic in the shape of a young girl's ghost; spells that arced and broke and tangled for no reason that they could discern.

The caster's look had sharpened. "The other ghost," she said. "She's interfering with the transfer?"

"Anya," the politician broke in. "I don't think we should encourage—"

"She's here because you thought she could help, Councilman," Anya snapped. "What does it matter what the girl believes so long as she helps get the job done? I don't know about you, but I'm out of ideas here—and we're running out of time. The Tower won't sustain much more of this." She gestured at Eridian's flaring heart.

Turning back to Xhea, she asked, "Can you remove the other ghost? Stop her from damaging the spells?"

"She's trying to get back to her body," Xhea protested. "You can't do this—you can't just kill her and take her body—" In her anger, she could feel the darkness rising, a surge of raging black. Her hands tingled with it, and the ever-present pressure of the bright magic against her skin, like airborne pins and needles, receded. Dark magic pushed against the boundaries of her flesh, begging for release—slipping into the air with her breath and her sweat, pushing for freedom.

Control it, she thought. Then: *Why?*

This wasn't a game. These people had taken advantage of the opportunity presented by a girl's terminal illness, consolidating Allenai's loans until the Tower was their financial dependent and all but crippled by magical debt. They had lied, fought for, and abducted Shai's ghost, and hurt Xhea in the process. They had murdered a girl for use of her body. And that was only the little Xhea knew.

Through the shifting light of the Tower's heart, Xhea could just see the crowd gathered in the garden far below, distant spots like freckles on an outstretched hand. Normal life in Eridian had ceased: every citizen was all but incapacitated; every bit of magic not necessary to keep their blood flowing, their lungs breathing, was being absorbed by the Tower to fuel this transfer.

All for power. All for altitude. Eridian's future—its status and economy, influence and trade potential, the future of each citizen's children—was being formed around her. It was future bathed in light and magic, yes, but one birthed in screams of terror, in torture and death. Yet here she stood, arguing semantics and morality, wasting what little time Shai had. Truly, she asked herself, was there anything at all she could say that would change their minds?

"Blight it," Xhea muttered. She tightened her grip on the iron pipe and swung, turning just far enough to hit Derren across his shoulder. He fell to his knees with a choked cry, his left hand clutching at his upper arm, while his right arm hung limply, twitching.

Her knee burned, but she pushed the pain away, hopping to keep her balance. She fought to keep hold of the vibrating pipe, her palms tingling from the force of that impact. The Councilman gaped, backing away with his hands raised defensively, while the exhausted Anya called for assistance. An aide scrambled toward them, some sort of spell half-woven through his fingers. He was careful to stay just outside the swinging range of Xhea's iron pipe—but it wasn't the iron that he should have worried about.

Magic responded to her call, boiling up the moment she relaxed her will to cascade from her like a dark waterfall. The sudden feel of it—the rush—the power—made Xhea laugh, giddy and furious, caught in a cresting wave of dark magic and anger and adrenaline. She was a thousand feet tall. She was all powerful, untouchable. Spirals of smoking black lifted from her hands, coiled up and out of her hair, wreathing her face with every breath. She felt like power incarnate, burning and glorious, and she was going to show them.

Xhea reached out a single hand, fingers spread. No spells for her, no complicated patterns of thought and command: only raw energy, the core of herself let free. Thick and black and angry.

"Hang on, Shai," she yelled over the sudden clamor. "I'm coming!"

Light flashed as some sort of defensive dome appeared around the Councilman, and a whip-like lash of energy uncoiled from Anya's hand, slicing the tide of darkness to tattered ribbons as it approached. The aide was slower. His spell caught on his fingers, tangled in his panic, and dark magic washed over him like a cresting fog. He fell without a sound.

There was no time to check if he was breathing.

Xhea cried out at a sudden pain in her bad leg: Derren's hand clamped around her calf and even the pipe wasn't enough to keep her from falling. She hit the ground and tried to roll, but Derren's grip was too tight, pinning her, a glow surrounding each finger. She felt the burn of his magic, searing through muscle to bone, and she screamed. Xhea's reach was instinctive, the rush of energy borne now by fear more than anger, but no less powerful. Black washed over Derren's head and he gasped, eyes rolling back in his head as he sagged limply to the floor.

Should have hit him in the face the first time, she thought, and dragged herself across the floor toward the platform.

The casters who had struggled to maintain the spells holding Shai were ready for her. Walls of shimmering light leapt up to enclose the platform with the girl's body and the two ghosts, the power's weave changing as she watched—preparing to repair itself from whatever assault she might attempt. Behind the walls, she could see one caster maintaining its strength, another preparing a more active assault, while one alone still worked on the spells binding Shai to the body.

But the platform wasn't her destination. Xhea stopped many body lengths from their defenses, lying on the glass floor above the edge of Eridian's living heart. Beneath her, magic pulsed and shifted, the light so close that she blinked back tears. *Bad timing*, she thought, watching as the heart flared: an arc of magic rose through the floor, up and over her like a sizzling-white rainbow. She braced as the arc reached its peak and collapsed, falling through her like a guillotine blade. Her scream was choked, and her back arched of its own volition as the power surged through her, burning, freezing, as she was suddenly, violently sick. But there was little in her stomach: only a thin spatter of water and bile slid across the floor while the world spun and twirled around her, darkness that had nothing to do with magic flickering before her eyes.

Don't pass out, she thought, panting. There was nothing to grab on to, nothing but cold glass and flickers of bright magic, and so she held tight to the cobweb-thin tether that joined her to Shai.

When the worst of the vertigo had passed Xhea looked up, craning her head as if she could somehow see through the room's crystalline structure, through Eridian's point and beyond to the space of sky where another Tower floated far above.

I told you I'd try to send a signal, Xhea thought, as if Councilwoman Nalani—and all of Allenai—might somehow hear her. *Here it is.*

Magic coiled in the pit of her stomach, that lake of stillness and black that she'd spent so many years trying to ignore and suppress, and attempted only recently—and futilely—to control. Since learning what her power could do, she had released her magic in thin wisps and fogs, in torrents as one might release floodwaters from a bursting dam. She'd let it escape and rush free—but never before had she called it.

Xhea placed her hands on the floor, the glass warm to the touch, and stared through to the glowing heart beyond. No breathing exercises now, no rhythm of thought—only need.

"Now," she whispered to herself, to her magic. She closed her eyes and *pulled*.

It felt as if her spirit were being forced through her hands, skin tearing, gushing blood and heat and freezing cold, as if her heart had been opened and she poured her life out on the glass. She felt something deep inside her breaking: a crack in the bedrock beneath that imagined lake. It hurt in ways that she had no way to name—yet she knew that she would live in this moment forever if she could, for in that pain and the surge of energy flowing from her, there was joy. Wholeness, the likes of which she'd never known.

A second passed . . . an eternity, and another.

Yet she did not die. She struggled to inhale and realized she was screaming, forcing the sound from her agonized throat with the same intensity that she willed forth her magic. She drew a shaking breath and heard the echo of her voice reverberate.

Xhea managed to open her eyes, blinking back tears and the veil of power that darkened her vision. Something in the depth of her had cracked, but so had the crystalline floor beneath her. A deep fissure now ran the length of her body, cracks spreading from the points where her hands touched. Yet even through the cracks' haze of white, she could still see her power flowing from her and into the Tower's heart below.

If her energy was like smoke, this was the smoke of the world burning: thick black and choking, a roiling cloud of darkness that enveloped all that lay before it—until it reached Eridian's heart. Where the cloud met the shifting magic that lit the Tower's core there was only turmoil. The black met the light and damped it, made the great rising arcs of magic sputter and fade into nothing. Yet so too did the brightness burn, shining all the brighter for the shadow cast against it, and beneath its light her magic was shredded to wispy tatters—nothing, less than nothing, and gone.

Xhea stared, one part of her shocked at what she had wrought. More: this was the deepest part of her set free, and it was this dark chaos, destroying everything bright and beautiful that lay in its path. She could feel it, as if that great boiling cloud were but her outstretched hand, her wind-blown hair. The more she concentrated, the more she felt she could slip from her body as one might remove a nightshirt upon waking, casting herself aside to live fully in the power, magic incarnate.

Within seconds it was clear that she could empty her whole self into Eridian's heart until she collapsed and died, nothing left to run the ruin of her body, and still the Tower would float, its lights on, its people warm and fed. Yet Eridian did not stand unscathed beneath her onslaught. No arcs of light rose through the cracking glass floor, and the light's intensity in the vast crystal room was manageable, even dim, compared to its past brilliance. She shook, but not just from exhaustion; the Tower itself trembled, an earthquake in a structure that knew no ground.

Had Eridian slipped, she wondered. Lost an inch or two of sky? Had its shimmering halo of spell exhaust thinned for but a moment, its displays of light and power grown faint? *Something*, she thought. *Anything*. And let it be enough.

It had to be; there was no second chance.

As her magic faded, oil-black darkness thinning to gray and shadow, a hand closed around her wrist and another grabbed her hair to haul her up. Then a cry—a man's voice made sharp with sudden pain—and the Councilman stumbled back from her, hands cradled to his chest. Anya was smarter: a swift kick, and Xhea rolled, gasping from the impact to her ribs. She clutched her side, her magic no more than a pale wisp of gray.

Slowly, the Councilman crouched on the cracked floor by her side, his hands palm-up, red and blistered. "We ask for your help," he said, voice heavy with recrimination. It was clear in his expression: he expected criminals to weep when he used such a tone, mothers to bow their heads and wail at the shame. "And this—" a gesture to the room around them, "*this* is what you do?"

Xhea coughed, hands still pressed to her throbbing side as she struggled to regain her breath. "Oh, spare me," she said scornfully.

But she followed his gesture, scanning the vast space around them. Cracks radiated from the place where she had lain, running riot through the floor and crazing the glass milk-white—and though the destruction's progress had slowed, it had not stopped. She watched as cracks ran up the walls toward the domed ceiling and further fractured the floor, the sounds in the sudden quiet like melting spring ice.

The protective walls around the pedestal had fallen, and the casters had scattered in three directions: one to the side of the young woman's body, still fighting with the spells, while the other two had hurried to the room's far edges where, unnoticed until now, two more platforms sat, hidden in shadow. Yet these, unlike the one atop which Shai struggled, were not clear sculptures of carved glass, but coffins: a body lay in each one, features hidden by the faceted sides; each was bright with magic that flowed from them into the walls of the Tower beyond.

No, not just bright: Radiant.

Xhea looked back the way she'd come. The opening to the lift tube gaped wide, an invitation to flee that she wished she could accept. Between her and the lift entry, Derren was slowly regaining his feet. Nearby, the Councilman's aide still lay on the floor, sprawled just as he'd fallen. Xhea looked quickly aside.

Whatever else the Councilman had been about to say was forgotten as the lights of message spells appeared, whirling about his head for his attention. He turned away, touching one after another, his eyes flickering closed as he absorbed the spells' energy and messages alike.

He glanced back. "Get rid of her," he said with a slight wave of his hand, his attention already elsewhere. To Derren, he added,

"Come on. We have imbalances all across the Tower, sections middle through base. Light only knows how many cases of energy shock we're dealing with. Of all the stupid . . ."

"What do you—" Anya began.

"I don't want to know. Just get her out of the way while we take care of this."

Anya reached for Xhea then hesitated, glancing at the fading blisters on the Councilman's hands. Her hesitation gave Xhea a chance to choke out, "Wait."

The Councilman made a disgusted face and turned away, ordering the enactment of a disaster plan whose name was composed more of numbers than words.

"Please wait." Xhea tried to sound desperate. "You don't understand. I wasn't trying to damage Eridian."

Anya's mouth twisted. She shook her head and pulled the long scarf from her hair. "You succeeded admirably, regardless." She wrapped the scarf's silken length around one hand in a makeshift glove. "Tell me," she said. "Who paid you for this attack?"

"This wasn't an attack. It wasn't *the* attack."

Anya gave Xhea an incredulous look and bent to grab her by the hair.

"Don't you get it yet?" Xhea wanted to laugh, shivering from the after-effects of magic and adrenaline, weak and numbed. "I'm not here to stop you. As if I could. I'm only the distraction."

At this, the Councilman paused and looked back. Xhea watched his brows draw down as his thoughts cascaded—watched him put the pieces together, one by one. By then it was far too late.

There was a sharp chime, and a woman's uninflected tones echoed throughout the great room. "*Proximity alert,*" the voice announced. "*Proximity alert. All citizens, please brace for impact. This is not a drill.*"

The Councilman did not brace but ran headlong toward the lift, spells flying from lips and hands. The spellcasters abandoned the pedestals and ran for the crystalline walls, placing their entire bodies against the glass as if the Tower might absorb them if only they pressed hard enough. Light flashed and flared around them, swirling into the Tower faster and brighter than Xhea could read. Defenses, Xhea supposed, and wondered what spells now flared around Eridian in a brief and desperate effort to maintain the Tower's independence.

Anya cursed, tore the scarf from her hands and rolled Xhea onto her side with her shoe. Xhea was too slow: before she could squirm away, Anya grabbed her arms and bound Xhea's hands with a few wrenching twists of the scarf. "Don't move," she commanded, then spun and sprinted to the lift tube.

Even tied, even exhausted, Xhea couldn't help but grin as she sagged to the floor.

"Battle stations," she whispered, and counted the seconds until Allenai's arrival.

Chapter Twenty-Four

Ten—did they have ten seconds? Xhea rolled onto her back, pinning her tied hands beneath her. On the platform, Shai had managed to free most of her right arm, the spellcasters' distraction allowing her to make some progress against her bindings.

Nine. Eridian's proximity chime continued to sound, the voice repeating its calm warning. *"All citizens, please brace—"*

Eight. Seven.

How many hostile takeovers had she watched from the ground? She couldn't begin to count. The fast, brutal battles lasted just long enough for vendors' stands to sprout on every street corner and public roof with a clear view of the action, selling snacks and magnification lenses in quantity. High entertainment, this. She had never wondered how a takeover looked—or felt—from the inside.

Six—

Xhea was thrown into the air in an explosion of light and noise. No time to think, no time to scream before the floor reclaimed her, impacting hard against her face and shoulder and injured leg. The world shook and spun, an unending assault of screaming metal, shattering glass, and an awful grinding noise that Xhea couldn't name. Shards of faceted glass rained down in a sharp, chiming hail.

Allenai hadn't just attacked but impacted, and if her flight path was any indication, they'd struck from directly above. Eridian's stabilizing spells had been totally overwhelmed by the force of an entire Tower falling upon them, aided by magic and gravity. If Allenai had already drilled through Eridian's layered defenses so that the two Towers now touched, then somewhere above the structures' flesh was beginning to meld, each battling for control of their combined shape. Each seeking to claim the other's heart.

Xhea lay limply, caught between the conflicting desires to whimper and to laugh hysterically. *Oh*, she thought. *It feels like that.*

"Xhea?" Shai's voice was halting, its raw sound testament to her screams. "Are you okay?"

It took a few attempts to respond: "Still breathing."

"Speak for yourself," Shai muttered, and then yelped. There was a snapping noise and a flash, and Xhea managed to turn just in time to see one line of the binding spell break away, the magic shimmering as it vanished. "I need help."

"Can you see the casters?"

"Emergency merger protocol," Shai managed.

"What?"

"They have to protect the Tower. Defend it."

Xhea tried to understand what that meant. Above, Shai continued to struggle, then made an exasperated sound. "They're being absorbed into the wall."

Xhea twisted, craning until she just caught sight of a human shape vanishing inside the crystalline structure. The aide's limp body had similarly been absorbed, and now was no more than a shadow inside the cracked floor.

"Huh," she said. "Good enough."

Unable to free her hands, Xhea wormed across the floor, doing her best to push aside the largest glass splinters before she lay on them. With her face but inches from the floor, she could see all too well what was happening below. Eridian's heart stuttered wildly, streamers of raw magic pulsing in every direction. Through the magic, she could just see the vast garden, and it looked a paler gray, as if the very life was being pulled from the trees and flowers and moss. Of the crowd, she could only see the dark spots of their bodies, all quiet and perfectly still. She hoped the Tower would absorb and protect them too.

Another tremor rocked Eridian, shaking the structure to its very bones. There was nowhere to hide, no way to protect herself from the splinters that fell, glittering, and so Xhea kept dragging herself forward, pushing with her good foot and inching along the ground as the shaking allowed. The surface beneath her continued to crack, thin fractures branching endlessly.

On the pedestal, the young woman's body had been tossed to the side and now lay in disarray, one arm hanging limply, the sheet slipped to expose a length of sickly-pale leg. Xhea could just see the side of Shai's face staring upward, one long arm and part of her chest; the rest of her had vanished inside the body. Whatever progress she made was constantly undone by the spells' pull.

"I'm stuck—" Shai said, squirming harder and whimpering at each move. It hurt, of that Xhea had no doubt, but without new spells being added it seemed the pain's intensity had faded, allowing panic to set in. "I can't manage—Xhea, Xhea it's pulling, and I can't—"

"Shai, you need to run through your breathing exercises." The familiar actions had always calmed her.

"Help," Shai cried as another tremor shook the Tower. Her free hand waved wildly, grasping at air as she fought for purchase. "Oh please, Xhea, you have to help me. I can't fight it and it's going to—"

"Shai, listen to me. You have to relax." Xhea tried to sound calm, struggling for the steady tone that Shai herself had so often used—and failed. Her heart pounded and her breath came too quickly, while Shai whimpered above. She could only think how good it was that the ghost couldn't see her, bound and beaten on the floor.

She changed tactics. "Shai," Xhea said, and this time she didn't try to hide her fear or exhaustion. "I need your help. My magic—it's out of control. It's too strong for me. Please—I can't remember which breathing exercise to do."

Shai whimpered again, arching against the bright lines that held her down. The body moved with her, muscles jerking spasmodically.

"Please," Xhea said, voice trembling. "Shai, I can't stop it. I don't know what to do."

Shai took a long and shuddering breath, the action echoed perfectly by the body. A pause, a breath. "You need . . . you need the first exercise."

"Which one was that? I don't remember."

"I . . ." Shai managed. "It's . . . I'll show you."

They began to breathe together as Eridian shook and shuddered around them. Shai's instructions began to come slower, her voice losing its panicked edge. What Xhea hadn't expected was the way her magic responded in truth to the now-familiar routine. She had thought her power exhausted, and yet as she ran through the patterns she felt a curl of dark in her stomach, a whisper beneath her breastbone. Carefully, as one might coax a flame from damp paper, Xhea guided it down her arm to her hands, letting it curl around her wrists as she breathed.

"Okay," Shai said at last. "I'm okay."

Xhea exhaled in a slow stream and tugged at her restrains. There was a rip of protesting fabric, and then her arms were free. "Real silk," she murmured. She raised her arms and let the ashy, blackened tatters of the scarf flutter to the floor.

Now stand, she told herself, staring up at the glass pedestal. *Don't think about it, just do it.*

She struggled, rose. It was only looking down at the mess of spells and tether lines that she saw the true problem that Eridian— and now she—faced. Countless spell-lines arched up and over and into Shai, dragging her down and binding her to the still-living body. Her struggles and flaring power had damaged some spells, tangled others—while through it all ran the other girl's tether, now so frayed that it was not one line but many, knotting wherever it touched. The ghost girl must have tried instinctively to reconnect with her body, and her tattered tether had indeed reached her body—but it had done so by impaling Shai through the chest.

The tether was a help, in a sense; even as the spells pulled Shai down, the other tether repelled her—likely a large part of why

Shai's fight had lasted so long. Yet the other ghost would only be able to return to her body by following the length of her tether— and unlike the near-invisible length of energy, there was no way one ghost could pass through another.

Xhea had thought only to ruin the spells binding Shai, freeing her; yet no matter how hard or long she stared, she saw no way to do so without untethering the other ghost entirely. Even with Shai lying still, the body doing nothing but breathing and shaking with the Tower's vibration, the lines moved and shifted.

Xhea reached into the tangle of magic, trying to separate spell from tether, but her attempts only agitated the lines. Shai gasped as a spell grabbed around her neck and tried to drag her down. A frantic struggle, and Shai managed to turn her head; a spark of light flew from her lips to the line, fraying it until it snapped. Yet after a fight that had clearly lasted hours, if not far longer, Shai looked as if she had little magic left to spare, the light of even her Radiant power dimming.

Xhea stared desperately as if a solution might rise from the knot. Wondering if there was time to attack the lines one by one, wondering if she still had the strength. She ached for the feel of her knife, the silver blade imbued with darkness, requiring no strength nor fuel but the movement of her hand. Even without the growing cracks in the floor and the crystalline walls' slow disintegration, she didn't imagine this space would remain safe for much longer, not with the tapered point of Allenai's main spire sliding knife-like toward Eridian's heart.

Eridian shook and the very walls seemed to scream as they trembled and buckled, fragments raining down. "Quickly now," Xhea murmured, trying to come to a decision. Save the young woman's ghost and risk letting Shai lose her battle with the spells; or save Shai and break the other ghost's tether in the process, letting both body and spirit die for a girl who was already dead.

Then: no. Not just a girl who was already dead. A friend.

Xhea's only friend.

"Shai," she said, touching the fine tether that still joined them and letting her voice reverberate along its length. "Shai, hold tight to me."

Xhea closed her eyes as she reached out, dug deep inside for the last wisps of her magic, and *pulled*. The darkness was thin and slow and sluggish, but it came, a chill touch that seeped from her fingers and palms, leaked from outstretched arms. There was no way to separate spells from ghost from tether; she simply directed her magic to encompass them all. A seeping fog, the creep of night: she set it free to do as it would.

Even as she forced her magic to flow, she thought of Shai. A fluttering dress, closed eyes and a meditative pose. A body like this one, young, hurting, dying under her hands. Those stupid little embroidered flowers on her shirt. Breathing exercises. A soft glow, quiet words in dark places. A voice screaming her name.

Xhea thought of everything Shai was, everything she knew and wished to learn, felt the tether that joined them and pulled with everything she had. She stopped only when she felt the last of her magic reach the young woman's body itself, pulling back before the flesh too began to die. She caught herself as her good leg gave way, and sagged over the pedestal and the still-breathing body—a body now empty of all but flesh and bone and breath. She could not stand, could not lift her head, her hands. Could not open her eyes.

Yet there was . . . a sound. The world broke and cracked and crumbled all around them, yes, and somewhere people screamed in fear and mindless panic—but closer. Closer. A thin sound. A whimper.

A cry.

Xhea forced open her eyes. On the ground beside her, the young woman's ghost stared at the severed tether that protruded from her chest, its end now cut cleanly. She looked at her hands, holding them before her—slender fingers with neat, painted nails: an artist's fingers, a musician's fingers, a spell-weaver's fingers. Trembling as they slowly became transparent, fading like mist in the morning sun.

"No," Xhea whispered and let herself all but slip from the pedestal's edge, grabbing for the thin length of tether that remained. No magic this, only a trick of hands long trained for such work. She fumbled, trying to get a grip on the bit of shimmering air as the Tower around them shuddered to its very bones. There was a loud crack and the fissure in the glass floor above Eridian's heart suddenly widened, snaking through the glass like something alive.

Tether in hand, it was all Xhea could do to hold tight and breathe. The ghost seemed to strengthen—and as Xhea clung to the tether's severed end, she felt herself steady as well, her breathing slowing, the trembling of her exhausted limbs easing, as if she somehow drew strength from the ghost as the ghost drew strength from her. She touched Shai's tether with a single finger and the room stopped spinning; the ringing in her ears faded, replaced by the sound of the Tower being transformed all around them.

As her energy returned, so too did the familiar pull of her magic toward the ghost. She knew she could weave the darkness around a ghost and send her away, as she had with the ghost in the hospital. Even now, but thin wisps and a shimmer of gray, it tugged toward the girl's spirit, wanting to offer her the same release. *No*, Xhea told it, a hesitant command, a whispered prayer. Instead, she showed it how to anchor, to stay.

Here, she said, and pulled on the tether, letting the energy stretch as wisps of her own darkness ringed around, coaxing, guiding its passage. She pressed her hand to the young woman's body; felt the beating heart beneath the flesh, the solid arches of her ribs, the warm softness of her skin. The tether shivered and hesitated, and again she coaxed it with darkness: *Here. Stay.*

The tether slipped from her hand, finding its true anchor anew.

The girl's ghost had watched the whole process, following Xhea's hands, and now she stared. "I'm . . . I'm dead," the ghost whispered. She looked at her own body, reaching so her fingers flickered in the air above her living mouth like a moth circling a flame.

"No," Shai said. She stepped forward and took the other ghost's hands in her own, clasping them together to stop their trembling. "No, not dead. You're only dreaming."

Another shudder and the crack in the floor widened. Xhea grabbed the pedestal's edge to keep from falling.

"Here," Shai said, as if oblivious to the Tower trying to shake itself apart around them. She pulled the ghost up beside her on the pedestal. "Just lie down here, that's right. Just lie down and close your eyes . . ." Xhea took the girl's ghostly hands and guided them toward their living counterparts; Shai cradled the ghost's head and allowed it to sink slowly into her body. Another whisper of power, a twining ribbon of gray: *Here. Stay.*

"Her name is Koiya," Shai said.

Xhea leaned down until her lips all but brushed the young woman's ear. "Koiya," she whispered. "Wake up."

A gasping breath and Koiya opened her eyes—a flutter of dark lashes, blinking back tears. Her lips, chapped and bleeding, opened and closed as if she were trying to speak but could find neither words nor the air with which to speak them

"*Shh*," Xhea said. "Remember later. For now you have to run— get out of here, okay? As fast as you can." Where would be safe? Xhea didn't know; yet the Tower could protect its own. Hostile takeovers were dangerous, but she'd never heard one spoken of as a mass slaughter.

Xhea took Koiya's hand and struggled to help her sit. The girl's movements were heavy and sluggish, her face dazed as if she were still lost in dream. "Come on," Xhea muttered as the Tower shook, hauling on Koiya's arm and urging her to stand. "I can't bloody well carry you out of here." She hopped back on her good leg, wondering where the iron pipe had rolled.

"Where did she go?" Koiya whispered. She stood unsteadily and looked around, confused; but whatever she saw in the trembling, cracked ruin of the room above Eridian's heart brought her no comfort. "The other girl. Where did she go?"

At Xhea's side, Shai pressed her fingers to her lips and turned away. Invisible.

"She's gone somewhere safe. This is a takeover, do you understand? You have to get out of here."

Koiya blinked once, twice, and comprehension blossomed. Her cracked lips opened in a perfect O. She took a step forward, clutching the sheet around herself, its long end trailing behind her like a train. She murmured her thanks without meeting Xhea's eyes and stumbled toward the lift tube, shards of glass dancing about her feet like diamonds. Even as the lift spells formed and carried her down, she still searched the room as if she might catch a glimpse of Shai if only she looked long enough.

It was only as Koiya vanished that Xhea realized her folly: "She was my only way down."

"I could try to call the elevator," Shai began, before another tremor drowned out her words. Unable to keep her balance, Xhea slipped from the pedestal, landing with her braced leg awkwardly beneath her. There was a crack like the world breaking, and the fissure made good its promise, rending the floor from end to end and raining its fragments through Eridian's sputtering heart to the garden far below.

Xhea stared. *No chance of an elevator now*, she thought, dazed. The gap divided the room in two, the pedestals on one side and the lift tube on the other. Even whole and healthy, she never could have made the leap. As she watched, magic began to rise from the crack, a bright fog no longer held at bay by the floor's barrier.

"Not good," she said, hearing the edge of her own fear, panic barely held in check. "This is not good."

And the point of Allenai's bottommost defensive spire broke through the ceiling.

Chapter Twenty-Five

Xhea cowered, wrapping her arms around her head for protection from the falling ceiling's debris. Yet though there was light and sound and the room vibrated as if it were a vast drum, nothing fell—no glass shards nor pieces of roof, no bits of broken Tower raining down. The echoing sounds weren't those of things smashing and tearing, but something she didn't know how to identify—something strange and primal and almost melodic.

After a shocked moment, she moved her hands and peered hesitantly upward. The tapered point of Allenai's main spire jutted into the crystalline room, the massive needle so dark it was all but black. Allenai's surface swirled in dizzying patterns, charcoal on midnight on black, and Eridian's walls shivered in response, fractures running riot through the clear facets.

But though they broke and splintered, the pieces did not fall but floated free, hovering in midair and quivering in time to the movements dictated by Allenai's liquid-oil patterns. Slowly they began to turn, faster and faster until it seemed that above her spun a spiral galaxy made from broken glass and fractured ceiling supports, strips of wire and plumbing pipe. Soon she could not tell one bit from the other, only watch the blur of their movement. And the sound they made—Xhea wanted to cringe and clasp her hands over her ears; she wanted to throw her head back and listen forever.

The Towers were singing. There were no words but those formed by the destruction, stressed metal and fracturing glass giving voice to the strange transformation above her. It was not the song of two political powers doing battle, but a sound from the structures themselves: a communion of living steel, grown walkways, and stone flesh given wingless flight.

"They're alive," Xhea whispered, unable to hear her voice over the Towers' song. Towers weren't just grown, shaped, and molded—they were *alive*. And the heart of living magic that she'd tried to poison was a heart in truth.

In time to their singing, the walls melted. The debris had become liquid in its dizzying turn about Allenai's point, and it now spiraled tighter and tighter in an upward-pointing tornado until it vanished into the other Tower's surface entirely. The rest of the ceiling overhead began to peel back like a lily opening, Eridian's surface stripped away layer by layer, melting and shifting and becoming absorbed into Allenai's very flesh.

Hostile takeover, Xhea thought, but the words were wrong. As terrifying and alien as the scene above her was—and as damaging to the lives in Eridian—this strange merging of the Towers was beautiful. If their meeting had been violent, their courtship rushed, it seemed they were no less grateful for the joining. Despite the chaos, the song that rose all around was one of joy.

"At least they'll be happy when they crush me," Xhea managed. She tried to get to her feet, but her legs wouldn't hold her.

No matter where she turned, she could see no escape. There was no hidden stairwell, no ramp, no door in a far wall previously unseen; only the crack in the floor and the long fall to the garden below. Even if there had been—could she have trusted such ways anymore? Where the Tower was not melting entirely, its walls were surely shifting, passages becoming unstable, rooms and halls moving within the confines of Eridian's outer boundaries, and redesigning themselves to meet Allenai's needs. Even in the throes of their joining, the Towers would not destroy anything with a magical signature—not, Xhea thought, that that'd do her any good.

Magic rose from Eridian's heart like steam on a winter morning. It surrounded Xhea, filling her lungs with every breath—breaths that hurt, hot and burning, before they numbed her from the inside out. Her skin too burned, and she shivered until she felt neither heat nor cold. Everything became strangely distant, as if reality were but a picture held at arm's length.

The darkness, she thought, and didn't know how to continue. There was no darkness here, only the light of the magic rising from Eridian's heart to meet Allenai, like two hands reaching out, touching. The magic rose between the two of them, a great turning pillar that grew with every moment, the force of the power like heat on her face, and they were singing, singing.

"Oh," she said, and stopped struggling. She could not stand, would not stand, and the world was breaking all around her. She was breaking. Broken.

"Xhea," Shai said, tugging sharply on the tether to get her attention. "Xhea, come on—we have to get out."

But there were rainbows, Xhea realized, shining up through the broken floor. Not just spots of brightness, but shards of rainbows that shimmered along the melting walls. She'd never seen a rainbow as anything but gradated shades of gray. There were so many colors, she thought, each the perfect version of itself. Now she knew why people stood on Lower City street corners and pointed them out to their children; why they watched them through the downpour and smiled.

Again Shai tugged, and Xhea tried to remember what she'd said. "Where?" she asked at last. "There is no out. No down. Only falling . . ." Oh, she wanted to sleep.

She looked up at Shai, the Radiant ghost, lit all around by rising power and rainbows, and that power seemed to fill her as if she were a vessel designed to hold only light. She was radiant in truth, and Xhea stared, unable to believe the depths of Shai's blue eyes.

The walls fell down around them. Absorbed, collapsed, she did not know, did not see them go—only saw their sudden absence. Felt the shock of a wind strong enough to steal her breath and whip her hair around her face; saw a light so bright it could only be the sun. There was no crystal room anymore, only the fractured ground on which they stood.

Where was the rest of Eridian, she wondered. She saw no green, no platform surface—where had it all gone? Or was it only that they were too high to see all of the Tower-that-was, the floating structure she'd known as Eridian and soon would be no more?

She looked up, letting the morning light fall full across her face as the cold wind bit her skin and tore at her clothes. All of Allenai stretched above her, an undulating pillar too vast to comprehend, its shadow enough to eclipse the world. So close she had but to reach out her hand . . .

She was dizzy, eyes too heavy . . .

"Xhea," Shai said, her voice clear over the wind's howl, the Towers' riotous song. "Take my hand."

"I . . . I can't . . ."

"Listen to me, okay? I'm getting you out of here."

"I can't stand," Xhea said. *Oh, to sleep*, she thought: to sleep, to dream, to drift away on those passing clouds, all breath and feathers and light. "I can't crawl."

"You can," Shai said. "Just take my hand."

Something in the ghost's desperation reached her. It was but one thing, Xhea thought at last. The one thing that Shai had asked. She hadn't asked to be saved or protected; she hadn't asked to die. Only this thing, this one small thing.

Xhea lifted her hand. She looked at the golden glow of her skin in the sunlight, dirty and smeared with blood—a perfect red, a rose's dark kiss—but golden still. Her windborne hair was black, and her eyes, as if she were both the sun and the shadows it cast.

A soft touch, a shiver like ice across her palm, and Shai's hand closed around hers. Did it hurt, that touch? The touch of the dead, of ghosts and memories; it should hurt, Xhea thought. Yet she felt only safe, that hand around hers, and the heartbeat echoing in her ears was steady and slow.

"Raise your foot, that's it," Shai said. "Now stand—I'll help you." Xhea felt Shai's hands guiding her, holding her strong, and struggled to be worthy of that help. Somewhere she felt something hurting, something in her knee tearing and raw, and some part of her was afraid. Yet it was a distant part, and though it screamed and cried warnings, it was too far from her to hear, too far to heed. Holding Shai's hand, she stood.

She glanced upward. The dark shape above them, Allenai-that-was—did it grow larger, or was it falling? She could not see its tapered tip, only the swell of its massive side, smooth like polished marble. Both, she thought. It descended slowly, steadily, impaling Eridian. The bottom swell of its lowest living platform eclipsed the sun like an unfathomably huge umbrella.

"Just these few steps. Walk with me now. I can do it, see? That's it, that's right." Murmured words, more comfort in their sound than content; a voice holding her strong against the wind and the terrible pain in her knee.

A step, another, never looking down, only up at the clear arc of the sky, the descending darkness of the Tower falling upon them in slow motion, the sun reflecting from Shai's pale hair. Another step, another.

"Shai," Xhea said. Her voice seemed to echo forever. "I'm going to die here, aren't I?"

"You're not."

"It's going to crush me. Allenai. Your Allenai." Up, she looked, up and up, but there was no need to peer or crane: the rounded platform of the landing bay was all but upon them, mere body lengths above and approaching without slowing. Perhaps it wouldn't be bad, dying.

Of all the questions she'd asked all the ghosts she'd ever known, she'd never asked what it tasted like to die. Whether their last breaths were sweet, like fresh blueberries stolen from the market, the juice of each so perfect it could only be experienced with eyes closed. Whether death smelled like the first violets blooming in spring, those thin stalks struggling to rise above asphalt and stone.

Whether there had been joy in their last moments, not in death or dying, but knowing, merely knowing, that they had lived.

"Look where we are."

Xhea looked down and saw the edge at her feet. No Towers hovered close but ringed them, providing distance between the merging structures and the magic that flared up and around them like fire. The Central Spire was a distant golden light, a thin pillar stretching from near-ground to sky, glowing like a second sun. Down, she looked, down and down, and saw all the way to the ground, an impossible distance below.

"Falling . . ." she said, *is just another death*; but she could not speak the words. Lips gone numb—from cold, from magic, she did not know.

"I know," Shai whispered. "But I need you to trust me. Can you do that?"

No words; no need for words. As the wind stole her breath, as Allenai came plunging toward them, Xhea wrapped her arms around Shai's ghostly body and clung, burying her face in that pale hair.

It was a very long way down.

There was only the wind as they fell. It was not wind as she knew it, not a sound, not a touch, but a physical force that seemed to encompass all that she was. Her ears roared with it, her body ached with the fierce fluttering of her clothing, her hair pulled back from her face so hard and fast that it seemed she'd leave it behind. It burned, the wind, as if its cold stripped the skin from her face layer by layer, though she kept it tucked against Shai's shoulder.

Ghostly shoulder. No protection at all. And she was falling.

A surge of sound as they passed a Tower: a sound like blown breath, the memory of a highway. And another, another. She could feel the City rushing past, even if she couldn't see it, the tears in her eyes obscuring all but the blur of passing aircars, the glow of road buoys, the intense colors that could only be Towers.

She was falling and then light spread around her, not worked energy, woven spells and controlled intent, but pure magic, radiant and true. They didn't glow but shone as if each were a line of distilled sunlight. Shai shouted words Xhea could neither hear nor understand, fierce in their volume and fear and joy.

The light unfurled.

Wings, Xhea thought, staring through dazzled, windblown tears. She was falling, and great bright wings spread around her, far wider than her arms could ever stretch, as wide as the sky. They surged and stretched as they cupped the air, fanning it in great strokes. The ground was coming up below her, a rising darkness of rooftops and roadways, and the wings beat, their pounding strong enough to replace the beat of her heart.

She was falling, flying, falling.

Impact.

Xhea lay still for a very long time. She breathed, that much she knew, but little else made sense. Was she warm, cold? She could not tell. How badly was she broken? Did she bleed? Questions flared and faded unanswered.

Easier to just lie as she had fallen, her arms spread wide and face hidden in the tangled veil of her hair, her cheek resting against a pillow of stone and broken concrete. She smelled soil and road dust, grass growing, a hint of garbage burning somewhere far distant.

Breathe, she thought. *Just breathe*. Let that be enough.

Unconsciousness drew near and pulled away, awareness sweeping in and out like the tide. Sometime, she knew not when, someone spoke her name.

"Xhea."

The sun was hot against the dark fabric of her jacket and her pants. The wind was cool and yet it seemed to drift over and around her, never more than stroking the back of one hand, whispering against a bit of exposed neck.

"Xhea? Are you okay?"

Sensation returned slowly, and she rather wished it wouldn't. It was easier to feel the small things: the sharp pebble on the ground beneath one hip, the stiffness in her arms, the swollen feeling of her lip and face and eye.

"Xhea, talk to me. Please talk to me. Oh, please be okay." The voice—Shai's voice. *Time to wake up now*, Xhea thought, and groaned.

As if the sound were a signal, feeling flooded back. Every part of her hurt, her knee screaming—and yet relief was there too, a cushion that, for but a brief moment, spared her the full awareness of pain. *Broken*, she thought, *and beaten, but not quite dead*. If it was as close as she could get to triumphant, she'd take it.

It was an effort beyond words to raise one hand and pull the hair away from her face. The sun was blinding, the knotted coins her fingers touched almost hot enough to burn. A moment—a breath, another breath. Then with a grunt and long whimper, she managed to roll onto her back.

Blinking back tears she stared upward, for a long time able to see only sky. It was blue—that perfect, heartbreaking blue—but color faded as she watched, leeching from the sky like pale clouds blooming. She was glad, almost, when it was gone.

Slowly, Xhea looked around, trying not to jar her throbbing head and neck. She lay just beyond the boundaries of the Lower City core, where untenanted buildings crumbled in sight of the skyscrapers, roofs sagging and collapsing inward, brick façades crumbling and falling like snow. Nearby, a section of broken overpass arched like a rainbow's concrete stump, the graffiti patterns on its sides almost dizzying in their layered complexity. *Xhea was here*, she thought; she'd write it only as a bloody handprint pressed against the wall. Statement enough.

Above, she could only now make out the shapes of Allenai and Eridian—though it was just Allenai now, she supposed. It looked like a strange monstrosity of a structure, the slender grace of Allenai-that-was meeting the pattern of Eridian's ever-widening platforms in a mess of shifting, living metal. It would take time for its shape to change and smooth, growing to once more become something beautiful. Something new. But whether her actions today would make her a hesitant ally of the new Allenai or an enemy, still hunted and feared, was as uncertain as the Tower's future.

At her side knelt Shai, ghostly hands clasped tightly in her lap, her face a study in hope and fear. She glowed silver and black and gray, a thousand shades of gray, every one of them radiant.

"That looked like it hurt," Shai whispered.

Weakly, all but soundlessly, Xhea began to laugh, the wet wheeze of her breath almost painful to hear. It hurt to laugh—a rib was surely broken, perhaps two—but it felt good too. It felt like being alive.

"A good observation," she managed at last, still laughing. She reached out and took Shai's hand in hers, the tingle of ghostly flesh against skin almost like warmth.

She still believed what she had always said: sometimes you have to leave someone behind; sometimes you're the one that gets left. *But not today*, Xhea thought, holding tight to Shai's hand, and her smile was faint and hesitant and true.

Not today.

Epilogue

Time passed.

Moving, Xhea decided, took entirely too much effort. It hurt to move—it hurt to even shift on the hard ground—and she was so very tired. Besides, the sun was warm for spring, warm and bright, and there were many long hours before night fell. Time enough to drag herself home, Xhea thought; time enough to just let herself rest. And so she lay against the ground, eyes closed, and shivered.

Reality seemed to draw close and pull away, sound rising and falling like waves, and Xhea drifted with it. Shai spoke to her, she knew that much, but the words themselves slipped from memory soon after they were spoken. Like the wind, she thought, shifting and changing; like water dripping from between outstretched fingers. Her own fingers twitched at the image, and it was only then that she realized she was still holding Shai's hand.

"Xhea," Shai said. "You're in shock."

It seemed, Xhea decided with a brain gone slow and clumsy, that Shai had said that before. Hadn't she? Was she remembering Shai speaking or only hearing those words echo, again and again, through the reaches of her mind?

"Okay," she murmured. For a moment there was blessed silence, broken only by the soft rustle of the wind.

"Listen to me, you can't fall asleep."

Xhea tried to force her eyes open again; she caught a glimpse of gray sky, of Shai's worried face, then her eyelids fluttered and fell closed.

"Okay," she said again, and lay still.

She could tell that Shai was close; she felt stronger with the ghost beside her, as if the tether were strengthening her. Strange—but she would think about that later.

"Later," she whispered. "Later, later, later."

There was a noise from somewhere that seemed far away. Too far away, surely, to matter. Yet her instincts plucked at her with tiny, worried fingers: she was unprotected, unhidden, lying exposed on a stretch of crumbling roadway. As if such worries were a spell in themselves, when Shai next spoke her voice had changed.

"Xhea," she said, tense, wary. "There's someone coming."

Okay, Xhea thought. *Time to get up*. And still she lay there.

"There are three of them," Shai added, and Xhea felt the ghost try ineffectively to tug at her hand. More urgently: "They've spotted us. . . . You. Whatever. Xhea, seriously—*wake up!*"

"Tell them . . ." Xhea took a long, slow breath, as if air could give her the strength that she seemed so suddenly to lack. "Tell them . . . that I want a sandwich." This struck her as terribly funny and she laughed, even though it hurt, the sound no more than a weak chuckle.

She heard the not-so-distant sound of a voice calling, and a moment later the crunch of gravel beneath a heavy heel grew closer and closer to her prone body.

"Oh Xhea," a low, rough voice said. Lorn's voice, heavy with a weight of sadness.

Though it took all her strength, Xhea opened her eyes; saw Lorn's shock—and yes, joy—that she was alive. The cut above his eye had been neatly stitched, though the flesh surrounding the wound was swollen and darkly mottled with bruises.

"Lorn," she whispered. Then softer, infinitely so, so that only the two of them could hear: "Addis." Naming the true spirit that lived within his brother's body.

"Yes," he said, coming to kneel at her side. "Xhea, how are you—I mean, I saw you fall."

She nodded—or tried to. "I don't like heights," she said sagely.

Lorn frowned. "You're in shock."

"So she keeps telling me." Xhea gestured limply at Shai, who hovered worriedly nearby, then let her hand fall back to the cold ground.

At that Lorn stilled, then glanced in the direction Xhea had pointed. "You actually found her, didn't you?" he murmured with a slow shake of his head. "Your friend, the Radiant. You saved her."

He searched for Shai; Xhea could just see the skin around his eyes crease as he squinted, attempting to see the ghost.

"I'm sorry," he said at last, speaking to what must have seemed like empty air. "I can't see you, or hear you but . . . I can almost feel you there. I'm Lorn."

"Hello," Shai replied. Her expression was strange; Xhea could not read it.

Lorn turned back to Xhea. He reached out a slow and hesitant hand, and brushed his fingers feather-light against her cheek. There was no shock, no feeling of twisting wrongness; just . . . an oddity. The touch of a living hand against her skin.

Perhaps it's gone, she thought. Her magic. Perhaps she had used it up in that final surge of dark—or perhaps there had been so much bright magic in the Towers' merging that her own had been burned away. She was surprised how much the thought saddened her.

Lorn glanced at his fingers and back to her face, then touched her again, letting his palm rest against her cheek, then her forehead.

"And you have a fever," he murmured.

Xhea laughed—or tried to. "Add it to the list." Her voice was so quiet that he had to lean forward to hear the words. She swallowed, struggling to wet her tongue, and spoke again: "I'm sorry about your car."

He smiled a little at that. "I am too." He turned and called over his shoulder: "She's alive! I need some water and blankets—and send Corrin to get the stretcher."

Xhea blinked at that, then struggled to rise.

"I don't need—" she started.

"Don't," Lorn said, and if his tone was kind the word was no less unyielding for it. "You are hurt and in shock, unable to walk, and clearly getting a monster of a fever. I'm taking you home, Xhea—and no, I don't mean to those cold and horrid tunnels."

She grimaced. "But—"

"No. No discussion. Do you actually think I would just leave you here?" A pause, and then he glared. "You did, didn't you? Foolish girl."

"I—but—" Xhea had no possible idea what to say.

A shadow fell across her face, and then Lorn was tucking a blanket around her—tattered and faded and nonetheless warm. A moment later and the stretcher had arrived; she whimpered and bit her lip to keep from crying out as they shifted her body onto the fabric between the stretcher's long metal poles. Still she tried to protest.

"This is about more than you, Xhea. You don't understand what you've done, do you?" Lorn glanced up at the merging Towers directly above them, then to the Central Spire and back down at her face. "You've brought a Radiant—a true Radiant—to the Lower City." He laughed incredulously, fear and hope threaded through the words, his voice deep and rich like old velvet. "Everything is about to change."

"But . . . what am I supposed to do?"

"For now?" Lorn said. "Rest. There will be time enough to talk tomorrow."

"Rest, Xhea," Shai whispered in echo, her voice by Xhea's ear. Shai's ghostly fingers reached out to curl around Xhea's own once more. "It's okay. I'm here."

Xhea let out a long, slow breath. She tightened her grip and held to Shai's hand as if she'd never let her go.

"Okay," she whispered. And it was.

Her stretcher was lifted and they began the slow walk back to the Lower City.

ACKNOWLEDGMENTS

I stared writing *Radiant* in 2008, and the journey from there to here has been a long one, with many unexpected turns. I never could have done it alone. I'd like to say thank you:

To my writing partner, Jana Paniccia, for countless hours of support, laughter, and advice. You read the rough and ragged first draft with its notes, missteps, and placeholders—"And then something interesting happens!"—and helped me turn it into a real story. I owe you so much more than a coffee.

To Greg Smyth, my surprise second reader, my husband, and my person, for . . . everything. For listening to my countless ideas and worries and rants, for your calm in the midst of unexpected storms, for the myriad cups of tea. For being awesome.

To Susan Mosser, my most perfect reader, for seeing the story I wanted to tell through all the chaos and misplaced words, and cheering me on until I brought it to life.

To my beta readers, Leah Bobet, Michelle Sagara, Terry Pearson, and Julie Czerneda, for all your helpful thoughts and feedback.

To Julie and Roger for opening your home and your family to me, and for providing such a perfect place to finish my first novel.

To my awesome agent, Sara Megibow, for your support and advice and unwavering enthusiasm.

To my family and friends for your love and mockery, your enthusiasm and sarcasm, your shared frustration and joy, and for the kind provision of baked goods. I'd list you all here if I could.

To the Canada Council for the Arts and the Toronto Arts Council for their generous support and funding, without which this novel might still not be finished.

And to you, the reader, for giving a new author a try. I know how many books vie for your time and attention, and am grateful beyond words that you took a chance on mine.